THE RADIANT CITY

LAUREN B. DAVIS

THE RADIANT CITY

To Donna,

Admit the light!

Love,
Lauren
Toronto
April 2005

HarperCollins*PublishersLtd*

The Radiant City

Published by HarperCollins Publishers Ltd

First edition

HarperCollins books may be purchased for educational, business, or sales promotional use through our Special Markets Department.

HarperCollins Publishers Ltd
2 Bloor Street East, 20th Floor
Toronto, Ontario, Canada
M4W 1A8

www.harpercollins.ca

Library and Archives Canada Cataloguing in Publication

Davis, Lauren B., 1955–
The radiant city / Lauren B. Davis. – 1st ed.

ISBN 0-00-200576-X

I. Title.

PS8557.A8384R33 2005 C813'.6 C2004-905844-4

HC 9 8 7 6 5 4 3 2 1

Printed and bound in the United States

Woe is me, for I sojourn in Meshech,
For I dwell among the tents of Kedar!
Too long has my soul had its dwelling
With those who hate peace.
I am for peace, but when I speak,
They are for war.

– Psalm 120

What we call fundamental truths are simply
the ones we discover after all the others.

– Albert Camus, *The Fall*

Cynicism is the last refuge of the broken-hearted.

– Ernest Hunt,
Canon, American Cathedral of Paris

CHAPTER ONE

The night is the wrong colour.

The first sound he heard was the horses. They sounded like eagles torn apart, like metal gears stripping, like speared whales. Matthew ran to the window. The barn was firelit from within, and orange tongues flickered up almost gently from the roof. His parents and his brother were already in the yard. His father strained to keep his mother from running headlong into the inferno. She twisted and turned in her husband's grip and Matthew knew there would be bruises up and down her arms tomorrow. Her cries mingled with the horses' shrieks. Ashes rose and swirled in the heated air. Hellish snowflakes. If he had wanted to, Matthew could have caught them on his tongue.

Everything made sense then—the kerosene can, the rags, his father's flustered irritation, his sharp, "Nothing, you hear! I'm doing nothing!" when Matthew asked him what he was up to yesterday in the tack room.

Matthew ran down the stairs and out the door to his mother's side and saw what she saw inside that burning barn. The horses' manes flashed and shrivelled, their teeth bared, their hooves flailed at the flames, the skin crisped, going black along their backs, chained in their stalls while the hay went up all around them, so hot they burned, denied even the cruel blessing of suffocation. Matthew stood his ground, faced his father and pointed his finger. He said what he knew.

Matthew's mother broke away from her husband and turned to her son. She slapped him in the face, so hard he fell to the ground. She had never hit him before and his shock left him speechless.

"Shut your mouth," she said. "You're lying. Don't ever say that again! You're lying."

Matthew looked up from the ground at her tear-streaked face, the skin so bright in the fire spray that she might have been burning. In her scalded eyes he saw she knew the truth, and that it made no difference, and that she would not forgive him for it. She would never forgive his father, either, but she would stay nonetheless, even if it killed her, which it would.

His father stood, fierce in his power, fierce in his victory. He did not smile. There was no need to hide anything behind smiles.

His brother took their mother by the arm and led her into the house. "We'll call the fire department," he said.

His father stared into the collapsing barn. "Go telling tales on me, will you, you little shit. All right, then. Let's see where that gets you."

Matthew pressed his face into the dust and begged the dust to swallow him, the ash to bury him.

And nothing was the same after that.

CHAPTER TWO

He wakes up in a hospital. There is pain, a lot of it, but it is over there, in the corner somewhere. It crouches and readies itself to spring into his gut. Someone is moaning. Ah, yes. *He* is moaning. A nurse's face appears, her skin like dusty paper, and then a warm liquid spreading, full of happy little massaging fingers. Good drugs, he thinks as he slips away from the crouching pain. Missed me, he thinks. But there is something to be remembered. Something worse even than this pain. But he can remember later. There will be all the time in the world for remembering.

Oblivion cannot last. Refuses to last. The doctors insist the morphine be tapered off. Matthew hates these doctors. And it is good to hate them, for it gives him something to hate other than himself.

His spleen is gone, the doctors tell him. He is a lucky man, they tell him. Another inch or so and the spine might have been severed.

Yes. Lucky. Lucky, Matthew.

The man in the square was not lucky. His daughter was not lucky.

Josh was not lucky.

More drugs please. Heads shake. So he begins screaming, and keeps on screaming, until they give him something and the black curtain tumbles over his eyes.

There are some people. Asking questions. Taking notes. There is a camera. A bright light. More questions. Then nurses are shooing people out. Raised voices. He wonders what he said. He screamed Josh's name. He knows that much.

Kate is here. Kate with her dark hair, and her vanilla and sandalwood scent, her long-fingered hands, her steel-and-sapphire eyes. Kate at the foot of his hospital bed, her white-knuckled fingers clutching the footboard.

"Hello," he says.

"I thought you were dead," she says and it is clear she has done much crying.

"I don't think so. I'm trying . . ."

She moves to the bedside to kiss him. Her lips feel chapped on his. Her hands are cold on his face. *How can anyone be cold in this country?*

"How long have you been here?" Time is an impenetrable grey cloud.

"Couple of days. It took a day for them to notify me. Planes, travel, you know."

"Such a long way to come."

Kate looks puzzled. "What did you expect?"

"I don't know." He fumbles with the sheet. Turns it back, pulls at it. Looking at her is painful. Being seen by her is worse.

"They say you're going to have to stay in hospital for a few weeks, anyway. Maybe longer. Three bullets, apparently. They did a bit of a dance around inside you." She wipes something off his face. "It's all right, baby, it's all right."

Oh, God, he thinks. I'm crying.

"Do you want to talk about it?"

He shakes his head. Language is helpless and helplessness destroys. A kid with his foot caught in a railway switch screams. The kid screams and tries to get out and the watcher knows he is not going to get out and the train whistle blows and it doesn't mean anything because that kid's as good as dead. *The question is, In that equation, which am I? Watcher? The kid caught in the track?* "I think I'm the train," he says.

"We'll get you back home soon," Kate murmurs as he cries. "I promise. Into a hospital in the U.S. and then home as soon as possible."

He cannot smell her scent, only disinfectant, bleach. Her hands feel like silken ice. He shivers. Sleeps. Dreams of Hebron. Bullets. Josh. Father and child. Sand between his teeth, coating his tongue.

Every time he wakes, she is there. Sitting in a grey chair against the pale yellow wall, which makes her skin look like mustard. Talking with the nurses. Drinking coffee from a Styrofoam cup. Petting him. Sometimes she clasps her hands under her chin and he thinks she might be praying. They do not talk about what happened. He's grateful for that. Talking is exhausting. Breathing is exhausting, but try as he might, he cannot get himself to stop. He cannot keep track of such things as days and nights. Everything is measured out in nightmares.

The phone rings. Far too often. People want to talk to him, interview him.

"Vivisectionists!" he yells.

They take the phone out of his room. There is some sort of a ruckus in the hall. Men with cameras. A security guard is posted at the door for a while. A big fellow who wears a skullcap. When he looks in on Matthew, he sneers as though he needs to spit.

From time to time, the older nurse, the one with the broken blood vessels in her cheeks, brings a plug-in phone into his room. Colleagues from the wire service ask how he is. They say they are sorry, but it is clear they want to get off the phone. Events like these make everyone uncomfortable. He pictures the way they take a deep breath before they call him. The way they gird themselves with concern. They are afraid of him. He can hear it in their voices. Then one evening the nurse comes in with the phone and says, "This is your father calling."

"Tell him I'm not here." He turns to the wall and pokes at a patch of peeling paint.

The nurse puts the phone on the bed and rests the handset on his ear. Matthew shrugs it off.

"Matthew! Goddamn it! Matthew Bowles!" His father was always loud.

Even at age thirty-nine, he feels like a defenceless boy at the sound of his father's voice. Matthew lets him yell for a few more seconds. Then sighs and picks up the phone. "Hello, Dad."

"That you?"

"Yes."

"I heard," the old man says.

"Oh? How?"

"You kidding? You're all over the news."

Matthew's gut churns, as though another bullet slices through him.

"Sure, you're on CNN, CBC, ATV, even seeing you up here in Truro. People in town are all talking about it."

"I see."

"I had a hell of a time tracking you down. You're a big fucking hero, eh?"

"Hero?"

"'Journalist tries to save father and child.'" His father snorts.

"I have to go, Dad."

"Yeah, well. This call's costing me a fucking fortune anyway.

You should have called me. Just wanted to see if you were all right."

"Sure. I'm just great. Thanks for the call." Matthew hangs up the phone.

"You want me to see if we can get a television in here, so you can see?" says the nurse.

"Hell, no!" He wonders if he can manage to swallow his pillowcase and choke to death before anyone gets to him.

Bandages are changed. Drainage tubes are adjusted. Urine and fecal output is monitored. Pain medication is still administered, but they are stingy, and so pain, of all kinds, in unimaginable doses, reappears. It takes root. It grows.

An army man visits. He is a slight, stiff man, younger than Matthew, maybe thirty, but very full of his authority; razor creases on trouser legs and sleeves. Matthew tries to keep track of things like name and rank, but gives up. It takes too much energy. The army is angry with him, this much he gleans. He is responsible for events. As if he didn't know that. As if he didn't know his own damnation. They understand, says the army man, that he has had some sort of a breakdown. They sympathize. Of course, even so, even so, even in his damaged mental state, he must see that the Israeli army is in no way culpable. Does he see that? *He does. Certainly. Whatever.* No. Not whatever. It must be crystal clear. *Fine. Crystal clear.* They also feel it would be best if he did not stay in Israel longer than is necessary.

"He'll be leaving as soon as he can. And don't worry. He won't be coming back."

Kate's voice, and her conclusions, surprise him.

The army man leaves. Matthew regards Kate. He will not be working as a journalist any time in the near future, at least not as he has been. Not in the conflict zones. That requires being trustworthy. It is a job best done at least in pairs. You go somewhere "hot." You find someone you know, or arrange it in advance. Someone you trust. You stick together. Better that way. Unless, of course, you cannot be trusted. Then no one will work with you. Too dangerous. I would not work with me, he thinks.

Kate seems to read his mind. "You'll come home with me. We'll have a life," she says. "No more war zones. No more of this. You have had enough, haven't you? Because I sure as hell have. I can't take any more, Matthew."

Part of him wishes he could say what she wants him to. She is beautiful, loyal and she is a tough woman. A defence lawyer—she has to be. She believes in Matthew and things like the future and children and all that. He's supposed to want a woman like that.

"No. You shouldn't have to," he says.

"So you're done, then?"

"I can't."

"You can't what? You can't *what,* Matthew?" Her head twitches. Her neck is full of tendons.

Washington. Life in that sun-drenched apartment. Kids and car pools and friends round for drinks and a nice steady job somewhere. A kitchen with a big steel fridge and an ice-maker in the door. Scented candles. Fluffy duvet on the bed. Everywhere softness, cleanliness, calm. He would go crazy from the smell of disinfectant. He would go crazy in the quiet order, with nothing to listen to except the sound of his memories scraping along the imported Italian tiles like a broom made out of bones.

It had all been fine when he had come and gone. All been undemanding and sweet when he had landed like a tattered carrier pigeon for a short rest stop. But as a permanent solution? He never intended the relationship to be forever. *I'm an asshole. Yes, well, that's not news.* He would last a year at most. Then he would break whatever promise she wanted him to make now. Break his word. Break her heart. Better to do it now. Get it over with.

In her eyes, he sees a tiny projection of what she thinks he is, this good heroic man. He cannot help himself. Wants to feel his hands squeezing the life out of his own false image.

In his head, there is the *thing;* that glinting something, like the after-glare from a flash bulb. The burn of horror. The ghost-flare of images. What he knows is that he cannot go back to any *where*, since there is no purpose to any *thing*.

How to explain?

How to explain he may not be alive a year from now?

He leaves out the last bit. He looks her straight in the eyes and then says, "I just don't love you, Kate."

"You're lying," she says.

He shakes his head.

"You're just saying that because you're sick. Because you're depressed."

He shakes his head.

It takes three days for her to believe him.

"If I go," she says on the third, "this is it, Matthew. I'm not going to sit waiting for the phone to ring. I've done enough fucking waiting. Enough sitting around. Wasted enough time on you. You're a real bastard, you know that?"

He does.

"Fine. You're a fool. You have no idea what you're turning down."

But he does.

"My life's been on hold, waiting for you. The number of times I've run to some fleabag dump in some godforsaken corner of the earth so we could have a couple of days together. The number of times I've believed your promises. Christ. What a fool I've been." She picks up her purse. "Hope you heal up okay. In every way. Leave a message at my office with Sherri. Let me know where you want your stuff sent."

She does not glance back. He does not blame her, of course. She is absolutely right. Kate, the only woman to whom he's talked of his mother's death; it was ruled not to be a suicide, but what else do you call starving yourself to death? Kate, who believes in lost causes like saving the rain forests or stopping the

AIDS epidemic in Africa, has no choice. At last she stops believing in him.

The next two days he spends alternately staring at the wall and at the bland expanse of white sheet that covers him. Both act as excellent projectors. All his nightmares find daytime viewing space. He simply cannot get enough sleeping pills.

The nurse comes in with the phone again. "A very insistent man," she says.

"Tell my father I died."

"Funny. It isn't your father." She puts the phone down and leaves.

He considers not answering it, and then decides it might be a diversion from the horror film playing in his head.

"Yes?"

"Matthew Bowles?" A man's voice. He does not recognize it. The line crackles. Long distance.

"Yes."

"Oh. My name is Brent Cappilini. I'm a literary agent." New York accent. He says "Brent" as though there were no "t" at the end.

"What can I do for you, Mr. Cappilini?"

"Call me Brent. And I'll tell you what you can do. You can write a book."

"What about?"

"About yourself. About what got you shot."

"Why would I do that?"

"Are you kidding? You are a hot ticket, pal. Am I the first agent to contact you?"

"Yes."

"Well, good for me, but I won't be the last. Believe me." He has a deep laugh. Deeper than his speaking voice. Matthew pictures a little man with a big cigar. "I can get you six figures, on spec."

"I'll think about it."

"I'll call you back tomorrow."

Matthew hangs up the phone and stares at the wall some more. His funds are less than limited. A few thousand. He is an independent, with no newspaper empire behind him. No long-term disability. His medical insurance will eat this up. He will never get any more. Bad risk. Very shortly, he will be destitute. *If I'm still alive. Like mother, like son?*

Writing a book might at least buy time in which he can sort through things and come to a decision. The knowledge he now carries, heavy as a sack of skulls, irrevocably changes the world. There is so little hope, and no purpose to anything. The world is exposed. It is horror, and all his belief in the power of observation proven to be folly. And if his mission fails, if it turns out there is nothing to understand, no answer, then he knows very well how to permanently stop the pain. Until then, he might as well write a book, maybe even explain a thing or two.

The agent calls again the next day. "I suppose we should talk," Matthew says.

"Good man," says Brent Cappilini.

CHAPTER THREE

Matthew wakes with a start. It is how he always wakes now, as though someone has yelled in his ear. He opens his eyes, looks out the bedroom window onto the courtyard. Dark out there, but that means nothing, it might be morning, might be afternoon even. The bed is as hard as an army cot. *That's the problem with furnished apartments. That and the crucifix over the bed. Must remove that.* He rolls onto his side, sits up slowly and hangs his head in his hands. *Coffee. Must have coffee.* He looks at his feet and notices for the first time the broken blood vessels around his ankles. *When had they appeared?* He feels sick to his stomach. Bathroom. The morning gag. Brush teeth. Do not look too closely in the mirror. Wash. Shaving optional. Forget shaving.

Shuffle into the kitchen. Root around in the sink for a semiclean cup. Plug in the coffee maker. While coffee brews, go into the living room. The two large windows here tell him it is morning. Turn on the pint-sized television. Blah-blah-blah. Turn it off again. Go back to the kitchen. Open the refrigerator. Steak. An old bag of salad. A wrinkling tomato. Half a dozen cans of beer. Some goat cheese. A bowl of fat green olives marinated in garlic. *Whoa. Stomach not ready for that one. Ah, milk.* Coffee in cup, milk in coffee. Cup in hand. Sip. *Ah. Coffee brain fizzle. There's a dance in the old boy yet.*

He carries the cup into the living room, to the cubbyhole on the other side of the main room. He congratulates himself again on finding a top-floor apartment at 11 bis, rue de Moscou. He sees the apartment as monastic, with aspirations. He is trying to step out of the husk of his past here and wants as little as possible tugging at his sleeve. If he is going to emerge, he must do so unencumbered. If he is *not* going to emerge, he wants to leave nothing behind. The price is right and more importantly it is a top floor, so his claustrophobia is not a garrotte across his throat. There is no bang-bang-bang of overhead footsteps, and the light is good. The syrupy light of late August flows in through the open window, across the cluttered, battered old table that serves as Matthew's desk. It soothes him, as does the view itself.

The place du Dublin is not a particularly pretty square and it is in a small corner of the 8th arrondissement behind the Gare Saint-Lazare where there isn't a single tourist attraction. Le Primavera Bistro on the corner sets up red tables and chairs and yellow umbrellas beneath the poplars whenever there is the least hope of suitable weather. There is also a green fountain that, like the quality of this morning's light, pleases him. There is something about the miniature temple, with its steady streams of water flowing over the upturned arms of the goddesses Simplicity, Temperance, Charity and Goodness, that gives Matthew hope. The sunlight sparkling on the water is like laughter, transmuted at this distance from sound to shards of prismatic encouragement.

Matthew has seen a great deal of light in his travels around the world, and he has come to the conclusion that it has different properties in different places: the harsh glare of a frozen icefield, the sweet veil in a bamboo thicket, the distortion of distance and depth that follows a thunderstorm when the sun's rays stab under the skin of cloud cover, the threatening gloom of a darkening prison cell. Light takes on the characteristics of the objects in its path, and this, he has come to believe, is what humans do as well. Light can blind as well as reveal. It can save someone who wanders too close to an unseen edge, but it can just as easily betray a person cowering in a hidden place. He has concluded that contrary to what religious imagery would try to persuade the populace, light is neutral, and indifferent.

The wounds in his body have closed over and physically, Matthew is as good as he is going to get. The mind is another matter. Diagnoses have been assigned. Post Traumatic Stress Disorder. Nervous Exhaustion. Still, the practical problem exists regardless of mental fragility: if you want to eat, you must have money. In a flurry of demented activity back in the United States the month before, he sold everything he owned. It put some money in the bank, but depressingly little. If he wants more, he must write the book. It is a simple equation, the execution of which has thus far evaded him.

And so, begin now. Start again. But first, scan the bookshelf above the desk to see if there is any inspiration to be had there or, failing that, any excuse to procrastinate. *Let Us Now Praise Famous Men* by James Agee, which is Matthew's bible. But not today. Some short stories by Grace Paley. A book by M.F.K. Fisher, a gift from someone now forgotten. *The Collected Stories of John Cheever*, some science fiction. Asimov, Frank Herbert, Heinlein, Ray Bradbury. *Nope. Sorry, pal. Nothing for you this morning. Pick up a pen and face the page.* It must be longhand, for he has long since learned the terrible temptation of the delete button. Breathe. Start where? Beirut? El Salvador? He writes about Beirut, and Sid Cameron, the Belgian photographer who wore a brown-and-yellow paisley vest he never washed. About the day Sid took him to the Palestinian refugee camp at Sabra, after the Lebanese Phalangists had slaughtered thousands. About the endless swelling bodies, the wandering, weeping women, the rubble, the mutilations. About how Sid had thoughtfully turned his head away as Matthew vomited and then offered him a half-bottle of warm Coke with which to wash out his mouth. "You'll get used to it," said Sid, who had survived his initiation in Vietnam and told stories about what napalm and bouncing-betty landmines could do.

Sabra was such a dusty place, and hot. Like Hebron. *Don't go there. Back away.* Next stop, El Salvador. Still hot, but wet, damp enough to flush the dust out of memory's mouth. The pen moves . . .

El Salvador. Carl showed me the ropes. He drove slowly, thoughtfully, on his daily rounds, taking photos of all the new corpses that appeared like weird night-blooming succulents, fresh each morning. Fresh too were the strange blisters that blossomed on my skin, spreading like a pale parasitic vine across my hands, my arms, and my chest. The rash grew with the rising sun and receded each night, only to begin again. The blisters didn't bother me much during the day, when they were nothing more than a soft burning, but at night, as they germinated under my skin, they itched like something crawling beneath the flesh.

Carl laughed at me as the blisters spread across my face, making me look like a pimply adolescent. "You should have seen the stuff that'd grow on you in Nam. It was like farm country in your boots," he said.

What ever happened to Carl? Matthew thinks, back again in his body, at his desk, in this Paris apartment. Oh yes, newscaster somewhere in the American Midwest, last anyone heard. And then, knowing he should not, he reads over what he's written. Frustration wells up from the bottom of his gut, bubbles over his chest and down to his fingertips. He thinks he should keep a large metal garbage bin next to his desk wherein he can have regular fires. It is difficult not to tear the page to shreds with his teeth. He has become, however, a very good crumpler, and his wastebasket is more than accepting.

So, there will be no more writing today. But what, then? He does not want to do what he mostly does. Mostly he sits and tries very hard not to remember things. Not Josh. Not the father. Not the daughter. Not Kate. Not his own father, brother, mother. Not Rwanda. Not Kosovo. Not Chechnya. Not so many places, not so many people. Not remembering them leaves very little room in his mind for anything else.

It is now eleven o'clock in the morning, and from the window, he watches the young man at Chez Elias, a tiny café on the square. The man wears a white apron and uses a long-handled brush to wash the glass. Now he whistles optimistically, but Matthew has seen him sitting at a table in the window, no customers in the café, poring over maps with a look of deep dissatisfaction on his face.

Matthew realizes he is jiggling his knee, tapping his foot, and he stops himself, because he knows from experience this nervous energy is not good for him. He tells himself he is adjusting to the tick-tock passing of time outside the crisis zones. He tells himself he is fine. He tells himself he should not have had that fourth cup of coffee. He tries to read the *International Herald Tribune*, a story about the North Africans, the *san-papiers*, who have occupied the Saint Bernard church in Barbès, demanding legal residence papers. It looks bad, with the government sounding tougher and tougher. It will not end well. He puts the paper aside. Folds it in a neat square and presses it flat. Looks around for somewhere to stuff his discontent.

The sweep of the clock's hands is agonizingly slow; the voices of the children on the street below are needles in his ears. He briefly considers calling Brent, back in New York, but it is too early, and besides, he already knows what Brent will say. *How's the book coming along? Come on, pal, get yourself together.*

Deciding what to do in a tourist town when one is not technically a tourist is a wretched task. Matthew has seen the Eiffel Tower and Notre Dame on previous trips; he has chased the ghosts of Joyce and Hemingway through the cafés and bookshops. He does not want to stroll up the Gap-and-Planet-Hollywood-infested Champs Élysées. He certainly does not want to go to a museum. He begins pacing, which is a bad sign.

Jack Saddler. Perhaps it is the morning's work, the memories of Sid and Carl that make him think of Jack Saddler, but the name now springs to mind and he is surprised he has not thought of it before. Jack Saddler. Vietnam vet, ex-mercenary, sometime combat photographer. The last time he saw Jack, back in Kosovo, Jack had said he was heading to Paris, in need of a break. Jack Saddler, who knew a thing or two about lugging a sack of skulls.

France Telecom proves helpful and a few minutes later Matthew dials a number for a mobile phone.

"Hello?"

"Jack?" There is a lot of noise in the background.

"Who's this?"

"Matthew Bowles."

"Hey! You in Paris?"

"Yup."

A moment's silence and then, "How you holding up?"

"Fair."

"I can imagine." The sound of car horns. "Fuck off! Not you, Matthew. You'd think we were in Tehran the way the French drive. Can you hear me?"

"I can hear you."

"Tell you what, you free later?"

"Absolutely."

"Meet me at this bar I know. Called the Bok-Bok." Jack chuckles. "You'll like the place. It never closes, and no one forces conversation if you don't feel sociable, know what I mean?"

"Just give me an address and a time," Matthew says.

When he gets off the phone Matthew looks at his watch, and then he takes a sleeping pill and strains toward unconsciousness until evening.

CHAPTER FOUR

Saida Ferhat wakes up as alert as a fox with the sound of hounds on the wind. It has been this way for a long time, started only weeks after her marriage to Anatole twelve years ago. It does not matter that, since Anatole is gone, she no longer has to worry about dodging an early morning boot thrown at her head. Waking this way has become a difficult habit to break. She waits for her heart to stop pounding, and then slips her legs from beneath the blankets, and pushes her wide, strong feet into the thick socks that serve as slippers. She wraps her dressing gown around her and quickly braids her hair, so that it hangs in an arm-thick rope down to the swell of her buttocks. Once, her hair had been black as the inside of an ebony box, but now there is silver in it. A strand here and there, and there another. Each one witness to a worried night, a wary day. At thirty-six, Saida suspects she will be snow-topped before she becomes craggy-faced.

She pulls the lapel of her robe up to cover the scars on her neck. It looks as though the skin is as malleable as clay there, as if a sculptor with no talent for creation has pushed it and pulled it, finally given up and left it unfinished. She flexes and straightens her right hand. The skin over the veins, stretched across the knuckle bones, is unnaturally smooth, and in the morning it is stiff, itches and pulls, no matter that she rubs almond and jojoba oil and aloe in each night.

Going to the bedroom door, she puts her hand against the jamb as she opens it, trying to be quiet for her son Joseph who is sixteen and sleeping on the couch in the room that serves as living room, dining room and kitchen. He did not get in until too late last night, and Saida knows she should be angry with the boy, running the streets, hanging out in Barbès, smoking and slouching around like a thug. She looks at him, and in sleep his face is sweet, beautiful almost—his soft lips open, his perfect skin flushed. He looks nothing like his stepfather, Anatole, who has thick features and a low hairline. Joseph looks like his father, Habib, buried fifteen years ago in Lebanese soil in a grave beside his Uncle Khalil—his eyes are thick-lashed and his nose is long and fine. Only his lower lip is imperfect. A slight malformation there; at the bottom right it looks perpetually stung and swollen. Saida has told him since he was a toddler that Gabriel, archangel of the cleansing fire, must have kissed him there. It makes him more beautiful, she says.

It is all she can do not to reach out and brush her hand over Joseph's head, the hair fashionably shaved as though he were a prisoner. Whatever anger there had been evaporates and she lets him sleep.

Saida uses the toilet and washes her face, brushes her teeth. She then leaves the apartment, stepping out into the dingy hall. Someone has ground a cigarette out on the floor and left the butt. A filterless Gitane and so it must be the fat man who lives with his ferret at the end of the hall. A filthy man. A filthy animal. Saida uses a tissue to pick it up. The man would shit in his own bed, she thinks. Two doors down, she lets herself into the apartment where her father and her brother, Ramzi, live. This apartment is also two rooms, with the men sharing a bedroom. The main room is slightly smaller than hers and there is a table with four chairs. There is also a larger armchair, bought second-hand for her father, covered in gold-and-blue damask, somewhat stained, and a round brass-topped table on which stands a silver tea set with a samovar that is not real silver. The tea set is the last remnant of life in Damour, of her mother's good taste and of promises betrayed.

Saida boils the coffee and sets out bread, cheese and oranges. Elias, her father, shuffles out of the bedroom, adjusting his dentures. They do not fit properly and they hurt him, she knows, but he is too proud to go without them. His hair sticks up at odd angles and his eyes have dark shadows under them.

Saida worries about her father, who has never found his way in this country, never healed—as though anyone could—from the loss of so many family members. His wife. His parents. His younger son, Khalil. His daughter-in-law, Farida. His son-in-law, Habib. His grandson, his namesake, Little Elias. He walks through the world now, his ear cocked to the cries of ghosts. Nor has he coped with the fall in status. No longer a civil engineer, respected, a landowner—but a café keeper, and less, the old man who sits by the door. She knows he misses the field, the oranges and the sun. She knows he misses being a man who understands his world. He is so often baffled now, sits gazing out the window.

He kisses her on both cheeks, pats her unscarred arm. "Good morning, Daughter."

"Did you sleep?"

He raises his eyebrows and makes a tsk-tsk sound. "*La.* Two hours, maybe three."

"So go back to bed, Father."

"Give me coffee. I'll be fine. An old man's complaint. A lack of sleep is nothing in this world. Nothing."

Saida pours the coffee, sweetens it and hands it to her father. He blows on it noisily and then sips. "Good. Your brother sleeps like a drunkard. Tanks could roll through the living room and he'd hear nothing."

"Is he up?"

Elias makes a face.

"He's going to miss the bread man."

"Get him up."

Saida goes to the door and opens it. "*Yalla!* Ramzi! Up!" Her brother lies on his back on one of the two narrow beds, long arms and legs dangling over the sides, his mouth open. She shakes him by the shoulder. Without waking, he reaches between his legs with both hands. Through the thin blanket Saida sees he has an erection and she feels blood come to her cheeks, bringing with it a flush of resentment. She slaps his arm. "Wake up! You're late again." His eyes spring open.

"What?"

"Get up, Ramzi. The bread man will come and you will not be there. What is he going to do? Leave the pita on the stones?"

"I'm not your son, Saida. Get Joseph up if you want to bully someone," he says, but he sits up and scratches his head, a sure sign he's moving in the right direction. "What time is it?"

"Seven-thirty."

"Shit." He scrambles out of bed. "I need a shower."

"Yes, you do," she says, wrinkling her nose as he pushes past her.

She goes back to the kitchen and pours more coffee for her father, puts food on a plate for him. "Do we have grapes?" says Elias.

"No grapes. Have an orange. I have to get Joseph up," she says.

"Are you taking me to the café, or is Ramzi?"

"I'll take you."

"The sheets should be changed today."

"I know, Father. You don't have to always tell me," she says as she leaves.

Back in her own apartment, Joseph has not yet stirred. She runs the back of her hand along his cheek. "Wake up. Come on. Wake up." He moans and turns away from her. "No, no, you don't. Up. You have to go to school."

"No school today. Teachers are on strike," he mumbles into the back of the sofa.

"You are a liar and a lazy boy," she says, but her voice is not angry.

Joseph tries to hide a smile. "Donkey boy."

"Yes, *walid himar.* Now get up or the donkey will bite your ass."

"Oh, that's terrible!" He laughs at the pun and rolls off the couch as his mother goes into the bedroom.

"I have to dress and get down to the café. Make sure Ramzi meets the delivery. And listen to me, Joseph," she calls to him as she pulls a navy blue dress from the closet, "I mean it. You go to school today. All day. And come to the café as soon as you're finished. I want to see what the homework is." She hears him in the bathroom. "Do you hear me?"

"I've got soccer after school."

Saida knows this is not true. She wants it to be true, but she knows he does not go to soccer, although it is an excuse he uses often. There are never any soccer clothes to wash. Never a soccer ball in the house. As far as she knows he owns no soccer shoes though he says he keeps them at school.

She does not want to call his bluff and telephone the school. Although she would never say this to her son, she dislikes the teachers at his school almost as much as he does. The tone of voice they use, as if their mouths are full of sour pickles, makes it clear they hold no respect for her—just another Arab woman raising a child alone, and one who bears the taint of her hardscrabble life in the texture of her very skin. The headmistress, Madame Brossard, lumps her into the same stew with Algerians, Tunisians, Moroccans. How can she explain who she is to the Parisians, who never go into Barbès let alone beyond the *périphérique*, into the housing projects where most of the immigrant population live? Her father once an engineer, her mother once a teacher just like them. Saida speaks three languages—how many do they speak? It's no use, and she suspects it's as little use for her son, who doubly condemns himself because he makes his friends among the *beurs*, those hard-eyed, slouching, baggy-clothed boys who try so hard to look like American rappers and who everyone assumes steal wallets on the subway whether they do or not. And her son does not. Of this she is sure.

She pulls her tights up under her dress. "I will call the school, Joseph. I will find out if you have soccer or not. Don't make me do that." He says something she can't hear over the flushing of the toilet. "What?"

"Call if you want. I have soccer."

"I will call. Don't you think I won't. And if I find out you are lying to me, I will tell your grandfather, I will tell your uncle. And you know what they will do. You'll be locked in your room for a month."

"I don't have a room. Besides, I'm too old for all that. I make my own decisions."

Saida wraps a scarf around her neck. She says nothing for a moment, letting him think about the consequences of his words. It's natural he would push the limits. It's his age.

"You can't treat me like a child anymore," Joseph says, standing in the doorway, his hands on his hips. Her beautiful son. Bold and brazen, as he should be. Saida smiles at him, then narrows her eyes, purses her lips and shakes her head at him in a parody of his own expression until he laughs.

"Such a mean man you'll grow up to be."

"I'm almost grown now." He shuffles back and forth, afraid to look foolish.

"Almost grown isn't grown. Be at the café this afternoon. I need you to take your grandfather to the doctor. He has to have his blood pressure checked." And Joseph sighs deeply so she will know how he suffers, but Saida understands she has won this round at least.

Oh, the men in my life, she thinks. So many men and always everyone needing something. Where is the air left for me to breathe, and when the time for me to breathe it in?

CHAPTER FIVE

It is just after nine o'clock when Matthew finds the Bok-Bok, in the mostly Arab neighbourhood known as Belleville, in the 20th arrondissement, where windows full of oriental pastries and shops selling prayer rugs and Korans line the streets. As he walks, he keeps his eye on a group of twenty-something North African men wearing track suits and smoking with practised nonchalance. They joke, slap palms and watch the passersby. Women keep their eyes downcast as they walk past them. When a blond in a short skirt and high-heeled sandals walks by, they toss out insults in Arabic and spit at her. The old women and the ones wearing traditional headscarves are treated with more respect. An old man comes out of his grocery shop and shakes his hands at them, as though they are a trip of goats he means to move along. He says something harsh in Arabic, but the young men take no notice.

Matthew gives them and their tangible disaffection a wide berth. There are young men like this in every city of the world, only the ethnicity is different. He knows that the angry, like the poor, will always be with us. He avoids eye contact and keeps his gait casual.

He is looking for a particular passageway that was part of Jack's instructions, and when he finds it he edges through a gate into a small discreet courtyard that smells of piss. He crosses to a door on the left, next to a wooden sign with the name of the bar on it and a Harley-Davidson logo sticker. The steps inside are absurdly steep, narrow and dark. He feels along the wall with his hands as he descends. The wall is damp.

When his eyes adjust to the shadows in the dimly lit room below, he sees that an attempt has been made to reproduce an in-country Vietnamese hooch. The floor is wooden, the bar is rough-hewn and the tattered remains of an army surplus camouflage net hangs from the ceiling, festooned with small red and green Christmas lights. The faces of Jimi Hendrix and Janis Joplin look down from the walls. There are dusty plastic palms in the corners and the air smells of cigarettes, beer, piss and the sort of centuries-old mould that is endemic to Paris basements.

Matthew waits a few seconds, knowing that eyes are on him, and then walks slowly toward the bar, nods to two men who nod back, but is careful not to stare at any face. He becomes still here, in the pin-drop tension, and he begins to relax for the first time in weeks. He feels as though he has stepped into water the same temperature as his skin. The jitters inside him begin to quiet. Home sweet home.

The bartender, a man wearing a porkpie hat over a scraggle of red hair, jerks his chin at Matthew, who orders a beer, whisky back, and drinks it, facing away from the room.

"You all right, then?" asks the bartender.

"Fine, thanks." The bartender nods and walks to the other end of the bar where he polishes a glass. The room's low buzz of conversation returns. It is a drone of speech not whispered, not under the men's breath exactly, but with awareness that not all things are meant to be heard by all people. A pale girl sits a few seats along the bar. She has black hair, which looks like a wig, and wears a tight, high-collared, Chinese-style dress. She smokes a cigarette and picks at chipped nail polish. There is a slit in the skirt and a dark bruise on her leg. She notices Matthew looking at her legs and stares at him but does not smile and so neither does he.

A man comes over and stands close to Matthew. He is not as tall as Matthew but is powerfully built, with tattoos of dragons on his arms. He says nothing.

"How you doing?" asks Matthew.

"You sure you're in the right place, friend?"

"I suspect so."

"No civilians here."

"Jack Saddler told me to meet him here."

"Ah," says the man and extends his hand. "Name's Charlie."

"Matthew."

Charlie and the bartender nod to each other and then Charlie returns to his table, where he says something to another man, who glances at Matthew and then turns away quickly.

After a few minutes, the door opens and Jack Saddler enters the room. As he approaches, a big grin under his droopy, greying moustache, Matthew notes he has put a few beer-pounds on his professional wrestler build. Being six foot one, Matthew does not look up at people often, but his neck tilts when Jack comes closer.

"Hey! The original bad penny," says Jack and he claps Matthew on the shoulder. His hand is the size and weight of a brick.

"You're looking prosperous," Matthew says.

Jack grabs his belly. "I look like a fucking Buddha."

"Suits you."

"How long you been in town?"

"Few weeks. You still carry that copy of St. Augustine's *Confessions*?"

Jack laughs. "Shit. You remember that? Well, I've got a confession of my own. I never read it. Just knew that one quote."

"Now I got it!" says a voice. They turn and see Charlie coming toward the bar. "I thought you looked familiar. Journalist, right? You're that guy. Hey, Dan," he calls to the bartender, "fuck me! This is the guy in Israel, you know, the guy with that man and his kid, on CNN!"

Matthew knocks back the whisky. "Time for me to go."

"Charlie, check yourself," Jack says, his voice low. "Now."

The man looks stricken. "Hey, hey. Listen." He puts his hand on Matthew's arm. "Sorry, man. No need to go. Rules around here. You don't want to talk, you don't have to talk. I fucked up. It's just not too often we get a . . . well, anyway, my mistake. You're welcome here." He holds out his other hand for Matthew to shake. Matthew hesitates. "Next drink's on me, for both of you."

Matthew looks at Jack, who nods.

"Fair enough," says Matthew and shakes the man's hand.

"Whisky, double," says Jack to the barman. "See you later, Charlie."

They take their drinks to a table, and before Matthew knows it, there are more drinks. The night ebbs and flows as people come and go. No one comes near the table. Jack asks no questions. Instead he talks of himself.

"Nearly fifty, can you believe it? I'm too old for that merc shit. Too old for the war photographer thing, too." Jack chews the side of his moustache, as he always did when he was uncomfortable. "I needed a break, you know?"

Yes, Matthew knows.

"I'm working in a hostel. Don't laugh. Sort of a receptionist-slash-bouncer. Gives me a little extra cash. And let's face it, there's something to be said for working in a place full of eighteen- to twenty-eight-year-olds. Especially the girls. All those belly rings and pierced tongues." His eyebrows waggle and Matthew laughs. "But that's not my real gig. I figure I'll do some stuff in Paris. Street-shot stuff, down and dirty. The Paris the tourists don't see. I'm thinking of a book of subterranean Paris. In fact, now that I consider it, you could even do the words. We could do it together. Me pictures, you words. What do you think?"

Matthew laughs. Josh's face swims before him. "Maybe," he says. "Maybe."

Later, when Matthew is back in his apartment, lying on his back, the bed gently rolling under the wave of booze, he wonders why it is that everywhere he goes he finds someone who's been in Vietnam. They pop up everywhere from El Salvador to Somalia. Soldiers turned mercenaries mostly, sometimes soldiers turned reporters, like Carl. Once in a rare while some guy, apparently just wandering.

The first time he met Jack had been in Peshawar. He was thinner back then, with red leathery skin, and a dog-eared, talismanic copy of *The Confessions of St. Augustine* that he wouldn't go anywhere without. Jack said he had come to the Afghan border to hook up with the legendary *mujahedeen* fighter Abdul-Haq. He stayed for a couple of weeks, making contacts and lining up guides to take him across the mountains. He showered in Matthew's hotel room and told stories about being a Ranger in Vietnam, Company F, 75th Infantry, trained at the Recondo School at Nha Trang. About the Saigon hookers who plied their trade in the cemeteries, about the ambushes and the unending sense of anticipation that came from never knowing when a piece of bamboo was going to jump out of the earth and impale you, or when a snake tied to a vine would swing into your face. About his well-earned psychological discharge. "Totally fucking *dinky dau,*" as Jack called it.

Jack had many stories and, at the time, Matthew thought most of them were probably true. Matthew was in awe of Jack's ability to move through his own terror, which Matthew had come to understand was the true definition of bravery.

"Aren't you afraid of getting killed?" he had asked.

"Immortality is health; this life is a long sickness," said Jack, quoting St. Augustine.

Jack vanished into the mountains and it was a long time before he resurfaced. In the interim, he became a sort of shining ghost, a sort of mythic questing figure. A doomed hero. Matthew winces. Jack would have picked up the gun in that square in Hebron. He would have let fly, and maybe then things would have been different.

CHAPTER SIX

Matthew and Jack arrange to meet at Odéon in the square in front of the movie theatres, to see if anything appeals to them, something to see later in the evening. From there they plan to head over to Square Tino Rossi, on the Seine across from the Institut du Monde Arabe, where Jack wants to photograph the tango dancers who gather late in the afternoons and into the evenings. As Matthew climbs the metro stairs, he is flushed and sticky with the afternoon's heat, which the sausage-casing constriction of the subway has only worsened. Even under the shade of the plane tree, he feels heat sick.

The street is a mass of people, and there is as much English spoken, it seems, as French. Everywhere he looks, wilted tourists in sensible shoes and track suits lumber along, taking pictures and gawking. The masses jostle and lurch and the cacophony from the car horns and the café crowds makes his head spin. He feels queasy, a combination of too much booze the night before and too little food today.

He looks around for a bakery, and spots one a few doors down. It is all chrome and glass and linoleum, the walls painted an eye-piercing shade of yellow. Plastic chairs circle three round metal tables and the air is thick with cigarette smoke from a group of well-dressed Italian teenagers drinking diet colas and speaking loudly. The cakes and baguettes look as far from those found in a traditional patisserie as Matthew can imagine. He is reminded of

Safeway Groceries back in Nova Scotia when he was a kid, and donuts with Plasticine icing in garish pink. His stomach growls again and he seeks the least offensive item in the display case.

The woman behind the counter puts her cigarette in the ashtray and steps over to him, hands on hips. She has orange hair and is heavily, if not improvingly, made up.

"Oui, monsieur?" She does not smile. Smiling is unnecessary in Parisian commercial transactions, purely discretionary, and today it seems Madame does not care to smile.

"Pain au chocolat," says Matthew.

"Quoi?" Madame frowns and squints as though he has a speech impediment, and so he repeats himself, adding a bottle of water to his order.

There is a shriek behind him. Matthew jumps and turns, legs bent, heart pounding. A young woman in a strapless sundress curses as she tries to manoeuvre a baby stroller containing a squealing toddler through the door. She rams the wheels against the door jamb, jarring the child. One of the young Italian girls, cigarette in hand, jumps up to help her, chattering away in Italian. The woman with the baby thanks her and then casts an evil look Matthew's way.

Matthew puts his money down on the glass, and the woman behind the counter scoops it up before he realizes she has handed him the wrong thing. He looks down at the bottle of water, and what appears to be an apple turnover. He briefly considers not making a fuss. However, even if he wanted an apple turnover, this one does not look in the least appetizing. Oozing industrial filling, the pastry gives the impression of papier mâché. The woman looks at him irritably, for he is not moving, and gestures with her hand for him to step aside so she can serve the mother with the still-screaming child.

"This is not a *pain au chocolat*," he says, in French.

"It is what you asked for," the woman says, looking past him.

"I asked for a *pain au chocolat*."

"Non!" She clicks her teeth and shakes her finger back and forth in front of him. "I gave you what you asked for."

"You misunderstood me, then." Matthew is aware of the young woman behind him; her impatience prickles the back of his neck. His anger rises, popping and fizzing in the veins, not quite at a boil, but fast approaching. He grits his teeth and tries to smile. "But I don't want this." He puts the offending pastry on the counter and nudges it toward her.

The woman takes a breath, as though readying herself to let lose a stream of vitriol. Perhaps it is some sliver of ice beneath his flushed skin, some shard of volatility that makes her hesitate. Perhaps she can sense he is holding onto the counter so as not to lunge across it and grab her by her supercilious throat.

She snorts. "It's not my fault you speak French so badly." She snatches the pastry off the counter, tosses it next to her pack of cigarettes near the register, grabs a pair of tongs and clamps the *pain au chocolat* in the case. She holds it out to him, but it is sadly dented. He takes it, turns and stomps out.

The pastry is dry as bark in his mouth and he washes it down with the water. His stomach feels better afterward, though, even if his palms are sweaty. He stands in the shade of the green-domed newspaper kiosk trying to get a little respite from the malodorous heat.

Matthew sees Jack lumbering along the sidewalk of Saint-Germain. His head is down slightly and his hands are stuffed in the pockets of his jeans. He carries a heavy camera slung across his chest. He nearly collides with a crumpled-looking old lady in front of him who stopped suddenly to let her Yorkshire terrier relieve itself. He says something, presumably "*Pardon*," and the woman pulls her dog toward her in mid-poop, the crap dangling from its trembling legs, as though she is afraid Jack might kick the creature. Jack steps around her and people move aside to let him pass. A mother yanks her little boy out of his path. A young man, big, but not as big as Jack, wearing a black T-shirt with the sleeves cut off, hesitates for a moment as though deciding whether or not to challenge Jack, whether or not to play a little sidewalk chicken and see who will move first. He makes a wise choice and at the last moment dodges.

At the corner, Jack waits for the light to change and there is a space around him that other pedestrians do not enter. A no-go zone, it seems, picked up by osmosis. Matthew wonders how he might cultivate one of those.

Matthew stands and they greet each other, shaking hands.

"How's it hanging?" says Jack.

"Too crowded. Too hot. Otherwise fine."

"Tourists, huh?" says Jack. "Any movies?"

They scan the offerings at the three nearby theatres—a selection of French comedies that neither speaks French well enough to enjoy and three American action films: *Independence Day*, *Chain Reaction*, *Mission Impossible*. They look at each other. "Nah," they say.

"Let's get out of here, then," says Jack. "Up to the Seine. It'll be less crowded there."

They head along Saint-Germain, but as they walk they hear a commotion of some sort ahead of them, and Matthew's skin tightens. He glances at Jack who, frowning, peers over the heads of the sidewalk crowd. There are voices, some shouting. Car horns. Someone has a bullhorn. Matthew tries to make out the words and cannot.

"Can you see what's going on?" he says.

"I don't know." Jack has picked up his pace, and as before, a space opens before him. "Demonstration of some sort, I think."

Matthew follows, thinking that they should be slowing down, should be running in the opposite direction, but they do not do that. They head into whatever is before them, on instinct, on adrenaline, on training.

People are unable to pass. Cars are at a standstill. Horns honk impatiently. A taxi driver gets out of his cab, yells something at the people in front, slaps his open palm on the roof of his cab, gets back in and slams the door. Then he presses the horn. The sound goes on and on until other drivers join in creating a furious clamour, and Matthew fights the urge to put his hands over his ears. People mill about, some turn back, some duck down side streets. Whistles blow. The bullhorn squawks and squeals.

Perspiration runs into Matthew's eyes and he wipes the salt-sting away. He feels the weird calm settling over top of the adrenaline, his vision distancing, as though looking at things through the wrong end of a telescope. Panic rises, but it is off to the left somewhere, happening to someone else. He follows Jack and within moments, they are at the corner of Saint Michel.

It is a large demonstration, thousands, probably. There is something pagan about it, like a parade of some sort. The crowd is mixed—French, North African, young, old. A number of women wear the hijab. The clothes of the Africans are like bright flags in the burning sun. Matthew knows immediately who they are. These are the *sans-papiers* and their sympathizers. A few days ago, riot police stormed the St. Bernard church, which three hundred illegal African immigrants had occupied for the previous seven weeks while they demanded the right to stay and work in France. People had been hurt. The papers had carried pictures of the police using tear gas and clubs on the immigrants and their supporters.

Now the demonstrators carry banners. *"XENOPHOBIE!"* *"Unies et solidaires!"* "*Sans papiers*—Made in France!" People play *djembe* drums carried around their necks. They shout slogans. They march arm in arm. Traffic snarls Saint-Germain as far as Matthew can see. Police in black jumpsuits and high-laced boots stand around in groups of five or six, talking to each other, smoking cigarettes. Their white vans are parked at the corners.

Jack begins snapping photos. "Good," he says to no one in particular. "That's good."

Matthew senses a change in the atmosphere, as though the air pressure has dropped. He scans the crowd—looking for the source, looking for conscious confirmation of what he has noticed at a subconscious, animal level. Finds it. A group of Frenchmen push their way to the front of the crowd. They yell taunts and jeers. It is easy to guess that these are Le Pen supporters—the political polar opposites of the demonstrators, dedicated to stopping immigration and "returning France to the French." Two years before, skinhead followers of Le Pen murdered Brahim Bouarram by throwing him into the Seine.

Within seconds, a group of demonstrators breaks ranks and confronts the Le Pen supporters. An African man walks calmly up to the biggest of the thugs and spits at him. The slime hits him squarely in the face. Although it takes only a nanosecond after that for all hell to break loose, Matthew sees it coming, as though in slow motion. People run, some of them scream. Someone shoulders Matthew and he spins around, and is struck again. This time he falls to the ground and immediately the weird calm of a moment before is shattered into a million explosive percussions that go off inside his head like machine-gun fire.

Paris disappears. He tastes dust. The world reduces to the need to seek cover. He hears shots, people screaming, sees small bursts of flame around him. He covers his head and crawls on his elbows and knees, kicking out where he must. If he can just get to the wall, inside a doorway, he will be safe. Everything pinpoints to the idea of this safety. He screams. Obscenities. Loudly. Someone trips on him and he scrapes his knuckles. Floundering, Matthew grabs a metal pole with one arm and holds onto it as though it is a wooden spar. He wraps his legs around the pole and puts his hands over his ears, closes his eyes. He wants the noise to stop. *Just make it fucking stop!*

Then there are hands on him, huge, heavy hands, lifting him up off the ground. He goes to swing, to strike out at whoever it is. Something traps his hands, a great bear hug traps his arms. Someone speaks to him.

"Okay, Matthew. All right, Matthew. Everything's fine, Matthew. You're in Paris, Matthew. Nice summer day. You're all right, Matthew."

Whose voice is that?

"Come on, pal. Come on. Come on back." The voice is familiar, but he cannot place it.

Gradually, the world begins to quiet.

"Breathe in. Breathe out. Not a problem. Okey-dokey. All right, Matthew."

Oh, yes. That's Jack.

"I'm gonna let you go now."

"Let me go."

"I'm gonna let you go."

The bands around Matthew's chest loosen, but the hands are on his shoulders, turning him around. Jack's face is close to his, looking into his eyes.

"How you doing, buddy?"

"Shots," says Matthew.

"No shots," says Jack.

"No shots?"

"Nope."

The world is quiet again, or at least, quieter. The altercation seems to have dissolved. The demonstrators are walking again. Even the car horns are muted. "Oh," says Matthew. The sidewalk dips and dances beneath his feet. He is afraid he may throw up. He reaches out and grabs the front of Jack's shirt. People pretend they are not looking at him.

Jack keeps an arm around Matthew's shoulders as he turns him toward two approaching cops. "Just be cool," he says.

"Ça va?" one of the cops says, nodding in Matthew's direction.

"Ab-so-lu-ment," says Jack, smiling broadly. "A little too much sun and *vin,*" he says, making a tilting gesture toward his mouth with his hand, thumb extended.

"No problems?" says the cop.

"No, no," says Jack.

The cop looks at Matthew. "Okay?"

"Sure. *Parfait.*" He feels glazed over, empty, a thin eggshell with nothing inside. If Jack moves away, the weight of the air will crush him.

"Okay. You stay out of sun, okay?"

"Sure," says Matthew, and the cops move slowly away.

"Let's get you out of here," says Jack.

Matthew lets Jack lead him up rue Hautefeuille to place Saint-Michel. They walk slowly, and Jack keeps talking to him. Nonsense talk. "Doing fine. Doing good. Just walking. Walking in Paris. On a nice sunny day." The way you would talk to a skittish horse. To a frightened child. Just the sound of the deep voice keeps Matthew moving forward.

Jack points to the underground pedestrian walkway, which will get them through the demonstration. "Think you can do that?"

"I think so," says Matthew, but he is not entirely sure.

"Atta boy," says Jack.

The underground passageway reeks of urine and is dark after the bright sunlight. Matthew stiffens as they descend, but Jack's hand on his shoulder is comforting. They pass only two other people, both women. They come up on the other side of place Saint-Michel, next to the Seine. The demonstrators pass behind them now, across the Saint-Michel bridge on their way to the Palais de Justice on Île de la Cité. Jack is protective, his hand on Matthew's upper arm, walking just slightly in front of him, clearing a path like a giant plough through a field of humanity. "See," he says. "All over now. Nothing to worry about. All over now."

They walk along the Seine, past the booksellers in front of their green wooden booths. The sun dazzles on the water. Notre Dame rises like a galleon. Matthew is afraid he may begin weeping and makes a sound. Jack gently squeezes his arm. It gives Matthew strength and the tears recede.

As they near the Square Tino Rossi Matthew hears music. Singing. A man's voice.

"Hmm," says Jack. "That's Gardel."

"Gardel?"

"Carlos Gardel. The Argentinian saint of tango. They don't dance to him in Argentina. Out of respect."

"How do you know that?" Matthew says.

"Picked it up in Argentina," says Jack. Then he smiles. "Along with a very pretty girl named Clara."

There is a blue-and-white striped awning set up for shade, and the dancers move about under it in that passionate, rhythmic foreplay that is tango. There are not many dancers at this time of day. Things do not really heat up until nighttime. Since they are not there to dance, Jack and Matthew do not pay the admission that would get them entrance to the actual dance floor. They take seats on the green metal chairs along one side of a railing that separates the dancers from the curious. Jack produces a slim flask from his back pocket.

"Drink."

Matthew does. Some time passes. Perhaps thirty minutes. Maybe more. They sit side by side watching the dancers prowl. Music changes, the sound like waves.

"So, nobody had a gun, I'm guessing," Matthew says at last.

"Not that I could see, anyway."

"I heard shots."

Jack reaches over and pats Matthew on the knee, as if he were a father and Matthew his son, although there is no more than ten years between them. "Listen, I've heard those very same shots before. Lots of times. And mortar fire. And don't get me started on low-flying airplanes." Jack laughs softly. "I'm better than I used to be, though. This the first time?"

"Third."

"Ah. Well, let me tell you. The trick is, as far as I can tell, and fuck what the doctors tell you—wait, you seeing a shrink?"

"Nope." Matthew's leg trembles only in fits and starts now. The shaking in his hands is practically unnoticeable.

A girl in a red dress, her hair short and slicked back, gleaming with pomade, dances backward past them in the arms of a wire-thin man who looks like a pimp. Their eyes remain locked onto each other and their bodies move in perfect harmony, as if they are preprogrammed. Jack raises the camera to his eye. At the last second, before she turns, the dancer snaps her head around and stares upward. Jack clicks the button. "Good," he says, and it is unclear if he means the shot, or the fact that Matthew is not seeing a therapist. "I guess they help some guys, but I gave up on 'em too. Anyway. The trick is not to let it define you. You get an episode, you get up, you dust yourself off, and you keep going on with your day. You don't let the fuckers live in your head. You don't let that present-tense thing get to you. You know what I mean?"

Matthew does not, and listens hard, for he suspects this is a secret he must learn.

"One good thing a shrink told me was this: there's a part of the brain that always lives in the present tense of the trauma, whatever it is. Like some little lizard part of your brain doesn't realize that whatever shit happened to you isn't still happening. So, if you have an episode, and you spend the rest of the day, or the week, or the fucking month dwelling on it, I figure you're reinforcing that shit. Key is to kick the little fucker out as soon as you can. See what I mean?"

"Yes, possibly."

Jack looks over at Matthew and then takes a handkerchief out of his pocket and polishes his lens. "It may do no good to talk about the fucking episodes, but sometimes it does help to talk about whatever's causing them. Say what happened, and then what happened next, you know? And then what happened after that. Train your brain to realize it isn't still going on, that you got past it. Like, I got shot, then I woke up in hospital, then I ate some crappy hospital eggs, pinched a nurse's ass and went back to sleep. Tell the story over and over again, lead the mind through, and convince your lizard brain that time's moved on." Jack pauses, holding the camera up to his eye. "So, if you do want to talk about what happened . . . well, you know."

"I'll keep it in mind."

A couple stops near them and executes a series of complex moves with their legs, intertwining them and stepping first right and then left at fantastic speed. They are both dressed in black, she with a red rose in her hair, he with a red rose in his lapel. Jack's camera clicks happily away.

"Anyway," says Matthew, feeling deeply vulnerable and foolish because of it, "thanks for saving my ass back there."

"No problem."

"Remember Kosovo? Seems like you're always saving my ass, doesn't it?"

"You can do the same for me one day. Have another drink."

And Matthew does, his hand damn near steady.

CHAPTER SEVEN

Saida swirls olive oil over the top of the *hummus* and sets it inside the refrigerated display case next to the bowls of eggplant *moutabal*, *taboulé*, *moujaddara* and spicy potato salad, as well as the platters of falafel, *safiha*—little pizzas with meat and pine nuts—two kinds of sausages, both *manakiche* and *makanek*. She arranges the pastries, the *baklava*, *maamou*, with either pistachios or dates, and macaroons flavoured with orange water. An oriental bakery near their apartment delivers fresh sweets to Chez Elias every morning. Saida herself is a fine pastry-maker and would prefer to make them herself, but there is no time for such things, nor is the kitchen nearly adequate. Already the savoury dishes must sometimes be cooked at home in the early hours of the morning. Since she left her husband, such responsibilities have fallen to her. Ramzi handles the coarser tasks, such as grilling the skewers of chicken and lamb or stuffing the pita with falafel while she makes the rest in the minuscule kitchen, just an alcove really, behind the counter. Saida does not mind that the kitchen is not private. She wants every customer to see how spotless and well organized the little space is.

In fact, the entire shop gleams. The floor, the four tabletops, and the counter—everything is spotless. Her father is her ally in this. She and Ramzi were raised to believe that a clean mind and clean body are intertwined, that a clean house is the outward manifestation of good spiritual health. If, however, Ramzi has relaxed his diligence as he grew into manhood, Saida lives with a bleached rag in one hand, ready to pounce.

Her father, of course, is not helpful in any practical sense. But he is her father and he is old and if he chooses to spend his days sitting by the window watching the world go by, reading Lebanese newspapers, then Saida feels he has earned the right.

She wishes Ramzi would leave her father alone. Every day the same thing and this morning is no exception. She listens with only half an ear to father and brother argue. The same old argument.

"We can't stay here forever," says Ramzi. "We'll never get ahead."

Her father shrugs. "No place is perfect. This is not so bad. We eat."

Ramzi makes a sound of disgust.

"You want to go back to Lebanon?"

"No. I didn't say that. But, well, maybe."

"I'll never go back. It is the land of the dead for me. And you are saying nothing. Wind across the sand."

"There are more opportunities elsewhere. There is more sunshine elsewhere."

"There are opportunities here. You think you have it so hard? You own this business. You can take a wife. Feed your children. The stores are full of things to buy."

"This city is depressing. People are so unhappy." Ramzi stands with his hands in his pockets, his stocky back and strong shoulders hunched. He looks out at the rain streaming down the window. "And unhappier still to see an Arab get ahead."

"Bitterness will only make your breath sour! I will not move again. How many times do I have to say this?" The old man strikes the table with the flat of his palm just as a girl walks in; she looks at them, hesitates.

"Good morning," Saida says with her friendliest smile and gestures with her hand to the sky. "Such dreadful weather."

"It's September, fall already," says the girl, stepping in, not looking at the men. "It's the season. October will be worse." She shakes her umbrella in the street and leaves it propped up against the door.

"What can I get you?"

"Espresso. A double to take out."

"Have a pastry to go with it, yes?"

"No. Just the coffee," says the girl, but she eyes the confections. "Oh, all right. Just one."

Saida wraps the *baklava* in wax paper, then she picks out a fat piece of pistachio *maamoul.* "I give it to you. For later. You'll like it."

After the girl leaves, the men resume their never-ending argument. To go. To stay. Finally, her father calls Ramzi ungrateful, which gives him an excuse to take off his apron and throw it on the floor. He walks out, leaving the old man in the doorway calling after him.

Elias turns to Saida; his arms open wide as if he could catch understanding trying to escape. "What does he want? What does he want?"

Saida shrugs. "A bigger life maybe. He's young."

"He needs a wife. Not to be married is unnatural."

Saida looks at him but says nothing. The old man makes a sound, of apology perhaps, or merely confusion at the strange new world in which he finds himself.

Ten minutes later Ramzi comes back again, and the day continues as all their days do, serving the customers who are only plentiful around lunchtime when they come in for falafels and *kebbé* of lamb or chicken. The rest of the time Ramzi makes plans behind his newspapers, Elias revisits grief-salted dreams of the past behind his, and Saida cleans, cooks, does the accounts and pays the bills.

At five-thirty, she hears someone come in and looks up from the ledger book, expecting Joseph, who is already late, but it is not her son. It is the tall American, thin as a drug addict, whom

Saida has seen in the square. She thought he was a tourist at first, but it seems he lives nearby.

"Good morning," she says. She decides when Joseph gets here she will skin him alive.

The man returns the greeting and nods to her father and brother. He orders a *café crème* and sits at the counter. Saida watches him. He does not look healthy. There are red blotches on his skin, such fair skin, and his coppery hair is dull. He has a good nose, though, straight and long. And his chin shows character and strength. He holds his hand up over his mouth when he is not drinking. He moves slowly, deliberately, as though he plans his movements in advance. It strikes her that he is someone who is working very hard to look relaxed.

Ramzi makes himself an espresso and sits down next to the American, flipping through a real estate paper from Montpellier. He runs his fingers down the page and picks at an ingrown hair on his jaw, near his ear. He makes small noises, which Saida knows indicate he would like to begin a conversation, but the man does not speak.

"You are American, yes?" Ramzi says, finally.

"Canadian."

"Canada? But not from Montreal, your French . . ."

"Not very good, is it? No, I'm from the Maritimes. East of Quebec. By the sea. Nova Scotia. Pretty much all English."

"That's all right. We speak English. Don't we?" Saida and Elias agree that they do. "My father insisted on our education. You never know where you will end up, do you? It is good to keep in practice. So we will speak English with you."

"Fine," says the Canadian and he smiles.

It is a good smile, Saida thinks. Not a smile that finds things funny, but a smile that tells the other person that they have done something good.

"You have been here before. You live on the square, yes? I have seen you. I am Ramzi. That is my father, and my sister."

"Matthew."

Ramzi and Matthew shake hands.

"America is a great country. Canada is the same, yes? Not like France. A man can get ahead in America. In France, it is a class system still. They say they kill off the aristocracy in their big revolution, but it is just a lie. You must be in one of their great schools, one of their great families—most of all, you must not be a Maghreb. You know this word?"

"North African," says Matthew. He looks at a photo on the wall of the last remaining forest of Biblical cedars, the Arz Ar-rab, near Bcharré, and at another of the Qadisha Gorge where Maronite monasteries are cut into the rock. "But that's Lebanon, isn't it?"

"Yes," says Ramzi, pleased. "We are Lebanese. But the French make no distinction."

"Lots of racism in North America too."

"If you have money, though, none of that matters, and you can get money in America. Here you are taxed to death. You cannot afford to hire anyone because of all the social security and health care and pension and such, and so you must do all the little work yourself and then you cannot make other plans. In America this is not the case." Ramzi says this with absolute assurance. "I will not stay here in Paris. I do not wish to stay in France, but if I do, I will go to the south, to Montpellier. At least it is not so grey there all the winter. A man could die from lack of sun."

In Arabic, Elias says, "Only the young have wings on their feet," and Saida hates the sadness in his voice.

"My father says he is too old to move again."

"Something to be said for staying in one place, I guess," says Matthew, and Saida thinks he says this without conviction.

"And this is why you are not in Canada, yes?" says Ramzi with a grin. "Some of us are born nomads, I think."

Matthew nods. "Some people are strangers wherever they go." He smiles again.

"Have you been to Lebanon?" says Saida.

Matthew looks at her and there is something in his eyes that makes her sorry she asked the question, which suddenly does not seem as harmless as she'd thought.

"Yes. Beirut. In 1982," he says and drops his eyes.

The silence in the café is quite loud then.

"We left in 1979," says Ramzi, and then they wait. "We were in Damour."

"I'm a reporter," says Matthew.

"So, you know why we left, then," says Saida.

Turning away into the kitchen alcove she busies herself cleaning the grill. She hears a noise and her son's voice.

"Marhaba," he says.

"You're late," she says, switching to Arabic.

"Not so much. A minute or two," Joseph says, also in Arabic.

"Where are your books?"

"I went home first, that's why I'm late."

"I called the school this afternoon. They said you were not there."

The way his eyes dart around the room, looking for a clue, an escape, gives him away.

"You shouldn't check up on me. It is humiliating. I was there."

"You want to add lying to your crimes?" He smells of cigarettes.

"What time did you call? I had to go to the pharmacy for aspirin. I had a terrible pain in my neck from sleeping on that couch. I might have stepped out and maybe that's when you called." He licks the mark on his lower lip. As he does whenever he lies.

"Stepped out?" Ramzi laughs. "The only pain in the neck around here is you!" He says it in English and looks pointedly in the direction of the Canadian. He uses a joking tone to diffuse the tension.

"What's happening?" Elias looked from his son to his daughter to his grandson, but no one answers him.

"Who are you running with in the street?" Saida comes around the counter now and stands in front of Joseph. She barely comes up to his shoulder. Her son is tall, like Habib. Strong through the arms and chest like him, too, and now he crosses his arms, making the muscles bigger. Only his eyes are his mother's. She stares into eyes so much like her own, dark-rimmed, but bright with anger. "What are you doing? Picking pockets on the metro? Smoking dope?"

"No!" he says.

"Where do you go—out to the *banlieue*? Your so-called friends are criminals?" Her hands fly like birds.

"My friends are my friends."

"And your family? What are we?" Fingers spread wide as though she would take hold of him.

"Saida, keep your voice down," says Ramzi, and flicks his eyes again toward the Canadian, whose own gaze is fixed firmly on his coffee cup. "You're embarrassing our customer."

"Oh, forgive me! God forbid! Of course, that's more important than your nephew. Fine. You deal with him, this tough man who skips school and lies."

"You didn't call the school. *You* lied," says Joseph.

"Joseph! You will not call your mother a liar. Apologize. Now," says Elias.

For a moment it is not clear if he will or not, and his uncle glares at him. "Joseph," he cautions.

"I'm sorry."

"Take your grandfather to the doctor, Joseph. We will talk at home. Go right back there. Your grandfather will call me and tell me. You will stay with him. Do your homework. Do *some* homework."

"What's going on?" says Elias. "Am I going to the doctor? Why so much shouting? Joseph, you are a good boy, aren't you?"

"Yes, *Jadd*. Don't worry," says Joseph and he goes over to the old man and kisses him.

Saida's heart burns in her chest.

"Sorry," says Ramzi to Matthew. "The boy, he misses his father."

"You think he misses his father?" says Saida.

"Well, Anatole."

"That man is not his father! His father is dead," says Saida in Arabic. If there was a pot within reach, Saida might very well have tossed it at her brother. "Anatole was never his father. Don't you dare say such a thing!" She glances at the Canadian and thinks it is to his credit that he says nothing.

"Have some tea with me," says Elias and motions to the boy to sit down.

"Do I have time?" he says to his mother, this time in English.

"If you're fast," she says and turns to boil the water. She shrugs. "Dr. Allouche always keeps you waiting at least forty-five minutes."

"Joseph, come and meet our new guest," says Ramzi. "This is Mr. Matthew. He is from Canada. A reporter."

They shake hands and Joseph is full of smiles. "Have you been to New York?"

"New York is not in Canada, Joseph," says Ramzi and slaps him lightly on the arm.

"I know that, but it is close. I love New York. I want to go there one day. Have you been?"

"Yes. Many times."

"Cool. Brooklyn Bridge. Times Square. Best rappers in the world come from Bronx."

"All that," says Matthew, nodding. "A lot of good jazz, too."

"Yes, jazz is good music. American Black music. So, you're a reporter. What kind of reporter?"

"Good question. I go where they send me. I report on conflicts."

"On wars, then. *Les points chaudes.*"

"Yes."

"What wars?"

"Drink your tea, Joseph. You have to go in a minute," says Saida. "Don't be so nosy."

"It's all right," says Matthew, and then to Joseph again, "I guess I've been to most of the wars in the past twenty years."

"Cool." The word is long, drawn out, and accompanied by head nodding.

"You think so, eh?"

"Sure. You get to be where history is making. See the truth of things."

"I guess."

"You in Iraq during the Desert Storm?"

"Yup."

Matthew begins to talk about being in the Rashid Hotel, about the bombs that fell, the whining thunder they made, about the great fires in the desert. Saida does not listen to the words which, being about war, sound like obscenities to her ears. Instead, she watches the two. Saida likes the way Matthew talks to her son. As though he were an adult, an equal. And she can see from the look on Joseph's face, the way he leans in to talk to the man and listens attentively to his tales, that Joseph is basking in the attention. He does miss his father, she thinks—or at least *a* father. *Misses Anatole, does he? Misses the beatings. Misses the drunkenness. Misses being told he is good for nothing, useless, born only for the garbage dump. What is that to miss?*

"Enough, Joseph," she says at last. "It's time."

When her son and father have gone she goes into the open courtyard across which is the toilet. She scrubs the sink and mops the floor. The rain has stopped now and she takes a moment to pick weeds out of the potted plants. There are a few late roses on the vine and if she dead-heads the old, perhaps there will be a few more. She likes to be here, in the open, with the miniature garden. It is her thinking place.

Her father thinks she should marry again. A nice Lebanese man this time, not a foreigner he said, as though they were not the ones who were foreign, as though it was not her father's idea that a Frenchman, albeit a Corsican, would make them less strange here.

They would integrate, become family here, her father had thought. Well, she has had enough of that. Besides, who would want a woman like her now, a widow *and* a divorcee with skin melted into shapes like pale mud over which many feet had walked? No, her son would have to be content with conversations with strangers, with a grandfather, with an uncle. This was why she has moved back to her father and brother and not gone off with her son, somewhere else, somewhere where a woman alone was not always tied to the belt of the men in her family.

That night, when at last she can sit and talk to Joseph alone, she means to talk to him as well about the school he has skipped, about the boys he runs the street with, but it is a good moment between them, and instead she talks about the Canadian.

"I liked his stories, didn't you?" she says.

Joseph shrugs. "They were okay."

He admits nothing to her, his mother. He falls asleep watching the television and she does not have the heart to wake him again. Tomorrow, she says to herself, putting the duvet over him and a pillow under his head. When she kisses him, he smells sharp, but sweet as well, like cinnamon and dates.

CHAPTER EIGHT

That night Matthew returns home after consuming a great deal of beer at the Bok-Bok. He lies in bed and considers the Ferhat family. Saida is a pretty woman. Her dark eyes are arresting, one might even say haunting, lit with sorrow, yes, but also with dignity and intelligence. Good bones, as they say, although it's obvious from the way she shields her scars that whatever happened to Saida has left her feeling unlovely, which is such a shame. Matthew likes the boy, who is growing into his skin, pushing out to find the limits of things. It is a tough age, sixteen. Matthew knows that only too well. So many things can change, some irrevocably, others only feel that way. So many things cannot be changed.

Matthew's own family lives in a carefully guarded compartment in his mind. It has been a long time since he has seen his father and brother, Bill, Jr. Bill has built a house on the same farm and lives there with his wife and three children. Matthew has never met his brother's wife, nor his children, God help them. He has not seen a picture of them; has never heard their voice on the phone.

Matthew's mother died two years after the barn burning. All her dreams of going to Halifax and studying to be a vet went up in smoke in that barn, as did her hope of a new life, away from her drunken, violent husband. She would not go so long as Matthew was still at home, but she had been planning. Saving a little here and there. Putting something aside for years, all the while trying to protect Matthew as best she could from her husband's drunken rages. It was always Matthew. Never Bill, Jr., and the reason was simple enough: Bill, Jr. was the perfect clone of his father. However, with Matthew getting ready to go off to college, she had confided in him. Told him she was planning to leave, too. Somehow, her husband got wind of those plans.

The day after the barn burning, the town constable, the insurance man and the fire marshal came to poke around and ask some questions. They all said there was no sense to things like this. Just plain fool bad luck. The insurance man asked if there was any motive for his good friend Bill Bowles to burn down his own barn. Matthew held his breath and stared at the man real hard, so he would know that hell, yes, there was a motive and just give him a moment alone without his father around and he'd sure tell him what it was. But then the insurance man shrugged, said, "There's just no figuring," and the men all looked solemn. A little later they had a drink together, Bill and Bill, Jr., and the constable and the fire marshal and the insurance man, and then the three men got back in the constable's car and went away, beeping the horn in a friendly way as they turned onto the main road.

Later the man from the county came to haul away the animal carcasses. The air was still thick with the smell of burned horseflesh; all his life Matthew would be haunted by the image of the black, bloated bodies hanging from a back leg as the knacker man winched them onto the back of his truck. And then the knacker man, too, was gone and the three Bowles men were left alone in the yard, amidst the smoulder and the stench.

Bill Bowles spit on the ground and then turned to look up at his wife's ashen face, staring down at them from the upstairs window. "Nobody goes anywhere," he said. "Not on my fucking watch." And although it was not clear whether his mother could hear the words or not, the message was indisputably clear. Bill Bowles, Senior held the reins of power and he was not going to give them up. The curtain fell and Matthew's mother's face disappeared.

After that, his mother remained in her room, mostly. She did what she was told and said little and cried not at all, not after that first night. The two or three friends she had from church came by from time to time, but his mother refused to see them, and so gradually the intervals between visits lengthened and then they stopped altogether. His mother did not wash and she didn't eat, or hardly anything, and then only when her husband threatened to force-feed her.

She was bent on dying. Had her mind set on getting out. One day she called Matthew into her room where she lay on the bed, a stick-doll under a faded quilt. "Get out now," she said to him, trailing her finger along the most recent bruise colouring his face. "Don't wait."

But he could not, of course. Not as long as she would be left behind.

It took her a long time to die.

A week after she had been laid in the ground Matthew packed his duffle bag and, closing the door softly behind him in the middle of the night, headed for Halifax and whatever fate he found, vowing he would spend his life pointing a finger at the brutal tyrants of the world. He would make people listen. He would make them see. He would make them do something.

And what has he done?

People see. People know. And so what? They do not care. They cannot care. It would rock their view of the world too much. People think that if it is true, what he and others like him have to say about the world, then the world is too horrible, too terrifying to continue living in. And so they look, but do not see. Hear, but do not listen. Know, but will not admit. *Admit.* To let in. To permit access to. Like light.

Matthew rolls over, buries his face in the pillow and weeps. He weeps for a long time, and when he is done he reaches for the sleeping pills he keeps handy and takes more than he should.

* * *

Matthew has developed a loose pattern to his days, one divided into blocks of time. He sleeps in the mornings, tries to write in the afternoons, and generally fails. Late afternoons are for Chez Elias, when he feels calm and friendly. Evenings are for the Bok-Bok. Unless he is in what he almost laughingly calls the Emotionally Hopeless Forest. Then it's alone in his apartment with the phone off the hook. Now he is on his way to the Bok-Bok. Or at least he was, until the phone rings.

"Hello?"

"Matthew!" Brent. Only Brent pronounces his name *Mat-you.*

"Hey, Brent."

"Don't hey me. What did you write today?"

"I'm working."

"So send me something."

"Fine, I'll send you something."

"You said that last week."

"And I sent you a chapter."

"I didn't get it. Big surprise. You didn't overnight it."

"French mail is whimsical."

"I'm laughing."

"I like to make you happy."

Brent heaves a huge sigh. "Listen, Matthew. Listen to me. You got an advance. A very nice advance. Your editor is expecting to see something from this. You are not an international charity. If you don't start producing—"

"I am producing. I'm just not ready to show anything yet."

"This isn't fiction, Matthew, where timing doesn't matter. Timing matters. You're hot for only so long and then somebody else comes along and does something else that everybody's talking about and nobody remembers you. If nobody remembers you, nobody buys the book, get it?"

It is Matthew's turn to sigh. "I get it. I get it, Brent. And really, I am working. It's just a little rough yet. I want to impress them, you know?" His insincerity is like thistles in his throat.

"Impress the hell out of us. Write something."

"I have to go."

"Don't make me come over there, Matthew."

"See you, Brent. I'll get you something in the next couple of days."

All the way over to the 20th on the metro, Matthew mutters to himself about avaricious agents and bloodsucking publishers. The seat next to him remains empty.

When he arrives at the bar, someone calls out to him. "Hey, Matthew, over here!"

His eyes have not adjusted and he cannot make out the face, but he knows Jack's voice.

"Hey," he says, blinking and squinting into the smoky gloom. Soon he can make out Jack's bulk, sitting at his usual table with his back to the wall. "I'll get a drink. You want one?"

"Draught," says Jack. "And bring a Coke for my pal, Anthony."

"Hey," says another voice.

"Fair enough."

Matthew orders two beers and a Coke from Dan, who pours them into thick glass mugs and hands them over without saying a word. There is a tired-looking woman sitting at the end of the bar, her blond wig slightly askew. Matthew nods and she smiles back. It takes him a moment to realize it is Suzi, the girl wearing the black wig the first time he came to the Bok-Bok. "Nice look for you," he says. "I like it."

"You're sweet. You buy me a drink, too?" She pats the seat next to her.

"Get Suzi whatever she wants, okay, Dan?"

Suzi gets up and comes over to him. Although he has lied about how flattering the wig is, it strikes him, not for the first time, what a pretty woman she is. Her eyes are huge and look even larger because of the dark circles underneath. Her mouth is very small, and overall she looks like a girl from another time, from the twenties, perhaps, when Betty Boop was the It girl.

"*Coupe de champagne,*" she says. "You join me, yes?"

"Maybe later, okay? I have to deliver drinks to the boys."

"Let me know, Matthew." She pronounces it in the French way, *Matte-u*—which, although similar to Brent's pronunciation, is infinitely more pleasing to the ear. She runs her green painted fingernail under his chin. "*Merci,*" she says and toasts him with her drink. Dan snorts.

Matthew makes his way between the tables, most of which are empty. John and Charlie sit together, as always, and, as always, before the end of the evening they will be arguing loudly. Three men Matthew has not seen before scribble something on the back of a paper napkin, and whisper. As he walks past, they stop talking and cover up the napkin. Matthew ignores them.

Jack takes his beer, drinks and wipes foam from his moustache. Three mugs stand empty on the table. Next to him is a man almost as large as Jack, wearing a broad-shouldered black leather coat. His forehead is high and his hair black, cut close to the scalp. His skin is the colour of red rice and strong tea. He wears an open, unguarded expression, which is unusual in a place like this. When he smiles, which he does as soon as Matthew approaches, his gums are predominant, and his teeth disproportionately small. There is no defence against such a sincere smile, and Matthew immediately smiles back.

"Thanks. I'll get the next round," says Anthony, and he holds out his hand for Matthew to shake.

"Pleased to meet you," says Matthew.

"Anthony's been down south in Marseilles."

"Ah," says Matthew.

"Anthony used to be a cop in New York City."

"Tough place to be a cop," says Matthew. He has trouble reconciling this occupation with the man who sits before him.

"All places are tough when you're a cop. It was a long time ago." He reaches up and taps his head. "Wound up with a metal plate."

"Ouch." Matthew winces.

"I was moonlighting as a guard at Bellevue. One of the inmates got all whacked out and picked up this big table. *Whammo!* Cold-cocked me."

"Jesus," says Matthew.

"I don't remember it."

"Anthony was in a coma for, what, two weeks?" says Jack.

"Thirteen days. When I woke up there were these spaces where things used to be. Can't plan things or remember some things like I used to. And I can't drink the way I used to. I'm better than I was. Some headaches, dizziness. Been eleven years. Now mostly I just have trouble with new situations. Like, when I'm travelling, right, I can read the train ticket fine, and I can read the station board where they list the track numbers. Problem is, sometimes I can't figure out how one thing relates to the other. Connection synapses don't fire."

"Doesn't mean he's stupid, though," says Jack.

"Well, no stupider than before." Anthony smiles. "I just like to tell new people what's what, so they don't draw the wrong conclusions if I draw a memory blank. Worse thing isn't the head, though, it's numbness." He flexes his fingers a few times. "Nerve damage. Not exactly conducive to handling a firearm. Not that I want to do that anymore. If I never see a gun again—fine by me."

"Hell of a story," says Matthew.

"It's not a story." Anthony looks puzzled.

"No, I didn't mean that it wasn't true, just that it's hard."

"I guess. But I got off light. You should have seen some of the guys in the head ward. Acting like five-year-olds in a grown man's body, or couldn't walk, or talk. Naw, a little confusion, a little numbness, it's all right. I get a cheque from the city of New York. I get to come to Paris and all. I'm studying food. That's what I was doing in the south, but it didn't work out. I got a job as a kitchen grunt. A crappy job, but it was a start. Good restaurant. But I didn't catch on fast enough."

"Sorry to hear that," says Matthew, but Anthony just shrugs.

"Language problem is the way I choose to see it. I make it a practice not to hang on to resentments. Keep calm. Kind of a vow I took when my life derailed. No more violence, you know?"

Jack snorts. "Anthony had a spiritual awakening. Turned over a new leaf. I knew Anthony back in New York. Made a fair penny together back in the day."

"Long time ago," says Anthony and he drops his eyes.

"Aw, don't get all remorseful," says Jack, punching him in the shoulder. "That was then. Now we're just three guys in Paris, right? No pasts."

"At least not in here," says Anthony. "Think that's why I took to this place, the first time Jack brought me."

"I'll drink to that," says Matthew.

Suzi passes their table on the way to the toilet and ruffles Jack's hair.

"Jack's got a girlfriend," Anthony says.

"Grow the fuck up," says Jack.

"Suzi's all right," says Matthew.

"Hell, yes. No problem there," says Jack. "I wouldn't mind a piece of that."

"Yours for the asking, I'd say." Matthew takes a long pull of his beer.

"Mine for the paying, actually. And I don't pay."

"I don't think she'd make you pay. She likes you," Anthony says, then smiles. "I got a girlfriend. Vietnamese girl."

"Anthony's new romance." Jack looks amused.

"What's her name?" says Matthew.

"Pawena. In fact, you should meet her. Come over for dinner. I'm going to cook, and Jack's coming. What do you say?"

"Sure, why not? Thanks for the offer."

"Jack, you working at the hostel Saturday night?"

"Nope."

"Okay, Saturday night, then." With that, Suzi comes out of the bathroom, and Anthony reaches out and takes her hand. "Suzi, you want to come to dinner with us? At my place? I'm cooking. You can meet my girlfriend."

"You want me to come to dinner?"

"You working Saturday night?"

"She always works nights, asshole," says Jack.

Suzi arches an eyebrow and puts her hand on her hip. "This Saturday I will take off. Can you really cook?"

"I can cook."

"I would love to come for dinner. Give me the address."

Anthony gives her an address and she whistles. "Oh-la-la! You live in an area I know very well. Good area for girls."

Anthony throws his head back and laughs. "Not on my street!"

When she walks away, Jack slaps Anthony on the back of the head. "What are you doing?"

"Pawena's going to bring her girlfriend, and with Matthew coming I thought it would be nice to have an even number. What?"

"Listen, Brainiac, how do you think your girlfriend's going to take to you inviting a hooker?"

"Oh, she won't mind."

"Geez, I hate cops."

"Present company . . ." says Anthony, and waits.

"Excepted," says Jack, rolling his eyes and grinning.

CHAPTER NINE

The Ferhat family live near the Barbès-Rochechouart Métro on rue du Faubourg Poissonnière, a street split down the middle between the 9th arrondissement and the 10th. So, technically, the Ferhats live in the 10th, which the bourgeoisie consider not as good a neighbourhood as the 9th, which in turn is not as good as the 8th. The Ferhats live on the top floor, the sixth floor, where former maids' and cooks' quarters have been converted into tiny apartments. The conversion happened in stages as the neighbourhood became less genteel. First, four or perhaps five decades ago, the tiny rooms under the eaves were rented out to people other than domestic servants. Then, thirty years ago, the landlord knocked down walls and made small independent rooms into four two-room apartments with kitchenettes. At that time the sole bathroom was down the hall, shared among the tenants. Now improvements have been made. Each apartment has a bathroom with a toilet and a shower—not an actual bath for, having been partitioned from a corner of the main room, there is no space. Still, they are pleased not to have to go down the hall, not to have to smell the shit of strangers.

The same cannot be said for all converted *chambres de bonne* in Paris. Immigrants, refugees, students, the poor in all forms, take what they can get. Wave after wave of people arrive from everywhere in the world, looking for safe haven, for inspiration, looking for the famous *liberté, egalité, fraternité.* They come from

America, from Romania, from Vietnam, from Algeria, from Cambodia, from Iran, Argentina, Russia . . . from everywhere life has been too dangerous, too difficult, or too dull.

They sleep in rooms too cold or too hot, rooms with no insulation between the walls, and they fall asleep to the sounds of someone else's snoring, or their lovemaking, or their weeping, their whimpers, their flatulence, their rage. They hang their clothes out of windows on racks to air out the stench of cooking fat and cigarettes. They grow geraniums and lavender and basil in pots on the sills. They put on extra socks before they go to bed in the winter and suck on ice in the summer when the pollution is so thick the inside of the mouth tastes of diesel fuel and all the wealthy people have closed up shop and gone to Deauville or Cannes or Annecy.

Some bedrooms are in the back of the building, facing the courtyard where it is relatively quiet—only the *gardienne* remains down below, shaking the dust off her broom, flapping her tablecloth, scolding her children. Or the sound of the neighbours' radios and guitars and, during the day, the sound of construction: jackhammers and drills and sandblasters that make up the endless soundtrack of Paris. Saida's bedroom, however, is at the front; she puts wax plugs in her ears so she can sleep through the rattle and clank of garbage trucks and car horns and the motorcycles and the arguing voices from the street below.

It is four o'clock in the morning now, and the garbagemen yell to each other, banging the large green bins against the side of the truck to empty them. Their yellow swirling lights send strange patterns across the walls. In her restless sleep, Saida rolls over onto her back and the sheet tangles around her crossed ankles.

She does not understand it is only the bedclothes that have imprisoned her and three beads of sweat appear on the top of her lip. She tries to kick her feet, but she cannot move them. She tries to reach down and see why she cannot move her feet, but her hands will not move. She hears her heart in her ears, loud with blood. With enormous effort she opens her eyes and it is then that she sees him. A figure in grey overalls, smeared in gas station grease. Something on his head. A hood? In a rush like electricity through her limbs she knows who it is. It is Anatole Mariani. It is her husband. Her ex-husband.

But it cannot be him. He is in jail. But it is him. *How did he get in?* She opens her mouth to scream, but no sound comes out. Her panic increases. She feels as though she is flailing, but her arms will not move, her legs will not move. She does not know if he has tied her down, because she cannot turn her head to look. She thinks perhaps he has drugged her.

Anatole has something in his hand. Saida does not need for him to step into the light slanting through the blinds to know what it is. She knows hot oil, hot enough nearly to be burning, by the metallic smell. Knows the smell of scorched iron from the pot, knows the other smell, the sick smell of melting skin. She hears his whispers in her head. *Arab garbage. I thought I was marrying a good girl, not a useless bitch like you. You're the reason I don't get ahead. I'm tainted by you.* In her head she screams for her father, for her brother, for her son. Joseph! She screams silently, willing him to hear her even if she makes no sound, *Joseph! Run! Run! Run!*

How did he get past Joseph without waking him? What has he done to Joseph? Anatole steps closer, so slowly, he is torturing her. He smiles, his thin pale tongue rubbing against his top teeth, as though she is something he will enjoy eating, once she is properly cooked. He stands over her, lifts the pot, his face is blackness, shiny, empty. . . . She hopes she will die this time, and quickly.

"*Maman! Maman!* Wake up. You're dreaming! You're dreaming again."

The sound coming from her is like that of an animal bellowing with the lion at its throat. Strangled. Wordless. As though her larynx had been cut. Joseph shakes her and then takes her in his arms and pushes her hair back from her sweaty forehead. Slowly she comes to herself and wraps her arms around her son.

"It's okay," she says. "I'm all right."

"Wake up, wake up," he murmurs. "Wake up."

Their tears are impossible to separate. Rain from the same sky, making the flames of her terror sizzle and hiss and steam, until they are nothing but grey ash.

CHAPTER TEN

It is Saturday and Matthew lies on his bed, staring up at the midday ceiling. The dull dishwater light shows up the cracks in the paint. Last night he dreamed about women. Ghost women with long fingers and pale, bruised legs. Friendly. He dreamed of Kate, and now he aches for her, knowing it is irrational. Something about holding each other. Forgiving each other. Tears. He presses the heels of his hands into his eyes and searches for an argument compelling enough to make him get out of bed. Here he is, come to the City of Light, and what does he do? Skulks in the shadows of basement bars with ex-mercenaries, with broken-down ex-cops, with hookers. Well, at least tonight he'll be going to dinner at Anthony's house. *A change of scene from the Bok-Bok, right?* Only sort of.

He moans. Sits up. *Enough. Get out of bed.* He smells sour. The bed smells sour. *Take a shower. Do a wash.* The idea of lugging his laundry to the launderette on rue de Clichy is enough to make him roll over and go back to sleep. *Agreed, then. No laundry.* But there must be something. There must be a reason to get out of bed.

You could write something. He moans again, louder this time. Brent leaves messages every second day. He should write something. Why not write anything and send it to him? Shut him up at least?

He drags himself to the bathroom, pisses loudly. Brushes his teeth and talks himself into taking a shower. The small shower is built into one of those fantastic French jokes, the sitz bath: a thigh-high square tub just large enough for one dainty Frenchmen to squat in, with a shelf for sitting, if one could figure out where to put one's legs. For Matthew, at his height, it is impossible. From the ceiling hangs a chrome ring with a white plastic curtain around it and a jury-rigged plastic hose attached to the faucet below. At least there's lots of hot water. He strips off his underpants and steps in. The water pricks at his skin and the steam softens the air. He looks down at his hard-on. Soaps up his hand. He begins to believe there may yet be hope for the day.

Half an hour later, coffee in hand, he sits at his desk. He picks up a pen. Begin where today? Try Srebrenica. Try Herzegovina. But his mind is on women. Ghost women. And as he tries to write they haunt him. . . .

There was a girl in Herzegovina. No more than sixteen or seventeen. She had a small wound on the side of her temple. So small it was astonishing to think it had killed her. By then I'd seen bodies ripped up so many times that it felt as though that was the way death should be. But this small spot, so little blood, seemed impossible. Her mother or grandmother (ages were hard to guess) knelt beside her, doubled over with arthritis, her thin grey strings of hair pulled up in an untidy knot, wearing a man's jacket and several layers of skirts. The old woman touched the girl's arm over and over again, as though trying to wake her. That girl was so beautiful. Death had made her beautiful. Pale and peaceful, completely lovely. Drained of all tension, all fear. So unspeakably frail and still and undefended. I wanted to touch her but when I put my hand out, the old woman grabbed me and bit the fleshy part beneath my thumb until she drew blood, and I hit her on the back of her head, hard enough to make her let go. I walked away, nursing my hand, weeping for this girl, whom I had never seen alive, whom I loved and who was dead. For days I dreamed of her and for weeks could not get her image out of my mind. I think she lives there still.

Later, when I came back to Kate from that time away, there was a moment when she lay sleeping on the couch. We had gone for a walk that afternoon, to see the cherry blossoms, pink and white, like a young girl's skin, the colour of a nipple, of a lip, of an earlobe. A man bumped into Kate on the sidewalk, and I was instantly enraged, pushing the man, challenging him, stupefied by the look of astonishment on his face as he apologized and said it was an accident. Kate stepped in front of me and made me look at her, her hands on the sides of my face, smiling as though smiles were a charm against bullies. "I'm fine," she said. "Look, no harm, no harm." And I saw that this was true and held out my hand to the man to shake, to say I was sorry, but the man scuttled away, muttering. We went home, Kate and I, and made love and I lost myself for a moment in her butterscotch skin. Then she'd dozed off with a book on her stomach, and her head tilted toward the sun coming in the window. It made her face look pale, too pale, pale as a phantom in the afternoon light. It was sudden, the way I couldn't stand to look at her and how I had to get out of the apartment right then, immediately, or I would choke. When I returned, drunk as Davy's sow, in the wee smalls, Kate was mad as hell and how could I explain?

Sack of skulls.

Matthew sits back, his fingers cramped around the plastic shaft of the ballpoint pen. *Don't read it back; don't read it back.* He opens the drawer, grabs an envelope, scribbles a note to Brent and stuffs it, and the pages he's just written, inside. Licks the seal. Flattens it with a pound of his fist. *Let's see what you make of that.* Matthew laughs out loud, addresses the envelope, and then sticks a stamp on the letter and grabs his jacket. He will mail the damn thing. He will. Still laughing, he heads for the door.

After mailing his pages to Brent, Matthew strolls back to his apartment, but realizes he does not want to go in. He stands at the heavy wooden door with his hands in his pockets. He has nowhere else to go, at least not until tonight and dinner at Anthony's. He wonders how this can be. How can a person live in Paris and have nowhere to go?

On previous visits to Paris over the years he had always been contemptuous of a certain type of expatriate and how the city supported their illusions. All the beachcombers, and soon-to-be novelists, painters, dancers, jazz musicians. They teach English or work as babysitters or moving men or at some other bad-paying job, or else they live off their trust funds or savings or, yes, disability cheques, and don't actually do any writing, painting, dancing, whatever. They sit in cafés and smoke Gitanes and they bolster each other's lies and they tell each other they are all Hemingways, or Josephine Bakers, or Picassos. Back in some place like New York, say, they would have to make it quick or be chewed up and spat out in record time and be back on a bus to Minnesota and the Mama's *lutefisk*. But not here. Here they slink along café to café. Now, he fears he is becoming one of them.

"Mr. Matthew!" The teenager from Chez Elias stands in the doorway of the café. He is dressed like any American teenager: baggy black track pants slung low on his hips, oversized jean jacket hanging almost to his knees. Trainers. He fills up the doorway. Matthew considers that if it were not for the ear-to-ear grin he would be a pretty intimidating kid, the kind old French ladies move away from in the metro, clutching their pocketbooks. That lower lip is strange. When Matthew first met Joseph he thought someone had given him a swollen lip, but it is clearly some sort of birth defect, as though someone has pulled down that side of flesh, turning it slightly inside out.

"Hello! My uncle says hello," he calls.

"Hello. It's Joseph, right?"

"Yes. Joseph. You busy?"

"Nope."

"Then you come. Have coffee."

Another café, another coffee. Matthew shrugs. "Sure," he says.

Ramzi greets him warmly and pulls out a chair at a table where the old man already sits.

"Sit with us. Joseph, you get the coffee."

Saida is behind the counter. She looks tired, with hollows under her eyes. Smiling at Matthew, she adjusts the scarf around her neck, and Matthew senses that this hiding of her scars is an automatic gesture. He has noticed that when she is not using her right hand, which is also badly scarred, she keeps it behind her back. When Saida smiles, the brightness of her teeth makes her skin look darker and the smudges under her eyes more pronounced. She says something to Joseph, and the boy comes back with a tray of tiny cups, a pot of Turkish coffee, a plate of dates, oranges and *baklava*.

Joseph sits and pours the coffee. Matthew looks at these three generations of men and can't help but wonder what it would be like to sit like this, with men of his own blood, of his own stories. To be known in that way. Where you come from. Who your people are. I know my people, he thinks, and I am not proud.

They ask him how he is and he says he is fine. They talk about the weather and about the *sans-papiers* and the recent strike by public employees, which brought the country to a near halt for one day, closing schools and grounding flights. Saida does not enter the conversation, but watches them and serves the occasional customer, wrapping packages of preserved lemons in jars, haloumi cheese, olives and pita. Matthew sips the coffee, rich and smoky, alive on his tongue after the sweetness of the date, the sparkle of the orange.

Joseph asks him questions about being a reporter, and at first he answers in monosyllables, not wanting to bring the dark memories into this place. Then he looks at the boy, who runs his hand self-consciously over his shaved head, his heavy eyebrows raised in eagerness, a smile of encouragement on that bruised-looking mouth—and Matthew sees himself as he never was, but would like to think he might have been: hopeful for the world, for tales of adventure, for someone to open a hand and show him a treasure from a far-off place. He sees how Joseph tries to be tough, dressing like that, with the swagger and the pout, but how he is, after all, just a boy champing at the bit and restless in this, the world of his family. Matthew finds he does not want to disappoint him and so he tells a tale or two—harmless stories of exotic places—the Khyber Pass, Beijing, New Guinea, Borneo. He tells of eating slugs with the Australian Aborigines, and snake meat in China. He tells of entering the bowl of a Hawaiian volcano with a film crew from *National Geographic* and of travelling with storm-chasers across the dust bowl of America on the trail of tornadoes big as mountains, moving at the speed of freight trains.

Matthew discovers he likes telling tales to Joseph, and when he looks at his watch he is surprised to find that three hours have passed.

"I have to go," he says.

"Stay for dinner," Elias says, his leathery face a mass of wrinkles when he smiles. "We make lemon chicken and spinach. Very good. Tell him, Saida."

"I'd love to but I can't." He is shy, suddenly, at the comfort he feels here, does not entirely trust it, and is therefore happy to have dinner at Anthony's to use as an excuse.

"You come back, then?" says Joseph.

"Sure."

"Tomorrow?"

"Joseph, do not be rude. Mr. Matthew is very busy," says Ramzi.

"I'll come back soon. Maybe tomorrow."

"Good," says Joseph, rubbing his head. "I'll be here."

As Matthew leaves, Saida calls out, "Thank you."

CHAPTER ELEVEN

Anthony lives in a rented house on a tiny road known as Villa des Tulipes, in the upper 18th arrondissement, at the porte de Clignancourt. From the metro, Matthew crosses rue Belliard, at the edge of the great flea market, Les Puces, through the throng of North Africans and Arabs selling everything from roasted corn on the cob to carpets from the back of vans. He finds Villa des Tulipes and as he turns onto it, is taken by the sense of calm on the tiny street. It is very old, and cobblestoned, the surface beneath his feet curving in an aged hump. Too narrow, really, for cars. If he reaches his arms out he can probably touch the iron fences and concrete steps on either side. The lane is a comfortably shabby assortment of small attached cottages, mostly one storey, but some with two, and is lit by the buttery light from old-fashioned street lamps.

Anthony lives on the bottom floor of one of the cottages, which is painted sky blue with dark green trim. A fig tree and a lilac bush grow in the postage-stamp garden. From an open window drift laughter, the smell of roasting meat, and Etta James's barrelhouse voice singing "At Last." Matthew flips the latch on the gate, crosses the tiny garden and knocks.

Suzi opens the door and kisses him on both cheeks. She smells of roses and, beneath that, something tangy, like lemons. She wears no wig and her hair is dark, cut in the short *gamine* style of Paris. She looks at least five years younger than usual, and Matthew realizes she is wearing almost no makeup other than a little lipstick. Her skin is pale and she has a few blemishes.

"Come on in. You are the last."

Matthew can't help but notice her eyes. The pupils are extremely small.

"Sorry I'm late. Hey, Jack."

"Hey. Good to see you. Suzi, get out of the way and let him in."

The entranceway is indeed so small that there is no room for the two of them. Suzi smiles and steps back. "Anthony is in the kitchen," she says. "So are we." Matthew follows her.

The walls in the hall are painted midnight blue and decorated with gold-foil stars. The kitchen, which Matthew can see at the end of the hall, is warm, pale terra cotta. The floor throughout is wooden. To the right is a small bedroom, the walls painted a serene shade of mossy green. Peeking in, he sees a large wooden cross hanging on the far wall over the futon bed, a bronze Buddha in the corner and stacks and stacks of books.

The kitchen is really part kitchen and part everything else. The back wall is made up almost entirely of paned glass and looks out onto a garden, only slightly larger than the one at the front, in which an ancient-looking olive tree grows. A low wall, topped with metal fencing, backs the garden; beyond that are apartments, but at some distance. Matthew assumes the rail tracks run between the apartments and the house, and that the house is built on the side of the drop. At the right side of the back wall is a fair-sized alcove that houses the refrigerator, the stove, the sink and the door that leads to the outside.

Anthony stands at the pot-cluttered stove, wearing a large white apron. The room itself is furnished with a low table, surrounded by cushions, at which sit two Asian girls. There is also a futon sofa covered in a colourful blanket and more cushions. Jack has taken possession of a big, battered leather chair near the back window, next to yet another pile of books and a reading lamp. Suzi dangles herself on the arm of the chair. In fact, all of her dangles, her legs, her arms, as though her spine is liquid. An intricately carved Moroccan lantern hangs from the ceiling.

"Matthew! Great to have you here!" Anthony comes toward him, waving a wooden spoon. "Let me introduce you. You know Suzi and Jack, and this is Paweena." He squats down next to a dainty girl sitting on a cushion at the table and dressed in a turquoise sweater with a high collar that frames her face. She is in her early twenties, perhaps twenty-five, her skin a mix of saffron and toffee. "Paweena, this is Matthew, the guy I told you about. He's a journalist, right? He was in Rwanda and Bosnia—just about every place."

"Nice to meet you," Matthew says, shaking her extended hand.

"Hi," Paweena says. Her hand is soft and cool and limp. "This is Jariya."

"Hello, Jariya. Pretty name."

"Thank you," says the girl, as she spits an olive pit into her palm before dropping it into the ashtray on the table. She has slightly bucked teeth. They give her an overly eager quality that doesn't blend with her eyes, which are as hard as black tacks. She makes no move to extend her hand and neither does Matthew. Jariya lights a cigarette and plays with a cheap pink lighter, twirling it on the top of the table.

"We are just now talking about Paweena's new apartment," says Suzi.

Matthew notices that Jack has his hand along Suzi's thigh, covering her knee. He notices, too, that there is something tricky in Suzi's voice. He looks at Anthony, who has his arm around Paweena, and he can't help but notice that Paweena is leaning slightly away from him, with a strange smile on her face.

"There is a new set of dishes I saw. I want them, and Anthony, he's going to buy them for me. And curtains. I need curtains."

"Sure, baby," says Anthony. He gets up and goes back to the stove.

Matthew notices that the doors have been taken off the kitchen cabinets, so that all one has to do is scan the shelves to see what's available.

"What's cooking?" Matthew's nose is practically twitching with the smells. Spices of some sort under the meat. Thyme? Nutmeg?

"Thought I'd do something for the hunting season. *Sanglier.* Wild boar. Marinated in wine and spices for two days. Potatoes gratin. Salad. Recipes from the Haute Savoie region."

"*Sanglier?* Really? Damn. I'm starving just thinking about it," Matthew says, and Anthony beams.

"Grab a seat, Matthew. Help yourself to some wine." Anthony points to an open bottle on the table.

"Thanks. So, where you girls from?" Matthew says.

"Thailand," says Paweena.

"Thailand?" says Jack. "That's not what Anthony said."

"Where he say we from?"

Anthony comes over and joins them at the table, folding his long legs easily.

"Someplace else," Jack mutters.

Suzi gets up and sits next to Matthew.

"Where'd I say?"

Paweena takes Anthony's jaw in her hand and brings his lips to hers. Then she turns to Matthew and says, "You ever been to Bangkok?"

Suzi snorts.

"Yup. I've been there."

"Lots of Americans, they think Thailand nothing but sex trade and cheap drugs."

"I don't think that."

"Uh-huh," she says.

"You married?" says Jariya.

"Married? Uh, no."

"Everybody hungry?" says Anthony, rising, and they all agree they are.

The food is splendid. The boar is served with a gravy *deglacé* and *"les herbes,"* greens baked with currants, lemon juice and a breadcrumb crust. The potatoes are thickly layered with cream. The salad has walnuts in it.

As dinner goes on and the wine flows, Matthew enjoys himself. Suzi sits between him and Jack and graces them with equal attention, a smile here, a nudge of the thigh there, a hand on the shoulder, a whisper. She asks Jack what it is like working at the hostel and where he goes to take photos. She asks Matthew where he is from and what Nova Scotia is like. Anthony sits on the other side of the table, bookended by the Asian girls. Jariya looks sullen and tries, unsuccessfully, to catch Matthew's attention more than once. They all compliment Anthony, who radiates pleasure and keeps up a running commentary on where the best butchers are and how to properly treat wild meats and why a light red wine is best with this meal. From time to time, Matthew catches Paweena staring thoughtfully at him.

As they move on to the dessert course, Matthew excuses himself to use the toilet. He walks up the hall and cannot resist peeking into Anthony's bedroom. As well as the Buddha and the wooden cross, Ganesh, smiling and elephant-headed, sits on a small table next to a pair of candles in gold altar sticks. A Thai spirit house with oranges, incense and a shallow bowl of water in front of it perches on the windowsill. He picks up one of the books that lie scattered about. *Thomas Merton: Spiritual Master.* He notices the Bible, and a book called *Of Water and Spirit*, by someone called Malidoma Patrice Somé about the life of an African shaman. The Koran. The Upanishads. *The Mishomis Book*, which, he learns from scanning the cover, is about the Midewiwin religion of the Ojibway people. There are works by Tagore, Chuang Tzu, Martin Burber and Loren Eisley. So many books. The room feels like sacred space. Matthew backs out, and hopes no one has seen him invade it.

On the wall in the hallway is a black-and-white photo. He stops to take a closer look. It is of the tango dancers in the park by the

Seine. Matthew remembers the dancers. The man holds the woman in the small of her back, their hands high over their heads. The woman is bent backward. The dress she wears has a tear under the arm through which a patch of dark hair is visible. The cords in her neck stand out even though her face is passive. The man looks as if he might sink his teeth into her. The light is filtered through the awning overhead, and at the same time reflects from the Seine below, making the faces both clear and softened.

When Matthew comes back to the main room it is evident that if Suzi had played no favourites early, she has now made her decision. She reclines between Jack's legs, leaning against his chest. His arms are folded around her and he smiles lazily at Matthew. Matthew raises his glass in a toast to them both and Suzi giggles. Other changes have taken place as well. Paweena has moved and now sits between Jariya and Anthony.

"Did you take that photo in the hall?" Matthew says to Jack.

"Yup."

"Here's to you. It's good. Better than good." He raises his glass again.

"A change from all the dead body shots, huh?"

They finish dinner with an apple *tarte* and caramel ice cream. Matthew hums along to Ry Cooder singing "Trouble, You Can't Fool Me." They are sipping coffee and brandy when Paweena says "I have it now." She keeps her eyes on Matthew and he feels an icicle twist along his spine.

"Have what, baby?" says Anthony.

"Where I know Matthew from. Jariya, you know who this is. This is the reporter who was shot in Israel."

"Wasn't me," says Matthew as Jariya's head snaps toward him.

"Shit," says Jack.

"Yes. Was you. I remember very good. You think you were Superman or something. Stepped in front of the bullets." She laughs. "Very foolish man."

"Hey, you that guy?" says Anthony.

"Wasn't me." He looks over at Jack, who meets his gaze.

"Man says it wasn't him," says Jack.

Matthew looks around the table into the faces of the people who, with the exception of Jack, instantly revert to strangers, all illusion of friendship shattered. Anthony regards him with open admiration, Paweena and Jariya with something like ghoulish curiosity, Suzi with slight embarrassment. What do they know about it? A father. A child. Gunfire. Dust and blood. The sharp taste in the mouth like copper pennies. The way the world dissolved in the noise. A gun within reach. The possibilities contained in the gun. Death and silence.

"Tell us about it," says Paweena, cocking her head and smiling.

The stem of the wineglass snaps. There is a skin-pop and then pain stitches through Matthew's palm. Wine spatters across the table. Blood drips, and someone shrieks.

"Put this on it," says Suzi and wraps her napkin around his hand.

"Sorry."

Matthew gets up and goes to the bathroom as Jack whispers something to Suzi.

"I'll get a bandage." Anthony starts to rise.

"No, let me," says Suzi as she disengages herself from Jack's arms.

While Matthew stands dripping over the sink, Suzi rummages in the medicine cabinet until she finds what she needs. Her small breasts strain against her T-shirt. The lace in her bra is outlined. She pushes up her sleeves and Matthew sees marks on her inner arm. She catches him looking, cocks an eyebrow, and he looks away. She takes his hand in hers and efficiently but gently cleans out the wound, which is narrow but deep. She puts the bandage over it.

"I did not know this was you," she says.

Matthew says nothing.

"We will get you a new drink," she says. "That girl is absurd."

"I think I better go."

"Sure. After a drink."

Her hands on his are oddly reassuring and he lets himself be led back to the party, where Jack hands him a large brandy.

"Drink up, buddy," he says and winks.

"Sorry," says Paweena. "You very sensitive."

"Yeah, that's me. Mr. Sensitive."

Matthew accepts the drink and leans back, wanting to be gone, but not wanting to be gone, allowing himself to sink into sullenness.

"You were a hero, man," says Anthony.

"Jesus, let it go," says Jack, with that growl in his voice again.

Anthony lets out a big laugh and they all look at him. His face is relaxed, composed.

"What's so fucking funny?" Jack scowls.

"You are. You sound like a bear. You're just like Saint Seraphim."

"Who's he when he's at home?" says Jack.

"If I was Catholic, he'd be my saint. He lived in the Russian forest and lugged a sack filled with heavy stones and sand across his back. Said it was to tire out what tired him out. Then he prayed for one thousand days and nights. Wrestling demons."

"And I'm like him? What are you, nuts?" Jack's laugh sounds forced.

Anthony raises his glass to Jack. "We both are. But he won, don't worry, and more than that, he made friends with a bear. He even looked like a bear. Sounded like one." Anthony smiles. "Just like you."

"Wonderful," says Jack. "How do you know all this shit?"

"I read."

"I don't believe in saints," says Matthew.

"Cynicism is the last refuge of the broken-hearted," says Anthony.

"You make that up?" It's Matthew's turn to laugh.

"No. The Canon at the American Cathedral said it."

"I think I like you better as a cop," says Jack.

"I thought you hated cops. Present company . . ."

"Excepted." Jack and Anthony clink glasses.

Paweena rolls her eyes and looks bored. Jariya holds a hand in front of her mouth while she discreetly picks her teeth.

"Anyway," says Matthew, and drains his glass. "Thanks for a great dinner. A fantastic dinner. I have to go."

"Don't go," says Anthony.

"Got to go. Have to get up early to work tomorrow."

"Sure?"

"Sure." He picks up his jacket, shakes Jack's hand and bends down to kiss Suzi on the cheek. "Thanks," he says.

"You are welcome," she says.

He turns to wave at Jariya and Paweena. He notices that Jariya has removed a shoe and her naked foot slowly caresses Paweena's leg.

"Uh, bye," he says.

"Bye-bye," they say in unison.

Matthew walks up to the metro, but once he descends into the underground, he knows he is not ready to go home. He needs to clear his head from the brandy and the talk, from the ghosts. He decides to head to the Seine. The platform is busy, even at this late hour. Couples. A group of young people joke loudly and flout the non-smoking rules. Two guys with a ghetto blaster try to be intimidating, with their French-Afro-rap music turned up loud. Everyone ignores them. At last the car arrives with an ear-piercing squeal of breaks.

He sits and a man sits next to him, wearing a fine blue-and-white striped *djellaba,* infused with amber and jasmine. At Strasbourg-Saint-Denis, Matthew transfers and heads in the direction of Porte de Sevrès. He gets off at Alma Marceau and makes for the quay. The night is star-scattered and cool, and as he walks down the stone steps that permit access to the river's edge he begins, if not to relax, then at least to decompress from the shock of the evening. He has been foolish, he now realizes, to think that his notoriety, his infamy, his *shame*, would not find him here. He will either have to learn to deal with it, or become a hermit. At the moment the latter is more appealing. He shakes his head to get the dusty images out and concentrates on his footsteps. One in front of the other. Just this. Stone under foot. Water. Stars. Houseboats.

This is what he has come to see. He loves the houseboats, some of them no more than rusty old barges, some gleaming showpieces. His favourite has an ancient wood-carved figurehead, bare-breasted, battered and proud, attached to a pole on the deck. Through the portals nestle tiny, efficient rooms filled with soft light. Water laps against the side of the boat as it rocks gently. Just looking at the boats calms him. He thinks it must be a grand life. He imagines pulling anchor and chugging away down the muddy river to a landscape full of new possibilities whenever the fancy takes hold.

He walks under the pont Alexandre II when he smells a whiff of something unpleasant, getting stronger. His nose twitches and he puts a finger under his nostrils. The acrid smell of urine is very bad. Catching a movement in the shadows, he jumps. As he turns, his skin prickles and his breath catches. Then he laughs. A sandy-coloured pup wriggles and begins to whine. It is tied to a ring in the wall next to a small alcove in one of the bridge's support columns. A light within flickers feebly; a candle. The dog cocks its head and barks once, short and sharp. From inside the alcove a raspy voice shushes the dog and Matthew realizes someone lives there, in the cramped nook in the wall. He can just make out a figure sitting on a stool, a muddle of blankets on the floor and, near the candle, an open book and a frying pan. He nods, but the figure simply stares, the message to stay away clearly articulated nonetheless.

A flood of loneliness abruptly overcomes Matthew, and he wants to speak to this man. He opens his mouth as the man blows out the candle, leaving Matthew pierced with a jolt of electric isolation.

CHAPTER TWELVE

It is nearly eleven o'clock when Saida climbs the stairs to her apartment two nights later. She has stayed late at the restaurant because dinner was busy and there was much to do afterward, cleaning up and getting things ready for the morning. When she left half an hour ago, Ramzi was still waiting for two tables of men who looked as though they were going to linger over their coffee and cigarettes. Usually Saida is home by eight. They do not generally get many people in after work. A few stragglers, a few of her brother's friends who come by after they have finished their meals at home, more to talk than anything else. But tonight they had all been hungry and so she had had no choice but to stay.

If this happens too often, she thinks, she will put her foot down and tell Ramzi he will have to make other arrangements, hire part-time help perhaps. Even under the table if they must take the risk. She cannot leave Joseph alone at night. But this is the least of her problems. Her son's grades had been very good, once. If only Joseph would stay home, as he promises he will, but rarely does. Ramzi tells her that at the boy's age it is normal to want to be with his friends rather than stuck in the house studying and looking after his grandfather. Her father tells her not to worry, that he is fine by himself, he is not so old yet that he can't take care of himself and that Joseph is a good boy. It is only her own gut that tells her there is much for a mother to fear in the twisting, turning, often dead-end streets of Paris.

Sometimes she wishes she had stayed in the old neighbourhood, in the 13th arrondissement where she had lived with Anatole. At least for a while there had been a few women to talk to. But that was before. They would not talk to her after she returned to the apartment, her bandages public notice of her failure. And now there is no time for friendships with women. There is work. There is family. It is safer that way.

Saida stops to catch her breath on the fourth-floor landing. Her legs are very tired after more than fourteen hours on her feet. She hopes Joseph is home. She called earlier, but there was no answer. Where does he go? He had stayed in the other night after his talk with Matthew Bowles, though. That evening she had sent him home with his grandfather right after dinner, telling him he must do his homework, that she would check it when she got home. And miracle of miracles, when she arrived a few hours later, there he was. Television off. Books on the table. He had been in such a good mood, chattering away about Matthew and his stories. Saida suspects many of these tales are exaggerations at the very least, but she could not help grinning to herself just the same. She even managed not to laugh when Joseph said he thought he might want to be a reporter himself one day.

Now, as she reaches the top floor she hears the music. *Rai* music. Too loud. *Oh, Joseph.* At least he is home. But how can he possibly work with the music at that level? She is a step beyond the first door when it opens and the fat man who lives there pops out. He wears no shirt, but only a grey, stained undershirt. He holds his rodent-pet, the ferret that is just a rat with delusions. It wriggles in his arms as though it were a squirming baby. Saida's skin goosebumps at the sight of its sharp little teeth.

"You hear that? This shit I have to listen to!" the man says as his watery eyes widen in indignation. He puffs on his cigarette.

"I'm sorry. He'll turn it down, Monsieur . . ." Saida tries to remember his name, Leclerc? Lévesque? Levigne? All these French names, they run together like paint.

"Turn it *down?* Turn it *off!* And keep it off or I'll call the police, I tell you. I'll call them on you. And I don't think you'd want that, would you? With what goes on in there?"

"I don't know what you're talking about. We do nothing wrong. He is just a teenager. You remember what it was like at that age." It is embarrassing to stand arguing in this way, in the hall, with that music and its thumping bass, which means they must raise their voices even more. Saida fumbles in her purse for her keys. Something sharp, a stray pin perhaps, jabs under her nail and she jumps with the crisp pain.

"You Arabs—" the man begins.

"Yes?" Saida bristles. "What about us Arabs?"

"Letting your children run the streets. Criminals and drug addicts. It will be the death of France!"

He slams the door before she can say anything more, and she is alone. It takes her a moment to realize she has found her key, that it is in her palm, digging in. She opens her fingers and sees a bright red imprint.

"At least we work!" she says to the closed door, but not so loudly. He could be capable of anything, a man like that.

As she puts the key in the lock the music stops. She swings open the door. Two strange boys look at her and she starts. Joseph steps out of the bathroom with something in his hand. He goes to the sink. One of the boys sits on the couch, a bandana tied around his shaven head, his huge feet in running shoes on her coffee table. He moves them. The other boy sits on the floor and wipes his eyes. But his mouth smiles. Laughing, then? Are they laughing at her argument with the neighbour?

Both boys are small and wiry. Handsome boys, but hard-looking, and older than she thought at first. Older than Joseph. Dark-skinned, Algerians maybe; the one who is laughing has a gold tooth. He sees her looking and puts his hand over his mouth.

"Imma," says Joseph, turning to her. "You're home earlier than you thought, eh?"

"No. Later."

Saida sees that he is rinsing whatever he had in his hand out at the sink. A shallow tin plate. The windows are open and it is cold in the room, but the air stinks nonetheless, sweet and acrid at the same time. "I don't want you smoking in the house. You know that."

"Sorry, *Imma*." *Imma*. Mama. Like he was a little boy again.

"Who are your friends?"

"This is Maloud, and Jamal."

Jamal, the one on the floor, gets up and extends his hand, which is delicate, with a thin wrist under a heavy imitation gold wristwatch. "Nice to meet you," he says. Maloud giggles.

Saida shakes his hand and says, "It's time to go home, boys. Don't you have school in the morning?"

"Oh, sure. We have to get up early for school," says Maloud.

Saida stands in the middle of her living-room floor and they must walk around her to get their backpacks and packages of Marlboroughs, their baseball caps and their jackets. Jamal brushes against her and apologizes.

"Okay, we'll see you tomorrow, Joseph," he says.

"Tomorrow," says Joseph.

When they are gone, she still does not move, and Joseph fusses around the small room, cleaning away cans of Coke and a bag of potato chips. "What?" he says, finally.

"Look in the mirror. Look at your eyes. That stupid grin on your face. You do this in my house?"

"What?"

"You think your mother is a fool? Shut the window. It's cold."

"I said I was sorry. I can't even have friends round now?"

"You cannot have these friends here. You cannot smoke drugs in my house."

"What are you saying? What are you accusing me of?"

"Not half of what I bet you are doing. What other drugs are you doing? Are you going to be one of the addict boys up the road, sleeping in their own piss, scabs all over their faces? Oh, my God."

Saida drops heavily onto the couch. There are ashes and crumbs under her table, ground into the carpet, which is not a good carpet, but still, it is a nice red colour and the pattern is pretty. "Is your life so terrible that you want to destroy it?" she says.

"*Imma*, it's just a little grass." Joseph sits down next to her. He speaks to her slowly, with a tolerant smile on his lips, as though she is incapable of understanding what matters. "It takes the edge off this shithole life."

Saida slaps her son's face with her open palm. She has not intended to do it. And as soon as it is done she bursts into tears. Joseph stands and looks down at her, the red mark on his cheek giving him more authority than his posture. She wishes he would say something.

She is still crying and her voice has hiccups in it. "So, that's what you think about the life you have? And it's just grass? But it's not a little anything. It is not. You are floating away, getting lost. I want you to go to university. You don't want my life? Well, fine. I do not want my life either. But my life or something a whole lot worse is all you'll get if you don't stop what you're doing." Her voice has risen and now she is standing, although she does not remember getting to her feet.

"Don't ever hit me again," Joseph says, and then, "Stop crying."

"Tell me I'll never come home and find you like this again."

"Fine."

"Tell me you'll stop doing drugs."

"Fine."

"Mean it," she says, taking hold of his sleeve. "Study. No more of these friends."

"Fine." His face is like his stepfather's then: impassive. A wall behind which he smugly hides. She could pound all day on a wall like that and break nothing but her own bones.

"I'll tell your uncle, your grandfather, too. We'll see what they have to say about this."

Still there is nothing, just the blank of him where she can find no purchase on which to pull herself into his heart. "What kind of a reporter do you think you'll make, stoned? Uneducated. Everything funny?"

It is just a flicker that she sees, then, in his dark eyes. Nothing more. But it is something.

CHAPTER THIRTEEN

Matthew sits at his desk with his head bent and his forehead resting on his fists. Occasionally he bounces his knuckles against his head, hoping to jar loose some words, no matter how inadequate. Anything to get started. Brent, it must be said, was not impressed with the pages Matthew had sent him.

"This is it?" he had said. "Some story about a dead chick? In all these weeks? Tell me, tell me, Matthew, that you have more than this. Tell me you are playing a sick little joke on old Brent? Tell me this, okay?"

"Okay."

"Okay, what the fuck?"

"There's more. That was just a sample."

"Matthew. How much are you drinking?"

"Not enough, apparently."

"I'm laughing. Hear my mirth."

Silence. Long. The sort of silence that was no doubt engineered to elicit a response.

Brent sighs. "So, there is more?"

"Sure."

"I want to see at least a hundred pages in my office by the end of the month. Clear?"

And so here Matthew sits. On page three.

He shuffles his feet under the desk and dislodges a small tumbleweed of dust and hair from its grip on the somewhat gummy floor.

He looks around and sees the apartment for what it is, a temporary cell, like a third-rate motel. The furniture is cheap, the sofa hard and armless, the chair wobbly. The shade on the overhead light is chipped. Dead flies and moths lie at the bottom of the glass bowl. He drinks coffee from a cracked cup. There is no comfort here.

When he was with Kate, she lit candles every morning for breakfast, white candles that smelled of rain. The snowy sheets were always pressed and inviting. They ate mangoes and drank wine lying on those sheets. Every Saturday morning she polished the wood with lemon oil and the apartment smelled of that and ginger muffins. She painted her toenails the colour of pale iridescent shell. He loved to run his hand along the arch of her instep, the fine bones of her ankle . . .

The phone rings.

"What are you doing?"

"Jack?"

"I got a bottle. Thought I'd come over. Shoot the shit."

The memory of Kate's toes dissolves and Matthew sees only the pages before him. "I was thinking about going across the street for some Lebanese food. Want to join me?"

"I'm coming over."

Half an hour later Matthew hears Jack thumping up the stairs. The footsteps, like battering rams, cannot be mistaken for anyone else's. Matthew shakes his head. It is a wonder Jack survived in the jungles of Vietnam, where Matthew thinks of stealth as a necessity. He opens the door as Jack hauls himself up the last few steps. He wears the jeans, jean jacket, black T-shirt and heavy boots that seem to be his uniform, no matter what the weather. He is sweaty and he screws his face up against the smoke trailing from the cigarette dangling between his lips.

"Hey," says Matthew.

Jack takes the cigarette out of his mouth, coughs and grinds the butt under his heel. "I gotta give these fucking things up," he says as Matthew steps back to let him in.

"You want to come in, or get something to eat?"

Jack hands Matthew a bottle of good scotch. "I'm starving. Put that someplace, we'll drink it later."

At Chez Elias they take a table by the back door so Jack can sit with his back to the wall. They share a bowl of pickled pink turnips, olives and a stack of warm pita bread with their beer. Matthew notices Joseph hovering hopefully near the counter and waves him over.

"Jack, this is Joseph," Matthew says and indicates the boy can sit down if he likes. He explains that Joseph is Ramzi's nephew and Saida's son.

Jack looks at Saida, who is in the kitchen. A bright blue scarf ties back her long hair. "Your mother's a pretty woman," says Jack.

"You Canadian, too?" asks Joseph.

"Hell, no," Jack laughs. "I'm American."

"You a reporter, like Matthew? You from New York?"

"Not far from there. I'm a photographer, among other things."

They order *chich taouk*, chicken marinated in lemon, and falafel and *taboulé*. When Joseph asks Jack if he is visiting Paris, Jack says, "I kinda go where the winds blow me."

"I would like to travel."

"You should travel. See the world. Have some adventures before you settle down."

"I want to go to Algeria. I have friends, and they have family there I can stay with."

"I've been there," says Jack. "Interesting place."

"Yeah? Where?" Joseph leans forward.

"Algiers. Biskra. El Golea. All over."

"What were you doing there?"

"This and that. How old are you?"

"Sixteen."

A small smile, no more than stretched skin under Jack's moustache, stains his eyes with something resembling loss. "I've got a son about your age," he says.

"You do?" says Matthew. Considering that this important fact is something Jack has so far withheld, it occurs to Matthew that, other than the war stories and battle scars, he does not know much about Jack. It has not seemed important before, this question of pasts and attachments.

"He is here?" says Joseph.

"No. Back in the States with his mom." Jack knocks a cigarette out of his pack. "Want one?" he says to Joseph. Joseph shakes his head and rolls his eyes toward his mother.

Matthew glances up and catches Saida watching them. The expression on her face is hard to read. He smiles at her and nods. She nods back but her smile is economical.

Jack lights his cigarette and blows smoke toward the ceiling. "Yeah, my kid's name's Jack, Jr. Maybe I'll bring him to Paris one day. Summer vacation or something. You think he'd like that?"

"Sure. I guess."

"You know, when I was in Algeria, there was this family, lived in a—what do you call it—a town built of earth?"

"Ksar," says Joseph.

"Yeah. A *ksar.* We lived with them for a month or so. Nice people."

"We? You took your son there?"

"Naw. Just some guys I was travelling with at the time. Stopped off there on the way to Libya. Now that was a hell of a dirty little secret war."

"Jack, maybe you should leave it," Matthew says.

"Why? Some people hired us, is all, to do some cleanup work for them. Lot of garbage lying around."

Saida brings their food over and says something to Joseph in Arabic. The boy shrugs and shakes his head. "She thinks I'm bothering you," he says as she brings a plate of *katfa* to another table.

The food smells wonderful. Lemons and olives and cheese. Matthew's mouth waters as he picks up a pita and breaks off a piece, shovelling it full of *hummus*. He looks at Jack, his cigarette in one hand, a forkful of chicken in the other, and considers what sort of father Jack would make. "You're not bothering us," Matthew says to Joseph. "But maybe your mother needs some help?"

"My uncle's helping. If she needs me, she tells me." He turns to Jack. "Anyway, you were working—you work in construction, like that?"

"More like de-construction, if you know what I mean." Jack taps the side of his nose with his finger.

Matthew watches the light switch click on in Joseph's head and his suspicions that he is a bright boy are confirmed. Joseph looks admiringly at Jack, as though Rambo has suddenly materialized in his very own café.

"Merde," he says, and whistles low. "It's true?"

"For Christ's sake, Jack."

"What? 'Course it's true."

Matthew is almost amused to find a little rat of jealousy scratching at the inside of his stomach. Amused to discover he would like Joseph to look at him with the same hero-worship.

Jack talks of travelling through the Sahara. Of a one-eyed man who led them in a convoy of camels and jeeps into the Sudan, of how he lay his head against the dunes at night and when Jack asked him what he was listening to, he said the music of the *djinn*.

They finish dinner with Joseph hanging on every word. He wants to bring his friends around, wants to introduce them to Jack. He wants to take Jack, and Matthew, he adds, into Barbès to see la Goutte d'Or neighbourhood, what he calls the real Paris.

Saida has been travelling in ever-decreasing circles, making sure she is near their table as often as possible. When Matthew meets her eye she glares at him and he winces, wishing he hadn't brought Jack along.

When the bill comes, Jack makes no move for his wallet so Matthew pays for them both, figuring Jack's bottle of Glenfiddich will even the score.

As they leave, Jack promises Joseph he'll come back sometime soon. "And maybe you can introduce me to some of your pals." They shake hands and as they do, Jack pulls the boy close and whispers something in his ear.

Joseph blinks and then smiles. "Sure," he says. "I can do that. Sure."

"What was that about?" Matthew says when they're on the street.

"What?"

"That bit at the end. What did you say to Joseph?"

"Nosey, aren't ya? I just told him not to let his mother catch him smoking."

Back in the apartment, Jack settles himself in the chair by the window as if he has been there before.

"Listen," says Jack. "Thanks for letting me crash on you like this."

"Not a problem."

Matthew waits for Jack to continue.

"Bad day, you know what I mean. One of those my-mind's-a-dangerous-place-better-not-to-go-in-alone days. You know."

Yes, Matthew knows. Jack sits with his arms folded and his hands under his armpits. His head is down and nodding, as though there is a conversation going on in his mind that Matthew cannot hear.

"Guess that's why I was telling the kid all those stories. Lots of memories today."

Matthew starts, unsettled by the fragility in Jack's voice. His own memories begin to twitter at him from the darkened corners of the room. Ah, to hell with the rest of the world, he thinks. Civilians. "You need a drink," he says.

"A truer word was never spoken."

Matthew opens the bottle.

"That's a pretty nice place, that restaurant. Nice people," says Jack.

"Joseph's a good kid," Matthew says.

"Seems to be."

"A bit troubled, maybe. His father's dead. Stepfather was a son of a bitch."

"Most are. Mother's pretty good-looking, if you don't mind the scars. You like the kid, huh? You acting big brother?"

"Just think he's impressionable, is all. Any more stories like tonight and he's going to want to go off and join the foreign legion."

"There are worse things." Jack reaches over and picks up a photo from the table. "Nice. Who is she?"

"Kate," Matthew says, on his way to the kitchen for glasses. He does not have to look; there is only one photo in the apartment.

"Who's Kate?"

"She's a lawyer. Lives in Washington."

"Right."

Matthew hands Jack a glass. He laughs and peels a price sticker off the bottom. "Guess you don't have many guests."

"Nope. Not many."

Jack nods and looks at Kate's picture again. "I was married once. I ever tell you that?"

"Not that I recall, but then you never mentioned you had a son, either." Matthew pours two healthy shots from the triangular green bottle.

Jack takes a deep gulp of scotch. "Judy. She's back in Arizona, in Sedona, land of the loony-tune, home of the harmonic convergence. She runs a place that sells tarot cards and books on angels and channelling and fake Zuni jewellery. She's Jack, Jr.'s mother. He's seventeen and already had some run-ins with the law. Chip off the old block, unfortunately."

"You see him much?"

"Haven't seen him in about a year, I guess." Jack pours himself more scotch and rolls the glass around in his palms.

"Miss him?"

"Hell, sure I miss him. I guess." The scowl on his face tells Matthew he doesn't want to talk about it anymore.

"How are things going at the hostel?" he says.

"Monday nights, Tuesday and Wednesday afternoons, Thursday nights. Some extra cash to pay for those little luxuries the state declines to provide for. Cigarette money. Not much more. Not enough more. Might have to find something else."

"Hmm."

"Has its benefits, though." He grins. "I believe part of my mandate is to make sure the little princesses out to seek adventure come to no harm. And there are plenty of eighteen-year-olds grateful for a big old lug like me to protect their beauty sleep. Forty-seven's not so bad. Nothing like experience." He chuckles and looks smug, the words sounding hollow in the bottom of his glass as he tips it to his mouth.

"There was this one little girl. Vietnamese of all fucking things. Said her name was Hang. Said it meant Angel in the Full Moon. Can you believe that shit? I mean, what can you do but fall in love with a girl who's got a name like that? She had size-three feet. Had to buy her shoes in the children's department. She was something else, man. You know, she was into all this kinky sex. She was a student at NYU, studying marketing or advertising or something. Travelling around Europe on her summer break. She had a website of her own and showed me. Pictures of her like you wouldn't believe." Jack runs his fingers over his moustache and stares off into the distance. "Tied up, man. Really tied up, so she couldn't wiggle a toe. Silk rope wrapped around her like a cocoon or something. She never would tell me who tied her up or who took the pictures, just that they sold real well. Said it was a Japanese erotic practice. It was her idea that I tie her up." Jack slides off the chair onto the floor. He lies on his back, a glass of scotch balanced on his stomach. "I thought those girls Anthony knew . . . I thought they were Vietnamese. He said they were."

"You looking for somebody to tie up again?" Matthew chuckles, makes a point of chuckling because as soon as the words have left his mouth he sees how imprudent they are. They would not have been spoken had he been completely sober.

"Fuck that. I'm looking for somebody who makes me *stop* thinking about tying them up." Jack laughs bitterly, then looks at Matthew. "Joke. It's a joke."

"How are things with you and Suzi?"

"Me and Suzi?"

"Yeah. I sort of figured you two might be starting something."

"She's a fucking hooker."

"So?"

"Yeah. I guess. So what." Then suddenly he throws his head back and roars, startling Matthew enough that he spills some of his drink. "I mean what the fuck am I? A fucking catch? Sure, for a deranged-Vet-ex-con-war-junkie with a drinking problem! Speaking of which. More please." He holds out his glass and Matthew obliges, and then refills his own.

"To Suzi. Belle of the ball," says Jack, raising his glass.

"To Suzi."

CHAPTER FOURTEEN

Evening falls and outside Matthew's window the place du Dublin is nearly deserted. A couple enter Le Primavera Bistro. An old woman walks her dog. A young girl strides along purposefully, a cigarette in one hand, a cell phone in the other. Matthew sits and stares out at the square, but his mind is on Suzi and how she looked that night at Anthony's. She reminded him of Edith Piaf, almost, or at least a Piaf in the making. She smelled of roses and lemons. He thinks of her breasts, of how they had looked under that T-shirt while she was so close to him in the bathroom, bandaging his hand. It has been a long time since he slept with a woman. Since before Hebron.

In his mind's eye, he sees himself walking across the room, dialling a number in Washington. Hearing Kate's voice on the other end. She would probably be sleeping now, one foot dangling outside the covers, for she always got too hot. She would pick up the phone, her voice velvet with sleep. She would say hello. Maybe he would hear hope in her voice, hope that it might be him, or hope that it would not be. He cannot imagine what he would say to her. He shakes the idea out of his head.

He considers going down to the Bok-Bok, and then dismisses it. If he is looking for a woman, better not to look there. Suzi is, apart from being a hooker, obviously shooting dope. Not to mention that she and Jack seem to be . . . something, although what is not exactly clear.

No. Not the Bok-Bok. But out, somewhere, where there are people.

Victoria Short. Every expat who passes through Paris hears about Victoria sooner or later. She has an apartment on rue Saint-André-des-Arts that she converts once every week to a *salon*, admission one hundred francs, which includes a buffet dinner, all the cheap wine you can drink, a poetry reading, or lecture on James Baldwin, or Bricktop, or Langston Hughes, or Miles Davis, and a few introductions. Victoria disguises the tang of sex with the perfume of jazz and literature. A black American journalist with whom he had been attending a conference on chemical warfare had first taken Matthew there seven years ago. Matthew had been back several times since, whenever he passed through and had a free Friday, and he usually bumped into someone he knew. Victoria's is a sort of informal meeting spot for the journalists who regularly pass through Paris.

An hour later Matthew climbs the stairs to the fifth-floor apartment, up a circular stairwell so steep and narrow he is dizzy by the time he reaches the top. Victoria's door, the only one on the floor, is open and she stands at the threshold.

"I know you! Matthew, if I remember right? Good to see you. Did I know you were in Paris? I thought you were in the Middle East. Yes, last I heard. Someone told me. Didn't I hear you got shot? Something heroic? Did you let me know you were coming? I ask everyone to reserve." Victoria is a large woman, with a barrel chest and imposing shoulders. Her wig, a somewhat ratty pageboy, fools no one. She runs her finger along a list of names. "People really must reserve in advance. Did you?"

"Nope. Last-minute decision."

She raises an eyebrow. "Something of a celebrity now. Still."

Matthew pulls two fifty-franc notes out of his pocket and holds them out to her. She is just about to take them when he jerks them away. "Listen, Victoria, do me a favour, will you? Can the celebrity shit. Seriously. Deal?"

She snatches the notes and slips them into the pocket of the red tunic she wears. "Next time call me in advance. Come in, come in! Carol Pratchard is reading from her new collection. Iowa Writer's School."

After adding his coat to the pile already heaped on the bed, Matthew makes his way through the crowd in the hall toward the living room. As he passes the tiny kitchen, he says hello to Eduardo, the Filipino chef who is everywhere Victoria is.

"Hey, Matthew, long time!" Eduardo chops onions with lightning speed, and Matthew fears for the man's stubby fingertips. Binko, Eduardo's monkey, chatters from his lookout atop the refrigerator. "Matthew," Eduardo says, "I hear about your trouble. You okay?"

"Sure, Eduardo. Where's the booze?"

Eduardo nods. "Okay, you're good. Take some wine—there." He points behind Matthew to a countertop covered in plastic glasses half full of red wine. Matthew takes one and makes his way into the crowded living room. People sit on folding chairs, perch on the deep casement windowsills and cram onto the brown corduroy sofa. Voices reveal the crowd as mostly Americans, expats and tourists. Matthew scans the faces to see if he knows anyone. Two men stand together, one wearing a blue tie-dyed *dashiki* and *kufi*, the other in waist-length dreadlocks and black leather. A number of couples, mostly straight. A too-thin woman with dyed blond hair smiles enthusiastically at him. Her nails are long and her fingers covered in expensive rings. He looks at his watch, does not smile back, and hopes she will assume he is waiting for someone. She turns away.

"Hey, stranger."

Matthew turns to find Denise Mumford grinning at him, her green eyes bright and fresh as spring's first leaves.

"Denise, you are a sight for sore eyes," he says, kissing her on the cheek. Jasmine, maybe. Camellias? Minty breath. God, but women smell great, he thinks. "I thought you were in New York."

"I've done New York. Restless feet—you know the syndrome."

"You coming back to the news?"

"Nope. As in never. Writing biographies suits me fine. I'm just here for a week or so, doing some research for the next project, a book about one of the big *fashionistas.*"

"Looks like it suits you. You look real good, Denise." She is almost as tall as Matthew is; her hair is jet-black and falls halfway down her back. She wears a pair of black, wide-legged pants and a white oversized shirt. It is loose, and most of the buttons are undone, revealing the curve of her breasts and the flash of white lace.

"I'm just a girl getting by on my wits and a few pretty dresses." She puts her arm through his. "You look more like Arthur Miller every time I see you."

"I don't think that's a compliment."

"Well, crossed with Sam Shepard. How's that?"

"I can live with that."

"Who's reading tonight?"

"Some bright young thing from Iowa."

They find a few square inches of wall to lean against just as Victoria makes her way to the front of the room to the bright young thing, who turns out to be a short, thin, earnest-looking girl who has just published a collection of short stories based on the life of Céleste Mogador, the nineteenth-century prostitute who transformed herself into a much-admired novelist and playwright.

The girl reads in a voice so monotone Matthew has trouble figuring out where one sentence ends and the next begins. Denise presses her breast against his arm. He does not think he'll have to sit through the whole reading.

Denise is staying at the Raphael on avenue Kleber. Her suite has a red velvet chaise lounge in a separate sitting room, art nouveau–mirrored armoires and a four-poster bed.

"Looks like the biography business is pretty good."

"You should see the bathroom."

"Only if you show it to me."

In the bathroom he says, "That's a good-sized tub."

"Yup. And deep, too," she says, unbuttoning her shirt. "You like bubbles?"

"One of my favourite things." He grins.

When they are settled, each comfortably at opposite ends of the tub, her legs over his, she asks, "How do you like living in Paris?" and blows a fluff of bubbles off the ends of her fingers.

"It's as good as any place, I guess." He massages her instep and she moans.

"Is it? Then why choose here?"

"Because it's a good city to be fucked up in." Matthew is surprised to hear the words come out of his mouth.

"Why?" Denise moves her foot away from his chest. When he does not answer, she says, "Really, Matthew. Tell me. I felt that way about New York once. In fact I think I chose it for that very reason, after I lost the baby and Peter all in one year."

"He was a louse. He should have stayed with you."

"No. I couldn't get over the miscarriage and he couldn't get over me not getting over it. I think I knew then that we'd only been together because we wanted a family, and since that wasn't going to happen . . ."

"You could have had another baby."

"I couldn't, actually."

"Sorry."

"It's all right. Now." She reaches out and traces a finger along the scar on his belly, making him shiver, then twists around in the tub so that she is leaning against him. "Come on, old friend. Tell me about being fucked up in Paris."

He runs his hands over her slippery breasts. They are very nice breasts, he thinks, with mauvish-pink nipples and spaced so that there is a lovely deep hollow in between. Maybe it is the warm water, the warm body relaxing him, or maybe it is that he has known Denise for so long that the familiarity feels like security, but he finds he wants to talk to her. "Parisians take depression as a sign of intelligence. There's none of that phoney American jolliness, none of that British stiff-upper-lip crap. Parisians respect someone who's figured out the world is a cesspool. They've built this visually perfect jewel of a city so that as you go down for the third time at least you have something beautiful to look at."

"Sounds like you're more committed to staying sad than to healing."

"Healing? I'm just trying not to bleed to death." He laughs and runs the palms of his hands over her hardening nipples.

"I should have been in touch after Hebron. You've become a symbol, you know. The man who tried to single-handedly end the Middle East conflict."

"Hey, cut that shit out."

"I didn't know what to say. I guess I still don't."

"Then why say anything at all?" Matthew bends her neck back and kisses her and they say no more. Sometime later, they are entwined on the bed's damp sheets.

Sometimes sex is like pulling the string back on a bow so far that when the arrow launches skyward, there is no telling when or where it will stop. Denise arches her back and buries her face in Matthew's shoulder just as his body stretches out and plunges into a toe-curling spasm of its own.

He rolls off her and she puts her hands up to her hair.

"My God, I haven't come like that in years," she sighs.

Matthew is horrified to find tears welling up behind his eyelids.

"Me either," he says. "Be right back."

"You okay?"

He makes it to the bathroom and turns on the shower fast, just as the sobs start. He has been in a multitude of bathrooms in his life, but never has he found one so ideally suited for weeping. The only light comes from a backlit alcove with glass shelves full of towels, giving the place the air of a marbled chapel or crypt. He grabs a towel the innocent colour and texture of sheep fleece. It perfectly muffles any sound not already drowned out by the rainstorm from the shower stall. He sits on the chair, a body-hugging padded wicker one next to the tub, buries his face and cries.

In the part of his brain not consumed with this sudden onslaught of grief, he wonders what on earth it is all about. He can think of nothing in the hour immediately past that would account for this deluge. He feels as though he is wrestling an ever-tightening net.

"Matthew? Are you all right?"

"Fine. Just taking a shower."

"Can I come in?"

"I'll be out in a second, Denise."

He steps into the shower stall and leans his forehead against the tiles. Oh, Christ, he thinks, you've got to get hold of yourself. The water is warm and the trembling in his legs and arms begins to subside. He tastes salt in his mouth. He places his palm on the white line that runs from his sternum to his belly button, then over to the nickel-sized pucker. *What happens to a man when he doesn't have a spleen anymore? A fit of non-spleen? A venting of non-spleen?*

He laughs some, through the tears, and then the tears are gone as quickly as they arrived. He imagines a line of grey, sleety squalls moving out to sea. It seems foolish to be standing in the shower alone when there is a warm friendly woman on the other side of the door. He dries himself and goes back to the bedroom with a towel wrapped around his waist. Denise sits in a chair by the window with a sheet draped around her, smoking.

"What the hell was that about?" She looks angry.

"I took a shower."

"You jumped out of bed as though I was some hooker you'd picked up."

Matthew sits on the edge of the bed. "You know me too well to think that," he says.

"Matthew, I don't know you at all. You are a master at not being known. Even Kate used to say that."

He is unprepared to hear Kate's name. "I just took a fucking shower."

Denise blows a smoke ring toward the ceiling. "What does *papak* mean?"

"*Papak?* What are you talking about?"

"You said it when you were in the bathroom. More than once."

"No, I didn't."

She grinds the cigarette out. "What does it mean, Matthew?"

"*Papci*. Trotters, literally. It's a Bosnian word. A *papak* is an oaf, a brute."

"Oh." She looks unsure if she should believe him or not. "So, why were you saying it?

"I wasn't." He looks around for his clothes. The room feels gaudy and oppressive. If Denise is going to go strange on him, he does not want to be there. He has enough trouble handling his own weirdness.

"Fine. I just pulled the word out of the air." She looks away, then back at him and her brown eyes show hurt. "I thought you were making remarks about me."

"About you? Why?"

"I thought, well . . . jumping into bed like that. . . . Maybe it wasn't the right thing to do. Oh, never mind. It seems you're leaving, so what difference does it make?" She turns her face to the window and pulls her arms and legs in tighter.

Matthew puts his pants on a chair and crosses the room to her. He squats and takes her hand between his. "I can stay."

"Do me no favours."

"I'd never say anything bad about you, Denise. I really don't know what you're talking about," he says, although he finds he cannot completely believe this. "Look, it is possible I said some things in the bathroom. Perhaps I said *papak*, but if I did, it certainly wasn't directed to you. Just leave it like that, all right?"

"I was happy to see you. I thought we could have some fun. That's all, really," she says, slipping out of the chair, away from Matthew and into a white terry-cloth robe that dwarfs her.

"Why don't we have dinner tomorrow?" he says.

"Can't. Work." It is her turn to head toward the bathroom.

"Well, the next night, then," he calls after her, thinking that he has always found women rather confusing.

"You don't need dinner, Matthew. You need a shrink." She stops in the doorway. "What are you going to do with yourself?"

"I'm writing a book."

"What sort of book?"

"You know. Journalistic memoir."

"Oh, God, Matthew." She turns and closes the bathroom door.

CHAPTER FIFTEEN

Saida scowls. Matthew's friend, this ungentle giant Jack, throws his head back and laughs at something he's said—laughter like the sound of a cannon being fired in a small stone room. Loud enough to break your eardrums. Even Joseph jumps, and sits staring wide-eyed at the big man.

"I'm telling ya, he picked the eye up and it was glass, right? Glass!" Jack slaps his leg.

It has been like this for two hours. Each story Jack tells is more lurid than the one before and his own part in the adventures more grandiose. Tales of fighting, of being a strong arm for hire, of battles in Afghanistan against the Russians, of scaling the perimeter of Somali fortresses, of Saigon, of Los Angeles prison cells. It is the stuff of James Bond movies—fantasy and testosterone.

This is the third time Jack has been in the restaurant; when he is here it feels too small, and Saida feels unprotected. Even though he has done nothing but talk, she feels the danger in him. Why, she wonders, is Matthew such good friends with this hulk? The pride in Jack's voice makes her wince.

He talks now of women, and she says, "*Alors*, enough!" as she slams one of the cupboard doors. Matthew looks at her and says something quietly to Jack, who glances at her, and then drops his voice. Saida watches him tilt his head closer to Joseph's, sees the eagerness in her son's eye.

Saida has had experience of men like this and has worked hard to forget. Jack stirs up her memories, like angry ants swarming out of a disturbed nest. She thinks, this man is a braggart, full of nothing but vicious wind.

She brings a cup of coffee to her father, who sits alone at a table by the window. He listlessly turns the pages of a newspaper.

"Are you tired, *Abba?*"

"No. Well, perhaps a little."

"I'll have Joseph take you home."

"And what will I do at home? I will wait until you are finished. We'll go home all together when Ramzi gets back."

"*If* Ramzi gets back."

Elias blows on his coffee, and then sips. "What makes you think he's not coming back?"

Saida looks toward her rapt and fervent son. "If you won't let Joseph take you home for your sake, then you take *him* home."

Her father follows her gaze and snorts. "Storyteller."

"I don't like his stories. Joseph," she calls, "come here."

Reluctantly, he shuffles over.

"Take your grandfather home. He's very tired and has a headache."

"Now?"

"Yes, of course now."

Joseph squats down and looks into his grandfather's face. "You want to go home?"

"Yes. I think I do."

Almost anything else, and Saida knows she might get an argument from Joseph, but not this. He cannot argue with his grandfather.

"Okay. Five minutes, okay?"

"Five minutes," she says, and her father nods.

"I'll finish my coffee."

The big man Jack does not stay long after Joseph and his grandfather leave. As Jack exits he makes a great show of saying good-bye to her, of bowing, exaggeratedly, with laughter in his eyes. She does not smile at him.

"I should get going, too," says Matthew.

"Wait," she says, and he does, nodding his head as though he expected her to ask. She puts together a package of stuffed vine leaves for him to eat at home later, and as she approaches his table he stands, as though to face her. It is hard to hold her ground and look up at him and say what she has to say.

"You are a good man, and I don't want to be rude, Matthew, but maybe your friend should spend more time with his own son."

"He doesn't mean any harm, Saida."

"Men like him never do. They just don't care if harm gets done." She will not smile, will not let her eyes fall.

"I know he seems rough. But he's all right."

Saida shrugs.

"You just have to get to know him a little, to understand him. He and I are alike in a lot of ways."

"I don't like his talk."

"He's just spinning yarns."

"What?"

"You know, talking big. He likes Joseph, and Joseph's good for him, I think." Matthew runs his hand through his hair. "He had it very bad after Vietnam. I know that was a long time ago, but . . . he pretty much saved my life once, in Kosovo. It's hard to explain. He's been through a lot."

"Lots of people have been through bad things."

Matthew blushes. "Of course, sorry. I didn't mean to imply anything."

"I have to think of what is right for Joseph. What kind of man he should want to be. We have had enough of war in our family, Matthew. Enough losses, you understand? To hear him talk, and the way Joseph listens, as though they were good stories, well, I cannot have that."

"Okay, look, I understand." Matthew squirms like an adolescent. "I just think Jack misses his own son, that's all. Makes him feel good to be around Joseph."

"There is money, too. Joseph has suddenly more than he should have."

"Where do you think he's getting it from?"

"On the streets there are many ways to get money you should not have. Especially with encouragement."

"You think Jack has something to do with it?"

"I think something is wrong. I don't want him near Joseph."

"We'll go somewhere else if you want."

"No, Matthew. *You* are always welcome here. Like family." Her eyes drop then. "I hope you like the vine leaves."

After that, she waits with some apprehension for the big man to come back, but he does not. Matthew comes in every day, but alone. Joseph does not stay with him so much, but does not ask for Jack either. Saida thinks he will forget the big man, given the chance.

It is early morning, before ten. Ramzi laughs with Matthew Bowles about something. The two sit at a table by the rain-streaked window and Saida watches them as she fills the napkin holders. Saida arranges pastries on a plate. It is good to have Matthew in the shop; it means her father and brother do not fight. Ramzi tells his dreams to Matthew and Matthew listens and discusses them seriously. A hotel in Ibiza. A chain of furniture stores catering to well-off Parisians who want their houses to look like Bedouin tents. A high-class restaurant in Montpellier.

Now, the time before lunch when it is quiet, it is just the three of them. Her father said he was not feeling well this morning and stayed home, which he is doing more and more these days, becoming, Saida worries, even more separated from the world. She prays Joseph is at school. Over the past several weeks,

Matthew has come to be almost like a cousin, perhaps, or an in-law. His presence is a relief from being just the four of them all the time, with the same conversations, the same worries, and the same grievances against one another.

Matthew is prone to fits of depression—Saida has noticed this, they all have. There are days when he does not come out of his apartment and then, when he does, he looks as though he has not slept, although the windows of his apartment have been shuttered. At such times Saida feeds him, for food is always good in the belly to bring the soul back to its centre, away from whatever dark place it has wandered into.

He has told her of the book he is trying to write, and when he talks about it he laughs, as though it were a foolish thing.

"Memory," he said, one afternoon when they were sitting together, picking at a plate of grapes. "It's like trying to use Medea's cauldron. You put in an old man and think a young one will come out, but all you get is, well, something you're ashamed of having done. It's so easy to remember horrible things. Why is that? Why is it so hard to remember the beautiful? I wish I'd taken time to write some of those things down as I went along."

She had had no answer to that, because she keeps her own bad things stuffed like damp tissues in the pockets of her skirt, ready to remind her every time she unthinkingly puts in her hand.

Saida sees a smear on the glass dome covering the plate of *baklava* and polishes it clear. Matthew seems all right today, his gestures less controlled than usual. His long legs are stretched out under the table, the foot not tapping. Ramzi and he look over a list Ramzi has drawn up of cities he is considering. Ramzi, in his fashionable jeans, his white shirt, his carefully blow-dried hair, is intent, chewing on the end of a pen, scratching himself behind his knee as he does when he is excited. She wonders what Ramzi would think if she suddenly pulled up a list of cities she might move to. Such a thing has never occurred to him—that, without a husband, she might decide to take Joseph and leave her father and brother behind. A daughter does not do such things. But sons do? It is hard not to hate the freedom men have.

On the other hand, one day, possibly soon, Ramzi will come home from one of his late-night dance-club forays with a girl. Someone bright and gentle and full of smiles. Someone who will settle her brother down, anchor him. Saida smiles at the thought. She could use not only the help, but the warmth a sisterly presence would bring. More babies perhaps, in-laws, a larger life. More laughter. In Lebanon, family was the touchstone, the North Star, the centre of everything; here in the turbulent sea that is Paris they drift apart like bits of flotsam after a shipwreck.

Her daydreams are interrupted when Matthew waves to someone outside. Saida stops polishing the glass in her hand. She hopes it is not Jack.

A very tall black man comes through the door, shaking water droplets like a wet dog, and slaps Matthew on the back.

"I was just going over to see you. You haven't been round to the Bok-Bok for a while."

"Thought I'd give daylight a try."

The Bok-Bok. Saida knows, from listening to their conversations, what this word means. So, this is another of these men. Saida folds the tea towel she is holding, folds it smoothly, the edges lined up perfectly.

Matthew introduces the man as Anthony, and he shakes hands with Ramzi. He wears a black leather jacket, with large padded shoulders. It hangs down to his knees, loose and sinister. Her brother looks so small beside these tall, giantlike men from another world. Ramzi calls for coffee.

The man sits with his hands between his legs, the palms pressed together, his shoulders hunched, leaning forward. He bounces his head a little. When Saida brings the tray, he turns around to look at her so far that she realizes he does not see out of one eye. He pushes his chair out and starts to stand.

"Let me give you a hand," he says, and his accent is thick, from New York, she thinks.

"No need."

"Anthony, this is Saida," says Matthew.

"She is my sister," says Ramzi.

"Pleased to meet you."

When she puts the tray down, he reaches out to take her hand but she jumps and quickly hides it behind her back.

"Does that hurt?" he says.

"Anthony, I don't think Saida wants to talk about it."

"I didn't mean anything. But, it looks like we've got a thing or two in common. I was hit in the head with a table. Big table, too. The corner cracked my skull right open, they said. Shattered the bones. You can see it." He bends his head down and shows her a dented place under the curly hair. He tells her she can touch it if she wants to, but she says she does not. "It's okay. There's a metal plate in there now."

"Someone hit you with a table?"

"Yup. Crazy guy. I used to be a cop."

"I'm sorry."

"It's okay. How'd you get burned?"

Ramzi starts to say something but Saida puts up her hand. "Someone threw a pot of boiling oil at me."

Matthew whistles low.

"Another crazy man, huh," says Anthony and his face is very serious.

"Yes. Exactly that."

Anthony nods. "At least you weren't blinded. And you're still very pretty."

"Thank you," says Saida. "Drink your tea."

The man smiles at her, and for a moment, she sees something under the smile, a struggle of some sort.

"Must be hard not to be angry," he says.

"Some days it is very hard."

He nods. "I agree." He pats his head, and she notices there is some grey in his hair. "I can cook. I'm an excellent cook," he says. A statement of fact with no conceit in it. "Maybe sometime I could come by here and help you in the kitchen. Not for any pay, but to learn how to cook Lebanese. What do you think?"

"He's a terrific cook," says Matthew.

She tries to picture him in the tiny alcove kitchen with her. "Maybe. We'll see."

"I wouldn't be in the way. Just be your sous-chef." He holds his pale-palmed hands wide and grins. It is as hard not to like this man as it is to like the other.

"Maybe."

As she turns to go he says, "Hey, you're Joseph's mother, right?"

"That's right," she says.

"Yeah, Jack told me about him. He really likes your son."

Matthew puts his hand on Anthony's arm. "Jack said that?"

"Yeah. Jack said Joseph took him down to see some place in Barbès—some Moroccan couscous place. But you knew that, didn't you?"

"No, I didn't," says Matthew.

"Oh. That's right. I guess you haven't seen Jack if you haven't been down to the Bok."

"I didn't know that either." Something cold, glassy and serpentine stirs in Saida's stomach. "Did you know this, Ramzi?"

"Maybe I knew he had Jack's phone number. The rest I didn't know."

Anthony looks at her and says, "You don't have to worry if your kid's with Jack. He's a very protective guy. He knows how to take care of situations."

The problem is, of course, that Saida does not want her son in situations that need taking care of.

"Did I say something wrong?" he says to Matthew as Saida turns away.

She stands in the kitchen alcove and chops parsley. She presses the back of the blade with her left hand and levers the handle down rapidly, harshly, as though she wants to cut right through the wooden block beneath. She pretends she cannot hear them.

"It's not your fault," says Ramzi. "She gets upset, my sister."

"She doesn't want her son around Jack?"

"I guess he's having some trouble in school. He's hanging around with some guys his mother's not real fond of," says Matthew.

"Oh."

"It's okay," says Ramzi. "Joseph is a good boy."

Saida looks over at Matthew then, and finds his eyes waiting for hers.

"It's going to be okay," he says.

She wants very much for this to be true.

CHAPTER SIXTEEN

Anthony and Matthew leave the café.

"So, where you headed, Anthony?" asks Matthew.

"I came to get you. Jack tried to call, but you didn't answer, so I said I'd come by to see if you're okay."

"I'm fine. Came to get me for what?"

"Graveyard visitation. Come with us. It'll cheer you up."

"You're kidding."

"Not at all. Death is good for the soul."

Matthew laughs. "Who's going?"

"Paweena and me, Jack and Suzi. We'll meet at the Passy Cemetery about three?"

"What's at the Passy Cemetery?"

"There's this great mausoleum. A Russian guy. You have to see it. Jack wants to take photos. So, come with us."

"Why not?"

"Okay. I'll see you then. I got to go meet Paweena at the Monoprix. She needs a new blender or something."

"Anthony, you're spending a lot of money on this girl, aren't you?"

Anthony puts his hands in his pockets and looks at his feet, turning them pigeon-toed first, and then pivoting on his heels so his toes turn out. When he looks up again, his face is serious. "Listen. I know Paweena's game. Don't think I don't. Like I said the first time we met, that whack on the skull may have knocked loose a few directional signals, but the engine still runs just fine, you understand?" Matthew begins to protest, but Anthony stops him. "It's all right. But you have to know where she's from, the sorts of things that have happened to her. Money changing hands means she's in control, and that feels safe for her. It doesn't matter to me. Man, look—you got some, you got none, you got a little, you got a lot. Sometimes you got to gorge yourself to see it isn't really the belly that's hungry at all, you know? Besides, she can ask all she wants, don't mean I buy her everything, you know?"

"Fair enough. Didn't mean to stick my nose in. Paweena's a lucky girl."

"Hell, yes, man. I am a catch!" Anthony punches him lightly on the shoulder, grins and heads down the street, saying he'll see Matthew later.

When Matthew walks into the apartment, the phone is ringing. It's Jack. Matthew tells him he has already spoken to Anthony.

"Tell you what, come by my place first and we'll take the subway together."

"Isn't that sort of backward? Don't you live over in the eleventh?" Matthew says.

"Come on. You can get on the metro at Europe and get off at Saint-Maur. One line. There's a great cheap Cambodian place around the corner, and then we can grab the nine line right back to Trocadéro. We can have a talk without the gaggle around."

Although this sounds like an extravagantly convoluted path, Matthew agrees, lured in part by curiosity about how Jack lives. All of their previous meetings out in the field have been on the temporary neutral ground of hotels and rented rooms.

The apartment is on Saint-Maur, a busy street made recently trendy by the relatively cheap rents and the resulting influx of those who call themselves artists. Across the street is an Arab bakery where a line of people wait to get in. Flaky date-filled morsels and assortments of pastries sprinkled with pale green pistachio nuts and almonds and sesame seeds fill the window. Saida comes to mind, as she had looked that morning, with a smear of icing sugar across her forehead. There are three cafés on the corner, all jammed with young customers, a sea of Marlborough cigarettes, colourful headscarves, dirty-blond dreadlocks and casual fashion that takes a significant amount of thought to achieve.

Matthew punches the security code into the metal pad on the wall, waits for the click and then swings open the heavy door. Inside, the entrance is littered with junk-mail flyers. The sound of someone's music, the bass far too loud, drifts down the stairwell. Through a doorway at the back he sees a minute courtyard, more of an airshaft, with a few dying plants in pots struggling toward the overcast sky. It smells of cat piss and old, mouldering plaster. He begins to climb the stairs and trips on the uneven, sloping second step. The handrail is sticky beneath his palm. He searches for the light switch, but when he finds it and presses, nothing happens.

As he passes the second floor the smell of marijuana drifts from the same bright blue door that hides the music source. Some sort of New World African–Cuban mix, overlaid by techno-bass. The floor shakes slightly in rhythmic response. On the third floor a baby cries, and Matthew notices a few more dead plants, geraniums, forgotten on a grimy windowsill. The wooden floors are wide-planked and shiny from centuries of feet. Here and there a nail rises up to snag an unwary boot. On the fourth floor there is silence, more sinister than the thoughtless noise, and Matthew imagines eyes pressed to peepholes and cracks in the wood. The sixth floor is where, in considerably better days, servants would have been housed. There are two doors, and a hall leading to more. To the left of the stairwell is a door with glass panels, one cracked and held together with electrical tape. Matthew knocks.

There is a shuffle inside and then the door opens. Jack fills the space completely.

"Come on in," he says.

The room is tiny and the door can't be opened all the way because of the wooden chair behind it. To the right is a single bed, with two shelves above filled with folded black T-shirts, jeans, a sweater and two shirts. At the end of the bed is a footlocker, atop which sits Jack's camera. To the left, next to the chair, is a square table on which sits a transistor radio, a copy of Tim O'Brien's *The Things They Carried*, an old copy of *Penthouse*, an overflowing ashtray, a plate with half a baguette and some cheese, and several packages of Camel cigarettes. Matthew notices a couple of hand-rolled butts in the ashtray, which account for the lingering aroma of marijuana. At the end of the room is a washstand with a sink, a hotplate and a cupboard beneath. There is no window; the only light comes from a bulb in the ceiling that has an imitation Japanese shade with a calligraphy symbol drawn on it in black ink. It throws a strange and unsettling shadow, as though a huge moth rests against the bulb.

Apart from its size, and the lack of natural light, what is unusual about the room is that, except for the overflowing ashtray, everything is impeccably, institutionally, neat. The bed looks like it has been made by a four-star general, the blanket and sheet so tight there is no doubt a dime would bounce to the ceiling. The clothes are folded and their edges aligned. A few clean dishes stand neatly stacked next to the minuscule sink. Three cereal boxes and a box of rice, arranged smallest to largest, are lined up like nutritional soldiers.

Matthew thinks of his own impossibly messy kitchen and shudders.

"You've got this place shipshape."

"I like to have things tidy. When you're my size you can't have a lot of clutter," says Jack, and there is something in his voice, as though he has been looking for approval, as though this were an inspection. "Hey, it's not much, but it's cheap."

"It's great."

"Yeah. A real château. You want a drink?"

"No. Too early, at least for today."

"Coffee?" Jack goes back to the sink and pulls out a pot from the cupboard beneath the hotplate. "I can boil water."

"Well, if you want one. Sure."

Matthew sits on the chair, wedged between the wall and the table, facing the bed. There isn't enough room to swing his legs under the table.

"Turn on the radio if you want," says Jack as he lights the gas burner.

The radio is tuned to a jazz station and the sounds of Coltrane's "Lush Life" waft into the room. Jack spoons instant coffee into two thick, white mugs.

"So, you looking forward to our journey into the city of the dead?" Matthew says.

"It's all right. Something to do," says Jack, giving voice to Matthew's own opinion.

Jack carries the coffee over and sets the mugs down in front of them. "You want milk?" Matthew says black is fine and Jack sits on the bed, his back ramrod straight. They talk about Jack's neighbours, old men mostly, and a couple of Filipina cleaning ladies who live together and avert their eyes whenever he passes them in the hall. "Like they're scared of me," Jack says, and chuckles.

Matthew finds it hard to relax in the room, and it dawns on him that it is as if they are sitting in a military prison cell. When Jack suggests they should get going if they want to eat, he feels nothing but relief.

At the Cambodian restaurant they eat ginger port with peanuts and *cambogee* beef. The only occidentals in the place, they sit on narrow benches and hunch over the bowls of steaming meat and rice. They drink beer and smile at the faces around them.

"I love this stuff," says Jack, shovelling it in.

When they finish they drink tea from small fragile cups with no handles.

"I hear Suzi's coming this afternoon," Matthew says. "So, you guys an item?"

"I don't know. She's all right. Smart, you know. Smarter than you'd think."

"I wouldn't think anything."

"Well, most hookers aren't smart. They're stupid or they wouldn't be in that job in the first place. I mean, they all think they're smart because they're getting the money, right, they think that's power. But it's not. That's just a pimp's con. Telling a woman how she can live off her womanhood and all that shit."

"Sounds like you've given it some thought."

Jack laughs. "Well, let's just say there was a time when a couple of girls didn't seem to mind making sure my rent was paid, know what I mean?"

Matthew pulls back. "You're not pimping Suzi?"

"Fuck, no!" Jack looks deeply offended. "I was never a real pimp. It was back in the seventies when that sort of thing was considered not such a big deal. Just a casual sort of thing, you know?"

Matthew doesn't, but keeps mum. Sips his tea.

"It's not like that. I like Suzi. I pay my own way. Not that I pay her, no fucking way, but you know what I mean. And it's none of my business what she does for a living, is it? I mean, not really."

"Don't suppose it is. But I have to say I don't think I'd like my girlfriend sleeping with other guys."

"It's just a job. Don't mean anything."

"If you say so. I suppose she could stop."

"Listen, Matthew, I like things the way they are. She stops hooking on account of me, then I own her, you know what I mean? I don't want the responsibility. It's just a for-now thing."

"Fair enough. I like Suzi. She's a nice girl."

"Yeah, well, she's nice enough for me."

There is something in his tone of voice that unsettles Matthew.

The bill comes. "I'll get that," says Jack.

Matthew can't help but notice the money in Jack's wallet. "That's quite a wad of cash."

"I sold a couple of photos," says Jack.

At the Passy Cemetery they wander through the paths set out like streets in this city of the dead. Over one of the graves a Pietà rises encased in fibreglass; over another is a statue of a naked woman kneeling, her hands palms-up on her thighs, her eyes closed in a face turned heavenward—the picture of despair and submission. There are angels and stone children and lambs and crosses carved to look as though they are made of wood. Trees line the paths and cast dappled shadows. The air smells fresh from the cedar trees but damp and earthy as well. Here and there old people stoop and kneel, dressed as though they're having lunch with friends. They tend the flowers, water the plants and polish the marble.

Anthony, his boots ringing on the stones, leads them to the mausoleum of the Russian count he's told them about. "He did everything," says Anthony. "Painted, sculpted, wrote poetry."

It is a massive tomb, easily the largest in the cemetery, with Cyrillic script engraved on the outside walls. They stand pressed up to the iron grille of the entrance, peering past the glass into the gloom within. The smell of cold stone and mould surrounds them. Inside there is a room decorated with a faded red-and-yellow carpet, a tasselled velvet chair, a candelabra, and a table on which stand two large stone vases holding wilted flowers. Over the table hangs a huge painting, presumably created by the talented count himself. In it, a black-hooded figure, face unseen, trudges up a bleak hill under a glowering sky.

"All very vampire Lestat," says Jack. "Very fucking Anne Rice." His camera shutter clicks; he checks the light setting and takes more shots.

Suzi, who wears red boots and a long black shirt with some

sort of complicated elastic at the hem that makes it poof around her calves, puts her arm through Jack's. "Does it frighten you?" she says.

Matthew notices that her pupils seem normal today, her skin less blemished.

Jack shrugs her off. "Why would you say that?"

"It gives me some—*comment dire . . .*?" She shivers.

"Willies," says Anthony.

She smiles at him, laughing.

Paweena, in jeans and a purple jacket, looks bored. "I don't like this place. Too many dead people." She has brought a baguette with her and picks at pieces of it, nibbling delicately. She behaves as if Suzi does not exist, looking through her or past her. It occurs to Matthew that he can't recall Paweena addressing any comments to Suzi when they were at Anthony's for dinner.

Suzi says, "Debussy is buried in here as well, you know." Her voice is high, girlish, like she is telling ghost stories, scaring herself and loving it. "Can you imagine it at night? Strains of *"La Mer"* drifting through the night as the count sits in his chair, listening."

Jack takes photographs of Suzi peering into the tomb.

"I want to go," says Paweena. She tosses the heel of her bread into a nearby garbage can. "This is no good, this place."

"In a minute." Anthony puts his arm around her. "Let's take a walk through, at least."

She turns away from his embrace. "No. You stay. This is your thing. You like all this mumbo-jumbo. Not me. For children. And fools." And with that she minces away, not waiting to see if he'll follow her.

Matthew is gratified to see he does not. Bitch, he thinks.

Anthony stares at the ground, his hands in his pockets. "Man, I just thought it would be interesting. There are times when it's very hard not to give her just the tiniest little slap," he says, and makes a feeble attempt at laughter. "But hey, I used to arrest guys for that, right?"

Jack punches him in the shoulder. "It is interesting. Weird. But, hey, I like weird, even if I don't like cops."

"Present company," says Anthony, his voice flat.

"Excepted." Jack nudges Anthony with his shoulder, once, twice, like an elephant trying to rouse a wounded member of the herd. "Come on," he says, "she'll meet up with us later, I bet. Not everybody gets this stuff. Come on. Give us the grand tour. Gimme the full bones, all that root doctor and hoodoo stuff."

"Yeah. What the fuck." Anthony smiles, although it is not his usual smile.

They wander away from the count and walk through the lanes. Matthew is oddly at peace here. It is like a town set out on fairy scale. Maybe, he thinks, my ghosts are socializing. Or maybe the world of death has finally become more his home than that of the living. It isn't a pleasant thought, and yet he finds himself thinking that he could bring a book, a Thermos of coffee, maybe, and spend an afternoon here.

Anthony has meandered off on his own, and Matthew watches Suzi and Jack. They hold hands. She looks so small next to him that she could be his child. Her neck, underneath the tousle of short hair, looks very fragile. She missteps on a loose stone and Jack steadies her, protectively reaching out with both arms. Matthew finds himself grappling with a sudden surge of jealousy.

He spots Anthony standing by a large monument in the corner of the graveyard. Anthony looks up at the statue of a heavy-limbed woman, who appears to droop under the weight of the stone cloth draped around her body. Anthony himself might be taken for a mourner, dressed all in black as he is.

"That's some statue," Matthew says as he reaches him. "Great stones." Around the upper rim of the stone square, at the feet of the figure that kneels over a central slab as though felled by sorrow, are a row of jewel-cut glass pieces the colour of amethysts.

"Look inside," says Anthony.

Inside, the light falls in mauve beams onto a reclining female figure carved from marble.

"It's beautiful, but . . ."

"But what?"

"It's well, it's sort of lonely."

"Yeah, you could see it that way. Although the light brings something in, don't you think?"

"No. I don't."

"Too bad," he says gently. The breeze shifts direction and the damp, truffle-y smell of the crypt floats around them.

"You all right, Anthony?"

"Thought I'd beaten down my old ways. All that anger." He sighs. "What do you think about Suzi and Jack?"

"I'm not sure. I think she might be good for him."

"I wonder who's going to be good for us, Matt? Who are we going to be good *for?*"

Anthony walks away then, just like that, and the place where he stood feels empty, a vacant spot in the shape of his body.

CHAPTER SEVENTEEN

"Sorry," says Anthony.

He says the word frequently because he and Saida often collide in the small kitchen. At first this upset her, flustered her, and she flapped tea towels at him to keep him at bay. Now, after more than a week of having him at Chez Elias, it has become something of a joke.

"Your feet," says Saida.

"Sorry," he says and looks down to see whose path he is blocking.

"Move back," says Saida, and she ducks in front of him to reach for a plate while he presses up against the counter behind him.

"Sorry," he says.

"Watch out," she says, and she swerves around him with a tray of glasses as he chops tomatoes on the big wooden board.

"Sorry," he says, and now she smiles at him.

She finds him funny, the big black man. Several days after their first meeting he had appeared at the café with a plastic container of delicious roast pumpkin soup. The day after that he had appeared again, this time with a grated apple tart. The next day, embarrassed by yet another offering—stuffed cèpe mushrooms this time—she had said, "You must stop. Our customers will begin wanting your food instead of ours."

"Might be to your advantage to put me to work, then, don't you think?"

"Why don't you chop those onions for me?" And he had. Which is how it began.

She had been unsure about him at first, but now she does not know what she would do without him. He is never late. He works with great concentration and enjoyment. He loves the food, loves everything about the restaurant, even the mundane chores like cleaning up and stacking dishes, which he arranges beautifully. It took some time for him to understand the way things work. He doesn't make connections like other people. He is unable, for example, to look at a menu and then find the corresponding item in the display case. However, once he knows the name of something he never forgets it. He learns in some mysterious way of his own and her explanations do not help, and so she leaves him to puzzle things out in his own way. What he lacks in associative ability, however, he makes up for in observational skills. His comments about customers make her laugh, particularly since they are delivered in a deeply serious voice.

"Maybe her pantyhose's too short," he says about the woman who refuses to smile and takes tiny mincing steps.

"I think he's afraid no one will listen to him," about a businessman who speaks far too loudly on his cell phone.

Altogether, he is a good employee, and since he works for free—well, for food that he mostly cooks himself—she is well pleased. The only problem is that now Ramzi feels he can do less. This morning, when Ramzi declined to show up at all, Saida decided Anthony would work only three days a week—she would be happy to have him there every day, but she fears if she agreed to that, Ramzi would stop coming in completely. Even before Anthony came to them, Ramzi worked less and less, his eyes fixed more firmly on the horizon every morning. There are nights he does not come home and Saida is sure there is a woman somewhere.

If once she thought her brother would help in raising her son, she no longer thinks so. Her son has become even more guarded, at least toward her, and she is frightened. She suspects he has a secret life somewhere that does not include her. And in the back of her mind a bulky shadow appears. He stopped talking about the big man Jack so easily. Too easily, perhaps. She has asked Matthew if he thinks Joseph sees Jack. He says he does not think so, but she is not convinced. And so she turns to Anthony at times, since there is no one else, really, for her to talk to. Her father is frailer with every day and the doctors say there is nothing to be done, that he is old and tired, and they shrug in a way that makes her want to pinch them. She cannot burden him more.

"Hey, there's Joseph," says Anthony, as he chops parsley. Saida wonders if thinking about her son has drawn him to her.

Saida looks up as he comes into the restaurant. His feet are so big in those sneakers. The laces are untied. She is sure he will trip but says nothing because he has already informed her that this is the style.

"Whattttzzzzuuuuup?" Joseph says, and Anthony laughs. This is also a style, apparently, something from an American television commercial.

"Are you hungry?" she says.

"Sure. *Chawarma?*"

"Cut it yourself," and she hands him a plate.

"Anthony, listen to this." He pulls the little silver disks that act as headphones from around his neck and puts one up against Anthony's ear. "Listen. Who is it?" he says, grinning.

Anthony listens for a minute, and then smiles. "Easy. That's Ice-T. 'Cop Killer.'"

"Ah, you're too good!"

"Cop killer?" Saida's hand rises involuntarily. "Who is a cop killer?"

"Nobody. It's the name of a song."

"That's terrible."

"It's political," says Joseph. "Right?"

"Well, since I used to be a cop, I don't know how down I am with the sentiment."

This talk baffles Saida. "How was school?"

Joseph wags his head back and forth.

"What is that? Yes and no? Good and bad?"

"Okay." He heaps his plate with marinated lamb.

"You have homework?"

"Not much."

"You must go to the only school in Paris that gives no homework."

"I didn't say I don't have any. I said I didn't have much."

"So, what do you have?"

He sits at the counter and shovels food into his mouth, his arm wrapped around the plate, as though he's afraid someone will steal it. "Some biology."

"Sit up, Joseph. You look like a gorilla. That's all?"

"I did the rest."

"Let me see."

He sighs and regards her from the great distance of long suffering. "I left it at a friend's house."

Saida folds her arms. "Why would you do that?"

"Imma," he rolls his eyes, which she chooses to ignore. "Pierre lives close to the school. I stop there sometimes on the way home and leave books there. You know we have no lockers at school. The books are heavy."

"I don't want you to do this. You know I want to see your homework. If the books are too heavy for a delicate boy like you, we can get you one of those carts the old ladies use to bring their groceries home. There, you see, I am smart too. I have come up with a good solution, yes?"

"Right." Finished with his food, he carries the plate to the dishwasher.

"Rinse it," Saida says. "I want you to get your books now, from this boy's house. I want to see your homework."

"I can't now. I have to go."

"What do you mean you have to go? You have to go where?"

"I'm meeting a guy."

"What guy?"

She can see him thinking, licking the bulge in his lip, searching for a plausible lie. It is so like him not to have something prepared. Her heart contracts with love.

"Some guys. We're going to play soccer."

"Soccer can wait."

"I have to go." Joseph puts his arms around her and kisses her on the top of the head. "I'll show you later. I promise."

"Joseph, do not patronize me," she says in Arabic. "I will not have it."

"I won't be late," he calls. "See you later, Anthony."

"See you." Anthony picks up Joseph's plate from beside the sink where he left it and puts it in the dishwasher.

Saida slaps her cleaning rag against the counter, and then goes to the door and watches her son. At the corner, two boys meet up with him and they go through some sort of hand-shaking ritual, all fists and thumbs and sliding palms. She faintly recognizes the boys. Are they not the boys she caught with Joseph in the apartment smoking dope? One of them, the larger one who wears a bandana around his shaved head, passes something to Joseph that he quickly puts in his pocket, and then they split up again. Joseph looks back, checking to see if he is watched. Saida ducks her head inside. *Silly boy! You should have looked before!* When she peeks again a moment later, he has disappeared. She turns and finds Anthony watching her.

"He's okay," says Anthony. "He's a teenager."

"This is normal in America? That a boy can do as he pleases at only sixteen, without any thought to his family? To his studies?"

"Teenagers are a pain in the butt the world over, I guess."

"You think he's going to play soccer?"

"He said he was. You don't believe him?"

She wants to tell Anthony what she has seen, ask him what it means. But it is family business, and already too many people are involved in her family. Again, it twitches, a hulking shape, dark in the corner of her mind. "He's spending time with that man Jack, isn't he?"

"Oh. I don't know. Jack's got a lady now. And the job at the hostel. I think he's pretty busy."

"I hope you're right," says Saida.

CHAPTER EIGHTEEN

"Matthew, pick up the phone. Pick up the phone. Pick up the phone. Pick up the phone. Pick up the phone." Brent speaks so quickly into the machine he sounds like a scat singer.

Matthew listens to the messages. The phone has rung six times in the two hours since noon. All of them Brent. He must have risen before dawn and vowed to make harassing Matthew his sole purpose for the day. As Matthew contemplates ripping the phone out of the wall, it rings again. He considers not answering it, but knows Brent will not give up.

"Hello," he says.

"Where have you been? I haven't heard from you in three weeks and you promised me you would check in every week."

"What's up?"

"What's up? I'll tell you what's up. Publisher says if they don't see a manuscript before Christmas the deal is off and you have to give back the advance. Which means you are screwed. *Screwed.* Do you get this?"

"Absolutely."

"And?"

"And what?"

"You are driving me fucking nuts! I'm gonna have a fucking coronary right here on the phone."

"I've got some stuff."

"Read me some."

"You want me to read you something? Now?"

"I do not believe you have anything. I believe you are lying to me. So prove me wrong. I love for people to prove me wrong. Make me happy. Read me, I don't know, three, four pages."

"Hang on." Matthew goes to the desk, pulls out some pages and brings them back to the phone. "Ready?"

"Am I ready, he says. Funny man."

Sarajevo. Josh, Philip and I sat in Camila's kitchen trying to ignore the incessant barking of Camila's dog standing just outside the door, legs splayed, neck thrusting, nearly choking on its tether. The sandy mixed-breed brute had gone crazy from the long months of gunfire and explosions, and lost its ability to differentiate between sounds that foretold danger and normal street noise. It just barked, all day, all night, relieved only by short periods of calm when it collapsed in a quivering heap, worn out by vigilance. Camila thought it would stop soon, because its throat was so raw. Flecks of blood spattered its muzzle now and she felt that in a day or two its vocal cords would blow out completely. She didn't have the heart to shoot the dog who had, she insisted, a hero's heart, and so we lived with the racket.

Josh, a photojournalist, was a short, wiry Londoner with a deep resonant voice that didn't match his blond, elfin face. I had worked with Josh before and was happy to be with him in Sarajevo. He was funny and smart and never seemed to panic or be affected by the dread that sometimes overcame me. Philip was also a Brit, from Guilford, with a shaved head and homemade tattoos on his arms. He chewed at the sides of his nails and spit bits of dried skin on the floor.

Josh and I had arrived in town looking for a cheap place to stay, and a man selling bread in the market told us about Camila Oric, a Muslim woman who took in boarders. Philip had already been there for a couple of weeks.

"Fucking dog," said Philip. "I should fucking shoot that dog."

"Poor old thing. I doubt his heart can take much more of that," said Josh.

Philip glared at the dog with undisguised hatred and fingered the pistol in his belt. "I hate fucking dogs. My mum'd never have one. Covered in fleas, they are." He wore filthy army surplus pants and jacket. He'd been fighting with the Muslims for three months and although he said he'd come in to take a bath, so far it didn't seem he'd found the tub.

I thought it best to get the guy's mind off the dog, off shooting anything. "So, tell me, Philip, what's a nice boy from Guilford doing in a place like this?" I said.

"Nothing for me in fucking Guilford, is there? Fucking dole as far back on the family tree as the eye can see and this dozy cow gets herself knocked up and I'm supposed to pay for it. Fucking hell." Philip sent a tiny missile of skin toward the dog. "More of the same, eh? I end up like my old man, in front of the telly with a lager and a takeaway and that's it? Not bloody likely. I want to know what the world's about, right? Everything." The way he pronounced the word, it sounded like "everyfing." "I want to know what it feels like to kill someone."

"Right," said Josh.

We had met young men like this before. I would rightly judge Philip a psychopath if he'd stood behind me in a lineup at the grocery store, but it was testament to the cruelty of the times and the place that, then and there, Philip was neither alone in his desire nor considered strange for speaking of it.

"And?" I asked.

"And it's fucking weird. This whole scene is fucked, man. Pack of fucking liars, all of them," said Philip.

I agreed with this masterstroke of understatement. I sifted through the murk to find the clear space of morality, for I wanted that more than I wanted anything. I could, and did, take sides. I was no pacifist. The problem was I took so many sides. I saw the right and wrong in a specific situation—the machete across the arm, the landmine under the foot, the cigarette in the palm—but once I stepped back, beyond the limits of any specific incident, the moral terrain became confusing. Motivation was a fog, obscuring everything. Truth hid behind a great rock of rage and sorrow and perspective, and the heart-rip of regret.

"None of us can afford to look too closely at the lies we tell ourselves," said Josh.

The next morning when we woke, Philip was gone and the house was strangely silent. We found Camila burying the dog in the garden, its throat slit.

"Is for the best, I think. I could not do this," she said, but her eyes were red-rimmed. "He was a good dog before. A very good dog once."

Brent is quiet on the other end of the phone.

"So?" Matthew says finally.

"This Josh, same Josh as in Hebron, I'm assuming."

"Yes. Same Josh."

"Right. Okay. It's good. I don't think I could have shot the dog either."

"No."

"You got more like that?"

"Yes, some. It's hard going, I'll admit it."

"Send what you got. It'll keep them quiet for a while."

"Bye, Brent."

"Ciao."

Matthew hangs up and spends the rest of the day sorting through the pages, scraps and fragments, organizing them as best he can. The structure, overall, is a problem. He digs narrow tunnels into the past then hits lumps of resistance which, when tapped, crumble. The cave-in begins and he has no option but to run, abandon the mine and begin again. At last, he stuffs a folder's worth into an envelope addressed to Brent. He looks at his watch. It is after eight. He will mail it tomorrow. This day is over, he thinks.

The next morning he drops the package to Brent off at the post office and decides to devote the rest of the day to being a *flâneur*, a wandering, idle, man-about-town.

It is late November now and November is not a merry month in Paris. It is grim. It is damp and chill, but not bracing. The leaves fall but do not turn the cheerful riot of colours he had always looked forward to in Canada. The days are shorter and it is full night by five-thirty. Matthew does not mind that so much, though, because during daylight hours he feels obliged to be doing something constructive and feels guilty when, like now, he is not.

He has made his way into the 6th arrondissement, and ambles down rue des Canette. It pleases him, this thirteenth-century street with its fine houses and the bas-relief of three ducklings playing in the water painted on No. 18. There is not much of this old sort of Paris left, and he tries to imagine what it must have been like when the priests of Saint-Sulpice frequented Miss Beety's famous brothel. Neither priests nor prostitutes seem to have much to do with the neighbourhood anymore. Fancy stores and fancy clothes and joggers in the Luxembourg Gardens and motor scooters everywhere, loud and arrogant.

He wanders into the place Saint-Sulpice to browse through the book fair. The square in front of the church bustles with merchants under tents fronted by book-covered tables. He meanders through the stalls, stopping to look at a nineteenth-century diary filled with drawings of flowers and poetry written in spidery, embellished script. He tries to translate the florid handwriting. He imagines some young Parisian woman, now long dead, trying to find something inspiring in her narrow world of high garden walls and the strictures of respectability. Judging from what he can make out—his French is almost as bad as the poetry—he concludes that she failed and remained trapped, and he pities her.

He puts the book down with a stab of regret, as he sometimes does with inanimate objects. It is an old childhood fantasy that he has never been able to shake completely, that things have feelings and careless abandonment harms them. As a young boy, he cried at the thought of toys left rusting and lost in the woods, wept to think of their terrible, immobile loneliness. His weakness irritates him.

He catches sight of a table of photography books and makes his way toward it. In the centre of the table is a book with a black-and-white photo on the cover. It is of a man Jack's size, his face like a piece of meat, fleshy, full of appetites. His shirt is open and his gut bulges rudely. One arm hugs a girl young enough to be his youngest daughter, a walleyed child in a low-cut dress. She holds her fisted hand up to the side of her neck between them. In the man's other arm he cradles a naked baby, the child's head thrown back, his arms limp and his mouth open. The proprietary, smug expression on the man's face makes it clear the baby is his. The grip of the man's blunt fingers on the girl, so fragile she looks as though she might snap, makes Matthew wonder what the man's relationship to her is. Daughter? Wife? Appalling. Fascinating.

A hand reaches out for the book at the same time his does and he looks to see who his competition might be.

"Anthony! I'll be damned. Go ahead."

"Paris is smaller than you think sometimes, isn't it?" He picks up the book and opens it. "Bill Burke. Quite a collection. White trash, man. Every photo's like staring at a car wreck." He flips through the pages and stops at one called, "Couple in a bar." A man, his face showing decades of abuse by harsh weather and hard liquor, wearing an undershirt, has his tattooed arms around an exhausted-looking, dark-haired woman with two black eyes. "These people are us, I guess. Reminds me of Jack, of his pictures, I mean. You seen any of them?"

"Just the one at your place," says Matthew.

"That's a good one. But a lot of them are like this. I don't want the book. Do you?"

"Yeah, I think I do."

Anthony hands it to him and waits while he pays. "I'm going into the church. You want to come?"

"In the church?"

Anthony smiles. "Yeah."

"I guess." And he follows Anthony in.

The day is dull, the sky an oddly rose-tinted grey. Inside the church, the light is such that it might have been deep night outside, the murk broken only by the flickering candles. It smells of incense and wood polish. Anthony closes his eyes and breathes deeply.

A few old people pray silently in the chairs in the nave and several tourists stroll about in the aisles. Above them is a magnificent organ loft and the walls are covered in murals. Matthew ambles along in tourist mode, reading the descriptions: St. Michael killing the demon, Heliodorus driven from the temple, Jacob struggling with the angels.

"You gotta see this. Follow me." Anthony leads Matthew to the back of the church, to an ornate niche containing the statue of the Virgin and Child standing in front of a great scalloped background, a serpent beneath her foot. "I brought Jack here once. He said it looked as though it had been built by a drunken Italian gardener, and maybe it is a bit over the top, but I kinda dig it."

"Well, it's impressive." Matthew thinks that whoever designed it might have been on acid.

Anthony takes a ten-franc piece out of his pocket and drops it in the little brass box before he lights a candle and closes his eyes in prayer.

Watching Anthony pray, Matthew is not sure what to do, and he feels like a voyeur. He wonders if he should just leave. At last, he sits down on a nearby chair and waits, wondering how long Anthony intends to pray and if he has brought Matthew here in the hopes of a conversion. He does not think so, and after seeing Anthony's room full of spiritual literature and paraphernalia, is not convinced he is even Catholic, but there are conversions and then there are conversions. Even if it is not Catholicism Anthony is recommending, but a more general sort of God-consciousness, Matthew remains unconvinced. The idea that he can be brought to God at this late date is laughable.

Still, the church atmosphere is soporific and he is lulled into a sort of waking trance after a few moments—the quiet, the candles, the placid expression of the Virgin, all creating an enchantment. Matthew might even have fallen asleep if not for a growing awareness of people behind him, laughter and voices, growing louder. Anthony opens his eyes and turns to look just as a priest, a bride and a groom, surrounded by a large group of friends and family, passes between them. Judging from their accents they are French North Africans. The bride's skin is the colour of mahogany against the white of her fabulously embroidered gown. One of the little boys pulls off his blue velvet tie, looks at Matthew and giggles.

Anthony says, "Come on." He follows the wedding procession and Matthew follows Anthony.

It is such a jolly ceremony that Matthew's spirits cannot help but lift, and it is only then that he realizes how glum he has been feeling. This happens often—that he is not aware of his emotions until the moment of their passing, or their intensification. It began out in the field, after some narrow escape, when he would look down at his hands and see them shaking, and then think, My God, that was terrible. Without the shaking, he might not have realized the depth of his terror. Now there are afternoons when he sits at his desk trying to work and finds himself near tears, when just a moment before he hadn't known he was sad, and with no reason, or none that he can name, like that night with Denise. But now he feels lightened as he watches the women who are like bright birds, their dresses peach and turquoise and daffodil. The priest is old and clearly delighted to be performing the rites. He jokes with the bride and groom, and although Matthew doesn't understand all of what is said he finds himself laughing too, as does Anthony, and he is happy to see so much joy.

Then the little boy who had been pulling at his tie a few minutes earlier throws himself down on the stone floor and lies there, his arms and legs spread out as though he were about to make snow angels. The grown-ups ignore him. A little forgotten body on the stones. Like the red-winged blackbirds that swept down on Matthew when he rode his bike beside the fields as a child, memories fly at him and he feels himself slipping, sliding, down into the sloping lands . . .

"I have to get out of here," he says and walks up the aisle to the front of the church, not waiting to see if Anthony is following, nor caring.

Outside, he stands on the church steps and looks upward, sucking the cold air into his lungs. A pair of kestrel hawks swirl in the air near one of the towers. One of them hovers. It gives Matthew the creeps.

Anthony comes up behind him. "The French say they're making the sign of the cross when they do that," he says.

Matthew keeps breathing, which is taking more effort than it ought to.

"Well, it's not my favourite church either, really," Anthony says, still watching the kestrels.

"The church is fine. Sorry."

"Nothing to be sorry for."

"Isn't there?"

Anthony turns from the hawks to Matthew, and then back to the sky again, but the kestrels have disappeared. "Matthew, listen, I'm glad I ran into you, man. You seen Suzi in the past couple of days?"

"No." Something begins to prickle in Matthew's chest.

"She's got a split lip. Some pretty bad bruises."

"What happened?"

Anthony shrugs. "She's not talking to Jack, I can tell you that."

"You think Jack—?"

"Yeah. I do."

The prickle turns to twitching heat. "What does he say?"

"Not much. He doesn't want to talk about it."

"What does she say?"

"Last I saw her, she threw a beer in his face and walked out of the Bok. I thought Dan was going to have to use the crowbar on him."

"I'd like to hear what happened from Suzi for myself, wouldn't you?"

"She won't talk to me." He looks pointedly at Matthew.

"Don't suppose you know where she lives, do you?"

"As a matter of fact, I do. I helped her carry a table home that she bought at the flea market near my place one day. I've got the door code, too." Anthony reaches into his inside jacket pocket and produces a ragged, swollen address book. He flips through it for several minutes because apparently there is no particular order to the entries, and at last comes up with Suzi's address.

Matthew copies it, and the code, onto a piece of paper.

"You want me to go with you?"

"No, thanks. I'll talk to her," Matthew says, and then wonders why he prefers to go alone.

CHAPTER NINETEEN

Suzi's apartment is in the 13th arrondissement, on the *rez de chaussée*. Matthew uses the code Anthony gave him to gain access to the hall. The tile floors need sweeping, but it is well lit from a skylight high above and the wide staircase has a graceful curve that tells him this must have been a good building, once. There is only one apartment on the ground floor. Originally, back when the building had aspirations, it had most likely the concierge's apartment. He hesitates at the door. The name on it is "M. Roussel." Perhaps Anthony has given him the wrong address. But no, the code worked, so that can't be it. The wrong apartment? But it is the only one on this floor. He knocks. No answer. He listens for any sound of life inside but hears only the meowing of a cat. This is stupid, he thinks.

He decides to wait outside for fifteen minutes. Let fate dictate what will happen next. He leans against the wall, staring at his shoes. Maybe Anthony is wrong. Maybe Suzi threw a drink in Jack's face because she was pissed at him for some reason totally unrelated to her bruises. Either way, like most things, it is none of his business. He looks at his watch. Five more minutes and he will leave.

"Matthew?" Suzi stands before him, her swollen lip discoloured, with a fair-sized scab. A bruise stains the skin on her neck, purple and green above the collar of her wool coat; another mars her cheek. Still, her face is not as bad as he imagined it would be if Jack had taken his fists to her. "What are you doing here?" She does not sound pleased.

"Anthony told me you'd been hurt. I wanted to see if you were all right."

"Anthony told you my address?"

"Yes. Is that a problem?" He is confused. This is not the Suzi he knows. The Suzi he knows is always happy to see him.

"I thought Anthony understood. I give my address out to people I want to have it. I do not expect them to pass it along like a number on a phone booth wall."

"I only came because I was concerned."

"Oh, you are worried about me? Is that it?"

"Well, yes."

She shrugs, in that way that only Frenchwomen can, pursing her lips, raising an eyebrow. "And now you see me. I'm fine."

"Somebody hit you."

Another shrug. "It is a dangerous profession."

An old lady pulling a shopping cart passes between them and gives Suzi a dirty look before entering the building.

"The neighbours talk too much." Her eyes are jittery and she rubs her finger under her nose. "What do you want? I am in a hurry."

He had not expected her to be angry with him, and does not know how to respond. "I guess this was a bad idea. Sorry. Just wanted to make sure you were all right."

She says nothing, but stands looking down the street to the right and then to the left and behind her. Anywhere but at him.

"Okay. Well. You're all right, then. Sorry." He turns to leave.

"Matthew." She reaches out. "*C'est moi.* A very bad mood is all. Don't pay attention to me. I suppose you better come in."

The apartment opens directly into a kitchen, painted white. There is a sink, cupboards and workspace with a hotplate on it, along the right wall. A few photos and a child's drawing are taped to the front of the refrigerator. Above the sink is a window, boarded over. At the back, a door leads to a paved courtyard. There is a table in the middle of the room, with two chairs, and a colourful braided rug on the floor. In the corner a spiral staircase leads down into what Matthew assumes is a below-ground bedroom. A box filled with worn stuffed animals stands in a corner. The walls are bare.

As they enter, Matthew can't help but ask, "Who's M. Roussel?"

"The last tenant, I suppose. I've only been here a few weeks."

"Oh, I thought for a minute . . . well, that it might be your name."

Suzi laughs. "You think Suzi is my real name? Men are such fools. You never see that movie, about the Chinese prostitute, *The World of Suzi Wong*? It is a name that works well for me at your bar."

"So, what is your name?"

She looks at him and frowns slightly. "Suzi, you call me Suzi, okay?" Leaving her coat on, she says she will be back in a minute and disappears down the spiral staircase.

Matthew sits at the table and a fat Himalayan cat pads up from the basement and jumps onto his lap. It purrs loudly and looks at him with proprietary eyes. After a few minutes, he hears a toilet flush and Suzi reappears. She looks much less jittery. She takes the cat from his lap and sits across from him. She has taken off her coat and shoes. She wears a short black skirt, black wool stockings that come just over her knee, and a red sweater, very low cut. She has not attempted to hide the damage. She curls one foot under the other, so her legs part slightly.

"Why are you here?" Her lids are heavy now and her mouth more relaxed.

"Did Jack do this?"

"What does it matter?"

"It matters to me."

"Why? What are you going to do? Beat him up for me?" She laughs.

"Maybe."

"He would kill you. You are too skinny."

"That's probably true."

Suzi arches an eyebrow. "What is a little violence between lovers, eh?"

"So Jack did hit you?"

"And so? I hit him back. I threw a drink in his face. I am not so fragile." She pulls down her sweater to reveal another storm-coloured bruise on her breast. "You Americans know nothing of passion."

Matthew opens his mouth to speak, but closes it again, for he can find nothing sensible to say. This is not what he had expected. Where were the tears? The anger? The fear? He watches her fingers caress the cat, gently tickling the fur, and then kneading, massaging. "That's ridiculous," he says at last. "Like something out of a bad French farce, all that slapped-face and slammed-door nonsense."

He stands and starts to leave but she pulls at his sleeve and he sits down again.

"No. It is not ridiculous. What is ridiculous is you coming here, acting the noble hero, when it is not nobility you want at all." She stands up, dropping the cat on the floor, and stands very close to Matthew, puts her hands on either side of his head. She straddles his thigh.

"Hey! Hey!" He stands up and steps back from her. "You've got the wrong idea."

In one quick motion, she pulls the sweater over her head. She is not wearing a bra and her nipples are brown and small. The bruises stand out like too-fresh tattoos. There are other bruises on her arms. She puts her hands over her breasts, and begins to caress herself. "I'm never wrong about such things."

Arousal flows through Matthew like a shot of whisky. He glances at the refrigerator with the child's drawing on it.

"We are alone," she says.

"Jack's my friend."

"This has nothing to do with that." She steps out of her skirt and stands before him, with only those black stockings on, and tiny white panties. There are more bruises on her thighs. "I can give you what you want, Matthew. What you came here for."

Her breasts rise out of her thin rib cage, all the bones visible. The bruises are vivid against her skin. The tale of violence they tell is pornographic, the images of brutal hands on her body. And then she puts her hand on the front of his pants and her tongue in his mouth. Her bones are tiny beneath his hands; her eyes, with their pinpoint pupils, are like those of something wicked.

He takes her up on the tabletop. She is very good at what she does and makes him believe her cries are real.

When he is finished, she goes downstairs and comes back wearing a Japanese kimono. "I'm sorry, Matthew, normally I arrange the price before." She names her price and he pays it, his face burning. "You are very silly," she says, kissing him on the cheek.

"I didn't come here for this, you know," he says, because he must say it, must say something.

"Of course you didn't. But still, it is a good idea, *non?*"

"I don't think we should tell Jack, do you?"

She throws back her tousled head and laughs. "Matthew. I am like a doctor. No, like a priest. *Absolument confidentiel!*" She puts her finger up to her damaged lip. "Shush," she says, and giggles.

He leaves her apartment, gets on the metro. A bunch of loud teenagers push and shove as they enter the car and he wants them to push him so he can feel someone's bones crack beneath his knuckles. Disappointingly, they keep their distance.

When he gets back to his apartment, he takes three times the recommended dosage of sleeping pills and still has to wait half an hour before unconsciousness overtakes him. He dreams of girls and soldiers and an old woman biting his hand.

CHAPTER TWENTY

Saturday mornings Saida shops at the open-air market on rue Dejean. She walks up rue de Faubourg Poissonnière toward the Barbès Métro and her thoughts are of Joseph. He had said little this morning, merely hunched over his bowl of café au lait. She suspects he was hung over, although he denied it. She tried to smell him, to discover the telltale sweetish sweat-reek of alcohol seeping through the skin, but he dove into the shower the moment she vacated the bathroom.

"Where are you going?" she had said as he put on his jacket. "I want you to take your grandfather to the restaurant."

"Can't. Soccer game."

"This morning? But we need you at the restaurant."

"I can't. I promised I'd be there."

"Where? Who with?"

He scooped change off the tabletop and stuffed it in his pocket, and then stooped to kiss her on the cheek. "Just some guys in Square Léon."

"I don't want you spending all your time up there. I want you at the restaurant this afternoon."

"Okay, okay," he said as he opened the door. His shoelaces dragged, untied, from his running shoes.

"Tie your shoes," she called after him.

Now, as she walks toward the market, pulling her cart behind her and with a basket on her arm, she decides to go by the square where the boys play soccer. Across the boulevard de Chapelle the streets become twice as congested, with both cars and pedestrian traffic. Outside the Tati department store, the sidewalks are nearly impassable because of the vendors hawking everything from pots and pans to hats to hams. She crosses Barbès and walks onto rue de la Goutte d'Or, entering the heart of the tiny, mostly Arab immigrant neighbourhood. At Le Case@Café, which is advertised as a cyber-café, the men inside are clearly more interested in the off-track betting that goes on than anything having to do with computers. The smoke drifts out of the grey-and-beige-tiled cubbyhole in a blue cloud. She stops and looks in the windows of the textile shops, with gloriously luxurious cloth from Algeria, from Tunisia, from Morocco, deep blue and rose and white and bright yellow, twinkling with gold thread and sequins. At Toualbi, she passes the Muslim butcher on the corner of rue de Chartres—sides of goat and lamb and waffled strips of tripe hang in the window. The lamb looks good, but she knows she can get it cheaper in the market.

She turns up rue des Gardes to the square and goes up the stairs past the metal gates, ignoring the four men drinking out of paper bags by the children's Jungle Gym to the right. The children of the area, being street smart, shun them as well, and high-pitched voices come from the other play area where there is a sandbox and teeter-totter. The older boys play soccer on two fenced-in, asphalt squares, one on a level lower. The intermittent shouts and soft thuds of footfalls make her smile. It will be nice to watch Joseph at play. When she looks over the waist-high concrete wall, however, she sees only black faces. All North Africans. No sign of Joseph. Perhaps on the upper square. She strains to see but cannot, and so climbs up to the next level. These are all Arabs. She scans them. No Joseph, and in truth she thinks these boys—ten, eleven, twelve at the most—are too young for her son. Three boys lean against the chain-link with their backs to her.

"Excuse me," she says.

The boys turn to her and stare blankly.

"I'm looking for my son. His name is Joseph Ferhat. Do you know him?"

"No, we don't know him," the boy nearest her says. He has a scar slicing through his left eyebrow, making it look as though he has one regular-sized and two smaller brows.

One of the other boys clears his throat, spits and smears the spittle on the ground with his shoe. It is clear that even if they do know Joseph, they will not tell her.

Saida has not really expected to find him here. She has hoped, of course, but did not really believe it. He lies to her. When had that begun? What was the first lie? Why doesn't he know it is wrong? Has he learned from his stepfather that this is the way a man is? She blames herself, for she waited too long to leave him, afraid of the shame her father would feel. Ashamed herself at the bad choice she'd made, the ridiculous belief they had all had, that marrying a Frenchman would make her, and by extension them, less strange here. She fears now that Joseph will pay the price for her stupidity. And how to stop it?

She goes into the church, Saint-Bernard de la Chapelle, to be quiet for a moment, to light a candle and ask Mary for intercession. As she walks up the aisle, toward the great statue of Mary behind the altar, the Holy Mother standing on a clouded crescent moon, she sees a jumble of rags on the steps. When she gets closer she realizes it is a person, a man, not old, sleeping but not sleeping, his shoes off, his feet on the warm-air grate. His head nods, he tilts incrementally, until he almost falls and then snaps up again. Nods, sways and begins the tilting journey once more. The caretaker, an Algerian, tries to move him, but the man is too much under the influence of whatever narcotic he has taken to be roused. Saida sees his face; he is younger than she thought. Not much older than Joseph.

She quickly lights a candle, murmurs a prayer and goes out the side door. It looks like rain. People have draped torn plastic garbage bags over laundry that hangs from racks out of second-storey windows. She passes the Hotel Myrha, advertising rooms with hot water and heat that rent for the month or for the day. Market shops sell dried fava beans, green tea in many varieties, pine nuts, pistachios, fermented milk in used Evian water bottles, rice, mangoes and dates. She passes the little shop that sells live chickens, its air powdery with feathers, and she sneezes.

A sharp voice calls out in Arabic and she hears the sound of palms slapping together. A group of young men spill onto the sidewalk. They do not move for people passing and so everyone, old ladies and women with baby strollers, must move around them out into the street. Farther along, the crowd parts for a large man, head and shoulders above the crowd. She sees the figure only from the back but it is familiar. Jack Saddler. There is no mistaking the bestial lumber of his walk. She strains her eyes after him, but he turns a corner and is gone.

The youths speak loudly and one of them, a big boy wearing a bright yellow jacket and a heavy gold medallion, flips a lit cigarette into the street. It narrowly misses a man carrying bags of groceries. Saida frowns, considers crossing the street, and then she spots him.

"Joseph! Joseph!"

He sees her; she knows he does, for he glances in her direction and then quickly turns away, a cigarette cupped in his palm.

"Joseph! Come here!"

"Oh, look, your *maman's* here!" The boys laugh and nudge each other, brave and sneering in the safety of their numbers, of their size, of their youth.

"Merde." He says this, and perhaps he thinks he speaks too low for her to hear, but she does hear it. He drops the cigarette, as though she will not see it. He slouches toward her, one shoulder down, moving as if he is limping, or dragging something, his hand on his crotch.

"What's wrong with you?" she says.

"Nothing. What do you want?"

"What do I want? What do you think, Joseph? What do you think?" Anger, and the cringing little worm of fear in her stomach, makes her repeat herself.

"I'm busy here. I said I would be by the restaurant later. You come looking for me?"

"I wanted to see you play soccer."

"The game got cancelled."

There is much laughter from the group at this. The indignation flickering like flames up her face makes Saida braver and she stands her ground.

"So this is what you do? Who was that I saw up the street? Was that Jack Saddler I saw just now?"

"No."

"It was."

"No."

"I want you to stay away from that man."

"I told you. It was not him. Look, I have to go now."

"You are going to go all right, you're going to come with me. Help me do the shopping. If you do not have a game you have no excuse, and besides, a *game,* what excuse is that? I let you get away with murder. Enough. It is over. You come with me."

"*Imma*, please. Not now. I'll come later." He says this under his breath almost, and she knows he does not want his friends to hear.

"Don't *Imma* me. Now. You can help Anthony."

Joseph stares at her, his handsome face becoming the impassive mask she hates so much. She scrambles, trying to find a way to get him out of there, and she knows if she is not careful now she will push him too far, he will baulk, flex his muscles, and she will lose him. "Listen, he told me he has a new CD he's made for you, blues musicians from America. He said you wanted it."

Joseph's face twitches as he struggles with his pride, and it is all Saida can do not to reach out and stroke his cheek. "He made it for me?"

"Yes. He told me he would bring it today for you, but he wanted to talk to you about someone named Robert Johnson and a pact he made"—she grins—"with the devil at a crossroads."

"Oh, yeah, that one!" He smiles now and her heart, which had been clinging like a bird to the side of her rib cage, flutters and relaxes. "Okay, I'll come. Wait a minute."

Joseph goes over to his friends and tells them a black American friend from New York wants to see him, has some blues music for him, he will get it and share it with them.

"You know a lot of Americans, *hein?*" says the boy with the yellow jacket.

Saida and Joseph walk together without speaking. They walk past the *téléboutique*, where customers who do not have phones can make cheap calls to Turkey, Romania, Poland, Algeria, Iran, Egypt, Cameroon, Senegal and more. They move into the Haitian and French-Caribbean sections of the neighbourhood. People lay out their wares on the tops of parked cars. Brightly coloured African cloth, carvings, jeans and cosmetics especially designed for African skin. Here the shops sell wigs and hair gel, manioc, plantains, taro, *igname,* gumbo and sweet potatoes. Green-and-grey metal construction barricades lay tipped over and flat on the torn-up street and people walk over them because it is impossible not to, there are so many people. As they pass the Paris Refugee Bar, Joseph waves back to a man with a thick black moustache and a cigar who calls his name from the doorway. Saida says nothing.

The market is crowded, as always, and smells of fish, meat and the faint rot of discarded greens. Stalls are set up, with plastic roofs on them, to sell every sort of vegetable and fruit, sweaters and boots, watches and linens. She gives Joseph some money and sends him off with a list. They will meet in twenty minutes.

"I'll take you for pizza after, if you want," she says, by way of reconciliation.

As he ambles through the market, she wonders if he will disappear into the crowd. While she shops, haggling with vendors over cracked wheat, rice, vine leaves, parsley and mint, she turns her head this way and that, trying to keep sight of him. When they meet at last at the far end of the market, she hugs him and kisses his cheek.

"You're a good boy," she says.

"*Imma,* please!"

CHAPTER TWENTY-ONE

Matthew does not leave his apartment for five days. He sleeps and writes, but sleeps more than he writes. All he sees is Suzi's rib cage, the points of her hips, the bruises on the inside of her thighs. On the fifth day, he watches Ramzi and Elias argue in the window of the café. Their arms wave, their faces redden. Finally, Ramzi flicks his hand skyward in a gesture of dismissal and turns away. The old man looks out the window. He rubs his hands over his face. Matthew wonders how long it will be before Ramzi takes his maps and hits the road.

He wonders if he should ask to come along, but he has no energy left for journeying. Turn to the page. *All right. Down to business.* For several hours he writes about Afghanistan, about being holed up in a cave with the *mujahedeen*, among them Zakirya, a one-eyed Tajik whom Matthew had considered a friend. Zakirya died, no, *evaporated* in a Russian mortar assault, after which Matthew found himself terrified of confined spaces for the first time. He writes about arriving in Peshawar and spending three days and four nights in Green's Hotel with two other reporters. They drank themselves blind with booze someone smuggled in from the United Nations Club in Islamabad. They took turns throwing shoes at the enormous but slow-moving cockroaches. They told stories about how brave they were, and special, and what important work they did. "But we're all right now, we're all right now," Matthew had said, repeatedly, and prayed that by the next morning the dread would be gone. It wasn't, but after the fourth night of incessant drinking and talking, it did reduce to a manageable level, a sort of spiritual tinnitus.

By evening his stomach burns. He goes to the medicine cabinet and chews a few chalky antacids. The mirror rattles when he slams it. In the living room, the walls bend in, pressing on him. Dust particles filter through the light like bacteria.

"Fuck it," Matthew says, "I've earned my fun."

Forty-five minutes later, he fans his hand in front of his eyes, watching the smoke swirl like grey ink through dark water in the Bok-Bok air. There is no sign of Suzi. Jack is at his usual table at the back of the room, sitting with Anthony and a guy Matthew doesn't recognize. The guy is of medium build, red-haired and young, probably no more than twenty-five. He wears combat pants and a bright red T-shirt. A leather jacket hangs on the back of his chair. As Matthew watches he leans back, balancing the chair on two legs, his thumbs hooked in his front pockets. He looks relaxed, which means he is probably just a guy and not a problem to be avoided, but you can never tell. Matthew lingers at the bar until he gets the lay of the land.

He does not see Suzi come up behind him. "Ah, Matthew, I missed you." She kisses him on both cheeks, and then rubs away a smear of red lipstick. She wears her black wig and her Chinese dress. Her fingers stink of nicotine. Her nails are ragged and covered in chipped blue nail polish. The smell of cigarettes, wine and heavy, musky perfume combine in a noxious ball.

"How are you?" Matthew says. Her eyes are too bright. She looks even thinner. There are bluish smudges under her eyes that thick makeup cannot hide, although the bruise on her cheek has faded away so that it is nothing more than a reproaching tint on her skin. "Are you all right?"

She shrugs. "I have my worries."

"Jack?" Matthew glances over to see if Jack is looking at them, but he seems engrossed in his conversation.

"Jack? No. Jack is nothing. Past history." She pats his hand. "Things come and go, Matthew. One does not dwell."

And with that he relaxes, slightly. Secrets will be kept where they belong.

"No. It is my daughter."

Matthew recalls the child's drawing on the fridge, the box of stuffed animals. "I didn't know you had a daughter. How old is she?"

"Ten. Eleven next month."

Matthew whistles. "You must have been a kid yourself."

"Of course I was. And she's like me. A wild one. She will not listen. Two months ago she goes to live with her father. He is a bastard. He will beat her, but she will not believe me. She is like her mother, eh? She has to learn the hard way. She'll end up in the *bois* if she's not careful," she says, referring to the hookers who ply their trade in the white vans lined up along the boulevards in the Boulogne forest and its environs. "She calls last night, all tears. But when I say come back and live with me, she refuses. I begged her. *Merde.* But she has made her bed, now. Let her father keep her. I do not care, I tell you. It does not matter to me at all." She puts her hand on Matthew's sleeve. "I am thirsty, Matthew."

"Sure. Dan, get the lady a drink."

"Thanks, Matthew," she says, and leaves him to sit next to a guy at the end of the bar with a huge grey beard and a belly the size of a basketball. Matthew cannot tell if he feels relieved or disappointed. A bit of both, he thinks.

The guy with Anthony and Jack says something that must be funny because both of them laugh but it is guarded, certainly not Jack's usual sonic boom.

"Jack, Anthony, how you doing?"

"Where you been?" says Jack.

"Downtime."

"Matthew, meet Brian Dance. He was in Bosnia, too." This close Matthew can see the slight narrowing of Jack's eyes, the tight smile. Matthew's stomach squirts acid. Brian Dance transfers his cigarette to his mouth and holds out his hand. It is a soft, small hand and Matthew does not like the feel of it against his palm.

"How are you?" Matthew sits down, fights the urge to wipe his hand against his pant leg. He risks a glance at Jack, who leans back in his chair, his arms folded over his chest. Jack keeps his clouded gaze on Brian Dance, which may mean his amiability toward the red-haired man is insincere or it may mean he does not, for some reason that does not bear examining, want to look at Matthew. Matthew's pulse quickens.

"Matthew's a war correspondent," says Anthony. "He knows Christiane Amanpour. Tell him, Matt."

"Yeah?" says Brian. "I hung out with her for a few days, in Srebrenica. Only woman I ever met who chain-smoked more than me. You know her too, huh?"

"Not really, but our paths have crossed a couple of times is all. What were you doing in Srebrenica?"

"I'm a reporter, man, like you. With FOX News—you?"

"I was freelance. AP, Reuters. When were you there?"

"I was in and out for a couple of years."

"Matthew goes all the way back to El Salvador," says Jack. "Nineteen eighty-three, right?"

Matthew listens intently to Jack's voice, searching for any clue as to what he is not saying. "Eighty-two, actually. Israeli invasion of Lebanon. I was about your age."

"I lost my cherry in Yugoslavia. Damn near lost more than that. Forty-four journalists died in that crappy little war, did you know that?"

"Yes," Matthew says, "I know that."

"I had some pretty close calls. I was just telling Jack and Tony here about the time in Tuzla the mortar fire came in and me and a couple of German guys were so drunk, holed up in this fleabag hotel, we couldn't tell if it was incoming or outgoing. This guy, Dieter, he was in his room with a hooker and the goddamn wall got blown out with him in mid-fuck. He ran out in the street with his ass hanging out, tripped over his own pants and passed out where he landed. We were pissing ourselves, man. Laughing, you know."

Jack cracks his knuckles, shoots Matthew a quick glance and says, "That so" with a wink.

It is obvious now that the cause of Jack's displeasure is Brian Dance and not, Matthew is relieved to conclude, himself. Relief is like fresh air, and he turns his concentration on Brian Dance. With each word, Matthew likes Brian less. He has met many young journalists like him. They popped in, interviewed all the top brass they could bribe, did a sound byte and ducked out again on the first convoy back to civilization. If they had stories to tell they were just as likely someone else's as their own, but to hear them talk they'd hung out with every media-darling from Amanpour to Arnett. Their ignorance of the real issues went out over the airwaves as gospel truth and was more dangerous than the propaganda the government tried to spit out. Some had the humility to learn. Others did not.

"So, Brian, when did you say you were in Srebrenica? What year?"

"Nineteen ninety-five." He shifts in his chair. "You know, there was this time a Serb guy . . ."

"You saying you were in Srebrenica in 1995?"

"Yeah. So? What's your point?"

"Just wondering."

Jack snorts.

"Matthew's been just about everywhere," says Anthony. "I'll bet you guys bumped into each other and don't even remember."

"That's probably true," says Brian. "It's hard to remember everyone."

Matthew cannot help himself. He wants to shut up and leave the guy alone, for it shouldn't matter to him one way or the other where Brian Dance has been and what he's done or hasn't, but it does. Matthew wants to form an alliance, him and Jack on the same side. "I'm really surprised I didn't hear about you. You must be some kind of *wunderkind*."

Brian looks at Matthew with outright suspicion, and he begins to sweat. Jack thumbs his nose and scowls impressively.

"No man, just trying to do a job."

"You must be really good at it, because—you remember Tony Birtley?"

"Yeah, the British ABC reporter, right?"

"Very good. Because Birtley's reports almost single-handedly saved Srebrenica back in 1993. Thing is, though, Brian, the Serbs got pissed off about that and let only a handful of journalists back into the enclave in 1994, and then barred everybody the following spring. In July 1995, everybody, including Christiane and me, was in Sarajevo. The peacekeepers and the Muslims were alone out there, without any public scrutiny, which, let's face it, is only occasionally effective anyway. One of the great fuck-ups of the war. The other, of *any* conflict come to think of it, is jacked-up little assholes who think they're reporters just because they have a press badge."

"You got a lot of fucking nerve," says Brian, rising to his feet.

"Not nearly as much as you have, standing up like that," says Jack. "I might mistake that move for an invitation to stand up myself. Which you wouldn't want."

"Gentlemen," cautions Dan from behind the bar. He cradles his crowbar in his arms.

"Maybe you better go, pal," says Anthony. "Might be for the best, if you know what I mean."

Brian takes stock of Jack and Anthony. "Fuck you. You're all fucking head cases." He slugs back the last of his beer and, looking at Matthew, says, "You're not even a real correspondent. Fucking stringer."

Matthew grabs his chest. "Oh, you got me! Ya got me!"

Brian picks up this jacket and storms out. Dan replaces the crowbar behind the bar. "Matthew, drinks are on you."

Matthew nods, bowing to tradition. He also notices that Suzi and the bearded guy are nowhere to be seen.

"I shouldn't have done that," he says, and thinks, Don't we all have our lies? Take Jack. If even half his stories are true, I'm the Queen of England.

"Done what?" says Jack, and the way he says it makes Matthew's stomach clench. Suzi probably said nothing. Probably. But what about Anthony?

"That guy. Fuck, what the hell do I know? He might have been there."

"It's a distant possibility," says Jack.

"If he was there he shouldn't have been," says Anthony. "Obvious."

"Kid probably has more credentials than me," says Matthew.

Jack slaps Matthew on the back and tells him to forget it, just forget it. "Let me buy you a real drink," says Jack. "You look like you could use it." And Matthew exhales, thinking everything is all right after all.

Several hours later, still feeling guilty, and on more than one level, Matthew has drunk more than he promised himself he would. He is on his sixth beer and fourth scotch back. It is nearly midnight and Anthony has left about an hour before, off to see the lovely Paweena.

Jack is talking about God, about Islam, the concept of fate, and submission to destiny. Matthew does not know how they have arrived at this subject, or why Jack seems to be making such profound sense. He suspects it is the booze, but does not mind.

Whatever it is, Matthew believes he has access to a clear window of truth. He decides they both do, that the moment is special, and should not be wasted. They need to talk about important things. It does not matter, suddenly, what happened between Matthew and Suzi, but it does matter what happened between Jack and Suzi. Matthew believes, as he views Jack through the topaz fog of whisky, that Jack must come clean, confess, make amends. "You know who knows about Mohammed?" he says. "Anthony. You know, he has got some weird pockets of learning. And insight. A very insightful guy."

"To Anthony. The only cop I can't seem to hate."

"To Anthony. May he gain insight into Paweena."

"Amen."

"Amen."

"Women," says Jack. "Fucking women."

"You and Suzi on the outs, huh?"

"You could say that."

"Anything to do with her split lip?" *In for a dime, in for a dollar.*

"Who told you what?"

Matthew shrugs. "It's a small bar."

Jack puts his beer down, leans back, folds his arms against his chest, and for a moment Matthew thinks he is going to explode. He braces himself, all his surety of the moment before evaporating. Then, just as quickly, Jack uncrosses his arms, puts his head down on the table and bangs his forehead three times. The glasses rattle.

"Fuck," he says, softly, once for every time his head hits the table.

Matthew realizes he has been holding his breath. He lets it out. "Yeah. Want to talk about it?"

"No."

"Okay."

"Yes."

"Okay."

Jack pulls his great shaggy head up from the table, intertwines his fingers and leans forward. "I had sort of an episode."

"An episode?"

"Yeah. A fucking *episode*. Like the kind some people get in crowds, at demonstrations, you know?" He chews on his moustache.

"Oh. Sure. Sure." The guilt is back then, a giant ball of grey gum in his stomach.

"I used to get them all the time, but I've been better. A lot better in the last few years."

"I didn't know."

"Don't look so worried. Everybody's different."

"I didn't mean that."

"Right." He sighs. "Fucking French and their fireworks. I don't even go to sleep anymore, ever, EVER, before two a.m. because that's when they can start, one o'clock in the morning because it's the end of someone's freaking birthday party or some shit. Goddamn!" He knocks back the rest of his drink. "I need a shot. You want one?"

"I'm good."

Jack nearly turns over his chair as he stands up. He moves through the other tables like a bull moose through a swamp. When he comes back, he has shots for both of them.

"To mental health," he says, and they raise their glasses.

"Anyway. It's like eight o'clock at night, right? We're sitting down to dinner. Suzi made this real nice meal. But it was the day of the storm, remember?"

Matthew nods. There had been a bad storm and it had kept him pacing back and forth in the apartment, jumping at every clap of thunder.

"Okay, so that had ended a few hours before, but then these kids from next door—Suzi's got this apartment—weird fucking place with the bedroom below-ground—it's on the ground floor, right, with this courtyard behind it—these kids, they're out there letting off these cherry bombs and I just about have a fucking heart attack, and I'm out yelling at them. I think I scared the hell out of them, but Christ! It was really loud. So, I drop a drink or two to quiet my nerves but I'm still wrangy, still squirrelly. And that goddamn wind's rattling all the shutters. Spooking me out. I'm trying not to show that I'm so edgy, right? Then, just when I think it's under control, some fucking kid lets one off right under the window and I swear the little fuck did it on purpose." His hands grip the tabletop.

"It's okay, Jack," Matthew says, hoping Jack can hear him.

Jack's hands relax their grip and he puts them to his eyes, rubbing hard. "Before I know it I picked up a lamp. Threw it through the window. I hear a kid screaming. The little snot with the firecracker. Musta been lurking around outside. Suzi flipped her nut. I slammed her up against a wall. I don't know why. I was pissed. I don't remember a lot after that. Next thing I know I'm in the apartment by myself, sitting in the fucking bathtub."

"She took off?"

"Yeah. She was out in the street. Madder than fuck. I felt like crap, you know? I didn't want to do that. I'm as bad as that ratshit of a prick, Joseph's stepfather."

"Saida's ex?" It is Matthew's turn to discover his hand gripping his glass tighter than is safe.

"I've never done that to a woman before. Never-ever." He shakes his head slowly and his eyes keep moving after his head stops.

Matthew sees how bad Jack feels about it, but he also knows that, given his size, a good wall-slamming by Jack could kill somebody. Especially somebody as tiny as Suzi.

"You know, I'd moved my stuff into her place."

"I didn't know that."

"Jesus, what the fuck's wrong with me?"

"Where you staying now?" Matthew hopes he has a place. He does not want to have to offer Jack a spot on his couch. He likes his windows and prefers not to have any lamps thrown through them.

"I got a room by the week, rue Veron, near Pigalle. For the time being, anyway." He grins sheepishly. "You never know, we might get back together. Could happen. Yessir."

This takes Matthew off guard. "She was here tonight. You talked to her?"

"Nah. What am I gonna say?"

"You might try an apology."

"Think that'd do it? Ya think? Well, maybe. But I don't know if I wanna start it all up again. You know what I mean? Maybe it's better. Yup, better this way."

Matthew says nothing.

Jack takes the tinfoil from the inside of his cigarette pack, folds it into a tiny square, then smoothes it out with his fingernail and folds it again.

"You ever think about death?" he says after a few minutes.

"Of course. Yes." With all the bodies piled up in his memory, how could he not?

"No, no! Not somebody else's death," says Jack, reading Matthew's mind. "*Your* death. The real death that's a-coming, the one you absolutely are going to have to deal with. I mean that second, man, those last few fucking minutes when it's coming down, coming at you, it's going to happen. Do you consider that? Con-tem-plate it?" He waggles his head as he says the last word, broken up into three syllables, mocking himself.

Matthew does not want to have this conversation. Jack stares at him.

"Do I think about it? Occasionally."

"And God? What about God?" Jack smoothes the foil out again, and keeps his eyes away from Matthew.

Matthew shifts uneasily in the chair, reaches over, jiggles a cigarette out of Jack's pack and lights it. The alcohol slides around inside him, weighing him down, dragging him to a place below, somewhere entirely unsuitable for a discussion of metaphysical subjects.

"What about Him?"

"Do you think, you know, whazzit, you know, what it's going to be like? Forgiveness, or Wrath of Judgment." He tries to sound glib beneath the blur of booze.

Sometimes, especially this late at night and seen through the haze of alcohol, Matthew thinks that Jack's face could be his own, with all his own malignant, unspeakable memories. Jack, more than anyone he knows, needs to believe in divine forgiveness, redemption. Peace. He wants to be able to offer him such things, but says only, "Maybe there's just oblivion. You know—dreamless sleep."

"Yeah," says Jack, and puts his hand up to cover his eyes. "I get tired, man. Sleep'd be all right, I guess. Aw, fuck it."

Guilt, Matthew thinks. The sack of skulls.

Matthew walks Jack home, for he is drunk enough to be vulnerable to muggers, even with his great bulk. They walk past the gauntlet of strip shows and live sex shows on boulevard de Clichy. A blond girl in too-tight shorts and a red bra under a long grey coat open to reveal her charms, steps from a doorway into their path. Behind her gleam large photos under pink neon. In one, a naked blond kneels over the face of an Asian girl. In another, a man takes a girl from behind, and the bent-over girl performs fellatio on a man standing with his hands in her hair.

"You like these photos, *oui?* Such pretty girls. Everything happening inside right now," says the girl in the shorts and bra. "Come in and talk to these girls."

Jack smiles wetly. He puts one of his hands over both of hers and holds them against his chest. The other arm goes around her waist, drawing her close. He sways, as though trying to dance, and Matthew is afraid he will lose his balance, fall, crush her.

"Okay," she says, "you like to dance, you come in, dance inside, yes?"

"Nope," says Jack. "You come home with me!"

"You hold me too tight," she says. "You let go."

"Let her go, big fella," Matthew says, trying to move his arm. It is like trying to bend a piece of wood. "Come on, eh, Jack? Release the lady."

From the corner of his eye, Matthew sees a very large, heavily muscled man open the door and move toward them. The man carries a wooden bat in his hand. Before he can reach them, however, Jack yelps and the girl lands on her rear on the sidewalk.

"Maudit con!" she yells, while Jack falls onto Matthew, so heavily that were it not for the lamppost, against which he finds himself pinned, they would both have fallen to the ground and Matthew would have been crushed. Jack rubs his shin, where a thin trail of blood shows through the torn leg of his pants.

"Fucking bitch," he growls. "Stabbed me with her fucking high heel."

The bouncer yanks the girl to her feet and shoves her toward the door, then turns to face Matthew and Jack, holding the bat loosely in his right hand.

"We have a problem, maybe?"

"No problem," Matthew says. "Going home."

Jack assumes the stance of a street fighter, legs slightly bent, the left in front of the right, hands in half-fists, one at the level of his chest, the other in front of his face. He tries to bounce on the balls of his feet, but is too drunk and falters, stumbling a few steps to his left.

"I think this is a very good idea," says the bouncer and he spits. "Take your friend."

Without another word he turns and disappears into the club,

closing the door behind him. A good bouncer, Matthew thinks—one who rarely has to throw a punch.

"I shoulda pummelled that shit into meat meal," says Jack.

"Let's go home." Matthew wanders up the street, knowing Jack will follow, hoping he will not kick out a window first.

The streets twist and turn in this somewhat neglected part of Paris, nestled between the great ivory towers of Sacré Coeur above and the Moulin Rouge, faded and tawdry, below. The streets are cobbled here and treacherous to the drunken or the lame. A transvestite wearing a cheap wig and a short skirt that reveals burly legs, leans up against a wall, talking to a short man. They pass a joint back and forth between them, the scent sharp and rich. The transvestite stares at them as they lurch past. Her lips are gold-flecked.

Matthew has to persuade Jack not to approach the crackheads and alcoholics lounging in various degrees of intoxication on the crooked stairs leading up to the place des Abbesses. They remind him of the mutilated corpses in Bosnia—impaled on the sides of barns, festooning the fences like tattered scarecrows, their eyes gouged out, their stomachs cut open. He shakes his head to scatter the ghosts.

Finally, they arrive at Jack's door. He wants Matthew to come up and have another drink, for apparently he has a bottle stashed. Matthew declines, but offers to help him up the stairs, a suggestion that offends Jack, and he leaves Matthew there, determined to prove he can make it up to the top-floor room under his own steam. Matthew waits outside the door, hears Jack stumble and curse, and then hears the anvil-drop of his feet climbing the steps.

Trudging toward home, Matthew is chilled and exhausted. All the doorways seem filled with hollow-eyed shadows. A memory of his mother comes to mind. There was a horse she had, a quarter horse with a bad temper and a habit of rolling, trying to pin a rider beneath him. He pitched a fit in his stall one day and damn near tore his eyelid off on a loose board. Bad-tempered as the horse was, Matthew's mother had spent days bathing the eye, binding it, calming the horse, trying to save the eye. When Matthew asked her why she bothered, she'd smiled and said, "I can't help but care *about* the things I care *for*."

CHAPTER TWENTY-TWO

All along, Matthew has known there are two subjects he must face if he is going to write the book: Rwanda and Hebron. As the watery December light falls across his desk, he picks up his pen and faces it. First things first. Do not worry about Hebron. First, there are other fields to cross.

The pen feels like a shard of ice in his hand. His fingers cramp. *In the Rwandan refugee camps, I came across a Tutsi woman, her head bandaged with a horrific wound and missing a hand.* Perspiration breaks out on his upper lip. *In her arms, she cradled a child whose eyes rolled aimlessly and whose jaw hung slack. There were three depressions in his skull. Deep, terrible dents, like dry pools with soft muddy bottoms. I could not understand why he was alive . . .*

"A boy he went to school with," the woman said, "found him alive in the pile of bodies. He used a hammer on him."

She was from Ntarama. She had hidden with her children in a little church, along with several thousand others, because the soldiers cut them off and they couldn't escape into the hills. "In years before, when the government killers came, they killed the men and left the women and children alone."

The gendarmes arrived and broke holes in the walls of the church. They threw grenades into the crowds of people and then fired shots into the congregation. "You cannot imagine the noise of screaming and the bodies everywhere. It was a terrible mess." Body parts everywhere. She lay covered with dying people, blood and filth.

The gendarmes broke down the doors then and walked through the piles, looking for anyone left still alive. "These people they finished off with machetes." She heard them, their blades slicing and her friends and neighbours moaning. She prayed to suffocate before they found her, but they did not find her and when everything was silent and dark she crawled out from under the stinking corpses. Her husband and three children died, also her parents, and brothers and sisters, and their children as well. She was the only survivor.

"And the boy?" I asked.

"Someone found him, a journalist, I think, and they brought him here. There was another boy with him, who saw it all, but he disappeared and I think he is dead. I will care for this boy now." The boy's head lolled helplessly beneath her handless arm.

Rooms upon rooms full of soul-scarred orphans.

The survivors of Ntarama chose not to bury their dead. They left the bodies and bones of their families lying on the floor of the church. They left them as a memorial so that no one will forget. I visited the church. It was a charnel house. I covered my mouth and nose with Vick's Mentholated Rub to cope with the stench. The flies formed an undulating blanket on the bodies. They were so thick, when I breathed in they filled my mouth.

Matthew stops writing and puts his head in his hands. The room festers with ghosts. They breathe on him, their breath icy and foul. He pours himself a large whisky and returns to the desk, gritting his teeth, shaking his shoulders to shrug the spectres away. They do not go far.

It is an impossible task. There is no word in the English language, not in any language that he knows, for the feeling. Horror. Rage. Grief. Impotence. Confusion. Terror. Disbelief. Guilt. This is not the first place, nor the first time, such savagery has been unleashed, nor will it be the last. Surely, humankind should have found the proper word for this by now. They created it; they should be able to name it.

He rocks back and forth, his hands clasped, his thumbs beating against his closed lips. He makes sounds. It tears him apart, the way he cannot find a word. But there is no word, no *words* that can do justice to the dead and maimed. There is only a list of atrocities. All he can do is transcribe the facts.

Nyanza. A mass grave. At least two thousand dead. Bodies bloated, contorted, covered in blood, in flies, in excrement, putrefying. Dogs everywhere, family pets turned feral and horribly well fed.

Ginkongoro. Mwulire. Mugonero. Kigali.

Then the cholera epidemics began. Hundreds of people in a blasted building, yellow vomit running from their mouths. No water anywhere. No help coming. A hillside of children near a hospital hut, thought at first to be dead, but not all dead. Crawling toward the hut as they died. In the hut nothing but the dead. Rivers full of bodies. Fields full of bodies. Bodies in decay. Bloated bodies. Fly-swarmed bodies. Decapitated children. Naked women and children tied together and tossed in the rushing Akagera River. Lake Victoria polluted with an estimated fifty thousand corpses.

Along with all the other journalists, he had cried out the numbers, pointed at the gashed and hacked bodies. He wrote his words and sent them along the wire, and nobody listened. Nobody came. Only clouds of ghosts, swarms of them, numerous as midges, as gnats, as rats, as flies, as maggots.

In the course of days, a million dead.

And so, the dreams of Rwanda—of lying under bodies, listening to the knife-man looking for anyone still breathing, nostrils clogged with matter. Dreams of the clawing dead. Dreams, once again, of burning barns and horses.

At last, he puts the pen down and covers his eyes. His head aches. He does not have the strength to pick the pen up again even if he wanted to. The walls arc in toward him. The air is too heavy, the room too small, the dark too oppressive. He practically runs to the door, down the stairs across the street and into the café.

The light spills out of the windows. Honey light. Golden light. Inside it is warm. It is fragrant with the smells of cooking. As the smells hit his nose, they mutate. They smell of decomposition and rot.

"Coffee," he says, as he claims a stool at the counter.

"You okay?" says Anthony, poking his head around the kitchen alcove.

Saida pours him coffee.

"Not really."

"You need to eat," says Saida. "I will get you something."

It is simple, these things: food, friends, coffee and light. He cannot eat, refuses food, asks for more coffee.

Ramzi sits at the counter too, watching the news on a small television. "Hello, Matthew," he says. "How are you working?"

"It's killing me."

"Ah, the artist's soul," Ramzi teases him. "You need an attic."

"I need something." He sees his hands are trembling, sees Ramzi noticing his trembling hands.

"You should come with me tonight. There is a good place for dancing that I know. Lots of girls."

"No thanks. Not my scene."

Ramzi turns to the screen. There are many lights flashing. People running. Police. Matthew's adrenaline pumps. He leans forward, trying to catch the words.

"What's that?"

"Ah, *mon Dieu,*" says Ramzi. "It is very bad. A bomb on the metro. Port-Royal Station."

Sirens are all over now, all through the streets, even in the café they can hear them.

"There are many injured," Saida says. "And there are dead. They are bringing bodies out. In the middle of rush hour on a busy line. They are animals, these people." Her voice is ragged and her hand is at her mouth. "It is starting all over again." The year before, a series of bombs had gone off in Paris, set by

Algerian fundamentalists. Eight people slaughtered on the metro, just two stops from the present bombing.

On the television screen people stumble about, covered in blood. Emergency workers run from one person to the next, swabbing, trying to calm them. The wounded thrash about on stretchers. Ambulances come and go, the wails rising and falling. The commentator sounds nearly hysterical. Early reports say police suspect the bomb was made of a canister filled with nails. Thick black smoke churns out of the metro entrance.

Matthew's pulse races and the room spins. He gets up, upsetting his coffee cup.

"Matthew?" Saida's eyes follow him as he backs toward the door.

"Gotta go."

"You going down there?" says Anthony. "Want me to come with you?"

If he does not get air, he will suffocate. "No. I'm not going there." He pushes through the door, past a couple on their way in.

When he is out on the street, he takes huge inhalations. He must get to his apartment.

But in his apartment it is worse. He can hear the sirens. And there are all those pages about Rwanda sitting on the desk. He knows it is impossible, but he feels as though he has summoned the horror through his writing. Unleashed it like a demon. Called it to them through the threads of his memory. The phone rings. He does not pick it up. He goes into the kitchen, finds a bottle of vodka, and does not bother with a glass. He finds his pills. Takes four. Stuffs wax earplugs in his ears. Takes the bottle and gets into bed. The phone rings again. He ignores it. He waits for unconsciousness. The demons can't get you when you're there. Good drugs, he thinks.

The next morning dawn refuses to break, refuses to take a stand against the night—it merely infuses itself through the watery light. Smoke-coloured mist envelops Paris. The day becomes simply less dark than night. The boundaries between things blur. Street, sky, stone, smoke from chimney pots, all have the same dull muffle of light. Shades of muffle it is, a damp wool scarf wrapped around Matthew's head. At noon, he downs another handful of sleeping pills and crawls back to bed.

The next day he does not get up at all.

And so it goes.

When hunger drives him from his nest of blankets, which begin to smell sour even to his nose, he eats pale green flageolet beans, salad shrimp, or corn, all direct from the can. He drinks vodka and when the vodka runs out he switches to scotch and then beer and finally just tap water and pills.

Seeking a fork, one afternoon (or is it evening?) he opens a kitchen drawer and shrieks when he sees what's inside. He jumps back, hitting the edge of the counter behind him with sharp force, right in the kidneys. There is a nutcracker in the drawer. And not even his nutcracker. Something left from a previous tenant that he had meant to throw out. *Why didn't I? Did I want to test myself?* Nutcracker nightmares from Tuzla. The man whose hands had been mangled by force of a nutcracker. It took hours, he told Matthew.

He avoids the stove because the thought of the blue gas burner makes him shudder, as do knives. He forces himself to pick up and throw out the bag of sinister oranges because they remind him that being hit repeatedly with a bag of oranges turns the organs to mush but the bruises do not show for days. The radiators are malevolent, whispering that a small body will cook if tied to a hot one for long enough.

He is afraid to look out the window, for there are too many cars out there and cars have hood ornaments. They all morph into the car of a Croat warlord who used the head of an *imam* for one. Cars also have antennas, which are the same as the one on the

Soviet jeep on the outskirts of Kabul with twenty or so human ears tied it. *Pull the fucking shutters!*

Matthew stands in the middle of the apartment and in the reflection of the windowpanes, he sees a little girl trapped against a wall in Hebron. He presses his hands to his eyes until pain shoots up into his brain, but still he sees things, sees faces, and hears blasts and the sound of screams. His skin is a fester of futility, a gangrene of guilt. He breaks out in small blisters.

He drinks another scotch and takes another pill, unaware that he calls out to Kate. He covers his head with the blankets. And so on.

CHAPTER TWENTY-THREE

Anthony is not working this morning but he telephones around ten.

"I'm still worried about Matthew. Now he doesn't pick up," he says. Several days ago, Anthony told her he had talked to Matthew briefly but that he had been, to use Anthony's words, distant and *muzzly*. "I went over yesterday after I left the restaurant. I knocked, but he wouldn't answer. Nobody's seen him."

"He has not been in for maybe four days now, is that right?"

"Five, I think."

The shutters on his windows had remained closed for the past three.

"Maybe he has gone away," says Saida.

"I don't think so," says Anthony. "I just don't."

"No, neither do I. He would have said."

"What should we do?"

"Can you go over? See if you can get him to come to the phone, at least?"

"Oh, Anthony. I don't think I can."

"I think you might be the best person for it. He won't answer Jack's calls either."

Well, good for him, she thinks.

"Jack says he'll break down the door if he has to."

It is Wednesday afternoon when there is no school in France, and so Joseph is in the restaurant. Saida has bullied him into helping her. Now he stands, listening to her, cocking his head, and trying to make out what Anthony says as well.

"I'll go over," says Joseph. "I'll go see him."

"No." Saida puts her hand on his arm to stop him. The look of those shutters, so tightly closed, so resolutely locked, hiding God knows what. No, it will not be Joseph who goes. "All right, Anthony. I will call you if I speak to him. What is the door code?"

She crosses the street briskly, with her shoulders back, pretending she is a woman capable of handling Difficult Situations. When she stands in front of his door her breathing is shallow, not because of the stairs, but because of the unwelcoming air that emanates from the other side. There is no sign saying "Keep Away," but there might as well be. The quality of silence that has seeped, even past the door, out here onto the landing, unsettles her. She fantasizes that something hungry and parasitic has hold of Matthew, and now sits smugly on his chest sensing her through the door.

A noise from within, a soft thump, startles her and her hand goes involuntarily to the scar on her neck. Quickly, before she loses her nerve, she knocks.

"Matthew, are you in there? I know you are. Please open."

She taps softly at first, and then louder.

"Matthew? I heard a noise. I know you are in there. Please. Open the door, just for a moment."

She pleads for several more minutes, and when he opens the door at last, it is all she can do not to step back in shock. His hair is greasy and flat against his skull. He is unshaven and so thin that his bones are visible under the fabric of his shirt.

"Are you all right?"

He blinks as though the red of her sweater hurts his eyes.

"Can I come in?"

"Come in," he says.

He looks embarrassed and she realizes she has wrinkled her nose at the smell of him, which is sweetish and thick. She blushes.

The room, too, is grimy and cluttered, the floor scattered with discarded pieces of clothing, shoes, sheets of paper, a spoon, a piece of hardened and crumbling toast. Sheets drape over the radiators and over the mirror, like in the house of a Jew in mourning. The air is musty and the odour of something unpleasant wafts from the kitchen. Her eyes follow her nose, and there on the table sits a half-eaten bowl of tomato soup and an open can of sardines mutating into a science project.

Saida stands in the centre of the room and slowly turns until she faces Matthew again. He steps past her and opens a window and then the shutter beyond. Although the day is overcast and gloomy, still the light spills in, invading the room, claiming territory.

"You want to sit down?" he says, shielding his eyes.

She clears herself a place on the worn brown leather couch and perches there. She tries to take stock of him. His voice, his way of moving is slower even than usual. He seems stunned, or drugged.

"You sit down, too, Matthew."

He picks up several sheets of paper lying on the floor and then opens the desk drawer, tossing the pages in as though he does not want her to get a good look at them.

"Please don't fuss because of me. Sit." Her voice is softer and he obeys. "Are you sick? Do you have a migraine? Do you need a doctor?"

She is shocked to see tears well up in his eyes. His Adam's apple bobs as he swallows.

"What are you doing here?" he says when he has regained control of himself.

"Anthony said he hasn't seen you and was worried. He came here. You did not answer. Apparently he called, and, sorry, but you were rather rude, and—how did he put it—*muzzly*. I understood you were not well."

"Anthony? He called here?"

"Yes, and Jack, but you didn't answer." She looks around for a phone, sees it, on top of an answering machine with a blinking red light. "Joseph wanted to come over, but I thought I should." She lowers her eyes to her hands resting in her lap.

"Maybe I forgot they called. Is that possible?" he says, more to himself than to her. "I've been in sort of a fog, I guess. I think I talked to Anthony, sure. Sure, I remember. A day or so ago, right? I don't know. Time seems to have taken on an elastic quality. The bombs. Have there been any more?"

"No. There is a lot of security. But no more bombs, Matthew."

He smiles, unconvincingly. "Do you want coffee or something?"

"Yes. That would be nice. Do you want me to make it?"

"No. I want to do it."

Saida watches him through the open kitchen door as he looks for the things necessary to make coffee. It seems like a very complicated process. Coffee maker. Filters. Coffee. Water. Cups. Sugar. He opens the refrigerator, pulls out a plastic bottle of milk, smells it and immediately drops it in the trash. He blows dust out of the mugs. He moves as though everything is stiff, from the taps to his wrist joints. He puts his finger up to his mouth and smacks his lips. Saida turns away as he comes back into the living room and she pretends to pick a hair off her skirt.

"Excuse me," he says as he walks into the hall. "Brush my teeth. My mouth tastes like somebody crept in there while I slept and put small woollen socks on my teeth."

When he returns, the coffee has brewed.

"What do you take?" He shakes his head. "Sorry, I should know. But it's always you getting me coffee, isn't it?"

"Just black."

Matthew hands her the coffee and she puts it to her mouth, blows on the steaming liquid and sips without checking the rim for dirt.

Matthew sits down across from her and keeps his hands

wrapped around the mug. She notices that, left to their own devices, they shake ever so slightly.

"We are worried about you."

"Don't be."

It takes some courage to speak. "Sometimes I think you are someone who is drifting. Not in a good way—but as though you will drift too far from shore. Look at my father. He has drifted. It is not very safe, always worrying these memories. Not good for you." She sips her coffee again. "Maybe I should stop talking. It is not my place."

"Look, I'm all right, okay?"

"I'm sorry. I am intruding."

"No, look, I'm sorry. I don't mean to bark at you. I appreciate it. The concern and all, really I do."

"I think . . . well, it is only that I think I know a little of what you are remembering. We have been through very much, my family. Joseph's father, my mother, my grandparents, my brother, his wife, their son . . . very many people. Terrible massacres. I know how bad dreams can be, sometimes not even when you sleep."

"Yes. Of course. I'm sorry."

"No, you do not have to be sorry, Matthew. I only say this to show I understand, maybe a little, yes? I have nightmares, sometimes, of things that have happened." Her left hand strokes her right, running her thumb along the burn-lines. "Sometimes it is good to talk about these things. I just say this, to tell you, if you want . . ."

"I think I want to leave it be, Saida."

"Ghosts do not like to be ignored." She wonders if she has gone too far. The only sound in the room is his ragged breathing and the angry bleating of car horns in the street. "How is your work going? This book you're writing?" she says, because the weight in the room is too much and she must cut through it with the only thing she has.

"I don't know. I mean, what's the point?"

"Can I use your phone? I said I would let Anthony know you were all right. And Joseph. He was worried, too."

"Jesus. Fine."

She makes the calls and keeps them brief, because it is embarrassing to say, "Yes, yes, he is fine. We are just having a cup of coffee," when the subject is in the room. She realizes her back is to him, and she turns, a smile of reassurance on her lips, but Matthew has put his cup down on the floor and his head in his hands, rubbing at the temples as though he has a headache. Hanging up, she can think of nothing to say and gazes around the room, trying to find a safe topic of conversation.

Matthew speaks first. "I don't know. I got an advance from a publisher. I start things. I can't seem to finish them."

"It must be very hard, writing." She sits down and leans toward him.

He speaks with his head hanging. "No. Sulphur mining, or coal mining, that's hard. Tarring a road when it's a hundred and twenty degrees out is hard. Working in a sawmill is hard. Being a ship breaker in Indonesia—now that's hard."

"Yes. Of course—"

"You know what Katherine Anne Porter said? I'm paraphrasing, but basically she said that human life is pure chaos, and the job of the artist—the only thing he's good for, incidentally—is to work that confusion into order. No one understands what's happening to them as it's happening, right? So writers have to remember for other people. We have to sift through experience until our disparate selves are reconciled, and by sharing it, offer the same opportunity for reconciliation to others. It's our duty. What do you think of that?"

"I think you should eat something."

"I think it's bullshit." He blinks. "What did you say?"

"I said that I think you should eat something."

Matthew laughs then and, even if it is not a very good laugh, but only something that scrapes the surface of sound, Saida feels better.

"Why not come over and have some food? I will cook for you."

"I don't think I can handle being around too many people just yet, Saida. Thanks, though."

"I do not want to be too pushy, but I think maybe you would feel better if you went out. Being around people you do not know is sometimes easier than being around people you do. There is a crêpe place around the corner if you do not want to go to my restaurant. I will not be offended. Sometimes I have had enough of my own cooking, too. It will do me good. It will be a break for me."

"You are rather pushy, you know that?"

"So Joseph tells me. And Ramzi. And my father, too."

"They usually do what you tell them?"

"Eventually. I am usually right."

He laughs again, a better laugh.

Encouraged, she says, "Yes, I think we should go for a walk, and then you should eat."

"I'm not much up for it. Honestly, I appreciate the concern, but I'm fine. I just tied one on and need some sleep."

"You are a worse liar than Joseph. Besides, I want to talk to you about him."

"About Joseph?"

"I am a mother. My son is very important to me. I worry about him, too. And he likes you. I want your advice."

"You are not only pushy. You are stubborn."

"Yes, this is also true."

"Oh, fuck it," he says and shuffles off to the shower, muttering all the way about meddlesome women. His voice is not harsh, however, and it makes her smile.

After a moment Saida hears the water running, hears him blowing his nose. The walls are very thin and the intimate proximity to a man she is not related to distresses her. She takes a small pad and pencil out of her purse and makes a list of things she must buy for her father. *Dish detergent. Toilet paper. Oranges.* The noise from the bathroom continues—wet noises of skin and soap. She cannot concentrate and would feel better doing something, but fears if she begins to tidy that it will offend him. And besides, this too, is personal. The things of a man, the sounds of a man, so near, and naked in the shower. She adds to the list for her father. *Milk. Kasha.*

When Matthew reappears, he wears a clean white shirt and black jeans. His skin is pale against the snowy cotton, but he looks scrubbed, if not pressed.

"Good," she says, relieved to see him back in an acceptable shell. "Now that is better, yes?"

Grumpily, he agrees.

When they are out on the street, she says, "I will just tell my father and Joseph. Wait."

Elias sits at the counter, and she is surprised to see Ramzi serving customers. They are not too busy. Three tables.

"How is he?" says Joseph.

"Sad. Fragile."

"Is he coming in?" says Ramzi.

"No. I am going for a walk with him. He needs fresh air."

"Now?" says Ramzi.

"You can handle the place by yourself. I manage by myself when you are not here. It is your turn."

"Fine. No need to raise your voice," says Ramzi, as he slices chicken off the cone of meat slowing turning on the grill.

"And besides, Joseph can help."

"I'm going out."

"Where out?"

"Out-out. Now that Uncle Ramzi's here. You don't need me."

"I want you here when I get back."

Joseph merely shrugs.

"You are going out with him?" Her father looks first to Saida and then to Matthew, who waits outside on the street, on the far sidewalk, with his back to them. "He is not coming here?"

"I will be back soon," she says, kissing him.

"He's okay, though?" says Joseph.

"I will try and bring him back later," she says and she kisses him, too.

As they walk, she can see the movement is doing Matthew good. His blood seems to be flowing again.

"Hear that? My stomach. I am hungry," he says.

His eyes still blink as though they hurt, probably from so much time spent in the dark, and, even though the day is dull, he pulls sunglasses out of his pocket and puts them on. They have to dodge people, as the sidewalk is narrow, and now and then he guides her with his hand on her arm.

The tiny restaurant is warm and steamy, and they get a spot in the corner near the window. The tables are rough-hewn wood and on the ceiling the old beams are exposed and have taken on a patina from years of steam and cooking grease. Matthew orders a crêpe with ham and cheese and tomatoes; Saida orders one with tuna and olives; they both ask for warm cider and a small salad. In a few short minutes, they are tucking in.

"So, what is it about Joseph?" he says.

"I do not know him anymore. I do not know where he goes, or who he sees. I do not know where he gets this money."

"He's a teenager. You're not supposed to know him. As I understand it, your job as the parent of a teenager is merely to embarrass him."

"I think he is spending time with your friend, Jack. I am sure I saw him the other day, in Barbès, when Joseph said he was going to play soccer. But there was no soccer."

"Have you talked to Joseph?"

"He does not talk to me anymore. I ask him where he is going; all he says is 'Out.'" Saida is afraid that now she might be the one who cries. She puts down her fork and smoothes the napkin across her lap. When she looks up again, their eyes meet.

"Okay, I'll talk to him. Jack, I mean. I can talk to Joseph too, if you want."

"I would appreciate it." She picks an olive up in her fingers and nibbles at it, depositing the pit on her plate. "Now, your turn. If you want to tell me what bothers you. I will listen."

"I'm all right."

"Have you ever noticed how much time you spend with your hand up in front of your mouth?" says Saida. She mimics him, three fingers curled over her mouth, the index finger held straight under her nose—like someone afraid of what she might say, and afraid of what she might breathe in.

Matthew puts his hand on the table and wills it to stay there; then he runs his fingers through his hair and tucks his hand under his left arm. "Seems to have a mind of its own," he says.

A look passes over his face then, as if he is considering something. "I feel better, though," he says, and still the look on his face is difficult to read. "That's down to you, I think."

Saida waits, hoping he might yet confide in her.

"Maybe I could do with a little more than listening; maybe we both could."

Matthew reaches out and runs his fingers along the side of her face. Saida jerks back in her chair.

"No. You have misunderstood," she says, somewhat more loudly than she had intended.

He draws his hand back as though her cheek were flame.

"Shit. I'm sorry. I don't know what I was thinking."

"Neither do I."

She thinks she will get up then, and leave him there. Leave him to his dark moods.

"Saida, forgive me. I'm an ass. I'm not myself. It's a guy reflex. There's no excuse . . . I'm really sorry."

He looks devastated, blasted with shame. He looks as though he is as shocked by his behaviour as she is. It is almost funny. Almost.

"Perhaps it does have a mind of its own," she says.

Then they laugh a little; she does not get up and leave him there. They drink coffee and talk about whether or not Ramzi will actually leave one day, and whether he has a girlfriend and about how grey the days in Paris can be, and how the tourists still flock there, filling the sidewalks and the cafés of Saint-Germain, lining up outside the museums in their sensible shoes and baseball caps, insisting on going up to the windy Eiffel Tower when everyone else is huddled over cups of *chocolat chaud* in the humid cafés.

When she leaves him an hour later in front of his door, she believes him when he says he feels better and that he will stop by and see Joseph tomorrow. She believes him when he says again how sorry he is.

"Never mind," she says. "We will not talk about it."

And that is how she intends to handle it, this thing that did not happen.

Joseph is not there when she returns. "Where did he go?"

"Out to meet some friends," says Ramzi. "Leave him be. It is his age. How is Matthew?"

"He will live, I think," she says. "It is what happened to him in Israel. He is still quite sick, I think."

"He is not very strong, is he?" Her brother says this as though *he* would have been stronger.

"And how would you be?"

He shrugs. "You move on."

It is Ramzi's way, this moving on. Always away from something. Saida knows what he does not: that he is not that strong either. She knows he is moving away from half-remembered images, whispered stories told at night when he was supposed to be sleeping. He was only a little boy when they left Lebanon. He remembers only in the bones, in the muscles that twitch to escape. She was older, she remembers more and maybe that is better after all, to know what it is that makes you what you are. A woman's way more than a man's, she thinks, all this sorting, sifting and measuring out the feelings of a life.

Finally, Ramzi is satisfied that there is no more to learn and they go back to their work. If he looks at her with unasked questions, she does not feel the need to offer explanations. He would like it if she found another man, someone to take his place here in the restaurant, someone to take hold of the end of the rope as he cuts himself free.

A pang twists like a sharp-clawed lizard in her stomach. They are a family broken. Other families cleave to each other in exile from their homeland. They cluster together at their church, Notre Dame de Liban, on rue d'Ulm. They hold each other closer because the world has become so wide. But the Ferhats are scattering. They are birds chasing seeds flying on the wind. In Lebanon, there was a celebration for everything, bringing everyone together, and there was work done together—like when the woman made *kechek* powder to cook in the winter with the lamb. Drying it on the roofs, grinding it, always together, talking, their voices like music. Here there was only the rustle of Ramzi's newspapers and her father's baffled expression.

Where does Matthew come from? Where are his people? All these people in Paris, wanderers without connection either to the place or to anyone else. It seems such a lonely life. How do you know yourself loved if there are only strangers around you, only the friends of this season? Saida keeps an eye on Matthew's windows, hoping to see them thrown back. It would be nice to feel she had made that happen, made him turn away from the dark loneliness inside him.

Except for the one shutter he opened when she was in the

apartment, they stay closed, and then his hand reaches out and that one closes as well. Without realizing she is doing it, her hand goes to her cheek. Then she shakes her head. Foolish thoughts. No one saves anyone else. They swim or sink alone.

CHAPTER TWENTY-FOUR

The next morning Matthew wakes up and, for the first time in a week, does not automatically reach for something to make him go back to sleep. He turns on the television and sees that no more bombs have gone off in Paris. Security is tight. Hundreds of soldiers and police patrol the streets carrying machine guns. Train stations, airports, the metro stations, all filled with law enforcement personnel. *Vigipirate*, the French emergency vigilance plan, is in effect and authorities caution commuters to be aware of any suspicious activities or items.

Matthew sits on the couch and stares at the plank floor, the dust balls, the ballpoint pen cap, the little turd of crumpled paper, the empty scotch bottle, a tea bag dried to rusty crispness. He cannot remember the last time he drank a cup of tea.

The stack of papers he wrote is still in the desk drawer. He takes it out and reads it over. Maybe he should not have tried writing about Rwanda; maybe it was too soon. Nonetheless, he did it. He remembered, and here he is. Kate would be proud of me, he thinks, and raises his eyebrows in surprise at the unbidden thought. He turns his hands over and looks at his wrists, the pale skin, the fragile veins like innocent blue rivers, and shudders.

He stands and shakes himself, plods into the bathroom, snatching sheets off radiators as he goes. After his shower he throws back the shutters, opens the window, letting in the cold air. Across the street Elias sits in the café window; he looks up, sees Matthew and waves, gestures for him to come over. Matthew waves back. He has promised to go and talk to Joseph and he will, but first he wants to see Jack.

The hostel where Jack works sits west of the Eiffel Tower, behind an unsightly group of high-rises in the 15th arrondissement. The New Friends Hostel is a yellow stucco building with a black-and-gold sign above a large window that looks into the somewhat shabby lobby. Matthew opens the door and steps in. The place smells of recent fumigation. To his right is a reception booth, but it is empty. In front of him, a door leads to a courtyard with a jungle of bamboo growing in it, and a scatter of white plastic chairs and tables, the chairs tilted forward and leaning on the tables. To the left, another door leads into what looks like a bar. Two kids speaking German scuffle down the stairs. The girl is chubby and packed tightly into hip-hugging jeans. A sausage of white stomach spills over the waistband below a short, fuzzy blue sweater, both visible under her unbuttoned jacket. The boy is acne-speckled and his hair stands in a series of spikes, so that he looks like he is wearing a wet hedgehog on his head. They smile at Matthew as they leave.

Matthew proceeds to the bar. It is a large room with a paned window overlooking the courtyard. A brick bar curves along the wall and the room is scattered with wooden pub chairs and tables. There is a video-game machine at the end of the room and T-shirts hang for sale on the walls. Three girls stand talking and drinking beer, Americans, Southern.

"I don't care what you say. I'm not staying here another night. Look at my legs," a thin blond girl says as she pulls up her pant leg and pulls down her sock. Angry-looking bites cover her calf. "I swear that's from bed bugs. I swear it."

"I know, I've got 'em too," says another girl with strange purple eyes, which Matthew assumes must be due to contacts.

The bartender, a young bulldoggish guy, comes over to Matthew. *"Est-ce que je peux vous aider?"* he says.

"I'm looking for Jack Saddler."

At the sound of Jack's name, the three girls turn toward him.

"Who isn't? He's not in the front?" says the bartender.

"Nobody's there."

"I don't know if he's working today. I thought he was, but maybe his shift's finished. Somebody should be out there, though. You want something?"

"No, it's all right. I'll wait in the lobby for a few minutes."

The girls whisper and giggle as Matthew steps out of the bar. A minute later, the tall girl with the long dark hair comes out.

"Hello," she says.

"Hello."

"We're waiting for Jack, too. He's not back yet?"

"Doesn't look like it."

She smiles and twirls a lock of hair around her finger. "Maybe he's up in one of the rooms. He goes up to take care of things sometimes."

"Does he?"

"You a friend of his, or what?"

"I'm a friend."

"I don't think he's here."

The two other girls come out of the bar and stand next to the dark girl. Matthew finds the mauve eyes unsettling. She looks like an alien.

"So?" she says.

The dark girl cocks her head and raises a warning eyebrow.

"Oh, for heaven's sake," says Purple Eyes. "Just ask him."

"Ask me what?"

"We're waiting for Jack because we were told he might have some grass to sell."

"Karen!" says the thin blond. "He might be a cop or something."

"He's American," says the dark girl. "He can't be a cop. Can you?"

"I'm not a cop."

A woman comes down the stairs and opens the counter into the reception booth. She has meaty arms in a sleeveless dress, which Matthew thinks must be chilly on a day like this. She is in her fifties, and her hair is not clean. It sticks to her head in greasy brown strands.

"Oui," she says as she pulls a packet of cigarettes out of her pocket. "This is a hostel, monsieur. For young people. Eighteen to twenty-eight only."

"I don't want a room. I'm looking for Jack Saddler."

"He not here today. Does not show up. Says he is sick." She makes a noise in her throat. "You see him, you tell him he don't show up tomorrow, he has no job."

"Thanks," Matthew says and opens the door to leave. The three girls follow him out.

"Okay, so, you know, we just thought that maybe if you were a friend of Jack's or something and if he's not going to show up, well, maybe you might know . . ." The dark girl's voice trails off as she twirls her hair around a finger.

"Can't help you."

"We have the money."

"I have nothing for you, believe me."

"Shit," says the thin blond girl.

He leaves them on the sidewalk, thinking he should take their money and leave them stranded. That would teach them a lesson. Stupid kids. Stupid *him*. Saida was probably right. If Jack is dealing drugs and Joseph is suddenly walking around with too much money there is most likely a connection. Not necessarily, of course. There are many places to get dope in the city and Jack would not have much trouble finding out who and where and when. *So why do I have a bad feeling?*

Matthew heads for the metro. As he steps off the curb, he hears an engine gun and turns to see a motor scooter not three feet away, swerving at a trajectory designed to run the red light and to miss him by inches, if his reflexes carry him in the right direction. They do, and he reaches out and flicks, ever so slightly he thinks, the shoulder of the driver. The motorcyclist wavers, nearly falls, rights himself and, with the agility of youth, is off his bike and in Matthew's face, flapping his hands around. With his helmet still on, he provides Matthew no opportunity to pop him one in the snoot, as he so longs to do.

In French, the rider asks, loudly, if Matthew is insane.

He replies that yes, he thinks it possible he is. This makes the rider pause. He then attacks Matthew's accent, telling him to go back to his own country before he gets the shit beaten out of him.

At this point, aware that people on the sidewalk are watching, that the drivers of cars stopped at a red light are gawking, Matthew advances a step toward the kid, who retreats. He taps the side of the boy's head with his knuckle. The boy jerks his head away, but does not remove the helmet. He steps toward Matthew, possibly checking to see if the tactic will work in reverse. It does not.

"American!" says the boy and makes the word sound foul. Matthew cocks an eyebrow and shrugs, arms open, waiting. The boy says, "Fuck you!" in a surprisingly good accent, gets back on his scooter and peels off, narrowly missing being flattened by a postal van.

Matthew wishes he had been able to throw at least one punch.

By the time he reaches the Bok-Bok, the feelings have dwindled and he is a little shaky, ambushed by his own impulses. He takes a place at the bar.

"Nice tree." Matthew gestures to the end of the bar where a foot-high plastic Christmas tree squats, garlanded with dog tags.

"Ho, ho, ho," says Dan.

It is only four o'clock, but Matthew orders a double scotch, and when Dan brings it, he takes a healthy slug, although even that does not prepare him for the shock of turning around and seeing Jack and Suzi sitting at the back of the room at Jack's usual table. Jack has his arm draped around her shoulder and looks well pleased. Suzi wears a white loose-necked blouse, something Mexican maybe. She wears no wig, and her short hair is tousled. Kohl lines her eyes and her lips are very red. She smiles and waves, her fingers fluttering. A leaf from the dull plastic palm next to her brushes against her neck and she giggles and flicks it away, sending a little cloud of dust motes into the smoky air.

"This is a surprise." He takes a seat across from Jack.

"You are too serious, Matthew." Suzi grins at him and snuggles closer under Jack's arm.

"Where you been holed up?" asks Jack.

"Taking some downtime is all."

"Anthony was worried about you," says Suzi, and when Matthew doesn't answer, she adds, "We all were."

"I tried calling. I was meaning to come by, too. See how you were doing," says Jack. "I was gonna kick in the door if I had to. Then Anthony called and told me you were okay."

Matthew shrugs. "So, you guys are all right again."

"Could not be better." Suzi leans over and kisses Jack on the cheek. "Aren't we, baby?"

"Yeah. We patched things up, you know. Thanks to you, really. I probably wouldn't have apologized if it wasn't for you, man."

"Listen, Jack, I have to ask you something."

"Yeah, so ask."

"I went down to the hostel today."

"I was supposed to work today, but Suzi and I . . . well, I thought I'd take the day off and celebrate." Jack raises his glass and so does Suzi and they clink. "Why'd you go there?"

"Curious, I guess. You've told me so many stories about the place."

Jack frowns, and smiles ever so slightly. "Curious about what?"

"There were some girls down there, looking for you."

"Why are girls looking for you, Jack?" says Suzi.

"I don't know. How the fuck should I know?"

"They were looking to make a buy."

"From me?"

"Yup. They were very clear about it."

"So?"

"So. Maybe it's none of my business—"

"Maybe it isn't."

"—and I really don't care if you are selling."

"That's good news."

Matthew rolls the glass between his hands. "But I do care if Joseph Ferhat's involved."

Jack removes his arm from behind Suzi and places his elbows on the table, entwining his fingers. "Now what's that supposed to mean?"

"Only this. Saida's worried about him. I've told you that before. And he's got some money, more than he should have. Won't say where he's getting it from. You don't happen to know anything about that, do you?"

"Maybe she's overprotective."

"I don't think so."

Jack leans back and folds his arms over his chest, looking at Matthew. Then he huffs, just a small chuckle. He spreads his hands out on the table, palms flat, the fingers splayed. They cover a good deal of the table. He looks up at Matthew, a big dumb-ass grin on his face. "You and Anthony, man. Even he's had a little chat with me. You'd think that kid was heir to the throne or something. Fine. Okay, you got me. But listen. He's not involved like you think. He just made one single introduction. That's it. And I paid him for it. It was a one-off. No continuing relationship. It happened awhile back. Over and done with. Okay?"

Matthew looks at Suzi, then back at Jack. "Isn't there anywhere else you can make a connection?"

"Meaning?"

"Leave the kid alone, Jack. Do me a favour."

Jack observes Matthew, his face unreadable, and then says, "Sure. No problem. He's not my kid, right? And it's not like I'm banging his mom."

"Nobody's banging his mom."

"Don't see why not. She's pretty good-looking even with those scars." Jack raises his glass and laughs. "Come on, man. No harm done. I said, come *on*."

"Don't be jealous, Matthew," says Suzi.

"What's he got to be jealous of?" says Jack.

"That you are friends with this boy. Such a nice boy."

"You met him?"

"Only a little." Suzi stands and smoothes her skirt. Matthew notices that her ankles look swollen. "He is a nice boy. Why, you don't think I'm good enough to meet a nice boy?"

"That's not what I said, Suzi."

"We bumped into him once is all," says Jack. "It wasn't anything. Jesus. Why am I defending this? You know me. If I give my word, it's my word, right?"

Matthew nods.

"So, are we cool, or do we have a problem?" Jack sips his drink.

"You tell me."

"No problem here. I don't have anything to do with the kid. All right?"

"All right."

"Excuse me. I must try and call my daughter. There is trouble at her school with other girls. They bully her." Suzi looks pointedly at Matthew. "I am a good mother," she says, and then rises, but she goes into the toilet rather than to the bar phone.

"She's a good girl," says Jack, and it is unclear if he means Suzi or her daughter. He finishes his drink. "You want another? I'm buying."

"No, thanks, I got work to do. Just wanted to get it straight."

"Straight it is." And they shake hands.

* * *

When Matthew arrives at the café, Joseph isn't there. Matthew sits with Elias and waits for Saida to speak to him, because he is not sure what his reception will be like, after the clumsy pass he made. She behaves, however, as though nothing has happened. Well, perhaps her expression is a hint more guarded than usual, but her welcome seems genuine enough. It isn't until she smiles at him as she puts coffee down for him that he realizes his shoulders have been up around his ears. He tells her he has seen Jack and feels confident Jack is not a problem. He promises to talk to Joseph soon. Saida clears the cups away, saying little, and it is obvious she is unconvinced.

"Do you want food?" she says.

"No, thanks," he says. "I think I want to do some work." And he is somewhat surprised to find it is true.

Back in his apartment his thoughts jump and snag on one thing after another. Suzi and her dark eyes. Her pale skin. That junkie love. Saida and the hope in her eyes. Looking for him to help when he is the last person to ask for such a thing. His fingers curl around the pen. What is the thread of his life? He wants to put it down on the paper. For the first time since starting this book, he actually wants to write it. He realizes that, in writing about Rwanda, he has released something. It is not all on the page yet, he knows that, but it is a marker, something crossed over. And so, not Hebron yet. No, not that. Make a little side trip.

It had been a bad day. I was travelling with Ray, from Texas, and Jack. It was one of those places. Best to travel in a group. We were driving south from Travnik when we saw a roadblock.

Ray was from Texas and had been studying to be a priest when he decided the Church was too passive and switched to the press corps. He looked at the delegation of eight thugs posing as army regulars and said, "Gentleman, I do believe we have a problem." He rubbed his hand over his jaw. "This is not good."

By then, it was too late to turn around. We came to a halt as men fanned out around us.

"Just stay calm," said Ray. He rolled down the window and one of the men, his thick beard flecked with old food, stuck his head in and looked around at the floor of the car.

"Afternoon," said Jack. The stench of beer wafted in on the man's breath. Another came around the passenger side and tapped on the glass. I rolled down the window. The rest of the men, all of them in Chetnik uniforms, stalked the vehicle the way a hustler stalks a pool table.

I felt my balls crawl up inside my belly. Hands grabbed and dragged us out of the car, slapped us around, guns in our faces. Jack took a lunge for his Leica and got a pistol butt across the back of the head. They took us out to a muddy field, made us kneel in the mud, hands behind our heads. The mud smelled like rotting hay and manure, and one of the Serbs pissed on Ray's legs while the rest of them roared with drunken laughter.

I tried to breathe through my open mouth. I couldn't believe I was going to die with that smell in my nostrils.

Then Jack said, "Well, I like a joke as much as the next guy," and he stood up, slapping at the mud on the knees of his jeans. "But if I stay down there any longer I'm going to go to bed tonight smelling like a pile of pig shit."

The men looked at one another and the first man, the one who had leaned his head in the car window, yelled something and gestured with his rifle that Jack should get back into the mud. Jack smiled, moved slowly and, never taking his eyes off the bearded man, he pulled a package of Camels out of his shirt pocket, offered them all around and grinned as though there was nothing wrong in the world.

Staying alive cost us three hundred Deutschmarks.

We climbed back into the car, smiled nicely and waved good-bye. Ray looked sheepish and said, "That smell may not just be from the fields, boys. I think I'm gonna rename this place the Brown Underpants Pass."

When we got into town, we dumped our gear at the hotel and cleaned up, especially Ray. Then we headed for a bar a soldier had told us about. As soon as I came through the door, I noticed a girl leaning up against the bar wearing thigh-high boots. Her hair was dyed several shades of blond and her face had the bone-white complexion of a vampire. I told her what had happened.

"Papci," said the un-dead girl. "Our beautiful country is raped by criminals spilled out from broken jails."

I drank a number of glasses of bitter wine. I told her I was brave. Told her I'd been the one who gave the papci *cigarettes and negotiated our release. She took me to her mother's house, where the second floor was nothing but rubble and wind and we fucked to the rumble and shriek of shells exploding and sniper fire. We fucked while Prince's "1999" played on a tinny cassette player. She smelled sour and her hair was dirty, but it didn't matter. I never knew her name, she didn't know mine, and when we were finished she asked me if I could get her some food. I said I'd try, although I knew I wouldn't and from the look on her face as I left, I thought she knew this, too. I put a few bills on the cassette player and left her lying on the mattress on the floor, her hands tightly clutching the blanket, even though she was asleep.*

A couple of weeks later, when I swung back that way again, I asked about the girl with the Nosferatu skin.

"You mean Mirjana," the busboy said and shrugged. "She don't come here no more since mother is shot." He put a pistol-shaped hand to his head. "Pow. Sniper."

I tried, then, to see if I could find her, just to see if she was all right, to bring her the food I'd promised her, but the house where she had lived was empty and no one knew where she had gone.

CHAPTER TWENTY-FIVE

She has turned on every light in the apartment. She has lighted four candles. It does not help. Anxiety has pushed, elbowed and hefted its way into the room as the hours pass, so that now there is no space for anything else, only the metallic sliver of fear when she realizes there is no one she can call. Ramzi is out. She cannot bother her father, who sleeps down the hall unaware that his grandson is not home in bed. She cannot call the mothers of Joseph's friends. The truth is that she does not know who Joseph's friends are. She is furious with herself and ashamed as well, for she has failed at being a good mother in so many ways. There is no other parent she can call in the middle of the night, in the middle of this night and say, "Is he there? Is my son with your son?" No one who can reassure her and say, "Do not worry, he is with us. He's safe."

She sits on the couch and pulls rhythmically at the end of her braided hair. How did it happen that she is so far out of his life? When she lived with Anatole, she used to know the boys in the neighbourhood who played soccer in the courtyard together. But that was then, when he was young; and it was there, in the 13th arrondissement. Another life. Maybe she should have stayed there, or gone back after Anatole went to jail. Joseph had had his little friends in that neighbourhood. Maybe it would have been worth the looks, the pity and the contempt the women in the building had felt for her, an Arab, a woman with more bruises than good sense. Would it have made a difference? Regrets and second-guesses flash into her mind like warning lights on a railway crossing, on a police car. Like lightning bolts, each one with its charge of danger.

She stands, walks to the bathroom and splashes water on her face. She straightens the towels. Takes a cloth and wipes at marks on the mirror. She returns to the couch, and almost at once is on her feet again. She turns the gas on the stove to heat water for coffee, takes out a mug and then turns the gas off again. Her stomach is already churning; coffee will only make it worse.

It is almost two o'clock in the morning. Where does a boy go at two o'clock in the morning? She has heard stories of boys who go down into the catacombs and play dangerous, drug-infested games; of packs of youths who pit themselves against each other in the cemeteries; of vacant houses overrun by drug addicts and perverts and pimps who buy and sell pretty children and teenage girls from places like Romania and Bosnia. She puts both hands over her mouth as her imagination conjures images too vivid to bear. She wonders if she should call the police, find out if they have—she can barely say the word, even to herself—arrested him for something. She shudders, pulls her sweater tighter and paces the floor.

The love she feels for Joseph is so great her ribs crack against the strain of her swollen heart. She gnaws at her nails. Every noise in the building makes her jump. There is never silence in this place. Always there is some hum, some rustle just beneath the surface of quiet. Like the noise of a refrigerator, you notice it only when it stops—except it never stops. A bump from somewhere down below. Footsteps. A door. Even at this hour. Do they never sleep? She has a headache from straining to hear his footsteps on the stairs.

She pulls back the red curtain, opens the window and sticks her head far out into the cold air, trying to catch sight of him swaggering down the street. The street is nearly deserted—a couple walk arm in arm, a man with a duffle bag and a bedroll ambles along, looking in doorways. She waits. Once she thinks it is Joseph, with three other boys, but she is mistaken and that clutches at her heart, too, that she could mistake her own son's walk. She lets the curtain fall, walks to the couch, sits, stands, and then sits again. She folds her hands in her lap and bends over so her chest rests on her knees, trapping her already-fidgeting fingers. *Still. If I stop acting like a lunatic, he will come home. I will count to one hundred. One, two, three . . .* At one hundred she decides, no, she has to count backwards. One hundred, ninety-nine, ninety-eight . . .

At three o'clock, she can stand it no longer. Something must be done. He does not stay out this late, not without phoning. Never has he done this before. But she cannot go out and look for him alone; she needs help. She considers Anthony, but she does not want to wake him. There is only one person she can think of who might help her, who will not be disturbed so late at night since he has said he is often up until nearly dawn.

In her little blue book she looks up Matthew's number, thankful that Anthony had given it to her during the time when Matthew was so depressed and they were worried about him. He picks up on the first ring and sounds neither surprised nor sleepy. She tells him what is wrong, the words spilling out like eggs from a basket, breaking everywhere.

"All right, Saida. Calm down. I'll be right over. What's your address? All right, then. Don't panic. He'll probably be there before I am, but if not, we'll find him."

She knows it is foolish, what he is saying, for how are they to find a boy in the midst of a city like this, with enough alleyways and subterranean vaults and hidden worlds to fill a whole other dimension?

It is less than half an hour later when his feet sound on the stairs. She has the door open before his head comes round the corner, and she tries to hide her disappointment.

"He back?" says Matthew.

"No. I am afraid. I did not know who else to call." The phrase sounds pathetic. He comes into the apartment and closes the door behind him. His presence in the room, the first man who is not a family member to be in her apartment since she moved in, makes him seem taller than usual. She walks to the table and chairs, puts a chair between them. Her hands clasp in front of her, under her chin, her elbows tight in beside her body. She is aware that every gesture she makes, every word she speaks, is a parody, a caricature. She puts her hands down, then behind her back, then in front again. "I shouldn't have called you. I panicked. I guess I panicked. He will be home any minute. I'm sure of that."

Matthew comes toward her, reaches out quickly and puts his arms around her, trapping her against his chest. "It's all right. And yes, he'll probably be home any minute. It isn't that late, for a boy his age, is it?"

She freezes against him, partly from shock and then for an instant she craves the comfort. Not to be alone anymore is a great temptation. But she knows where such temptations lead. She pushes away from him, from the pressure of his hands, and their eyes meet briefly, and if there were room for another emotion she thinks he, too, might be embarrassed by the implications of such an embrace. Saida looks out the window. "He comes home no later than one o'clock. But then, yes, sometimes he is later. He calls, though. Most always he calls."

"So why is this different?"

Why is it so different? This is a reasonable question. It is different because it is three o'clock in the morning now and she does not know where her son is and she should know, and she has been afraid, more every day, of the way he slips through her fingers like angry smoke. "It is too late. He should be home."

"Okay, so where does he hang out? You've called his friends?"

"Yes. I called. No"—she looks down, shakes her head—"I do

not know many of them. They are not from this neighbourhood. I do not know them. There is no one to call."

"Did you call the police?"

"For a teenaged Arab boy gone not even twenty-four hours?" He knows nothing. As if they would care.

Matthew runs his fingers over his skull. "All right. Okay. Where does he go?"

"If I knew that, don't you think I'd go there?" She has made a mistake calling him. She wants him to leave.

"Listen to me, Saida. I'll go out and look for him, if you can give me some clue, anything, about where he might be."

She tries to think, her mind a whirl of streets and doorways and parks and alleys and bodegas and fetid apartments in the *banlieue*. "He is often in Barbès, I think. He might be there, anywhere. There is a park, Square Léon. The boys hang out there. But any of the streets . . . out in the suburbs with a gang, if he's gone out there he can't get back, the metro has stopped—oh, I do not know!" She must calm herself. If she crumples now . . .

Matthew steps toward the door. "I'll start there, then."

She turns and reaches for her coat.

"I think I should go alone," he says.

"No. I am going with you."

"What if he comes home? What if he calls?"

She does not want to see the good sense in this, for if she has to stay, has to sit and do nothing, she will surely go crazy. "I cannot."

"Look, Saida, I know you're worried, but there's really no reason to go off the rails. Joseph's probably just running the streets with his friends, or maybe he's with a girl or something. Believe me, sixteen-year-old boys can find a million reasons not to call their mothers and ask permission to stay out for the night. I'll call you in an hour, but you need to stay here."

He puts his arm around her shoulders and, whereas before she wanted only to scurry away, now it is different and she does not like that it is different. She wants to pull away and wants, at the same time, to grab the front of his jacket and bury her burning forehead there. The indecision means she stands still.

"It is okay," she says. "He is fine. He is fine. You will call me every hour, or more, yes?" In her mind, she sees the minutes, a flight of steep stairs, each riser three-feet tall, climbing up into the night. She will never be able to haul herself up that far. She looks up at Matthew. His eyes, shadows and light, hold hers. "Please, Matthew. I am so sorry to involve you."

He gives her a strong squeeze. "Look, no worries, all right? I'll take a look up the street in Barbès, and call you from there, either way, okay? Write your number down for me. Tell you what, how about making us something to eat? When we get back I bet he'll be hungry. I sure as hell will be. Soup or something, okay?"

She smiles a little. "Busy hands, is that it?"

"Empty stomachs is more like it."

"Thank you," she says, and in her mind she sees herself kissing his cheek, feels the prickle of stubble under her lips. *No. This is only need. This is only fear.* She pats the front of his coat, buttoning the top button for him. "Thank you."

CHAPTER TWENTY-SIX

On the street, he heads toward Barbès, and with every step his conviction that he is out of his mind grows. One tall, thin, white guy roaming the streets of Barbès in the middle of the night is an invitation for trouble.

Why is he out here? *Because Saida asked me.* Saida, who works so hard and came to drag me up from the pit. Saida, who was burned and is still beautiful. Saida, who cooks lemon and chicken, serves customers, and washes dishes while her brother reads the paper and her father stares out the window, and Saida, who still has time to grow jasmine in the courtyard. Saida, who smells of sandalwood and whose hair is like a black velvet rope. Saida. *Because she needs me. Because her son needs me too, maybe.*

Think of the son. Don't think of the mother. Matthew remembers what it feels like to be one of the lost boys. Never Never Land is not all it is cracked up to be. Especially if it never ends.

Paris this late at night is a different world. Vacant and hidden. The quiet unsettles Matthew. Few cars. A lone, half-frozen bicyclist along the boulevard de Rochechouart. Symbolically, ironically, inevitably, a lone black cat in an alleyway. As he crosses Rochechouart he notices the bums in the doorways, set up for the night in sleeping bags laid over cardboard and scattered with empty bottles and plastic bags, their half-wild dogs at the watch. The homeless can't be forced into shelters if they have dogs, and so, of course, they all have them. Yellow eyes follow him as he walks, hackles raised, soft growls. Farther on, several men stand, waiting, watching for business, he assumes.

Turning right on rue de la Goutte d'Or he hears voices from somewhere nearby. His hearing becomes more acute with every step and he finally identifies the voices as coming from a television on a third floor. Metal security gates cover shop windows and graffiti emblazons the walls: dozens of different tags in red, orange, white and black paint. Light spills softly from a half-open shutter and along with it the voice of Cheb Hasni, the young *rai* singer gunned down by Islamic radicals in the streets of Oran a couple of years before. A pair of drug addicts, quietly nodding away the night, slouch against each other in front of the butcher's. The air smells different here than in Matthew's neighbourhood, full of leftover lamb *tagine,* cumin and incense mixed with the garbage and the smell of drains. *Parfum des égouts.*

He passes the police station just as two cars pull up. Out of the first the police haul a blond girl with a wide-boned Slavic face. She is no more than twenty, in tight jeans and sneakers, her hair a rat's nest falling over her eyes, and she is handcuffed. Two more police get out of the front of the second car and two girls get out of the back—one Arab, one African. These girls are not handcuffed, and the African looks pleased, the smile on her face and the swollen eye telling most of the story.

Even before he climbs the steps to the Square Léon, he hears more voices. Louder, slurry. Three drunks wrestle with a bottle, until it falls to the ground and shatters, the smash followed by loud curses. One man tries to slap another, only to misjudge the distance and land on his hands and knees, where he quietly, effortlessly, vomits. The soccer grounds are empty; the houses around the square locked up tight.

A group of young men loiter at the corner of rue Myrha. He counts six but cannot tell if Joseph is among them.

"Hey," he calls, "Joseph? *C'est moi.*"

He is answered in French. "Who you looking for?" says a small man with sharp eyes and two missing teeth.

"Friend of mine. Joseph Ferhat."

"What you want?"

"Said I'd meet up with him, but I can't find him."

"We don't know him," says another man.

"You don't know Joseph? I thought everybody knew him. Sixteen? Lebanese?"

"You looking for boys, you *pede!*"

Matthew laughs at the accusation. "No, no, nothing like that." It is important not to look flustered, not to move too quickly in any direction.

"Get out of here!"

Joseph is not there, and they are not going to tell him anything. He raises his hand to say thanks and walks away slowly, not looking back.

He searches a few more streets and sees no one who looks like Joseph, nothing but remnants of human beings and the scavengers that feed off them. It is a needle in a fucking haystack. At a public phone he dials Saida's number. It is nearly four a.m., and no sign of him. Surely he'd be holed up with a girl somewhere by now. Matthew's earlier protective instincts are replaced by a desire to strangle the kid when he sees him next.

In the phone booth, he wracks his brain for other options. There is someone who just might know, and although it rankles him no end to have to call Jack on this subject, he is desperate. He dials Jack's number and for a moment, when a woman's voice answers, he thinks he has the wrong number.

"Suzi?" he says after a pause.

"Oui?"

"It's Matthew."

"What time is it?"

"It's late. Listen, is Jack there?"

"No. I got in a couple of hours ago. He is not here." If she is miffed at Jack's absence, it does not show in her voice.

"Joseph Ferhat hasn't come home tonight. His mother's going nuts. I don't know where to look. Suzi, listen, do you have any ideas?"

"Why are you asking me?"

"I'd ask Jack if he were there."

There is silence on the end of the phone, then the sound of a match scraping against a box and smoke sucked into lungs. "Suzi, you're a mother. How would you feel?"

"I am sure he's fine."

"Where should I look?"

There is a long exhalation at the other end of the line. "There is a squat full of artists. It is on rue de Châteaudun, near the Gare Saint-Lazare, I think. They call it La Source."

"I've heard of it. Jack pointed it out to me awhile back. They put out some kind of a lit mag."

"I think there is a party. I would try there if I were you."

"Thanks, Suzi."

"You did not hear this from me. It is not good for a mother to be looking for a child," she says and then hangs up.

He decides to look at the squat, if he can even find it, and then call it a night. Maybe Joseph is hanging out on the Champs Élysées, maybe he is in an all-night club, maybe he is in jail, but there was only so much Matthew can do. He stuffs his hands in his pockets and heads back down rue du Faubourg Poissonnière toward rue de Maubeuge, which leads him directly to Châteaudun, at the church of Notre Dame de Lorette.

At the taxi stand in front of Notre Dame de Lorette, three drivers doze in their cars while the blue light on the stand's column flashes unnoticed. Whoever is calling for a cab at this hour is unlikely to get one. Matthew walks in the direction of the train station, trying to remember exactly where the squat is.

He need not have worried. It is unmistakable.

The squat stands on the south side of the street and is a large building, modern, though abandoned by the insurance company that once occupied it. The double glass-and-metal doors lead to a long hall lit with fluorescent lights, festooned, in honour of the season, in red and green tinsel garlands. To the right of the door a large storefront window displays a television playing a video. In it, a grey-haired stocky man in plaid shirt and jeans, who reminds Matthew of a Nebraska farmer, jumps up and down in what looks like a prison exercise yard, endlessly trying to reach a blue milk carton that hovers above his head. Behind the television, a pink neon sign blinks on and off. "This is not ART!" and then "This is ART!" Bass-booming music thrums from somewhere high up. When Matthew puts his hand on the glass, he feels it vibrate.

Behind the doors sits a large red-haired, red-bearded man, so fat his stomach falls across his thighs and his buttocks spill over the seat of his chair, which tilts back on two legs and leans precariously against the wall. He wears a red beret with a black band and a parka with a Canadian-flag decal of dubious origin. His eyes are closed.

Matthew taps on the glass, and the fat man opens his right eye, screwing up his face as he does so. He regards Matthew for a moment and then closes the eye again.

"Pardon." Matthew taps again.

"What?" the man says in English through the glass, not opening either eye this time.

"You going to let me in?"

"Why should I?"

"Why shouldn't you?"

"Because I don't know you. And because it's very late."

"I heard the party's only just starting round about now."

"You don't look like much of a party animal. Who would have told you such a thing?"

"Jack. Jack Saddler." He throws out the only name he knows.

The man's eyes open slowly. "You know Jack?"

"I know Jack."

In slow motion, the man straightens his chair onto four legs and stands. His legs are short, but his arms are long. It gives him the appearance of an overdressed orangutan. He puts his arms behind his back and stretches loudly, and then flips the lock on the door. As Matthew squeezes past him, he says, "Jack's upstairs if I'm not mistaken. Top floor. Don't go to the first or second floor, or the third, or the fourth, or the fifth. Those are private. The party's on the top floor."

"Thanks."

The man takes Matthew by the elbow. The music's beat is stronger here, although oddly it is no louder. Just the vibrations coming off the walls, the floor, as though the building has a heart-beat. As though the building is beginning to panic. He feels it in the pulse of the man's fingers.

"On second thought, wait. There." He points to a spot on the floor, and then opens a door and sticks his head in. "Jean-Marc. *Viens.*" He turns back to Matthew and says, "Jean-Marc will take you up."

A man appears, with so many piercings in his lower lip it is a wonder it stays attached. He motions for Matthew to follow and he does, just as the border guard turns to let in two girls, one with green hair.

The building is a labyrinth of halls and doorways. The squatters have hooked up the electricity somehow, and wires run in complete disorder; extension cords connect to extension cords stapled around doorways and along the floor, but the elevator does not work. Matthew follows The Pierced Man up the stairs. The music is louder, and when he puts his hand on his sternum, Matthew feels it there as though it is trying to influence his internal organs.

A dark girl in a bright blue scarf and with huge gold rings in her ears passes them and she and The Pierced Man greet each other. On the second floor, he turns back to Matthew and says, in French, "First time here?"

Matthew tells him it is.

"This is a good place," The Pierced Man says, switching to English. "Not like other squats, eh? This is organized. We have committees. We're going to the mayor. We're going to get things right here, so they can't throw us out. This is for artists, eh? Not for drug addicts. Not for *clochards*. You're an artist?"

"No." The beat grows incrementally stronger with every vertical foot.

"Writer?"

"Sort of."

"Ah. Me, too." When the man smiles under the cold lights, Matthew swears he can see little bits of white tooth through the holes stretched in his lower lip.

Matthew looks down the hallways as they pass. Lights are on in some rooms and he sees canvases, bits of twisted metal, paints and mattresses. Artists have used the walls as well. Great swaths of red and black on one wall; figures, fairly well drawn, in a scene from one of the political demonstrations on another, the angry faces and wide-open mouths seeming to reach out toward him. Three buckets with painted eyes on them, attached to metal poles, stand against a wall. Halfway down the poles someone has tied bananas and plums. The fruit has blackened and fruit flies swarm.

On the third floor, they set off down the hall, turn left, then right, past door after door. Then they take another flight of stairs and turn right. They go a long way. So long that Matthew is sure they must have crossed the whole building and must now be in some other building altogether. He imagines the sound follows them. He imagines something sinister and heavy, hunting them with a stone club. In one room, a shooting party is underway, the junkies lounging on mattresses, leaning on each other, scratching themselves and twitching. Candles dot the floor around the mattresses and blankets, their flames flickering either from drafts or from the pulse of bass in the floor, the walls. A fine sprinkle of dust flutters down from the ceiling. "I thought you said there was no dope here."

The Pierced Man shrugs. "What can you do? Two of them have lived here for a long time, since before we took over. They don't hurt anybody."

There seems to be no end to the hallways, and perhaps it is just because the lights are out at the end of them, but to Matthew they look like they lead to nothing, or rather, they lead only into darkness. The music is loud enough that now, had he wanted to talk, he would have had to raise his voice above the inexorable rhythm. Something electronic and soulless. He has the growing sense of many people above them and in his imagination it is a looming, writhing entity. His breathing is shallow.

They come into a cavernous space full of bodies. Walls have been knocked down here, leaving only the support beams. Lighting is uneven, provided mostly from bare bulbs hung from raw connections in the ceiling, or from construction torches, the kind with metal half-backs and wire grilles, hanging from hooks around the walls. Couches form a large square in the centre, and these are crowded. Lots of low-slung jeans and belly rings and little tops on the girls that push their breasts up into the presentation position. The air is so pungent with smoke, Matthew's eyes water. The crowd is young, early twenties mostly, and he feels like a dinosaur in his fraying, unfashionable jeans.

The Pierced Man abandons him the minute they walk in and wanders away in the direction of a boy who dances shirtless, his six-pack stomach glistening with sweat. Matthew tries to get his bearings as he feels the floor beneath his feet bounce in time to the music, to the mass of dancers at the far end of the room. It is important to remember to breathe deeply. He hopes the redecorating that has gone on has not compromised the beams holding up the floor.

The question rolls through his head again. And the answer: *Because Saida asked me.*

Four mismatched tables along the right wall, in front of what looks like offices, are laden with electronic equipment—turntables, mixing boards, video equipment and projectors that spray a series of moving pictures on a screen hanging over the crowd. The pictures are of someone diving into water, someone diving backward out of the water, a man on a bicycle riding along a wall, a man falling. A rangy young DJ with his head shaved to disguise his receding hairline wears headphones and works two turntables at once. Water-filled bottles cover another long table.

Matthew scans the crowd for either Jack or Joseph but the lights are uneven and it is hard to see clearly through the smoke, which is as much grass as tobacco. So much so, in fact, that he suspects he'll be getting a contact high within minutes.

There is a ruckus of some sort going on in the corner and Matthew's heart hammers, thinking a fight has broken out. Then he sees flames and hears screams even above the pumping bass and thinks a fire has started, but there immediately follows a flurry of diving and stamping and swatting. The sound of metal on wood and banging and crashing. He walks over.

"Quelle horreur!" A girl stands in front of him, shaking her hands in the air.

"What's going on?" Matthew shouts through cupped hands.

"Les cafards!" she shrieks and shakes her hands some more.

Matthew moves in for a closer look. A woman with long hair, a long face and a pockmarked complexion stands near the wall with a blowtorch. Matthew's skin ripples with goosebumps as though someone rubbed an ice cube on the back of his neck. He imagines grabbing the blowtorch, a device suitable for so many diabolical activities for which it was not designed, and bending it irreparably in two.

In a semicircle around the long-haired woman, fifteen to twenty people cluster, each armed with something heavy—boots, a frying pan, a telephone book. Another man grips a crowbar and bends over the baseboard.

"One . . . Two . . . Three!" the man calls, and then pries away the wood.

Hundreds of small brown insects scatter and scurry in all directions. People yell like warriors lunging into battle. The woman with the blowtorch dashes frantically this way and that against the wall, trying to nuke as many cockroaches as possible. Matthew may have shrieked as well, but the audio avalanche buries the sound. Everywhere people stamp and hurl and hit and mash. He catches a glimpse of someone who looks like Joseph, dancing a cockroach-killing tarantella next to a girl with short bleached-blond hair. Matthew tries to keep sight of him, but people push, some toward, some away from the frenzy and all Matthew sees are feet and scurrying things and the red flash of fire. His chest feels like it is in an ever-tightening vice.

They could be ganging up on anything, with shoes, with bricks, rocks, knives, with blowtorches. It could be anyone on the ground there under their feet, their flames.

Matthew pushes through the crowd then, toward the door, trying to get air. Faces leap in front of him; they look like masks, with wide eyes and wide mouths, and lips too red and teeth too white and shiny skin, and all around him is noise.

He may hear his name. He may not. His hands fly up and out, trying to clear space. His legs tingle with the desire to kick.

He pushes someone hard, a tall, beak-nosed man with an orange scarf around his neck who bumps into someone else, then bounces back toward Matthew and curses. Matthew mutters something about claustrophobia and getting out of his fucking way and then he is in the stairwell and it is dark, descending into somewhere cellar-ish and inhabited and he does not want to go down and cannot go back. He presses up against the wall.

A shout, something barely riding the crest of the techno sound wave. "Matthew! Hold up!"

For a moment, he wonders if someone who knows his name is

going to mug him. He scrabbles to find something to defend himself with—a piece of wood, a bottle, anything. The figure is backlit, looming above him.

"Matthew?"

The voice is familiar, the stance. The figure steps down onto the stairs. The mouth, something about the mouth.

"Joseph?"

"You all right?"

"Yes. No." He does not want to run, but he has to put more distance between him and those blowtorch bearers. He retreats another flight, not caring if Joseph follows him or not. And with another floor between him and *that*, he sits down on the stairs.

Joseph comes down and sits next to him. "I thought I saw you. What's wrong? Are you sick?"

It is important to sound sane.

"Lunatic asylum," he says.

"What?"

Breathing takes up all his concentration. He counts. One-two-three, in. One-two-three-four, out. He runs his hands through his hair, willing them to be steady. "I just don't like crowds is all."

"This isn't a good place to come if you don't like crowds."

"It wasn't my idea." His pulse begins to return to something like normal. He will be home in an hour, he tells himself. Just an hour. Back inside the nest. Just do the next right thing, finish the job and get the hell out. He takes a good look at Joseph—his eyes are bloodshot, he is pale and his breath stinks of beer. "What's with the goddamn blowtorch?"

"Crazy place, huh?"

"Crazy place." Matthew wipes sweat off his upper lip.

"Well, hello campers." Jack stands at the top of the landing and he looks like a sequoia. A swaying sequoia.

If someone yells "Timber," Matthew plans to dive over the banister and take his chances in freefall. "Hello," Matthew says.

"Want a drink? They got Red Stripe Beer of all fucking things."

"What are you doing here, Jack?"

"Me? This is the place. My place, like. Kids from the hostel turned me on to this place. They love me here. I am a legion, a ledge . . ." Jack blows out his lips. "I am a legend here. This is a Christmas party. You need a drink." The blond girl appears beside him. "Hi, honey," Jack says to her.

"I was just telling young Joseph here that I don't much care for this place."

"So, what are you doing here?" Joseph's eyes dart in the direction of the girl.

"We should talk about that. Somebody's worried, you know?"

"That is Farida." Joseph points to the girl.

"Hello, Farida."

"'Lo, Farda. No. Firda?" says Jack.

"She doesn't speak English," says Joseph. He beckons to her to come down and she does.

"Enchantée," Matthew says and tries very hard not to sound sarcastic. The girl smiling at him is about as sweet as a girl can be, early twenties maybe, her eyes the colour and shape of brown almonds, with lips that look bruised, slightly swollen. Matthew is about to ruin Joseph's night.

"Listen," he says in English, his mouth close to Joseph's ear. "Why don't we call it a night, eh? Give your mom a call, drop the young lady off if you want."

"My mother?" Joseph's mouth opens and he goes red. If there has been any doubt in Farida's mind about how old he is, he has just blown it. He looks twelve.

"She called me, Joseph. She's fucking frantic."

"*Merde!* She has no right to call you, what is this? What *is* this?"

"Is 'er a problem?" says Jack, and he pats Farida on the ass as she goes back up the stairs.

"Fuck!" says Joseph, and it is unclear if it is because of Saida or the pat, or Farida's parting in general.

"What do you expect? No need to blow a gasket. You're lucky

she didn't insist on coming with me." Terror replaces anger. "Look, I know this is bad. I know it's embarrassing. But it's nearly morning, Joseph. It's nearly four-thirty in the morning and I'm getting mighty tired."

"Is it that late?" Joseph stands and cranes his neck to watch Farida glide away, her bottom swaying in skin-tight black pants.

"Let's get you out of here without blowing your cover."

"My cover?"

"Yeah," says Jack. "Without making it look like Mama sent Matthew here all the way after you." He snorts and sways and then reaches out to steady himself against the wall.

"I guess my cover doesn't much matter now, does it? *Merde.* And what if I don't want to go?"

"I'm not going to drag you out. Fuck that. You're old enough to make your own decisions. I'll let her know you're alive and you can do what you like."

Jack comes down the stairs, his heel slipping on the fourth step forcing Joseph and Matthew to grab him. He only laughs and slaps Matthew on the back. "You missed the poetry. You missed the *performance* art." He says the word in such a way that Matthew assumes the performance must have involved human excrement, or toads, or someone squeezing blackheads.

"I thought we talked about this. Was this your idea?"

"What? Was what my idea?"

"He's sixteen! His mother's going out of her tree. For Christ's sake, Jack!"

"Didn't know it was that late. Want a toke?" He holds out a soggy joint in the fingers of a hand that also holds a bottle of beer. He's been drinking for so long his sweat smells of it.

"C'mon, Joseph. We're getting out of here."

Joseph's shoulder stiffens under Matthew's hand.

"I don't want to go. What is this? You are now my mother's . . ."

"Her what?" says Matthew.

"Her . . . *flic*."

Cop. Matthew can live with that. In the wide ocean of possibilities, it is not so bad.

"Like I said. You make your own decisions."

Jack stands in their path, swaying. "Aw, man, let him stay awhile, *Dad*. He's got a thing going." He puts his finger up to the side of his nose and grins, his eyes wandering from side to side.

"Maybe you should call it a night as well, Jack." Someone yells from upstairs and there is the crashing sound of metal chairs collapsing. Matthew's stomach squinches up into his throat. "I didn't think this'd be your kind of crowd."

Jack's head tilts back and he chews on the inside of his mouth. "Don't think I fit in with an artistic crowd? That's the truth, right? Is it? You know what I think?" he says and folds his arms across his chest. As he does so, his hands get tangled in some complicated manoeuvre designed to keep him from burning himself with the joint. In the transaction the beer slips to the floor and the glass shatters. Jack looks at it sadly; he looks at Matthew and smiles lopsidedly. "Maybe you're right." And then he laughs. The Jack Laugh, the one that makes heads appear in the stairwell, even over the music.

Joseph's muscles relax under Matthew's hand.

The three of them make it out of the building slowly, picking their way through the maze of halls and half-lit doorways, the pulse gradually diminishing as they descend. Once, they get lost and find themselves in a bathroom of sorts where someone has set up a child's wading pool and a hose from the sink. It smells of bleach and mildew in equal measure. "Just like a Turkish jail," says Jack. They retrace their steps and find the stairs.

"I see you found him," says the border guard.

"Was I lost?" says Jack.

"You never know," says the guard and unlocks the door.

The air is colder than Matthew remembers. He buttons up his

jacket, but Jack seems immune. Joseph looks tired and a little pasty.

"I have to find a phone to let your mother know you're all right."

Joseph hangs his head.

"Tell you what," says Jack. "I'm coming home with you. Sure. Explain it was my fault."

"I don't think that's a good idea," says Matthew.

"She's going to be very mad." Joseph's eyes cloud, sulky under heavy brows. "She treats me like a child. It is impossible."

"She'll be glad you're all right, but I suspect that yes, you are going to have to face the music, my friend."

"Yup. Coming with you," says Jack again.

"Listen, let me talk to you." Matthew pulls Jack aside and tries to remember that taking a pop at Jack is not a wise thing to do. "This has got to stop, all right? You got to leave this kid alone. You said he had nothing to do with your selling dope."

"Yeah. I said that. That's what I said."

"Would you want Jack, Jr., mixed up in shit like this? Hanging out in a place like this?"

"If he's with me, why not?" says Jack, but he doesn't sound convinced. He takes a cigarette out of his pack and tries to light it. The match falls to the ground. "Oops," he says and tries again. "Aw, what the fuck. What am I doing hanging around with a kid anyway? This place is a rat hole, full of pertenti . . . perntentious . . . full of shits. I miss the ole Bok-Bok."

"So do I, as a matter of fact."

Jack puts his arm around Matthew. It feels like a sack of wet sand.

"We need a good drunk up, the two of us. *Joseph!*" he calls. "Come here! Joe!"

Joseph comes over and Jack puts his hands on either side of the boy's head, and lets his hands slide onto his shoulders, leaning into him, swaying on his feet. Joseph looks at Matthew, puzzled, and braces himself against Jack's weight.

"Gonna tell you a story," Jack slurs. "My dad gimme a piece of advice, see? He said if I was inna bar fight, always need to remember it would be a dirty fucking fight. Fighting dirty. So the thing to do, see, you gotta grab an ashtray—one of those big heavy mutherfucking bar ashtrays, metal, or glass'll do I guess. If it's heavy enough—and stuff it down my pants in front of my dick. Get it? Protecting the boys." He takes his hands off Joseph's shoulder and gestures as to correct ashtray placement. Matthew and Joseph steady him. "So, few years later here I am. Okinawa, drinking in this bar with a bunch of fucking Danes—they are big mothers, right, big as me, all of 'em, or bigger. And this fight breaks out. Nasty. Very nasty. So I remember my dear ole daddy's words of wisendom and I grab me this big metal ashtray off the bar and pooshisin . . . pussin . . . make it nice and tight over the boys." He stands back and splays his feet, balancing, blocking out the action. "I'm getting ready now to do some seerus damage to this Norwegie guy who's pissing me off, when I get this feeling. This really bad shensation. Next thing I know I'm clawing at my dick, pulling my pants down and rolling on the floor trying to get the fucking ashtray off my dick. Everybody's stopped fighting to watch me have this fucking epi fit." He takes a deep breath. "Fuckin' epi-lep-tic fit or whatever they think is happening and then they're all laughing at me so hard the fight's over. Bartender sure was happy and I'm drinking free for a week. But, and this is the point. Let me tell you now, I was feeling mighty sore." He claps his arm around Joseph. "So, I will leave you with this: Always, always, every time, make sure the ashtray's empty. Burning butts are the temporary ruin of a man."

Jack slaps Joseph on the chest and Matthew on the shoulder and ambles uncertainly off into the night.

"Is he all right?" asks Joseph.

"He's fine," Matthew says, and points to the phone booth. "Come on, we have to phone your mother."

They call Saida. Once she knows he is safe her voice becomes icy with anger.

For the next couple of blocks, Joseph is quiet. He shuffles and tries to look unconcerned, but Matthew sees he is worried about what his mother will say. Now that he is back on the street, reality settles in.

"Anthony was there tonight, too," he says, as though this would make it all right.

"I didn't see him."

"He left early."

"Smart guy." Matthew tries to remember what it is like to be sixteen, to feel tied down and impatient and invincible. "Tell me about the squat. Why do you like it there?"

He shrugs. "I don't know."

"What do you do there?"

"Hang out. Nothing. I don't know. There are people who care about things, who understand what's going on in the world and aren't always talking money, money, money, school, school, school, work, work, work. It's boring. It's capitalist bullshit. All my mother and uncle care about is, are they making enough money. This is no kind of life. I'm going to be different. My life will mean something. I'm going to travel, see the world. I want to go to America and see these roadside attractions. Like Carhenge."

"What the hell is that?"

"Brian at the squat told me about this. It's in the Nebraska flatlands. Like Stonehenge, but made from cars. Also, I want to see the world's largest ball of twine and Paul Bunyan the giant. And Route 66."

"Well, I agree with you on that last one, anyway."

"The point is to travel. To drive through deserts alone. Jack says a man has to know he can stand alone."

"Jack says that, huh?"

"Yes. He says a man doesn't really know what he's made of until he has only himself to depend on. If he can survive this, being alone and facing death, then he will never be afraid again.

You must agree. You've been all over the world, in very much danger. You told me stories."

"Well, I can talk an awful lot of shit. And, I hate to break it to you, but so can Jack. And believe me, Jack's a good friend of mine. But he can be one hell of a gasbag."

"A gasbag?"

"Full of hot air. Tells a good story, but doesn't make a lot of sense. Not all the stories add up. It goes with the territory, Joseph."

"What territory? You are telling me he is a liar? That you are?"

"Not exactly. Just that sometimes for guys like Jack, and like me I guess, after a certain amount of alcohol, or whatever, the stories can get a bit shinier in the telling than they were in the living."

"No. I don't think he's like that at all." He shakes his head. "No."

"I know you made some introductions for Jack. For his sideline money."

Joseph says nothing.

"You don't know what I'm talking about?"

"I know."

"Don't get involved with that shit, Joseph."

"I am not involved with anything."

"That's good. Because you get caught, you'll end up in a world of trouble. It'd kill your mother."

"I am not involved. I introduced him to a friend. It's no big deal. It's not heroin. Not crack. Just a little grass."

"Be that as it may. Stay away, you understand?"

"Sure." Joseph stopped and pulled at Matthew's sleeve. "Does my mother know?"

"She suspects. I'm not going to tell her any more, as long as you promise me it's over, agreed?"

"Yes. Agreed."

So, they walk, lost in their own thoughts, along the quiet streets, past the blinkered bakeries, past pharmacies with their green crosses dull and dark, past bookstores and butcher shops and travel agents with photos of Tunisian beaches in their unlit windows.

They arrive at Joseph's apartment building. "Well, we're about to see what kind of man you are, Joseph. Can you step up?"

"I'm not afraid of my mother. What can she do to me? I'm old enough now to make my own life."

"If you say so."

He presses the code and opens the door.

"Are you coming up?" Joseph says, and it is difficult to know whether he wants Matthew to or not.

"I just want to say good-night and make sure she's all right."

"I can make sure she's all right."

"I won't stay long." Matthew gives him a gentle push into the dark entranceway. He wants to see him to the door. He follows him up the stairs, smiling. He wants to see Saida's face. Then he stops smiling, unsettled. Apparently, he wants her to be pleased with him.

CHAPTER TWENTY-SEVEN

Now that she knows he is alive, is free and unharmed, Saida's hands tremble. There is nowhere to put the futility, nothing to wrap her fingers around that will help her make her son see sense.

When Matthew first suggested she make soup, she thought he was a fool. When he left, she sat and looked out the window. She had watched him walk away, had seen him hesitate at the corner and had been afraid he would not look for Joseph, that he would go home to his bed, and she could not blame him. And then he had disappeared, and she sat in the apartment watching the candles that didn't help at all, or did they? Did Mary send her Matthew? She had tried to pray again, but the words were a scatter across her mind.

She began to make the soup.

It was something to do with her hands. Cilantro, cinnamon, garlic, onions. Lentils, spinach and potatoes. The rhythm of chopping, the smell of the spices, clean and hopeful. Make something good to eat and your men will find their way home. Her mother had said that. Oh, *Imma*, bring your grandson home, she prayed, picturing her mother's face, wide mouth and eyes like the sweep of a bird's wing, like calligraphy, her brow smooth, without a worry line.

Then the phone rang and he was not found. Not in the playground. But Matthew would keep looking.

I miss you, Imma. Tears are a blessing, her mother had said. Tears wash us clean, they are holy water, too, she said. And I am well blessed tonight, thought Saida, wiping her face with a tea towel. Everything into the pot, simmer and stir, simmer and stir. Steam on her face like a reassuring hand.

The kitchen smelled good, although the idea of eating felt like stones on her teeth. She set two bowls out and cut bread. She stirred the pot. Tasted. Added salt. Squeezed in lemon. And then the phone.

"He's with me."

She wanted to speak but there was only a sound, feather against air as something tethered took flight.

"Saida?"

"Is he all right?"

"He's fine. We'll be back in a few minutes."

"Where was he?"

"He was at a party."

"And where was this party?"

He hesitated for only a moment. "At an artists' squat."

"A what?"

"Sort of a commune."

"I'll be waiting," she said.

"He's okay."

"I'll be waiting."

And now she sits, her hands folding napkins, curling up the edge of the tablecloth, picking at her clothes and dusting surfaces that have no dust on them. At the sound of feet in the hall she stands, looking at the door. She steps forward, reaching for the lock, and then stops, lets Joseph use his key. As the handle twists, she turns back to the stove, anxious that they find her doing something, anything.

"Hey, Mom, we're home," says Matthew.

She keeps her face over the cinnamon-and-garlic soup steam. She hears cloth against cloth, a coat being removed. She waits for her son to speak—the sound of his voice will inform her, give her a clue.

"Smells good in here," says Matthew. "Doesn't it smell good?"

"Very good." Joseph's voice low, subdued, but by what?

"Are you hungry?" she says in Arabic.

"A little, yes."

"Matthew, do you want some soup?"

"Oh, maybe I should be going. I'm pretty tired."

"You should eat first. Sit." She carries the soup to the table, ladles it into red bowls.

They sit at the table. Joseph blows on his soup. Matthew dips bread into his.

"It's good," says Joseph.

"Why do you make me send someone to look for you?" she says.

"You didn't have to. Nothing was wrong."

"*La!* Stop." She slaps her hand on the table. "Do not play games with me, Joseph. You know what is right. What is wrong. You have done something wrong. It is not a discussion."

"It was just a party."

"You are not a cruel boy. But you are turning into a liar. I can smell the alcohol on you. You have been unkind tonight. To me. I have to tell you this?"

"Tay-yib, Imma. Tay-yib." He glances at Matthew, who has his eyes on his soup and bread.

Saida knows her son is embarrassed in front of the Canadian, but she does not mind that. He should be embarrassed. He should be ashamed.

"Okay? This is what you have to say?" If Matthew were not there, she would slap him; her hand is a thing with a mind of its own and it wants to slap him. She puts it under her arm to quiet it. "You are crossing a line, Joseph. Are you sure? Are you sure you want to cross it?"

"La."

"And so?"

"Ana asif."

"I hope you *are* sorry." There had been so many words she had wanted to scream at him in the dark hours when she waited, not knowing. They are evaporating on her hot skin. "I was afraid, Joseph. I was afraid you were dead."

"You worry too much."

"Hey," says Matthew. "You should be glad your mother worries about you."

Joseph puts his spoon beside the bowl and leans back, his hands in his lap. There are little spots of red high on his cheeks and his eyes are pink and look sore. "You don't remember what it was like when you were my age. I bet you wanted to . . . to have your freedom, too. Get away from your mother all the time looking for you."

Matthew sucks his teeth. "I remember exactly what it was like."

"So what are you taking her side for? Tell her it's not good the way she keeps me too close. Your mother, she was the same?"

For a moment, it is as though a bird flies above Matthew's face, casting shadows. "My mother died when I was about your age. She died of a broken heart." He tears his bread into tiny pieces. "Don't be a jerk. You'll be out on your own soon enough. May not feel like it now. But it's the truth. Before you know it."

It is only the slight raising of Joseph's eyebrow, the way he presses his lips together, as he has done since he was a little boy and something worried him, that shows feeling. A quick flick of his eyes back and forth. A feeling he does not want anyone to know he has, as though he is afraid they might catch him at something, might discover something. And Saida thinks that still, she knows her son, he is not such a stranger, yet.

He opens his mouth to speak and then shuts it again.

"What?" says Matthew.

Joseph pulls his misshapen lip between his teeth and chews it.

"What?" Matthew says again.

"You . . . you broke your mother's heart?"

"No, my father did."

It is clear from the look on Matthew's face that he does not want them to ask any questions.

They eat their soup. Saida has a little, too. "It needs more salt," she says, but they assure her it is fine.

When, not long after, Matthew says he is leaving, Joseph's head droops on his chest.

"Make up your bed," she says to him.

She walks Matthew to the stairwell.

"You are a good friend to us," she says.

"Your family's been good to me," he says, and then he says, "Well."

"Thank you. I cannot thank you enough. I do not know what I would have done."

"He would have come home in a little while."

"But you found him. And to know someone was looking for him, it made a difference to me."

"Good night," he says.

She takes him by the shoulders and kisses him on one cheek and then the other. "You are like family now," she says. "Like a brother to me."

His smile is uncertain and perhaps she has embarrassed him.

He nods. "Thanks," he says, and then he is gone.

When she steps back in the apartment, Joseph is already asleep under the blanket, his back turned to her. His pants and shoes lie on the floor beside the couch, which he has not bothered to unfold. Here in the darkest part of winter it will not be morning for another hour or so. He sleeps with his neck on the armrest and she knows he will have a crick in it when he wakes.

She does not get him a pillow. Serves him right, she thinks.

CHAPTER TWENTY-EIGHT

Two days later Matthew goes back to the New Friends Hostel. A tree with flickering lights is in the lobby. It is topped with a beer can rather than an angel. There is grime in the corners of the room and the paint peels off the ceiling. This time he finds Jack sitting in his place behind the reception desk. A girl leans on the counter talking to him and when she turns to look at Matthew he sees it is the girl with the purple eyes. She has dyed her hair a bizarre shade of aubergine.

"I've been meaning to call you," says Jack, rising.

"Thought we should have a talk."

Jack nods. "You want a coffee?"

"Sure."

"I'll get 'em. Karen, take off, okay, honey? I'll catch you later." Jack comes around the counter and pats the girl on the behind.

"You'll remember what I said?"

"Yeah, sure I will."

"Thanks, Jack." Purple Eyes reaches up and gives Jack a peck on the cheek. "You're a sweetheart."

"That's me."

Matthew waits while Jack gets the coffee from the bar. He hears voices, and a group of Spanish travellers, three boys and two girls, descend from the rooms above, ignore him and leave in a whirl of laughter and Gitanes smoke.

Jack pushes the door from the bar open with his back, holding two coffees in plastic cups. He hands one to Matthew and motions for him to come back around the counter. He pulls out a chair beside a small wooden table. Matthew sits, but Jack remains standing at the counter.

"So, have we got a problem?" Jack licks his thumb and leafs through a stack of paper.

"I hope not," says Matthew.

"So do I. Joseph's mom settled down?"

"She's fine."

"Good. Look, Matthew. I consider you a friend. I don't have many of those. You're a good guy. You've got a lot of integrity. That means something."

"Jack—" He is in no mood to be conned.

"No. I mean it. Guys like you and me, we've been through some shit, right? And we understand each other."

"I just want to be clear about Joseph."

"You made yourself clear."

"I hope so."

Jack turns his back to Matthew and seems fixated on the papers in front of him. Matthew wonders if he's reading. Jack's head twitches, and he lifts one shoulder and then the other, as though to loosen the muscles. Finally, he says, "He's all yours, Dad. All yours."

There is bitterness in Jack's voice and something suppressed, clenched between his teeth, but before Matthew can respond, he turns, smiles as though nothing is wrong and says, "Let me show you something." Jack reaches under the counter and pulls out a portfolio case. "You never ask to see my work, you know that? I want to show you my work."

The mood shift is so swift, Matthew decides he was mistaken.

Jack unzips the case and lays it on the table for Matthew to see. The photo is of a wino on the banks of the Seine. He sits with his back up against the stone wall, his feet straight out in front of him. He is a tatter of rags, newspaper stuffed beneath his open shirt. His hair sticks out and he grins at the camera like a lunatic. His hands are between his legs. His fly is open and his penis, surprisingly large, is in his hand. In the foreground the river carries the flotsam and jetsam of Paris. The next shot is a stone figure, the one from the Passy Cemetery. Her head is bowed under the weight of grief, the folds of her dress heavy as wet velvet, hair falling like a hood and hiding her face. Light filters through the branches of a nearby willow tree and combines with the lines of the draping fabric of her garment to create a mood of mourning.

Matthew blinks and looks again. The photo emits a sense of chances lost, grief and decay. "Good light. Who does the developing?"

"I do. At the squat. They have a darkroom. And yes, Joseph's been around. He's interested in this stuff, he says. But that's all. And I hadn't seen him for a while before the party. That was just a coincidence, all right?"

Matthew concentrates on the photos. The next is of Anthony with Paweena and Jariya in a booth at a café. Anthony and Paweena sit on one side, Jariya on the other. The contrast is dark, making the booth, the wall and the table all look slightly unclean, sordid—and the girls' faces look sinister, secretive. Anthony's face is the one bright spot, paradoxically, given the darkness of his skin. It is as though he was in the presence of unknown entities. Matthew doesn't want to look too closely.

There are a series of shots of circus performers from one of the Romany circuses that set up from time to time on the outskirts of the city. A young girl wearing an outfit cobbled together from a bikini and a pair of tights. Her makeup is very thick and doesn't hide her pimples. She stands in front of a trailer. A grinning man, his teeth broken, holds out a thick snake. The man wears a battered top hat. A circus horse, his legs splayed with age or fatigue, eyes the camera warily. A dwarf scowls, his stubby fingers under his nose.

There are other photos, of cemeteries, funerals, prostitutes in white vans by the porte Dauphine, crack addicts in the metros and back alleys. Skulls lining the catacombs. A woman dancing in a church. All the lighting is at once dark and unforgiving—every mangled defect showing, merciless and frail. Reality peels away layers from the subjects, exposing them in all their unconscious vulnerability.

There is one of Joseph. He is standing in a shop doorway. Slouching, his eyes half-closed. The room behind him is all darkness. In front of him the street is littered, with broken glass and dog shit in the gutter. A sign in the shop window says, "*A louer.*" For rent. Matthew winces.

The last is a triptych of Jack himself. In the centre panel he stands knee-deep in black water, looking straight at the camera. Shirtless. Powerful and battered. There are scars on his chest. Old wounds from knives, at least one that may be a gunshot. To the left is a scorched landscape, still smouldering, strewn with bodies. To the right is a graveyard with three newly dug, as yet unoccupied, graves. There is no expression on Jack's face, his mouth is open and slack-jawed, his hands droop at his sides.

Matthew feels a great weight fall to the pit of his stomach, and at the same time he has the sensation of cold air around him. "Jesus," he says.

"So, what do you think?" Jack sits before him, his hands clasped so tight the knuckles are white.

"I think they're incredible. Hard to look at, to be honest, but impossible not to look at. Have you shown these to anybody else, like to a gallery?"

"I'm doing the rounds. No takers yet."

"Won't be long. You have real talent."

Jack's face breaks into a huge grin, which he tries to suppress. "You think?"

"I know."

"Well, I wanted to show them to you."

Matthew isn't certain, but it's just possible that Jack is blushing. "I'm glad you did."

CHAPTER TWENTY-NINE

They are in the trough, past the longest night of winter, but not yet broken through to a new year. The sky looks like a drawing taken from the pages of a child's bedtime story. Something about Dream Weavers perhaps, with cloud ships, their sails billows of ether-silk, ready to set out for the Land of Nod. The full midwinter moon is so bright it gives the impression the clouds are backlit and outlined in orange as the city lights bounce off their underbellies. The vast space beyond is nearly purple, and the stars, the airplanes twinkling red and green, the satellites moving across the heavens, are ludicrously crisp and clear. On such a night it is easy to see why poets have long flocked to live in Paris.

Matthew and Jack stroll across the city—the Eiffel Tower, the Trocadéro, the grey-and-gold lantern-bedecked bridges spanning the Seine—it all looks as though it has been staged by the world's best cinematographer. The air is cold, but the vision of the white platinum moon has drawn many people out on this night between Christmas and New Year's. Bundled up in scarves and hats, they meander about, slightly drunk on beauty.

Matthew and Jack have finished off a dinner of steaks, *frites* and salad topped off with a fine red wine and a *tarte fine* at a good, cheap bistro on boulevard de Grenelle. Now, with a flask safely snuggled against Jack's belly in the pocket of an army surplus jacket that was a Christmas gift from Suzi, they head off in the direction of what Jack has described as his in-country cave.

Matthew doesn't know what he means by that, but the spell of the night is upon him and he surrenders to Jack's lead.

"I talked to my ex over the holidays," says Jack.

"How's your son?"

Jack looks disgusted. "Felony-stupid."

"Something happen?"

"Aw, he broke into his school, trashed some computers and stuff. The thing is, the kid's so dumb he decided it wasn't enough to just screw around, right? He had to have a little something to show for it, so he steals the security video camera—while the camera's recording to a remote. I mean, he doesn't steal the videotape of him and his buddies jacking the camera—no, that's someplace in the basement. He steals the actual camera, leaving the videotape so the cops have a real good shot of him, close up, hands reaching for the goddamn thing. Jesus." He glares at Matthew. "What are you laughing at?"

"Sorry, Jack. But you gotta admit—"

"Yeah, I guess. He got expelled but they're not going to press charges apparently."

"Well, there's that at least."

"What the fuck's he going to do with no education? Go into the army for Christ's sake? He's talking about it and just hangs up the phone when I tell him he's crazy."

"Sorry, Jack."

"I don't want him to end up like me, you know? Not that I'm doing so bad, but this kid's got a world of possibility and no draft to fuck him up. Why does he want to risk ending up in Yemen or Somalia or something? I thought I'd see him be somebody, you know?" He looks sideways at Matthew. "Same way Joseph's mother feels about him, I guess."

From what Matthew understands, Jack has been keeping his distance from Saida's son and there is no point in picking at a scab. "Jack, Junior's just a kid," Matthew says. "Kids get in trouble. He'll probably pull himself out."

"Last time I called, his mother couldn't even get him to talk to me. Said he was just going someplace. I said I'd come back and kick the crap out of him but she said no, that's the last thing he needed. She's got him believing I'm some whack job. I gotta get back there sometime soon. Real soon."

"So why don't you go back? Maybe she'll change her mind if you make the effort to go all that way."

"Well, there's other reasons. I shouldn't probably go back right now."

They walk toward la porte de la Muette, handing Jack's flask back and forth.

"What about you?" Jack asks. "Any yuletide greetings?"

"No."

"Nothing from the woman in the photo?"

"Nope." In fact, Matthew has put the photo away. He has not thrown it out, but it is no longer on his shelf. It is in a box, along with a photo of his mother, a collection of coins from various lands, a Swiss Army knife he got as a kid, and a yellowed copy of the first story he ever published. It had taken him a whole night to put that photo away. A whole night, three almost-dialled phone calls and a bottle of scotch.

"That okay with you?" Jack says.

"It's the way it needs to be." Matthew sees no reason to tell Jack he spent Christmas Eve with Saida and her family. They took him to midnight mass at the Lebanese church, where they sat not on pews but on straight-backed chairs, and the pictures around the walls of saints were all black-haired and bearded and far more biblical-looking than the blond blue-eyed Jesus of Matthew's Protestant youth. Then they went back to Saida's little apartment, the five of them, and ate stuffed crêpes called *attayef* and S-shaped shortbread cookies called *ghrybeh*. They gave him a navy-blue-and-green plaid scarf, which he now wears tucked up inside his coat. Matthew gave Joseph a Buddy Guy CD and a book of *American Roadside Attractions* that kept them all laughing.

He gave Saida a cedar-scented candle in a glass holder. The next day he went back with Anthony, they ate lamb, vine leaves and the sweet-potato pie Anthony had made. They sang songs and ended the evening playing, of all things, Monopoly. Matthew lost his shirt even though he owned the three green properties and all the railroads. Saida's father won.

The main traffic artery separating that-which-is-Paris from that-which-is-not-Paris is called the *périphérique*, and even at this late hour it is a rush of rubber and metal below them as Matthew and Jack cross the footbridge to the outer boundary of the great Boulogne woods. During the day the forest is mostly joggers and dog walkers and pram pushers, spattered here and there with white vans along the roadsides in which burly, silicone-breasted prostitutes ply their trade. There are pockets of land where men stand next to trees and shrubs, allowing themselves to be perused by other men, who wander the pathways like gourmets through a truffle market.

As twilight falls, however, the fresh-air fanatics and families disappear. The homeless, who move into the city during the day, return at nightfall and creep into the dark recesses of the wood, where smoke can sometimes be seen rising from their campfires. They shy away from the paths and roads—these are strictly the domain of the prostitutes who are dropped off by pimps in cars, vans and minibuses, and the sexual adventurers who often arrive in Jaguars and Mercedes. A fleet of flesh that, until this night, Matthew had only heard about in stories.

They are not a hundred metres inside the woods when the first figure steps into their path. She is tall, wide in the shoulders and slim in the hips, and she wears a fake fur coat open to show long legs encased in high black boots and black stockings hooked to the garters of a red-and-black corset. A tiny scrap of lace covers her sex. She purrs at them and reaches for them and Matthew thinks this is why Jack has led them here, and he doesn't want it. The wood is full of such forms—wearing dog collars and leather, leopard skin and tiny skirts—and some look like men beneath the makeup. Matthew swarms with contradictions. He is repulsed and yet intrigued, embarrassed and yet emboldened. He is also, he realizes, slightly afraid, for the woods are dark even with the shining moon, and the voices call out like perverse mermaids, singing from the shoals of his self-loathing.

Jack puts his hands up to ward them off, like beggars in a market, and is harsh with them and they sense something in him and back off. The two men continue and at a certain distance Matthew looks over his shoulder and is amazed at the carnival of sexual possibility. The sirens sway and touch themselves, cup their breasts in their palms, put their hands between their legs and touch themselves, and the feminine ways are often too delicate, too practised to be true so that Matthew wonders what is beneath those tiny skirts and scraps of lace. He thinks how cold they must be.

"*This* is your favourite place?" he says.

Jack laughs. "Wild, ain't it? But no, not here."

As they near one of the main roads Matthew sees that cars move slowly, crawling, as the men and sometimes couples choose and shop and compare. Now and then a door opens and someone gets in, someone gets out. It is a bustling, bursting place and Matthew's head spins. He looks around at the sad-eyed, weary, slightly desperate faces, pro and john alike; he wishes they looked as though they were having a better time. Several women appear to be ill, with track marks and bruises on their legs and arms, sores on their faces. Wads of tissues and used condoms shine white and wet on the hard earth. Without the cover of summer foliage, couplings are only semihidden by the shadows. A figure on her knees, in front of a man wearing jodhpurs and riding boots, and there, another pair, one with her face pressed to tree bark. In his pants, against his will, his penis flickers, twitches, stirs, and he shoves his hands in his pockets and looks away.

Jack leads them to a crossroad near a restaurant where every path is filled and every tree root seems to writhe and moan. A sign on the restaurant advertises itself as a venue for conferences and wedding receptions. Jack points to the Pré Catalan Garden gates.

"Through there," he says.

The gates are locked, but are not high and pose no major obstacle.

The garden is serene, a circular parkland with a path leading around pristine lawns and flowerbeds. Weeping willows dip their branches into a stream to the right, and on the far side a small log house built to look like an alpine chalet nestles under beech and poplar trees. To their left, at the far edge of the grass circle, a huge, perfectly symmetrical tree grows, its branches a fan of black lace against the eggplant sky. There is not a sound here, as though all the furtive mumbles and moans of a few feet away are barred at the gate. The moon is a weird fairy-light as they amble along the path.

"Quite a transition," Matthew says. "You'd think this place would be more popular, even at night."

"Guess the hookers don't see any reason to make their customers hop the gate when they've got the wide, wide woods to play in, and the homeless guys seem to prefer the deep forest. I guess it's harder to roust them from there. Although I never have seen a cop in here." Jack's breath forms a soft cloud around his face.

"You come here often?"

"When I need to be alone. When I need to think."

A noise in the bush to their left makes Matthew's heart thud. "What was *that?*"

"You spook too easy." Jack kicks the bush. There is a squawk and a chicken runs into the path. It is white with black spots and a red comb. It glares at Jack with an indignant eye.

"What's a chicken doing in here?" Matthew says.

"Somebody probably had it as a pet and dumped it."

"A chicken?"

Jack shrugs. "Some people think snakes make good pets."

The chicken pecks at the ground and takes a few steps toward them.

"If it's still there when we come back maybe I'll take it home," says Jack. "Maybe give it to Anthony. If we leave it here, one of the homeless guys'll cook it."

Jack fumbles in his army surplus jacket, which seems to have a thousand pockets, until he finally produces a packet of crushed soup crackers. He tears it open and scatters crumbs for the bird, and it wastes no time. "Attila the Hen," he says.

They leave the chicken, which scuttles back under the bush as they continue along the path.

"The air smells different here," Matthew says, breathing deep. "Good. Clean." He thinks of how snow smells—light and pure—and how it squeaks under your boots when the temperature is very low.

Jack points to another gate at the curve of the path. "In there."

A small sign reads "Jardin de Shakespeare." This gate is somewhat higher and they scramble up the rock wall to get footing. As they jump down on the other side, Matthew sucks the blood off his palm where he caught his hand on a jagged stone.

"What do you think?" Jack looks as proud as if he had built the place himself.

They stand at the entrance to a garden, which is a microcosm of the one outside. It is smaller, denser, and in the moonlight, undeniably magical. In front is another circle of grass, but sloping to either side lie banked flowerbeds with paths on two levels. The beds and paths gradually slant upwards until they meet at the far side of the grass over a stone hill with a flat space in front.

"It's a stage," says Jack. "They put on plays during the summer. It gets better. Come on."

As they walk, Matthew realizes the garden is named after Shakespeare not only because they put plays on here, but also because the plantings are done on themes from the plays. They walk through Macbeth's heather and twisted trees. There is a bronze plaque in the ground with words etched on it in both French and English. Matthew bends close to read it in the moonlight. The witches' speech. *"Double, double, toil and trouble; Fire burn, and cauldron bubble."* As they near a hill of stone they enter the Midsummer's Night Dream, lush flowering plants slumbering now in deep midwinter. Jack steps down from the path onto a stone by a small pond. Matthew hears sounds—clinking and the rasp of metal—as Jack fiddles with something. A lock, he presumes. A loud clank and Jack disappears. For a second Matthew doesn't know what has happened and then Jack's great shaggy head reappears.

"This is the best part. Come on in." He shoves metal bits back in his pockets. Matthew can't help but wonder what else is stored in the multitude of pouches and compartments and zippered sacs.

He steps down and sees that the hill is actually a cave, used as a backstage area, no doubt, when plays are performed. As he ducks in he has to feel his way, then he hears Jack strike a match. He has produced a candle from his pocket and lit it. It is primitive—two men in a cave by a flickering light. Matthew thinks of Neanderthals, of smugglers' caves, and foxes' dens. Jack grins and his glasses gleam with flame. He holds the candle out and turns, showing Matthew his lair. There are several wooden crates, a spool of wire, a couple of two-by-fours, a rake, a green plastic garbage can, a shovel, a cane chair. There is a set of rough stairs.

"There's an opening up top." Jack puts the candle in a nook in the stone wall and sits on the spool, gesturing that Matthew should take the chair. "Sometimes I come here and sit. I don't know if you'll get this. But it feels right to be here. Like it was made for me, sort of."

"How did you find it?"

"I roam around. But I saw it, and right away I started thinking about what it would feel like to be inside here, looking out, with earth and stone behind me. I had a place like this in Arizona.

Out in the old cliff dwellings. People said it was a shaman's cave but all I knew was that there were times it was the only place I could be. Like this place. I think—you know—I could hold a place like this."

"What do you need to hold a place for? From what?"

"Nothing. It's just a feeling. Look, I know people think that we should get over it. I know that. They say, 'The war's been over for decades. Get over it. Move on.' Well, it's not something you move on from, it's something you move on *with*—it's memory but it's more than memory—and sometimes finding a place like this, a landscape that suits you, no matter how weird, it's like floating in saltwater. It takes the weight off, lets you feel lighter. You get that, right?"

Jack's eyes are fixed on Matthew, searching for something, and Matthew wishes he knew what it was so he might give it.

"Get over it? I'd love to get over it," Matthew says. "The things you see . . ."

"The things you do . . ." says Jack and he hangs his head, his shoulders hunched and his hands dangling between his knees.

Matthew turns away from Jack. It is fearful, this attraction to the underground, and yet at the same time it is an alluring slip out of rational skin, away from the brazen head of civilization. He looks out the barred entrance of the cave onto the garden beyond. The light is silver, the shadows deep. He hears a sound behind him, but does not turn to look.

Later, Jack speaks of the Ho Bo woods and Cu Chi and Vietcong who lived for years, down below in the dark labyrinthine tunnels. How they seemed like ghosts to the Americans and Australians who searched for them. How he, being so large, couldn't fit into the tiny entrances, but he stood guard for the small guys who volunteered to go down into the earth—the tunnel rats. The ones who came back told tales of bamboo *punji* spikes smeared with dung, of roots that might be tripwires, of Vietcong who waited in alcoves with a garrotte or a knife to lay against an outstretched throat, of tomb bats and spiders, fire ants, giant centipedes and booby-trap boxes full of dozens of scorpions, of bamboo vipers and kraits. Over time, he said, he came to appreciate the perilous, perverse beauty of it, appreciated the lure of underneath.

When the moon has reached its apex and begun to slide, they emerge from the cave. Jack clicks the lock back into place. They cross the boundary from inner garden to outer and when they reach the right spot Jack bends down and makes a clicking with his tongue. The chicken, however, does not appear.

"Huh," says Jack. "Dumb bird."

At the gate, the prostitutes are even more plentiful than before, the woods alive with sound and skin. Matthew leaves Jack, who, laughing, says he's going to get himself some chicken yet. Matthew keeps his arm out, like a quarterback running for a long goal, fending off the invitations, the insistences, the taunts. Open mouths, wet tongues, open arms, red nails, the dark tangle of hair, the smell of perfume, of hairspray, the musky scent of sex mixed with mouldering leaves.

He walks faster, wanting to break into a run but holding back, for he doesn't want to look ridiculous. He is a boy again, lost in a sinister enchanted wood, full of dark magic, and he is convinced that if he hesitates for a moment, surrenders to the lure, he will be eternally ensnared. He follows his ears to the noise of the *périphérique*, is guided by the lights on the other side. When he steps out of the wood he is shaking.

CHAPTER THIRTY

It is Saida's birthday celebration. In her bedroom, she stands in bra, underwear and a new pair of black pantyhose. She chooses a skirt, orange wool with black embroidery around the hem. She holds it next to her body, trying to smooth it into something that will do, and then places it next to the other discarded items of clothing on the bed. She opens a drawer and pulls out a black long-sleeved T-shirt. It is no good. The neck is too low and she doesn't have a scarf in the right colours to hide the scars. There is a rust-coloured turtleneck, but it clashes with the skirt.

She presses her lips together in frustration and determination. It is the brasserie at the Hotel Lutetia she is going to, after all. The famous name conjures up images in her head of a Paris that dangles just outside the reach of her fingertips. A mirage that would melt away if she tried to grab it. Picasso, it is said, stayed at Lutetia. And Matisse, and de Gaulle on his honeymoon. Of course, it is not one of the spots that today's fashionable crowd flocks to; it is a place past its best days. But still, she imagines the time when it was the gathering place of writers and painters who drank fine wine and wore chic black clothes.

Yes, that's it, she thinks. Something black, with which there can be no argument. A turtleneck, a skirt—the one with the little gold coins, fake of course, dangling from the hem. An old skirt, but it will do. Anatole bought it for her not long after they were married, but she mustn't hold that against the skirt. She will wear gold earrings in her ears and put her hair in a simple braid and colour her lips red.

"*Imma,* are you ready? Matthew will be here any minute." Joseph's voice is excited, although he scrambles it with annoyance.

"I am almost ready." She steps into her skirt, pulls the sweater over her head and works her fingers quickly through her hair. When it is done she looks in the mirror above her dresser. She looks like a gypsy in mourning. It will not do. She must not embarrass Joseph. She hears footsteps in the hall.

"*Imma!*"

"Yes, yes, I am coming. Let him in." She twists her hair around her hand, uses combs and pins, and anchors it at the back of her neck, a great rope of braided hair that creates a complicated-looking twist, tendrils falling. She studies herself. It looks as though she has not gone to much trouble. Almost as if her stomach was not as knotted as her hair. She puts on lipstick and a little kohl around her eyes.

"Wow," says Matthew, as she steps into the living room. "You look great."

Joseph whistles, and she hides her smile behind her hand. "I will do?"

"You are beautiful," says her son.

Matthew is in black pants and a charcoal sweater over a white shirt. Joseph wears his usual uniform of baggy pants and sweatshirt and running shoes. "Oh Joseph, is that what you want to wear?"

"What's wrong with it?"

"It's fine," says Matthew, and she can see he means it and is glad, because she doesn't know what else Joseph has anyway. "Anthony's going to meet us there. You ready?"

She takes a deep breath. "Yes, ready."

They walk to the metro at Barbès and she tries to think of the last time she was in the 6th arrondissement. A walk through the

Luxembourg Gardens last summer after church on Sunday? Or was it the summer before? She has never gone into the Bon Marché, never to buy herself so much as a pair of gloves, let alone a dress or blouse. Never gone into La Grande Épicerie attached to Bon Marché, with its windows crammed full of sparkling sapphire-blue bottles of water, boxes of chocolates in gold foil, and silver tins of tea from India. But now she will go to Lutetia, and eat a fancy dinner with her son and her friends, like Parisians do. No, like *other* Parisians do.

As they wait on the raised outdoor platform for the train to come, three boys tumble up the stairs, their Algerian-accented voices loud. They smoke cigarettes even though smoking is not permitted in the station and slap each other's palms, laughing. From the corner of her eye Saida notices Joseph take a step away. Not so far as to be too obvious, but far enough that it might be assumed he is not with her and Matthew. As the boys pass, they look her up and down and one of them sneers and spits onto the track. She knows that they mistakenly assume she is a Muslim woman, not Catholic, and that she is fallen from grace, little more than a prostitute in their eyes, by virtue of her proximity to this non-Arab, this non-Muslim man. They remind her of her ex-husband, Anatole, who called her a filthy Arab. They are opposite sides of the same coin. He abused her because she was too much like them; these boys despise her because she is too little like them. She holds her head high and arches a brow at them, daring them to speak. She has a mother's look in her eye. They amble past in silence and when they are midway down the platform, she turns back to Matthew, picking up his words.

"I hope you like this place," he is saying. "The food's quite good. Well, I haven't been there in years. But it used to be good. We could have gone to the hotel's gourmet restaurant—The Paris—instead of the brasserie, but to tell you the truth, I prefer the brasserie. The restaurant's too formal and the food's no better—it's just snob value. Of course, we could go to the restaurant if you want. I'm sure they'd have room on a Sunday night. I could use the payphone and see."

"No, Matthew. I wouldn't like the restaurant either. The brasserie is wonderful. I would not feel comfortable in the restaurant. It's already far too generous of you."

"That's not what I meant," he says. "I just meant I want you both to do what you want tonight." And he puts his hand over his mouth as though that is not exactly what he means either.

"We know what you mean," says Saida, and it makes her relax a little, to see how nervous he is. "Don't we, Joseph?"

"Sure. It's cool," he says, his hands in his pockets. Saida and Matthew share a smile.

The train comes and at Pigalle, just two stops, they change trains to the 12 line heading south across the river to the Left Bank. It is such a world away, a completely different Paris from that of Pigalle, or Barbès, or Belleville, a universe away from the *banlieue*, the concrete suburbs around Paris—the word that literally translates as the place of banishment.

They come out of the metro at Sevrès-Babylone. Here in the 6th arrondissement there are chic shops and cafés full of pretty people and wide boulevards like Saint-Germain, with stores like Rodier, Gap, Max Mara, Crabtree & Evelyn and Burberry. It feels like Babylon, mythical and decadent. In Barbès, women tote plastic shopping bags. They wear scarves tied in knots around their heads and sandals on their swollen feet, even in the coldest weather. Here the women dangle Louis Vuitton handbags too small to carry anything of use. They dye their hair to look like they have spent the winter in the sun and wear high heels to make their legs look long and put a sexy sway in their backs. In Barbès the men sit on cement blocks on the corners, they smoke and argue about politics and why their children live without hope of good jobs. In Saint-Germain the tourists wear expensive, sensible shoes, and take pictures with digital cameras of church spires and bridges, and search for Frenchmen on bicycles carrying baguettes.

The Hotel Lutetia is on the corner; the entrance has a large striped awning and white planters with topiary puffball trees guard each side of the door. A red carpet covers the steps.

"You want to take a look in the lobby?" says Matthew, and she nods.

He takes her elbow and leads her up the stairs, chatting away to Joseph about the hotel. It was used, he says, to house the Jews who were brought back to France after surviving the concentration camps. At the entrance a man in a top hat holds the door open for them. His eyes skim smoothly over Saida, but trip slightly on Joseph.

Inside the revolving doors, the lobby is a gleaming place, with black-and-white tiles on the floor, red velvet chairs, more potted trees entwined by white roses, highly polished wooden columns and gold-and-glass display cases full of jewellery, shoes, handbags and pens. The cases stretch out in a long hall to the left and it seems infinite to Saida, like a mirror facing another mirror. In front of them the imposing reception area beckons, a curving desk of mahogany in front of three sets of dual columns in some sort of pale burled wood. Lush orchids grace the tables.

They walk past well-dressed men in dark suits and women who smell of expensive perfume. Two women stand near each other, talking into cell phones. None of these people pay them the slightest bit of attention. *We might be anyone. We might belong here.* Matthew leads them through the hotel bar, opulent with black-and-white carpet in an intricate mosaic design, and the same red velvet chairs. Groups of three and four sip cocktails and Saida notices a woman in jeans and black stiletto shoes with rhinestone buckles smoking a cigar. Joseph cranes his head to look at the ceiling, which is inlaid wood of different varieties and structured in such a way as to look almost three-dimensional. Mirrors in gold frames line the walls and soft lighting gives the room an air of quiet elegance and comfort provided. Joseph adjusts the collar of his jacket, turning it up around his ears, and looks sidelong in the mirror at the effect.

Through another door and they are in the brasserie. Having come through the lobby they are now at the main entrance of the restaurant, which is across from the bank of windows facing the street. The tables all have white cloths and the banquettes are black leather. Again, mirrors line the walls, in front of which hang brightly coloured posters in chrome frames. The carpet is red, the colour of ripened summer grapes, as are the leather cushions on the curved wooden chairs. The lights are large frosted globes.

Matthew speaks to a tall girl in a black pantsuit, gives her his name and says they have a reservation. She tells them one of their party has already arrived and asks them to follow her. She leads them to a table in the corner, on a banquette, set for four.

Anthony stands when he sees them, a huge smile on his face. He wears a red tie and white shirt under his leather jacket. "Hey," he says, "happy birthday, Saida."

"Technically my birthday was a few days ago," says Saida, but she smiles.

"Listen, make it last as long as you can."

They settle themselves and a waiter arrives to take their drink order.

"Oh, champagne, I think. Don't you?" Matthew looks at her and she can only nod. "Good, champagne it is. And Joseph, what do you want?"

"Coke?" he says.

When the champagne comes, and colas for Joseph and Anthony, they toast Saida and wish her well.

"Have you seen this menu?" says Anthony. "It says the guy who runs this restaurant is Philippe Renard. He studied at Troisgros in Rouen."

"Is that good?" Joseph asks.

"Oh, yeah. He won the Prosper Montagné Prize and the Coq Saint-Honoré." Anthony points to something on the menu. "I know what I'm having. *Dorade* with seasonal vegetables in *pistou* sauce. What about you?"

"The chicken?" says Joseph.

"A good choice. Garlic, thyme. Mashed potatoes. Why not try the snails and mushroom *cassolette* to start?"

"Okay. Sure."

"I can't imagine a North American sixteen-year-old eating snails." Matthew shakes his head.

"Why not?" Joseph watches Anthony unfold the napkin and put it on his lap, and then he does the same thing.

"We are a squeamish lot. What are you going to have, Saida?"

"It all looks very good. But perhaps the *dorade*, like Anthony? What do you call this in English?"

"Sea bream," says Anthony.

"What about the figs with goat cheese to start?"

"Yes, fine."

"What about wine?" says Matthew.

The waiter comes, recommends a wine and takes their order. Everything around Saida seems to shine and flutter. It is just a brasserie, nothing special, full of tourists in comfortable clothes and a few older Parisians. But to her eyes it sparkles and gleams. A small silver bowl is filled with tiny orange and yellow roses. The tablecloths, clean as bleached sails. Polished wood, chrome, silver. Silverware that is heavy and pleasing in the palm. Delicate wineglasses. The room is a still point from the storm of traffic outside breaking like waves against the curb, just on the other side of the window.

When the figs come they are purple and plump and the colour of yellow cream inside, brown seeds a sprinkle of popping texture. The goat cheese is crumbly and dense. Fruit and cheese rest on a bed of bitter greens. Their taste, soft and sweet on Saida's tongue, leans into expectancy and is not disappointed by the sharp smoke of the chèvre cheese. There is fig vinegar on the greens.

"So?" says Anthony. "Taste this, too." The *cassolette* with a pastry top has arrived in a small earthenware pot. He holds out a fat grey snail atop a mushroom that drips butter and cups his hand underneath so as not to spot the tablecloth. She closes her eyes and takes the meat between her teeth. A little butter dribbles down her chin. The snail is hot and rich and chewy and oozing garlic; the mushroom is a kiss of something almost sweet.

She opens her eyes and grins at Anthony, Matthew and Joseph, who laugh at her. She gives Anthony and Joseph a piece of fig, a mouthful of cheese and they groan with pleasure.

"You know, I think I might go back to New York one day and maybe open a restaurant of my own," Anthony says. "Like this, you know? Something really classy, but not so classy you can't just go and hang out with your family, right? Someplace that's about the food, not the glitz, you know?"

"I could be your sous-chef," says Joseph. "New York. The Bronx, yes!"

"The Bronx? No. Manhattan, my man. But sous-chef? Step back, now. I just don't see you in that capacity."

"No?"

Anthony punches him on the shoulder. "Naw, baby. You're more an out-front kind of guy. You can be my partner. Handle all the money and such. I'm not so good at that. Yes, sir. I can see it now. 'Joe and Tony's Brasserie Français.' I am dead serious about this. What do you think? Are you with me? Take you too, Mom. Naturally we'd need your expertise, since you are already an experienced restauranteur. Man, I could do it up right." Anthony leans back and rests his arms along the back of the banquette. Without meaning to, he brushes the head of the woman at the next table, who wears her silvery hair in a rigid swoop of hairspray and bobby pins.

"Oh! Alors!" she says and makes a sucking noise with her teeth. Her companion, a grey-skinned man with broken blood vessels along his cheeks, glares at their party. Rather, not at their party. He glares at Anthony. He glares at Joseph.

"Sorry," says Anthony, patting the lady on the shoulder. "Sorry."

"Zut!" she says and jerks her shoulder away.

The man continues to glare.

"Do I know you?" says Joseph, in French.

"Joseph!" Saida puts her hand on her son's arm.

"No?" says Joseph to the man. "Then what are you staring at?"

Saida's grip tightens. The man blinks slowly and then leans in close to his female companion to say something Saida cannot catch. The woman nods and her lips purse, her eyebrow arches.

"Aw, shit," says Anthony.

"Fucking racists!" says Joseph.

"Joseph, please." Saida looks from Joseph to Anthony to Matthew. She has never seen this expression on Anthony's face. It frightens her. Such a lovely dinner.

"BHLF," says Matthew.

"What?" says Joseph. His eyes flash beneath the frown.

"Bald Headed Little Fart. The problem is, it's gender-specific. Good for the guys only."

"Not necessarily," says Joseph, and then he laughs, and Anthony, after a moment, laughs as well.

"How about a little glass of wine for Joseph, even though it's not his birthday? Mom, what do you say?"

"I say, yes, fine."

When the main course comes, the couple next to them leave, and they all toast their parting. "To BHLF's past," says Anthony. A young German couple who smile and say "good evening" take their place.

The fish is like salted honey in a savoury, milky sauce. The vegetables are jewels—emerald asparagus, beans and spinach and bright orange baby carrots. Saida and Joseph share bits of food. Perhaps it is the wine, but Joseph talks more than Saida has heard him speak in weeks. He talks about his friends who live in the *banlieue*, as though he does not remember telling her he had no friends who live there.

"Rashid's mother is a cleaning lady for these rich women in the 16th, and now she loses half her customers to Portuguese and Filipina cleaning ladies, and they don't say so, but she knows it's because they don't want Arabs around them."

She tries not to interrupt him, not to make him stop speaking. She breaks crusty bread into small pieces and dips them in the sauce.

"There are kids who live in this garage out there. They're really screwed up. Glue and gasoline all day long. One looks about nine, but he's almost my age. He won't live long."

"No parents?" says Matthew.

"Not that he wants to go home to."

He talks about the police who won't go in these neighbourhoods and when they do, maybe once, maybe twice a year, they find all kinds of assault weapons and sometimes even explosives. Saida meets Matthew's eyes and he winks at her.

"Just because a guy walks down the street without his papers, the *flics* should not have the right to hassle him, heh? What if he just forgot them? A guy should have the right to just forget sometimes without being called a criminal." He points at Matthew with his fork. "I bet you do not get stopped, checked, do you?"

"Nope, can't say I do."

"That is what I mean. It is different for us." Joseph tilts his head from side to side and cracks his neck. The sound makes Saida wince. "In my world, just because a guy's got a record, it doesn't make him a bad guy."

"It doesn't make him a good guy either, you know?" says Anthony.

"What?"

"Everybody in the world's got it hard one way or the other. Stay mad at the injustice, let go of the resentment. That stuff will give you cancer."

"You don't understand," says Joseph.

Anthony laughs. "Yeah, the black man with the metal plate in his skull doesn't have a clue. I want the plum tart for dessert, what about you?"

The waiter, tipped off, she suspects, by Matthew, has put a candle in her tart.

Later, when Saida and Joseph are at home, Joseph looks at her and says, "Do you think Anthony meant it, when he said he'd take me to New York one day?"

Joseph lies on the couch, his arms behind his head. The blanket is pulled up to his waist and he is naked above. The hair under his arms is very thick and there is hair on his chest, a silky thatch over his muscles. His eyes are focused somewhere on the ceiling and he chews his lower lip, the fleshy, slightly misshapen bulge. Saida remembers the fig and thinks that one day very soon, if not already, there will be a girl nibbling on this fruit. It will not be long, she thinks, before he moves beyond his mother's house forever. *Oh, let him be safe!*

"I think Anthony says only things he means. But you mustn't raise your hopes, Joseph. Sometimes we can't make things happen no matter how much we want to."

"I think he means it, too," says Joseph.

CHAPTER THIRTY-ONE

The phone rings at five o'clock in the afternoon.

"Saida," calls out Anthony, "it's for you."

She is up to her elbows in minced lamb. "Can you take a message?" She never gets phone calls, unless it is her father or Ramzi, and they are both here. It can only be someone selling something she does not want.

"They say they have to talk to you. Saida?" Something in his voice makes her look up. "I think you better take it."

She rinses her hands under the tap and wipes them with a paper towel as she crooks the phone up next to her ear. *"Oui? Allo?"*

"Is this Madame Saida Ferhat?" A man's voice. Deep. Official. Her heart skips.

"Yes."

"This is Inspector Bertrand of the BDM. We have your son Joseph here."

The BDM. Brigade des Mineurs. The Police Youth Brigade.

"What has happened? What is wrong? Is he all right?"

Anthony reaches for her, and she holds up her hand to ward him off.

"He's fine. You need to come and get him. We'll want to have a chat. We are on the quai de Gesvres. Perhaps you know where?"

"Where are you?"

His voice is impatient. "Quai de Gesvres, madame. At Hôtel de Ville Métro. You will be coming now, I assume."

"Yes," and she wants to tell him she has never been there before, never to a jail to pick up her son, or for any reason, never to the Office of Public Assistance, but he has already hung up.

"What is it?" says Ramzi, who has come up behind Anthony. She looks from one face to the other, to her father sitting at the table near the counter, his coffee cup halfway to his grey lips.

"Joseph. He is at the police station—" Her voice cracks. "I have to go. Now."

"You want me to come with you?" says Anthony.

"No, I will go with her," says Ramzi.

"No one will go with me," she says and she grabs her coat and runs headlong into the street, where car horns and her brother's voice calling after her barely register. She runs up the street, her heart racing, her fingers tingling, her breath short.

In the metro there is a delay, a passenger is sick and Saida bites her knuckles to keep from screaming. There is no air in the metro and the woman in front of her smells of cigarettes and coffee. She stamps her foot and the man next to her takes a step away. She transfers at Concorde, cramming her way onto the car, pushing at rush-hour commuters who huff with disapproval.

At Hôtel de Ville the square in front of the mayor's office is oddly empty after the crush in the metro. The people crossing the square hurry with their heads down into a wind that has come up, its cold scent foretelling rain. The sky is a charcoal glower that nearly matches the dark rooftops of the ornate building. Statues of soldiers holding flags stand guard on the roof peak. Statues in every niche and along every ledge. A building guarded by heartless stones. The lamps are old, wrought iron, each post holding four glass chambers that flicker on when Saida half-jogs past, as though they are security lights searching for her.

At the quai de Gesvres the traffic going across the bridge from the Île St. Louis is backed up into gridlock and the horns scream. The building she seeks is a new one and looks severe, harsh, impersonal. She puts her hand to her heart and says a quick prayer as she skitters up the steps. The door is heavy and she must use two hands to pull it open.

Inside the air is overheated and dry. It smells of men, sweat and cigarettes. Police walk about as though nothing upsetting happens here. Three Eastern European–looking women sit on a bench against the wall. They seem old and tired, like potatoes that have sat too long in the bin. There is a glassed-in booth and a man presides behind it talking into a phone. She waits for him to finish.

"Yes?" The man has a large nose and he puts his finger in the right nostril, flicking.

"I am Saida Ferhat. I was called. My son is here."

"Name?"

"Saida Ferhat."

"His name."

"Oh. Of course. Joseph Ferhat."

"Wait there." He points to the bench where the three women sit.

There is no room for her on the bench and so she stands next to it. The women talk to each other in a language that may be Russian and do not look at her.

After a few minutes a small policeman comes out of a door with a file in his hand. He holds the door open and calls her name. She steps forward.

"Come with me, please."

He does not say anything else, and Saida follows him down a hall. There is a large room to the left full of desks and computers. On the right are more doors. There are more police here and there are boys sitting on chairs. One is wearing handcuffs. Some are smoking. Some are Arab. Some are not. One is crying and one is trying not to. One lounges with his legs far out into the corridor. The policeman kicks his foot as he walks past and tells him to sit up. The boy does.

They go into a small room where there is a metal table and four chairs. He indicates she should sit down. When she sits she holds onto her purse tightly so the shaking in her hands does not show.

"Madame Ferhat. I am Inspector Bertrand. As I said on the phone, we have Joseph here." He is a tidy man, this policeman, with hair in a crewcut, his scalp showing beneath. He has small hands and his nails are very clean. There are lines around his dark eyes, but not so much between his brows, which means he must smile a good deal, although he is not smiling now.

"Yes."

"He was detained by the police on the Champs Élysées with two other boys."

"What was he arrested for?"

"I didn't say he was arrested. I said he was detained." There is almost a smile.

"What was he doing?"

"Do you know what tagging is?"

"No." *Was he cutting tags off things?*

"Tagging is when they spray paint something, graffiti if you like, on the walls. But it is not mindless graffiti. It has a meaning. A way of staking out territory. Rather like dogs. Each tagger has a special symbol. This is his 'tag,' you understand?"

"Yes. I think so."

"Good. Is your son in a gang, madame?"

Saida's purse drops to the floor. "No! Joseph is a good boy. He is not a gang boy."

"We have all the tags, all these images, in a computer, madame. We know to whom they belong. This particular one is the tag of Rashid Charef. He is a known member of one of the Aubervilliers gangs," he said, naming one of the more dangerous *banlieue* to the north of Paris.

"But Joseph is not in the *banlieue*, there must be a mistake."

Inspector Bertrand taps his pencil on the tabletop, turning it in his short fingers so that first the eraser touches, and then the graphite point. He watches the pencil turn as though this movement is out of his control, something apart that he merely observes.

"We do not believe there is a mistake, madame. Rashid Charef was with your son."

"God! This cannot be true!"

The policeman shrugs. Then he walks around the desk and picks up her purse and, handing it to her, says, "Is Joseph's father with the family?"

Saida blushes and adjusts the collar of her coat over her scars. "No. I am with my brother and my father. There are good men in Joseph's life."

"That's good. Very good. Madame Ferhat, I'm going to be straight with you. Joseph had a can of spray paint in his pocket. We found it on him. But he wasn't doing the actual tagging. At least not when they were seen. Rashid was, and another boy, who is also known to us. Your son has not been apprehended before. He has no record." He sits on the edge of the table and leans forward with his arm across his chest so that their eyes are almost level. "Yet. This is a crucial day for your son, madame. And for you. This day I am letting him go home with only a warning. The next time we are not going to be so kind. And now his name is here, with us, you understand. We will know him the next time. You do not want us to know him. Do you understand?"

"I understand." She wishes he would not sit so close to her. His small eyes never leave her face, but trap her, pin her, and she cannot break away.

Abruptly, he smiles, pats her on the shoulder and stands up, moving to the door.

"I'll go get your son," he says.

Saida is left alone in the little room. Her knuckles are white on the straps of her purse. Her breath comes in small puffs, as though something thick and rubbery wraps around her lungs. She cannot move the weight with her breath.

When the door opens behind her she jumps up. Joseph is in the door, taller than the inspector, who holds him by the upper arm. There is a bruise on Joseph's cheek. She wants to press her palm to that bruise, to pull all the blood out of the darkening stain. She wants to slap him.

"Hi," he says.

"Oh, Joseph," she says.

"You have to sign a few papers and then you can take him home," says the inspector. "Let's go."

They walk down the hall past the boys. Following behind them, Saida sees one of the boys wink at Joseph, and smile. She has never seen this feral-looking boy before, with his bad skin and bald head and gold tooth. She stops in front of him and says, in Arabic, "And where is your family to come for you, tell me that?" But the boy just looks at her as though she were a stone, a tree, a wall.

"Madame Ferhat," the inspector says, "do not tease the animals, please."

She signs a paper that says she has been fully informed of the incident and that her son is in good physical condition and has not been harmed and that he has been warned.

"You're lucky we're not making you pay for the cleaning," says the inspector at the door. "You're lucky you're not scraping dog shit from the sidewalks for a month or two."

"What do you say, Joseph?"

"What?" He looks at her blankly.

"I said . . ." She grips his arm and pinches, but he does not flinch. "What do you say? You do not thank him for not charging you? For letting you go home instead of to the detention centre?"

"Thank you," says Joseph, but he skews his eyes away to the left as he says it.

"Don't come back," Inspector Bertrand says as they step out. "Make me lose my bet."

They do not speak on the way home. Saida begins to speak a hundred times but the words catch behind her teeth and twist into screams, and so she clamps her jaws around them. She manages not to cry until she gets off the metro and crosses le boulevard de Rochechouart to rue du Faubourg Poissonnière. Then the tears spill out. She wipes them away, but they are faster than she is and soon they drip down her chin.

"Imma," Joseph says, and he puts his arm around her.

"No," she chokes.

"I'm sorry."

"No," she says and tastes salt.

In the apartment, she lurches into her bedroom and closes the door, saying only, "Call your uncle. Tell him what has happened. You tell him." She lies on the bed, pulls the pillow over her head and cries herself to sleep.

CHAPTER THIRTY-TWO

It was the worst kind of night, not one in which Matthew couldn't sleep, precisely, but rather one when he could not *stay* asleep. He would fall unconscious and suddenly awaken ten minutes later, his stinging nerves hypervigilant; then he was wide awake for half an hour or more of restlessness followed by ten minutes' black and finally the giant, full-body twitch. At five o'clock, he gave up and stood in a warm shower until the ghosts melted down the drain.

He leaves the apartment before nine, stalking a landscape that fits his mood and at last wanders over to the Medici Fountain in the Luxembourg Gardens. He sits on a green metal chair by the side of the long reflecting pool that is surrounded by plane trees. At the end of the pool in a tumble of stone looms the statue of Polyphemus, the jealous Cyclops, spying on the lovers Acis and Galatea as they embrace. Stone walls border the pool, rising as they approach the statue. And at the same time the ornamental vases on the wall get smaller, creating an optical illusion that the water slopes downwards. Matthew meditates on the brooding, disturbing statue. It is the moment before murder. Its stasis is a mercy for the lovers, however it is a cruel piece of amber in which to catch Polyphemus, doomed forever to watch his beloved, the uncaring Galatea, in the arms of the man she has chosen instead of him. In the myth there is no such reprieve for love or for revenge, because moments later, the tale tells, Polyphemus lets out a great anguished cry and Galatea escapes by flinging herself into the sea, but Acis is not so lucky. The Cyclops hurls an enormous boulder at him, crushing him to death. The place is a reminder of the inevitable slaughter of joy, a bower dedicated to melancholy.

Matthew's muscles begin to relax as he sits there staring at the moment just before brutality wins. Yet he cannot help sympathizing with the Cyclops. Betrayed by the tyranny of unrequited love, he could not help what he became, neither his nature nor his horrible passions. Matthew wonders whether it is his compassion for these volatile, malleable creatures, irrevocably transformed into brutes, that cripples him. He wonders too if he is becoming one of them.

He thinks about Joseph. The truth is, there probably are not many possibilities for Joseph, who clearly is not going on to one of the *grandes écoles* and will not be a lawyer, doctor or politician. He will work in the restaurant, or as a house painter or construction worker and there is nothing wrong with that in principle; but Matthew senses Joseph will be unhappy, is already unhappy, and impatient to boot.

Saida was beautiful that night at the restaurant. Her mouth had looked like a soft ruby. Several times her knee grazed Matthew's under the table. Or had his grazed hers? Since the cops picked up Joseph, she is a mere ghost of herself. On one hand, Matthew tells himself, it is no big deal—just a little graffiti—but on the other hand, it may be the tip of the iceberg. *Banlieue* gangs. He is familiar with all the stories—stolen cars chopped and sold to Russian mobs in exchange for guns. Young girls gang-raped and burned alive. House invasions. Caches of Kalashnikovs. Drug lords. Pickpocket rings are the least of it. Graffiti a mere addendum. Two days ago a blaze lured police and firemen to one of the housing estates and when emergency vehicles arrived, rocks and Molotov cocktails and gunfire greeted them. Two cops are in hospital.

Trouble everywhere. Ghosts.

Every time he closed his eyes the night before, he had seen the faces of a father and daughter huddled up against a wall in Hebron. Begging for mercy. He had seen again the glint of gunmetal and all the possibilities—for redemption, for damnation—that glimmer contained. Yes. *I should have picked up the gun.* No. *Reporters don't pick up guns.* Pick it up or let it lie. What did it matter? He had walked out of the shadows, crossed over into the circle of hell. Blood in the sand. On his hands. The memory is fire.

You're getting closer, he thinks.

Yes. The book moves along. Brent is a happy agent. Enough sent to him to keep the publishers happy. Soon, Matthew is going to have to write about Hebron. And so . . . But not yet.

A light drizzle begins to fall from a dirty, towel-rough sky. He sits until the damp seeps into his clothes and then on a whim he decides to wander over to the Abbey Bookshop in the Latin Quarter on rue de la Parcheminerie. He looks for something about God and sex and sorrow by Morley Callaghan, or something by Orwell, or Beckett even, something worth a second reading. In his present state of mind, nothing is, and he turns away from the stacks, disgusted. He walks to the Square du Vert-Galant, the small park shaped like the bow of a ship, at the end of Île de la Cité. The drizzle has stopped and a cluster of tramps shares a bottle of wine, sitting precariously with their legs dangling from the stone wall. A young couple loll on a bench, he leaning back on his elbows, she straddling him, her hand on his groin. A woman walks a long-haired, bristly-looking dachshund. Matthew looks down the Seine. The vast brooding bulk of the Louvre is to his right, the Eiffel Tower pierces the grey sky in the distance, all the dark, muddy water is below him. The water is mesmerizing. Hypnotic. An empty plastic water bottle bobs by. He watches it float downstream and disappear. It takes some effort, but at last he turns away and heads home. Not Hebron yet. One chapter left before he has to face it. Chechnya.

As I strolled through the medieval-looking market, I thought the name of the town was still apt. In 1818, General Alexei Yermolov built a fortress in the North Caucasus. His aim was to intimidate the wild and rebellious people living there. He named his fortress Grozny, which means "Terrible."

I walked the unpaved road, over the stone and mud, crowded with livestock and an occasional Eldorado or Mercedes. Women shook cabbages and bunches of pale carrots at me from behind their vegetable carts. Men wore sheepskin hats and carried knives in their belts. Ruslan, my Chechen guide, and I walked past the stalls where people sold turnips, lamb carcasses, bricks of hard black bread and vodka, to the arms market next door where men haggled over Kalashnikovs and rocket-launchers.

"They get these guns from the Russian soldiers," said Ruslan. "Ironic, no? This is the good word? They barter for these guns. Russians—they love their vodka." He spit on the ground. "They go trade their guns for bottle. The gun is sold to a Chechen and he use it to kill this same guy later."

Almost all the windows in the buildings were gone. The remains of a ten-storey apartment building with a missing façade tilted and hung, defying the laws of gravity in such a way that it seemed drawn by a surrealist. Next to it stood, or partially stood, the corpse of what was once probably a concrete-block garage or workshop. Now half the building was nothing but a shambles of caved-in rubble and the other half had only part of the roof and walls intact. Words were painted on the outside wall. Ruslan told me what the words meant, "People they are living here."

The air was bad. Water service was sporadic at best and the odour of sewage was over everything, including the blood-and-meat smell of the markets. We passed a small coffee shop, no more than an alcove in the bottom of a structure that looked as though it might collapse at any moment. Strings of coloured wool hung from the doorway.

"We go in," said Ruslan, holding the makeshift curtain back. "I know them."

Inside, the air was heavy with unwashed flesh and smoke and the perfume of the thick coffee rising from tiny chipped cups. A man with a face so wrinkled he looked like an apple doll set bowls of stew in front of us. It smelled of mutton and was mostly grease.

Ruslan said something to the man, who nodded, laughed and made a gesture, holding up his hand to indicate Ruslan should wait there.

"What's up?" I said.

"There is a woman—a fortune teller here. I am hearing she is to be good." Ruslan shrugged. "We will see."

A small woman came out from behind a flowered sheet tacked up at the back of the room. She beckoned us to come.

"Bring you coffee," said Ruslan.

"You go. I'm not interested in knowing the future."

"No. You come. Pick up you cup." The Chechen walked away and I followed as was expected. Men looked at me from the corners of their eyes, tense, suspicious. Ruslan said something and the men relaxed. The press was welcome. They knew reporters generally favoured the little guy with the big foot on his throat.

We sat on stools around a barrel the old woman used as a table. She wore a red-and-yellow scarf over her head and layers of dresses, shirts and sweaters, all of different colours and all unwashed. Her hands were farmer's hands, gnarled, strong and thick.

Ruslan told me to give her some coins. She had us drink our coffee, and when we were finished, she emptied my cup and then overturned it. She waited and spoke to Ruslan, shaking her head and holding her hands upward.

"What's she saying?"

"She tell me her nephew he picked up a tape-recorder he find on the ground. It explode in his face. Russian booby trap. Lose an eye. And he blind now, his right hand probably never work good again."

"Tell her I'm sorry."

"Husband killed by the Russians, both sons taken away. She don't know where."

"Tell her I'm sorry for her."

"She knows. She want you to know is all. To tell people what happen here."

"I'll do my best."

"She say they hate us because we are Muslim."

The woman picked the cup up and held it in the bowl of her hands. The grounds had dried and left patterns on its sides, at which she peered intently. She began to speak and Ruslan translated.

"You have fire in your past, fire in your future, she say." The woman rubbed her belly. "You must be careful of you stomach. She see sickness there."

"Why do you think I'm not eating that stew?"

"She see a broken chain—a love broken—and a beetle, so there will to be hard challenges."

"Nothing good, then?"

Ruslan spoke to the woman and she shook her head, shrugged, said something.

"She see an owl—what we call night eagles—see things of the darkness. And a bat, not good things. But also she see a tent and a tree, shelter and life, but not now, later, far down the cup, away from the handle. Not here. She say maybe you shouldn't look so much into the flames. Burn the eyes, then you see nothing but shadows."

Ruslan's fortune said he would have grief, but that he would travel, "Maybe to America," he said. A sword foretold his enemies would fall and a wheel meant fortunes would change. The old woman said a dark man would find him a good bride, which made him laugh.

As we left, she told us to stay away from water.

"Not really a problem around here," I said.

The next day as we travelled south, with Leon from The Times, *toward the checkpoint Assinovskaya, we came upon a bridge that only moments before had been the target of a Russian bombing raid. People, at least those who could, ran through the streets. Leon and I got out of the Volvo to take a look. Bodies were scattered about, and body parts. A shopping bag, with turnips and bread and potatoes leaking out, looked as though someone had dropped it in haste, and then I realized an arm was still attached to it. The bridge was only partially destroyed, and before we knew it the planes returned. We barely had time to dash back to the battered old Volvo, which was missing the doors on the driver's side. Even as we spun the wheels trying to turn, an explosion rocked the vehicle. Ruslan screamed, his leg full of shrapnel.*

I drove to the small hospital for war veterans in Staraya Sunzha.

"That fortune teller was no good," said Ruslan, as the nurses worked on his wound. "She told you to stay away from water, not me."

"Maybe she was right about the bride," I said.

A huge chunk of flesh was missing from Ruslan's calf. There was no anaesthetic and he broke out in a sweat when a nurse began cleaning it, but he did not cry out. It was not clear when he would be walking again, but whenever that was, the doctor said, he'd never again be free of a limp.

"You need a new driver. Try my cousin, Shaikhan."

I left Ruslan with some money and my thanks and went looking for the cousin. But Shaikhan had already disappeared into the mountains to join the rebel forces.

By the time Matthew finishes, it is evening. He eats some bread and cheese, washes it down with tap water and goes to sleep. He does not dream.

CHAPTER THIRTY-THREE

A week has passed since Matthew wrote about Chechnya. He is already getting back the first chapters from the publisher with editorial comments. Change this. Change that. Take out this. Put that in. It's not fiction, he thinks, how can I change what happened? If only he could.

He sits at his desk in the predawn darkness. He feels he must begin as the sun is coming up, for it will give him as lengthy a time as possible of daylight in which to write. He does not want to write this part in the dark.

He goes to the kitchen and plugs in the kettle. Boils water for an egg. Pushes down the toaster button. Simple things. Good rules for beginning: Have something in the belly to ground yourself. Do it slow, but when the time comes—do it.

When he finishes in the kitchen, he carries a large cup of coffee and a plate with a boiled egg and toast to the table by the window. He eats while the sun begins to rise.

And so. The time has come.

Begin with the beginning of that day. He writes a sentence. *I woke up in a puddle of sweat and tears, my heart hammering.* He wills himself not to read it back. He writes two more. *The fire dream had come back. It came back after Rwanda.* The pen begins to move of its own volition. *The narrow bed was hard and damp. My hair was plastered to my skull and my sinuses throbbed from the smell of disinfectant in the room.*

I hadn't had a good sleep in so long it was hard to remember what being rested felt like. I was thinner even than normal, and there was a patch of festering skin on my right thumb, at which I couldn't stop picking. Slowly the words come. Light moves across his desk. He discovers he is chilled and pulls a sweatshirt over his head. Pages begin to pile up beside him. He keeps writing. Moving through the day like someone drugged. The phone rings and he lets the machine get it.

"Matthew? You in there? Pick up if you're in there." Jack's voice floats from the machine. "Where you at, man?"

Matthew ignores it. His pen runs out of ink and he finds another and keeps on writing. It gets dark and he turns on a light. The phone rings again and he disconnects it. He vows to keep the pen in his hand and keep writing until it is done. He falls asleep at some point and the next day begins again. He hears noises in the hallway. Someone knocks and slips a note under the door. He reads it much later. "I came by to see you. I'll come by tomorrow. Just checking to see if you're okay. Anthony." Matthew writes, "Fine. See you later," on the back and tacks it to the door. Anthony returns the next day, sits outside on the step and sings. He sings Leadbelly songs. "In the Pines," and "Good Night, Irene," and "Easy Rider." For a time in the afternoon as the shadows lengthen, Matthew sits on the other side of the door, listening, but he still does not open it.

It is the smell, finally, that makes him open the door. He is hungry and the scent of meat is too much for him. Anthony smiles as if they have seen each other yesterday and holds out a heavy Dutch oven.

"Smells good," Matthew says and his voice sounds as though it comes from someone else, from somewhere else.

"It's a three-beef daube. The trick is the cloves and nutmeg. It's like a perfume, you know, it brings out the scent of the flesh. Plus the orange zest. You can leave it out, but it doesn't taste right."

In the kitchen, Anthony tucks a tea towel in his belt and serves up the stew while Matthew watches him from a chair. Anthony moves quickly. He opens drawers, looking for cutlery; he opens cupboards, looking for plates. He has brought salad in a bag and a crusty loaf that he cuts into thick slices.

"See," says Anthony, "you have to make the daube the day before and let it rest so you can get all the fat off, but leave the flavour." The scent of thyme and bay, oranges, nutmeg and onions mingle with the beef and fill the kitchen. Matthew finds his hands are shaking and is afraid he might faint before the food reaches his lips.

They are quiet while they eat. Billie Holiday sings about blessing the child. Matthew is not ready for spoken words yet. All his words are scribbled on the pages strewn around the room. It is not until Anthony puts coffee down in front of him that he is wholly back in the residence of his body.

"This is wonderful," he says. "Thanks. I don't get it, though. Why bother? Why sit outside my door?"

"Because you wouldn't open up."

"Ah."

"Didn't want you getting lost. I've been lost. Not such a good place."

"True."

"Paweena left me."

"Aw, shit. I'm sorry, Anthony. Here I am all wrapped up in myself."

"No, it's all right. I think I would have ended it myself soon. Doesn't matter what I gave, it was never enough. I don't think that girl's ever going to be satisfied. She pitched a major fit about me being late one night, but I think she was mad 'cause I wouldn't buy her some furniture she wanted. Just came to the end of the line on this one. I think it surprised her that I didn't cave, you know? I'd bet she thought threatening to leave would scare me into paying up." Anthony laughs softly. "But you have to know when to call it quits."

"Sorry. I'm really sorry."

Anthony shrugs, as though trying to shake off the hurt. "Nothing to be done. Gotta suck it up. So, looks like you've been working."

"Yes. I've been working." Matthew is still trying to figure out the complicated process involved in moving his teeth and tongue and lips and producing sound.

"How's it going?"

"Well. I got past the graveyard this time."

"What's it all about?"

Matthew holds the coffee mug in his hands, looking down into the liquid, as much a mirror as a well. "It might be about what you said. Getting lost. Losing things you didn't know you could lose."

"Things get lost, things get found. That's what I learned when I got my head whacked open."

"Yeah?"

"The world looked different after, let me tell you. The first few years I was like a kid, emotions all over the place. Like a thirteen-year-old. Depressed as hell, most of the time. My people, they didn't understand. I wasn't the same person. My personality had changed. I knew that, just couldn't do anything about it, and I couldn't reconcile myself to life the way it was. That kind of shit just wasn't supposed to happen to me. Only thing I ever wanted to be was a cop. Had to deal with a lot of rage. Still do, some days. Rage and confusion." Anthony stands. "Come on, let's clean up while we're finishing the coffee."

Matthew follows him into the kitchen and pours apple-scented liquid soap into the porcelain sink, runs hot water over it until the sink is half-full. He pats the bubbles, liking the feel of buoyant, springy softness. "So, how did you finally come to accept the way things are?"

"Some days I don't. But, believe it or not, there's a trade-off. It's like looking at things from a different place. Maybe not better, but not worse. From the top of a different mountain, is what my auntie used to say. I used to look at my fingers and see them, right? See them clear. Four fingers and a thumb." He holds his hand up in front of his face, but looks past it, at Matthew. "What was beyond was there, too, but . . ."—he pauses, looking for a word—"unnoticed. Now I sometimes don't see my fingers, but I see you."

"I don't get it."

"Sometimes it's better to forget about myself. Truth is, maybe I wasn't that squeaky clean before. Maybe a personality change wasn't such a bad thing. Seeing the truth hurts, man. It always hurts. I left some damage in my wake, back in the day. I look back on who I was, and I don't recognize that dude. Well, most of the time, anyway. I mean, I know he's still in there somewhere, but long as he stays where he should, well, *that* I can reconcile myself to." Anthony laughs softly as he dries a plate. "Truth is, I consider my accident a sort of redemption. Something like a back-assed state of grace.

"The only thing I remember about the attack was a light, like an explosion of light, inside my head. Streaks, shooting out every which way. Zigzagging. I kept seeing it, this map, this design, like a city of light. Maybe that's why I came to Paris." He laughs softly. "City of God. City of Lights. Something dazzling. Something that radiates. Something sending out rays of light."

It is somewhat surreal, the comfort Matthew takes in the washing of a dish, the shine of a clean glass, the feeling of a full belly and the conversation of a friend. "You ever heard of Le Corbusier?" he asks.

"Nope."

"An architect who developed a plan he called The Radiant City. He proposed razing the centre of Paris, building skyscrapers and turning it into a 'vertical city,' free of the bustle, the congestion, the dirt. Everything nice and clean and orderly and regimented, full of happy, smiling citizens."

"Vertical city? Sounds like the projects." Anthony chuckles.

"Exactly. It's what North American public housing was based on. He imagined Utopia and created blasted neighbourhoods, social destruction. His idea of saving us all. Sorry, Anthony, but I just don't think I believe in redemption."

Anthony smiles. "To free from distress," he says, as though quoting from the dictionary. "To remove the obligation of payment, and to exchange for something of value."

They finish cleaning the kitchen. Anthony insists on spraying the counters with Javel and running first a broom and then a damp mop over the floor, which is how, he says, a good restaurant kitchen always does it. The kitchen is now cleaner than it has been in weeks, maybe months.

"That's fine," Anthony says, proudly surveying the shining surfaces. "So, can I read it?"

"What?"

"What you wrote. Can I read it?"

It is absurd, of course, that he has not considered this, not considered that someone must read what he has written, that someone other than he will render judgment. "Oh, I don't know."

"I'd like to."

Who better, really, than Anthony?

"Well, all right, then." Matthew hands him the papers.

"Have you read it over yet?"

"No, actually, I haven't."

"So, let's do it this way. You read it to me."

"I don't think I can."

"Sure you can," says Anthony. "It's better that way."

He will have to read it sometime, he realizes, and what better place than here, what better time than now? His mouth is dry and he pours them both a scotch before he begins.

The fire dream had come back. It came back after Rwanda. The narrow bed was hard and damp. My hair was plastered to my skull and my sinuses throbbed from the smell of disinfectant in the room. I hadn't slept much the past few nights. In fact, I hadn't had a good sleep in so long it was hard to remember what being rested felt like. I was thinner even than normal, and there was a patch of festering skin on my right thumb, at which I couldn't stop picking.

I got up. Urinated. Splashed water on my face. Threw back the curtains. Light helped.

An hour later Josh Anderson and I sat on a small terrace. Josh was a photojournalist, and not happy to be in Hebron. He had allowed me to talk him into shooting this story about the Christian Peacemaker Teams only because nothing else was going on at the moment. "No photo ops," he said. Photo opportunities or not, tensions ran high in Hebron, and the air was thick with random anxiety, but this was the way of things in the West Bank. We sipped coffee and talked, wasting the two hours until our scheduled meeting with Susan Carver.

The Christian Peacemaker Teams had arrived in Hebron, as they put it, to put themselves in the way of violence. A nonpartisan group of mostly Quakers and Mennonites, they came to Hebron not only to try to calm the tensions, but also to document human rights violations, and I admired them, even if I thought they were too idealistic for their own good. They had been escorting both Palestinian and Israeli children to and from school.

A Palestinian suicide bomber had blown up a bus in the area two weeks before and died, along with five other people—including three from the same family, one of them an infant. The next week Israeli settlers had attacked CPT volunteer Susan Carver and two Palestinian schoolgirls. They kicked the girls to the ground and dragged them through the streets by their hair. The settlers hurled threats and abuse at them. A man knocked Carver's glasses off, threw her down and kicked her repeatedly in the back. Another pointed an Uzi and said, "This is my country and any foreigner who comes to be with these Nazis will pay with their life." Now the Israeli soldiers had arrested one of the settlers, a teenaged boy, for taking part in the assault.

There was to be a trial. I wanted to do a story on both sides of the incident because it seemed to me to be the perfect metaphor for the insanity of the unending conflict.

It was hot and dusty and my skin felt gritty. Josh had just told a joke involving a cameraman, a camel and a cactus, and I was in mid-laugh when I heard gunfire. Shrieks came from the balcony above us. Looking up, I saw a man pointing and when I followed the sightline I saw an Israeli soldier, who looked to be barely out of his teens, standing with his foot pressed against the neck of a young Palestinian. The soldier put his gun against the boy's forehead. At the same moment, a stone hit the soldier solidly in the mouth, producing an instant bloom of blood and teeth. He stumbled backward and the boy got up and ran. The soldier fired and the boy fell, screaming. Other soldiers shot into an alley that led to a mosque.

"Fuck, fuck, fuck," cried Josh, clicking off shot after shot with his camera. "I don't know if I got that. I don't fucking know."

We ran toward the action. The soldiers were taken by surprise by a number of youths armed with slingshots, weapons that are far more deadly than they sound. Think of David and Goliath. The Israelis, some no older than the rock-hurling Palestinians, turned to defend themselves. Women screamed and ran for cover in every direction. The soldiers took refuge behind a building in which the shutters quickly slammed shut. I imagined the occupants cowering behind upturned furniture in darkened rooms. There were Palestinian gunmen, at least three of them, on the rooftops and the air rained stones. I grabbed a couple of trash-can lids and tried to shield our heads. My ears buzzed with the lethal whine of gunfire, the ping of ricocheting bullets and the thud-crack of stones. The soldiers moved back to the marketplace, trying to make it to the army post. We followed them, Josh with his camera up to his eye. I attempted to keep us under cover while at the same time making sure Josh didn't stumble.

"Holy fuck," said Josh and pointed across the square. There, huddling behind a low concrete partition wall, was a man and a child. The little girl looked no older than seven. She wore a red thob and had a white scarf on her head. The two were trapped in the crossfire. The man screamed and took the

little girl's scarf to wave like a flag over his head. He kept his right arm and leg extended, bent backward around the little girl, trying to pull her behind his body. The concrete wall offered little protection. Bullets zinged around them, hitting the ground in soft puffs of dust and stone shards.

"Oh, shit," I said, as Josh and I crouched behind the corner of a market stall.

It went on for a long time. Both sides were entrenched, well covered and unyielding. Minutes ticked. The man never stopped crying out, calling that there was a child there, his daughter, don't shoot, don't shoot. It was unclear whether either group of shooters could hear him over the sound of gunfire. More time passed. The man tried to make more room behind his body for the little girl. He was crying. For a long time she shrieked, her tiny mouth wide open, her eyes shut, her hands at her ears. There was a momentary lull in the shooting and the man tentatively raised his hand, began to stand.

"Come on," I urged them under my breath, "come on."

A volley of bullets made the man duck back down. A body fell from the rooftop, landing on the ground nearby with a thud. A Kalashnikov automatic rifle clattered next to it, the strap still wrapped around the wrist. Puffs of brown dirt floated in the air. The ground changed colour as blood, dark as garnet, seeped from mouth and ear and nose.

"Stop fucking shooting, you assholes!" I yelled. "Stop! Stop shooting!"

The little girl went silent, and for a moment, I thought she had been shot, but no, she was probably so terrified she'd gone catatonic. The man waved the white scarf again, crying out to both sides to hold their fire, just for a moment, just a small moment.

They did not hold their fire.

Fifteen minutes went by like this. My heart raced, my stomach clenched in a knot of futile rage. I looked at the gun lying in the sand. Now and then I yelled, but it was useless. I couldn't bear it. Again, the rifle lying near the body of the Palestinian drew my eyes. I couldn't stand by and watch. It was impossible, when the answer was right there in front of them, so simple, so perfect. I decided that if someone explained it to them they could not fail to see the rightness of it.

I stood up.

"What the fuck are you doing?" Josh tried to pull me down, but I shook him off.

"They'll get killed."

"You'll *get killed!"*

"I have to make them stop," I said, stepping into the open space. I held my hands up and turned slowly. "Stop!" I shrieked, my voice sharp with fury. "If you bastards want to blow each other to kingdom come, be my fucking guest! But leave these people alone. Do you hear me? Leave them ALONE!" The gun was so near my foot. I wondered if I would pick up the gun. I wondered what I would do with it if I did pick it up. Part of my brain told me that reporters do not pick up guns; another part of my brain told me that these petty distinctions did not matter in a world such as this one. If I picked up the gun I could shoot the shooters, never mind which side. They all deserved to die for what they were doing to the little girl.

I heard a noise and turned to see Josh stepping behind me, the camera swinging around his neck, Josh's hands outstretched toward me.

"Matthew, for Christ's sake!" he hissed, as though speaking softly would draw less attention.

"Leave me alone. I'm okay," I said. "They're going to fucking stop, I tell you."

For a moment, it seemed as though they would. There was a pause, perhaps because both sides were in shock at the sight of lunatics in their midst. It was a choice between gun and girl. I turned and smiled at the man and the little girl. The man's eyes were glazed and frozen and his face was drenched in tears. He made an infinitesimally small move.

The shock of the impact sat me down on my ass in the dust. It was as though someone had jammed a hot iron rod into my middle. I heard screaming, a lot of gunfire, and then less screaming. And then, only I was left to scream, the sound—the squeal of a pig being slaughtered—came from my own mouth. I raised my head and looked toward Josh who lay in the dust and blood, next to the Palestinian and the gun. Whatever I had intended, I would never reach the gun now. Then I turned my head, which took a great deal of effort, and looked at the father and daughter, crumpled in each other's arms. They were as still as the stone wall behind them.

And nothing was the same after that.

Matthew begins to cry.

Anthony reaches over and pats him on the shoulder. "Hey, Matthew," he says, as he pats him. "Hey there, hey there."

CHAPTER THIRTY-FOUR

The next night Matthew goes to the Bok-Bok to celebrate the breakthrough and to buy Anthony a few drinks by way of thanks. He feels lighter, as though the world is crisper, clearer. The wraith light of memory that had blurred his vision is no longer so powerful. He has spent the day editing, and is convinced the centre will hold. He has spoken to Brent. His future is, if not aglow with possibility, at least not such a lump of dark coal. Although the burden of guilt has not lessened, he feels, for the first time, as though he may be capable of shouldering his share.

It is early in the evening and the bar is not yet as full as it will be in a few hours. Anthony and Matthew sit at a table past the bar. Anthony talks of his new morning ritual. He walks up to Sacré Coeur each morning and watches the sun rise. He talks of how the city glows and how even on days when it rains there is a moment as the sun comes up over the horizon when, below the cloud cover, a band of gold appears under the metal-grey blanket above. Matthew listens and considers getting himself such a ritual, something to set him up for the day, to put it in perspective.

Anthony nudges Matthew and points with his chin to the door.

Jack comes in with Suzi. She looks worse, much worse, than the last time Matthew saw her. Although she wears no wig, which usually makes her look younger and fresher, she now looks like a prisoner of some sort. Grey and hollow-cheeked. Her eyes are wide and scrambled. Muscles intermittently jerk, and even beneath the oversized coat she wears, her body shivers.

"Somebody needs a fix," says Matthew. Like a bag of sand with a hole punched in it, he can feel the optimism of a few minutes before drizzling out of him.

Suzi makes for the bathroom without greeting either of them. Dan, clearly displeased, says something to Jack. Jack merely shrugs and comes toward them, his hands in his pockets. Dan stands scowling, looking after him.

"She all right?" says Matthew.

"She will be," says Jack, and his eyes flick to the bathroom door. "What's up?"

"We're celebrating Matthew's writing," says Anthony.

"Oh yeah, why?"

"Because he's writing."

"I got over a hump." Matthew kicks a chair back with his foot for Jack to sit down. "Hebron."

Jack smiles and holds out his hand. "You wrote about Hebron? Hey, well done!" Matthew takes his hand; Jack encloses it in both of his, and shakes it. "Big step, man, big step."

"Thanks, Jack. Really. Not a big deal to many people, I guess, but, well."

"Yeah. I know. I *know*."

"Let me get you a drink. What'll it be?"

"Just a beer, thanks."

At the bar, Dan brings him another round of drinks and says, "I don't like this shit in here. Jack knows that. So does Suzi. She's always kept it in line. Until recently."

Matthew nods but says nothing. He hands Dan the money.

Dan crumples the bills in his fist. "Cops leave me alone. We have an understanding. I don't want that upset. She's gonna get banned."

"Where else would she go?"

Dan snorts. "Are you kidding me? Chick like that, she'll always find some stinking hole to climb into." He turns away to the register.

He brings the drinks back to the table. "Listen, Jack. None of my business maybe. Probably. But what's up with Suzi? She seems pretty strung out."

"Some thing with her kid. She was living with Suzi's ex and now she's run away. You know what junkies do when the shit hits the fan. I don't know. I've had about enough, to tell you the truth."

"She's been in the bathroom a long time. Maybe you should check on her," says Anthony.

"Leave her. She's nodded out is all. She'll stumble through in a while." Jack licks the foam off his moustache.

"Dan's not happy," says Matthew.

"Dan's never happy."

They say nothing after that, for it is hard to talk when Suzi is so close to them in the bathroom with a needle in her arm. Dan keeps looking at the bathroom door as well. Old Charlie, sitting at the bar next to John, has stopped arguing with him and the two sit quietly, watching Dan, watching the bathroom door.

"I better go check," says Jack after a few minutes.

"Might be a good idea," says Anthony. "You want me to go?"

"Nope."

Jack disappears into the bathroom and Matthew fights the urge to get up and walk out of the bar, all his equilibrium gone, nothing but an empty sack inside his chest now.

They can hear Jack calling Suzi's name. And then there is a loud bang and the sound of cursing. Matthew and Anthony stand. Dan comes around the bar with his crowbar in his hand.

Jack comes out of the bathroom. His face is ashen. "Call an ambulance. She's fucking OD'd."

"Not in here," says Dan.

"What?" says Matthew.

"No ambulances, no cops in here. You get her out. I'll make

the call. Tell them there's an overdose in the courtyard. Not in here."

"Are you serious?"

But Jack has already run back into the bathroom and reappears a moment later with Suzi in his arms. Her tights are around her knees. The skin on her thighs is mottled and the veins are red and blue. Her face is blue, her eyes rolled up. Her mouth is open and a trickle of thin vomit dangles. There is more vomit on her chest.

"Make the call," Jack growls at Dan as he shoulders past him.

Anthony and Matthew follow Jack up the stairs. It is cold outside and garbage bedecks the courtyard. "Where's her coat?" says Matthew.

"I'll get it," says Anthony as he disappears down the stairs.

"Is she breathing?" says Matthew.

"I don't know. I think so." Jack holds her until Anthony comes running back upstairs with her coat. Then he kicks a piece of cardboard to flatten it out and lays Suzi on it. He covers her with the coat.

"She's dead," Matthew says. There is no movement, nothing. He looks at her lying there and she has become just another body, another mass of tissue, another corpse. He steps back.

Anthony leans down and puts his head to her chest. "Not quite."

"You guys go," says Jack. "I'll stay. I'll say I found her here. It's okay. There's nothing you can do." He rubs his hands over his face. His features have sagged, fallen, and he looks ten years older. He looks back at the Bok-Bok, as though considering returning to the bar.

"I'll stay too," says Anthony.

"Sure, me too," says Matthew, although all he wants to do is run. Though shame burns him, presses into him like a red-hot poker, he does not think he can bear to see another body. Suzi's shoe has fallen off somewhere and her foot is so small, twisted in. She looked like an ungainly, pigeon-toed teenager.

Jack turns on Matthew and thuds him on the shoulder. The blow knocks him back several feet. "No! Fuck that. No. I don't want you here. She's my girl. She's not yours! Don't touch her."

"What?" Matthew looks at Jack and sees it then. Sees what Jack knows. The inside of his stomach feels as if a tin cat has dug its nails in.

"You have to be fucking everywhere, don't you?" Jack stands his ground, his hands in fists, white flecks at the corners of his mouth. "There's nobody you leave alone. Matthew's fucking little entourage! You're supposed to be my fucking *friend,* not some goddamn *asshole!* You're supposed to be on my SIDE!"

"Jack, listen . . ." Matthew takes a step toward him.

"NO!" The violence in his voice stops Matthew cold. Jack crosses his arms and keeps his hands under his armpits. He rocks back and forth as though he is freezing, trying to keep warm. His mouth twists. "Get the fuck out of my face, Matthew. You don't want to be here now."

Matthew opens his mouth, but cannot think of anything to say.

Jack takes his fists and hits himself on either side of his head. "Jesus! Jesus! I need a drink." And he walks back to the Bok-Bok, kicking open the door. He vanishes into the darkness.

"Go on, Matthew," says Anthony, who kneels beside Suzi and slaps her face quickly, over and over again. He smiles sadly. "It'll be all right."

And although Matthew doesn't think so, he turns and half runs out of the courtyard, down the street. People get out of his way. He can hear the sirens now, although they are still a long way off.

CHAPTER THIRTY-FIVE

"What are you doing coming here by yourself?" Saida says to her father as soon as she sees him in the doorway of the restaurant. "Come and sit down."

His coat is wet and his hair sticks to his head. There is blue around his lips and bright patches of red around his eyes.

"I do not want to sit down," Elias says.

He trembles; she can feel it when she takes his arm.

"Are you ill? Do you want me to call a doctor?"

He shakes her off. "No. I have to tell you."

"Where is Ramzi?"

"I woke up to an empty house." There are scabs on the back of her father's hand. He does not heal well anymore.

"He didn't come home last night?" He has turned into a tomcat, she thinks.

"He came home. Like a thief in the night he came, and then he went again."

"What are you talking about?" Saida stands in front of her father, her right hand pressed to her stomach, her left hand rubbing her right. The hard-boiled eggs she ate for breakfast churn in her belly.

"I am telling you. Ramzi has gone to Nice." Her father slumps against the counter and she helps him to a chair.

"Anthony, get my father some water, please."

"Is everything okay?"

"I don't know. He says Ramzi's gone to Nice." She pulls a chair close to her father. "How can he just take a vacation when he feels like it? When did he say he was coming back?"

"He left this." Elias hands her a sheet of paper. "I found it taped to the refrigerator."

I am sorry it has to be like this. I tried to tell you I could not stay in Paris. It will never be my home. I am moving. I know this will be difficult for you, and for Saida, but you will manage, and Joseph can begin to work now. You must know that I have been unhappy and I will never be happy in Paris. Celine has family in Nice. I will be in touch when we're settled. I love you, Abba. Your son, Ramzi

"What does he mean, 'when he's settled'? Who is this Celine?"

Anthony puts the glass of water on the table. "Is everything all right?" he asks again.

"I don't think he's coming back, Daughter." Elias's lower lip begins to quiver. "I have failed as a father. My family is scattered."

"How could he do this? Are you sure?"

"He took all his clothes. I woke up. He was gone. And this is what he leaves me. A note. Not even a kiss. I will never see him again, not even his wedding. I'll be dead and I won't see his face again."

"Morning!"

Saida looks up and sees Matthew in the doorway, shaking the rain off his jacket.

"How's everybody?" he says and then stops. "Saida?"

"Oh, that selfish bastard! He has run away from home!"

"Who? Joseph?"

"No, Ramzi, I am telling you! He has run off and left us for some girl!"

Matthew looks at her. His mouth opens and then closes. He

looks terrible, and although Saida registers this, she has no time for his troubles today.

"Oh, I know what you are going to say." She grips her father's shoulder and he puts his hand over hers and pats, trying to calm her down, but what is the point of calming down? Why should she not scream and yell since she is left with everything to do and no one to help her? "You are going to say that he is young and he is restless and has never wanted to be here. Well, who gets to be where they want to be? Who gets to do what they want to do? That is too damn bad, I tell you. He is a selfish little playboy and he can go to hell, for all I care."

"Saida," says Elias, and he begins to cough.

"*Abba, Abba,* drink this." She holds the water to his mouth and rubs circles on his back. She feels the ribs through his sweater. This will kill him, she thinks. She sits down and puts her head in her hands. "I cannot do this. There is not enough of me."

"I can help," says Anthony.

"You'll be all right," says Matthew. "Look, he'll probably be back. Just gone off on an adventure, right?"

"He's gone. All those maps. All those want ads." Oh, how her head throbs.

"I'm not going anywhere." Anthony crosses his arms and stands in front of her as though trying to block anything harmful.

Saida wishes it were that simple. "I could sell the place," she says.

"I do not want to sell, Daughter. Where would we go?" Elias looks like a frightened, wizened child, his lower lip trembling. "The restaurant is in my name, isn't it? It is all we have now. The only thing we have. I do not want to sell."

"No, *Abba,* don't mind me. I am talking nonsense is all. We will be all right."

"Listen, Saida," says Matthew, looking at Anthony out of the corner of his eyes. "I hate to say it, but you've been pulling the lion's share of the work around here anyway, haven't you? I mean, Ramzi had sort of drifted away before now, hadn't he?"

This is true. He has been useless for the past few months. What would change?

Anthony squats down in front of her. "And I'll help," he says.

Saida looks at these three men. Mutilated, each of them in their own way. Misfits. The three un-wise men. She looks down at her hand. She is also a member of their tribe. She puts her hands on either side of Anthony's face and kisses him on each cheek. "You are a great help, Anthony. I could not do it without you. In fact, I'm going to start paying you."

"You don't have to. I've got my pension."

"We don't pay Ramzi anymore. We pay you." Saida picks up her father's cold hands and warms them between hers. "We'll be all right, *Abba*."

"I'm very tired, Daughter."

"Do you want to go home? Shall Anthony take you home? Anthony, would you?"

"Sure. I'll get a cab."

"The metro is fine for me," says Elias.

"I'll get a cab," says Anthony.

"Hang on, Anthony," says Matthew. "I'll come with you. I need to talk to you."

They leave, and after a few minutes, Matthew comes back. He looks different. As though he has heard something he did not expect. The whole world is awash in bad news. There is no cure for it. She says, "I made some *ghoraybeh*. Do you want some?"

"I've never turned down one of your cookies before, have I?"

She is halfway to the kitchen when she stops and starts to cry. She stands in the middle of the restaurant and covers her face with her hands.

Matthew comes up behind her, starts to put his arm around her and then stops. “It’ll be okay,” he says.

Saida puts her scarred hand behind her back and stops crying. “Sit down. I’ll bring you a coffee,” she says.

CHAPTER THIRTY-SIX

Matthew had gone looking for Anthony, prepared to hear the worst. Prepared to go to funerals, to take whatever punishment Jack wished to deal out. He deserved it. After leaving the courtyard, after leaving Suzi lying on the wet cardboard with her tights around her ankles and the sound of sirens on the wind, Matthew had walked aimlessly, walked and walked until there was nothing to do but stop walking, take a pill and sleep. The coward's oblivion. Pull the blanket of shame up over his head. He had done nothing for the woman he had fucked, whose lips had been put to use for his pleasure. He had betrayed his friend, and if he could fool himself into thinking it had not felt like it at the time he was surrendering to Suzi's somewhat professional ministrations, there was no denying it when he looked into Jack's face. Had he told himself Jack didn't care much about Suzi? Yes. Had he told himself Jack wasn't capable of caring? Yes.

But she wasn't dead.

Anthony had told him, however, that she was done with Jack. Done with them all, in fact. She was done with the Bok-Bok, with the life and the drugs. God willing. She was waiting to get into a treatment centre. Doing outpatient until then. It might be six weeks or more before she could get in anywhere, for of course she couldn't afford a private clinic. Until then, Anthony said, she was at Saint-Rita's.

And what, Matthew had asked, is Saint-Rita's? And then, "Ah," when he was told.

"If you want to talk to her," Anthony had said without prompting, "you'll find her there most afternoons. Mornings I think she's at the walk-in clinic. Evenings she's got meetings, you know, recovery—twelve-step."

"You think I should? I mean, would she want to see me?" Matthew had said as Anthony got into the cab with Elias.

"I think that's kind of up to you," said Anthony. "But you need to talk to Jack, too, don't you think?"

First things first. Saint-Rita, patron saint of desperate cases and prostitutes. Her chapel is on the boulevard de Clichy. Henry Miller used to hang out there. It is nearly five-thirty and dark by the time Matthew finds it. It is a strange little storefront chapel. On one side of the door is a display window with a painting of the saint. A large thorn sticks out of her forehead. On the other side of the door are two large modern, rather lurid, stained-glass windows, murky with street grime. Matthew goes in. To the right is an office, to the left, the chapel itself.

Inside the chapel a nondescript brown-haired girl in a navy pea jacket stands in front of a bank of yellow, red and green votive candles, in the middle of which Saint-Rita's wooden statue rests against a blue wall. As Matthew passes behind the girl, she places a scrap of paper in a small basket at the statue's feet.

The room is small and no one else is in it. Matthew admits relief to himself. He has made the effort. What more is required? *You must make sure. Wait a while, it won't kill you.* And so he prepares himself to stay, not long, but long enough to walk out clean.

To the left are the stained-glass windows Matthew saw from the street and to his right is a confessional; before him rows of plain wooden chairs are set up in front of a modest, slightly raised altar with another statue of Saint-Rita and a gold-painted icon hanging above it. Farther along the confessional wall, he notices a small statue placed on a piece of wood above eye level, behind a piece of protective glass. Upon closer inspection he sees that it is a Black Madonna wearing a blue dress, the kind little girls would dress a Barbie doll in, the space around her feet cluttered with bits of paper that have been tucked over the top of the glass.

The room, he realizes as he walks farther in, is actually an L-shape. In the back of the far angle a twig of a figure perches in the last row of chairs. She leans forward onto the back of the seat in front of her. Her head rests on her folded hands. There is no mistaking that tousled head of dark hair. Matthew cannot tell if she is praying or crying. He does not want to disturb her, he tells himself, as his heart hammers. *I am afraid of her.* He backs away and takes a seat near the altar. He tries to focus on the gold-painted icon of mother and child. Tries to think about what to say to Suzi, since all the words he had have disappeared now that she is before him.

He tries to pray. It does not take long before he realizes that he has no idea how to go about it. The prayers of his childhood hardly seem appropriate. *Now I lay me down to sleep. I pray the Lord my soul to keep.* Or maybe it is appropriate. Snippets come to him from other places, places not his own. . . . *Hail Mary, full of grace . . . God grant me the serenity to accept the things I cannot change. Our Father, Who art in heaven.* He settles on the Our Father and closes his eyes, thinking the words while he keeps a picture of Suzi in his mind.

The images that rise, of breasts and thighs in black tights and soft wet places, are not suitable. He shakes his head and tries again. Gets needle marks and sores around her mouth. He starts again, this time with, *This is for Suzi* . . . but of course that's not her real name and he doesn't know her real name.

He hears a sound, like a laugh, and opens his eyes.

Suzi looks at him, and the expression on her face is of such terrible need that his breath is sucked out of him. He rises and walks to her, taking a seat, but leaving an empty one between them. Her eyes never leave his face.

"I'm glad to see you," he says. "I wanted . . . I wanted to say I was sorry."

"What for?" Her voice sounds rough, like her mouth is very dry.

"I left you." Her brows knit and her mouth opens. "I left you, when you OD'd. I didn't stay."

She shuts her eyes. "Oh. That doesn't matter."

"And about Jack."

Her eyes open again. Her hands are in her lap and she holds them very tight. "I am done with Jack."

"I'm sorry," Matthew says.

"Fuck him. I am done with all of you!" She spits the words out at him. *"Tu comprends? Fini!"*

"Okay," he says. "That's probably best."

"My daughter is gone. Run away again and this time she does not come home. Her father washes his hands of her, but I will not. I will not give up on her. I will find her."

"Sure you will."

She glares at him. "I will stay clean. Five days I sweated and tore myself and screamed until my throat was raw. I shit myself. I lay in my own shit and my own vomit and my own sweat. Do you know what that is like? Among strangers? Can you imagine this?"

"No."

"Anthony visited me. We talked. But I don't want to talk anymore. This time will be different. I will find my daughter, *hein?* And we will be a family, her and me." Her eyes are wild and desperate, as though she is watching a killer approach, something glinting in his hand. "I have to."

"That's good."

"Why did you come here? What do you want?"

"Can I help?"

"What are you going to do, Matthew? Take me home? Hold my hand. Give me money? Fuck me again?"

"No, I mean, sure, if you need money . . ." He fumbles in his pocket.

"*Oh, mon Dieu,* don't give me money!" She recoils as though he has offered her a live snake.

"Okay, okay." And he wishes she would keep her voice down. She frightens him. The look in her eye. The savageness in her. "Anything . . ."

"Nothing." She whispers it, as though the strength is leaving her. "Go away."

"Suzi, I'm—"

"Micheline."

"What?"

"My name is Micheline."

"I'm sorry, Micheline. If you every need anything, call me."

"Go away, Matthew. No more of you, no more Bok-Bok, no more dope, no more of you, no more Bok-Bok, no more dope . . ." She closes her eyes, begins to rock back and forth, and presses her palms together, putting them against her forehead, chanting the words, making them a prayer.

Matthew thinks about leaving her money, but knows she is right, knows what she would do with it. He gets up, and although the chair scrapes loudly on the floor, she does not open her eyes.

As he walks up the aisle, he meets the eyes of a young woman. She stands below the Black Madonna. She wears a leather jacket and a short black skirt. Blue streaks her hair and heavy blue shadow on her eyes.

"Qu'est-ce que tu veux ici?" she says, her voice ragged with too-many cigarettes. *What do you want here?* "You can't even wait until we get outside? *Con!*" She turns on her heel and stalks out before Matthew can say anything, although of course there is nothing to say.

Back out on the street there is no sign of the girl with the blue eyeshadow, but there are three other women standing near the door. None of them look at him as they file in. There are also two men slouching and rubbing their hands, commerce in their eyes, waiting for someone else to come out of the church.

CHAPTER THIRTY-SEVEN

Matthew looks out his window toward Chez Elias. There is no Elias at the front table anymore. Since Ramzi's disappearance, the old man does not want to come to the restaurant. He stays in his apartment and watches television, and Matthew feels oddly bereft, not being able to watch him and Ramzi argue about the Next Great Move. If he feels that way, it is easy to imagine what Saida feels, what Elias feels.

He picks up the phone. It is a call he's been trying to make for a couple of days now. He did call once, but no one answered, sparing him.

Today Jack answers on the second ring.

"It's me," says Matthew.

"Yeah," says Jack. Matthew hears him inhale, but cannot tell if it is a cigarette he is smoking. "What's up?"

"I've been meaning to call."

"Uh-huh."

"I think I owe you an apology."

"You do, huh?"

"I'm really sorry, Jack. About everything."

"Listen, everybody fucks up from time to time. You just caught me off guard, all right? Bad moment."

"I crossed over a line."

"She's a fucking hooker. You think I'm the only guy she was sleeping with? You think you were?"

"Well, no, but . . ." Matthew stammers. He had not expected Jack to let him off the hook. He remembers the look on Jack's face that day in the courtyard.

"But what? You and me, we're all right. Let's leave it there."

"If you say so. Just want you to know I feel bad about it."

"Well, don't beat yourself up over it. Like I say, I didn't own her. Besides, she's history. Disappeared into thin air. Gone from the apartment, just gone." Another inhalation. "Fucking junkies. Whack jobs every one. Death on a stick." It does not matter what Jack says, Matthew can hear the regret in his voice. And something else. Anger. But at whom?

"Sorry, Jack."

"Stop fucking saying that. Maybe she'll get clean. Maybe it'll be for the best. Maybe life with me scared her straight." A laugh, low and tired. "So, how's the book going?"

"Good. I'm editing. How's the photography?"

"Haven't done much the last week or so. But I'm talking to people. About that book I wanted to do—*Subterranean Paris*. You think you might still be interested in doing the words?"

"Yes. Maybe, when I get through this."

"Fair enough. Listen, I'm going to see the late showing of *Men in Black* tonight. You should come. We can talk about it."

"Yeah, all right. What about Anthony?" Somehow, Matthew thinks it will be better if Anthony is there. Something between them in case they need a buffer.

They agree to meet on the Champs Élysées and then go to the café on the top floor of the Virgin Megastore around nine-thirty, grab a coffee and then head to the theatre.

It is nearly nine-thirty when Matthew and Anthony come up the steps at the Franklin D. Roosevelt metro. They walk toward the music store. It is a Wednesday night and the wide sidewalk is not as crowded as it will be later in the week. Young people hang about in small groups, smoking and flirting with one another.

Well-dressed Parisian couples stroll along, waiting for friends, picking a movie to see from the dozen or so films available in a three-block strip. Little kids run among the pedestrians, laughing. A never-ending roll of traffic lurches up the generous avenue. A man saunters toward them, a pit bull wearing a studded collar straining at the leash on his right side, a beautiful thin girl with long chestnut hair on his left.

"There's Jack," says Anthony.

Matthew looks and at first, all he can see is a group of young *beurs*. They stand in the entranceway to a small *centre commercial*. There are three of them, and then, yes, the big man is Jack, shaking hands with one of them, and tucking something into the inside of his jacket. Matthew frowns. "Is that Joseph?"

They approach and as they do, two of the young men take a step back, nudge each other. The third turns to see what they are looking at. His eyebrows shoot up involuntarily as his eyes widen. He sucks in his misshapen lip. Jack turns more slowly and as he does he smiles, smiles before he even sees who is behind him, because of course he knows who it will be.

"Hey," says Jack. He lifts a cigarette to his lips, smiles lopsidedly through the smoke as he squints.

"What's this?" Matthew says. The ends of his fingers tingle. "Hello, Joseph. Didn't know you'd be here tonight."

"And I did not know you'd be here." He looks quickly at Jack and then at the ground in front of him.

One of the boys has a bandana around his head and a gold tooth. The other is smaller, although neither is as big as Joseph. And their skin is darker. Algerians? The two take another step back. They take their hands out of their pockets.

"Who are your friends?"

"This is Maloud, and Jamal." He turns to his friends. "This is Matthew. He is a friend of the family. And Anthony. He works for my mother."

Matthew nods at them, but neither one extends his hand.

"What's going on here?" asks Anthony. His voice is monotone, flat, controlled.

"Just doing a little business. All done now," says Jack.

"Thought you weren't doing that kind of business with Joseph anymore," says Matthew. He cannot see it, cannot see why Jack has arranged things this way, for it is obvious he has arranged them. Why show him, why rub his nose in it? Anger rises up, rising like sour vomit, like black bile.

Jack smiles. "Why? Have I crossed a line, Dad?"

It makes sense then, and Matthew thinks, Oh, God, but I've been a fool.

"Joseph, get the fuck out of here. Go home." Matthew will not drop his eyes from Jack's.

"Now hold on," says Anthony. "Everybody cool down."

"You can't tell me what to do," says Joseph.

"No big deal here, Matthew. We're all friends. Aren't we all friends?" Jack holds his hands out, palms up.

"I don't know, Jack. You tell me. What the fuck is going on here?" Matthew's voice has risen. "Are you crazy? You pissed off at me, you tell me, you don't drag a kid into it."

"I'm not a kid," says Joseph. He steps between Matthew and Jack. "Don't call me that."

"Easy," says Anthony.

People on the street are beginning to move away. Maloud and Jamal look around nervously.

"Stay out of this," says Jack. His eyes are riveted on Matthew now, and he throws the cigarette to the ground. "This is between Matthew and me."

"What, all this because I slept with Suzi? You'd get Joseph fucked up because of that?" It is not making sense, is not adding up.

Jack pushes Joseph out of the way and pokes his finger in Matthew's chest. "Mr. Hero, right? Mr. Do-Right. Taking care of young Joseph here. Taking care of Joseph's mom. Getting Anthony a job. Writing the big fucking book. Where'd you get the time to fuck Suzi? That's what I want to know." He spits the words, his face inches from Matthew. Jack keeps poking him in the chest, hard enough to hurt, hard enough to leave bruises. "But you see, I know you, I've seen you. Seen you crawling around on the ground, looking for a place to get out of the gunfire when there wasn't any fucking gunfire. I know you. You're not such a fucking big man, Matt, not so fucking brave as you'd like young Joseph to believe, now are you?" Matthew knows he should step back, but he does not. He pushes Jack. Just to get him out of his face.

It happens very quickly. The two boys take off running into the maze of shops and disappear. Joseph lunges at Jack just as he goes for Matthew. Jack's arm shoots out and he connects with Joseph's cheek, and Joseph goes down, his cheek spilling blood. For one stupid moment Matthew thinks it will all be over, just like that. The insanity purged by Joseph's blood. Matthew turns to Joseph and in that moment Jack grabs him. He has his hands around Matthew's throat and his hands tighten. Matthew chokes, clawing at Jack, trying to get purchase on his thumbs, his fingers, anything.

"Jack! Stop. Now! You'll kill him!"

It is Anthony's voice. Then there is another bellow. Matthew does not see exactly what Anthony does; his eyes are fixed only on Jack's face, which is suddenly purple with pain. Anthony has his thumb behind Jack's ear. Whatever he does makes Jack let go, and Matthew thinks, Oh, this will be the end of it now. And then Jack groans, and he and Anthony struggle. Anthony tries to calm Jack down. "It's okay, it's okay," he keeps saying, looking into Jack's eyes, as Jack had once looked into Matthew's. But it is clear. Jack does not see him. Matthew, coughing and choking still, makes a lunge for Jack, but he is not quick enough.

It is just one punch. The hand at the end of Jack's arm is an anvil. Anthony comes off his feet. Goes backward. Stumbling. Crumpling. Legs buckling. But his arms are limp. His eyes. They are all white. And then there is the sound. His head against the concrete wall. And blood. As though a blood spring has opened in the rock. Anthony lies with his legs in a diamond shape, the soles of his feet nearly touching, his knees bent wide. His arms are wilted at his sides. His head is raised slightly, leaning against the concrete wall. Blood runs down his neck, his shoulders, pools like a cape along his arms. His mouth hangs open in a foolish and ugly expression. His eyes are no longer all whites. They are half-open, unfocused, slightly crossed. They are dull as mud.

Matthew stands in a stasis of heaving disbelief. A membrane between worlds has been rent, a sliver of icy paralysis through which the soul cries, *Make it not so, MAKE IT NOT SO!* A great wall of sound comes from behind Matthew. A roar, like a lion being torn apart. A disembowelling. Matthew also screams. People call for the police. People yell. Some run. Matthew stands at the centre of his own twisting universe. He is at the core again and it is quiet here, even with the screaming, as it had been quiet in another square, near another concrete wall. Everything on the outside of this nucleus looks the way it does on a merry-go-round, fast, blurred, indistinct, turning. It is as though a centrifugal force—call it refusal—pushes the outside farther away, leaving the inner hub empty and still.

He kneels beside Anthony. He looks into his eyes, trying to see some fading light, some flicker receding. Anything. But there is nothing bright and nothing even dark. His eyes hold no secrets. They just are not Anthony anymore.

Matthew stands up. He looks around, abruptly and acutely aware that Jack might attack again.

Where is Jack?

He is not where he had been. Joseph is on all fours on the sidewalk, staring like a wild animal at Anthony. Jack is not with him. Matthew scans the street. Nothing. And everyone is looking at

Anthony and Joseph and Matthew. Jack has vanished into the crowd, into the metro, maybe. Into the shadows.

Matthew goes to Joseph and hauls him to his feet. "Joseph. Go home. Go home now. Run." There will be police. A young Arab man cannot be here. "Run," Matthew says, shaking him, pushing him, and then he too is gone.

Matthew is freezing cold all of a sudden and he begins to shake. A man comes near and puts his coat over Anthony, trying to keep him warm. As though that would help. A surge of guilt goes through Matthew. He should have taken off *his* coat.

"The *flics* will be here in a minute," says the man.

Matthew's stomach roils. "I'm going to be sick," he says. With his hand over his mouth, he heads for the alley. No one stops him.

In the alley, it occurs to him that he might kill Jack. That he might find him and kill him. The thought pulls him up and slams him against the wall. There is horror in leaving Anthony, his friend, there on the sidewalk. Anthony, who came to look for him when he wandered in the emotional wastelands, who cooked daube and sang Leadbelly songs to him through the door. Anthony, who believed in redemption.

Anthony, who would not want him to kill Jack, and would not want Jack to kill himself. For that is the other possibility. Matthew still hears the sound that rose behind him as he stood over Anthony's body. The sound of someone being disembowelled. The sound of Jack's howl. Death sang in that voice. Anthony's. Maybe Jack's. Maybe Matthew's. That too, is possible. Matthew considers this. Yes, it is possible, also, it is acceptable. An acceptable solution.

He ducks through the Galerie Rond Point and back along Franklin D. Roosevelt to the taxi stand. When the driver asks him where he wants to go, he is not sure what to tell him. Jack will not go back to his own apartment; Matthew knows this. Suzi has vanished, apparently, and so he will not go there.

"Belleville," he says.

The driver looks unhappy. Taxi drivers do not like to dawdle in areas like Belleville too late at night. Matthew gives him the address and turns away. Let him be unhappy. He tries to think, but his thoughts scatter like marbles on a tombstone. Glancing around, he catches the driver looking at him in the rear-view. Matthew is thumping the door with the side of his fist. *"Pardon,"* he mutters. He wonders if he has been talking to himself. It is possible.

In his head, he plays out what he will do when he finds Jack. He pictures his hands around Jack's throat. He pictures his fist in his face. He pictures making his eyes roll back in his head the way Anthony's had. He pictures arriving too late, finding Jack hanging from a street lamp, with a bullet in his brain, with a needle in his arm. He pictures Jack gone mad. He pictures Jack broken, crushed under grief, the sack of skulls now, finally, one skull too many. He does not know which scenario frightens him more. He does not know which one satisfies him more.

The traffic at this time of night is light and they make it to the Bok-Bok almost faster than Matthew wants to. He pays the driver and watches him take off hurriedly, making for the safer, better-lit areas of Paris. He half stumbles down the stairs. Charlie and John sit in a corner. Three men he does not know huddle in the back. A new girl sits at the bar, dressed in a cheap gold halter dress, the skirt so short her panties show above her crossed legs.

"What's up?" says Dan.

"Jack. Have you seen him?"

"He was in this afternoon."

"Not just now?"

"Nope." Dan tilts his porkpie back on his head and looks at Matthew suspiciously. Then he pulls out the crowbar. "Am I going to need this?"

"I don't know. Don't suppose you have another one of those, do you?"

"You want a drink? Looks like you could use one."

Thankful that Dan is not the kind of man to ask questions, for he would break down if he has to say the words, he takes a double scotch, no ice. He holds his forearm close to his body to lessen the shaking in his hand. He sits at the back of the room and waits, sipping, for fifteen minutes. Then he waits twenty more.

"If he shows up," he says to Dan as he leaves, "try and keep him here. I'll call in half an hour."

"Don't suppose I could stop Jack if he wanted to leave," Dan said. "And I'd be a fool to try. Anyone would be."

"Do your best. It's important. And Dan . . . watch yourself."

"Matthew, wait." Dan reaches under the bar and then holds something out to him. "Take this."

It is a sap. Heavy as only a ball of lead in a leather casing can be.

Matthew cannot find a cab and has to walk blocks, until finally he hails one on rue de Gambetta. He jumps in, gives the address on Châteaudun and has the driver wait while he talks to the border guard at the squat. No luck. Jack's not there. The guard says Matthew is free to come on in, but Matthew believes him and does not bother. He really does not think Jack would want to be in a crowd just now.

He calls Dan. No sign of Jack.

And then it comes to him. He has no doubt in his mind where Jack has gone.

CHAPTER THIRTY-EIGHT

The girls and almost-girls swarm the taxi even before it comes to a halt. A pair of breasts press against one window and through another, hands lift a skirt—proving the pantyless owner is at least technically a woman. A girl hops up on the hood and the driver curses, saying the paint will be scratched; however, when he turns to face Matthew to accept his payment he grins. Matthew fights the urge to grind the francs into his face and eradicate that smirk. He gives him no tip, which earns him an insult he ignores. He opens the door and pushes into the wall of lace-covered, rubber-corseted, leather-wrapped flesh.

They call out to him in French. "Come with me, I give the best head." "No, don't listen to her, she's too old. I'll make you come until you scream for mercy." "You are so pretty. You want to see my pretty little pussy? The real thing, *cherie*." Their hands on his arms, their hands everywhere. He clutches his back pocket, guarding his wallet, and with the other hand he reaches in his jacket pocket and finds the sap there, waiting like a sleeping demon, heavy and dense.

"Fuck off!" he yells and throws his arms up, shaking them off. His hand swings back, threatening. The hot ember of a cigarette on his neck burns and he slaps it away.

"Con!" Bastard, calls a deep voice. A sharp heel kicks him.

He breaks through, jogs to the fence and hops over into the

Pré Catalan Garden. Unlike the last time he was here, this night is not clear; there are no stars overhead, no moon. The terrain is dark and deeply shadowed. He senses he is not alone. The great tree in the centre of the lawn creaks as the wind blows. He heads across the grass in a straight line toward Shakespeare's Garden and the cave. His passing startles a crow roosting in a birch tree and its caw is a mocking rasp in the veiled night. Matthew's nerves jump like downed electrical wires. There is the flap and flutter of wings above him. Dark shapes only, bats or birds. Sentinels, raising the alarm. Not that he thought it would be possible to come upon Jack without warning. He tells himself it doesn't matter.

At the next fence he calls, "Jack? You in there? I'm coming in." Bravery boosted by bravado.

He climbs the fence and drops to the other side. As before, he tears his palm, which gives him a new focus for his anger. Sucking on it, he slowly walks across the centre of the circle of grass. He catches a faint whiff of tobacco on the wind, but it is gone so quickly he can't be sure. As he reaches the edge of the grass he hunkers down, resting on his heels.

He waits as his breath slowly returns to normal. The rage leaches out of him, spreading across the hard earth, the cold stones. He gazes into the cave mouth, not even a real cave, but a make-believe cave, although the stones are real enough. It looks impoverished, lonely, more a place for a scared twelve-year-old to go than the hulking man he is looking for. Soul-piercing sorrow slinks in to claim ground beside his anger.

It is hard to tell what, if anything, lies beyond the cave's mouth, and from where he sits he can't tell if the lock has been jimmied.

"Come out, come out, wherever you are." He thinks of the endless nights Jack has spent standing in the green jungles, still as a held breath. The minutes tick by and nothing moves. From beyond the confines of the garden come the distant sounds of car tires and now and then the voice of the prostitutes. It is as though a transparent dome, a bell jar, has settled over the Jardin de Shakespeare. The place becomes a microcosm of other places, specific to the truth—the isolation and danger—of all other places and yet removed from their reality.

Of course, it is possible Jack is nowhere near this place.

"What's the matter, Jack? Waiting to sneak up on me? Finish me off? Is that the plan? Well, give it a try. I'm not going anywhere."

The darkness remains merely darkness.

More time passes, perhaps a quarter of an hour, perhaps half an hour—it is difficult to keep track the way his thoughts race. Anthony's face swims before him in the dark. The sound of his laugh floats in on the wind. Guilt like a sack of squirming snakes writhes in his gut. He fingers the sap, heavy in his pocket, uses his coat sleeve to dry tears he hasn't noticed crying. His fury grows with the tears.

He stands up. "Fuck you, Jack," he shouts into the cave. "You fucking psycho." He braces himself, one foot in front of the other, balanced for impact.

The cave entrance is opaque as a piece of coal.

"I'm not going in that cave of yours, so if you want me, you're going to have to come out. And you'll have to come out sometime. I can wait until daylight. People will be here then. Is that what you want?"

Another ten minutes, fifteen minutes.

"So what? Have you offed yourself? Done us a favour? Is that it?" *Aw, shit. Regret.* With the words the taut wire of rage begins to sag. He wants a drink the size of a gallon drum, something he can fall into and drown. He has to know if his friend has found a permanent solution to his terrible troubles. *My friend?* The thought knocks Matthew as surely as a hammer blow to the head. Fucked up. Kindred soul. For it is possible, isn't it? That look on Jack's face as he strangled Matthew? The blind look that sees only ghosts. Tries to kill the ghost. Matthew has worn that look.

Jack. Betrayer. Comforter. Corrupter. Killer. Friend. One way or another. It must be settled.

"Fuck it. I'm coming in there."

He walks slowly, straining to see. The lock at the barred entrance to the cave, although replaced on the hook, is not clicked shut. His mouth dries up and the nausea churns. He touches the lock.

"Matthew," a voice says.

Matthew nearly tumbles backward. The voice is Jack's but it doesn't come from inside the cave, it comes from above the cave. He steps back and looks up. Jack sits cross-legged on the roof of the cave. His face is covered in what looks like mud and only his eyes and teeth shine. He looks like a nightmare version of the Cheshire cat.

Matthew tries to keep the fear from his voice. "How long have you been up there?"

"Watched you walk across the grass. Didn't want you to see me. What do you want?"

"Anthony's dead." There, let it be said for the first time. Let it find its target like a bullet. There is the sound of something being stifled, swallowed, choked down. "Come down." Matthew tries to see if Jack has anything in his hands.

"You scared of me?"

There is no point in lying. "Yes. But not so scared I don't want to fucking kill you myself."

Jack nods. "I'm not going to hurt you. I'm better than I was. Some. When you first got here, well, I think it's good you didn't come all the way in." He uncurls himself with an ease Matthew didn't think possible in a middle-aged man who has apparently sat on the cold earth completely motionless for the past hour at least. He disappears behind a bush and then soundlessly reappears to Matthew's right. Matthew's hands form involuntary fists.

"Where's Anthony?"

"What do you mean?"

"What's happened to his body?"

"I don't know."

"Why don't you know?" Jack's voice is flat.

"I guess I left—came after you before the police got there."

"You shouldn't have done that. You should have stayed with him. What happened to Joseph?"

"He took off. Went home, I think."

Jack nods. He pulls a package of cigarettes out of his pocket and offers them to Matthew. Matthew takes one. Jack flicks a match on his thumbnail and cups the flame so it is hidden.

"So you want to kill me?" Jack says.

"I don't know." Matthew's hand shakes as he lifts the cigarette to his mouth.

Jack sits with his back to the cave wall and indicates Matthew should do the same. They look out across the garden. A pair of rabbits nibble on the grass. Jack straightens his left arm and raises his right, squinting along the line, miming the action of looking down a gunsight. He aims at one of the rabbits. "Pow," he says.

"Have you got a gun?" Matthew says. It will move things along, asking this question, get to the heart of why they are here together.

"No gun. I said I'd never have a gun again." Jack's teeth are very white against his darkened skin. "I was afraid somebody'd get hurt. Bad joke, huh? I kinda wish now I had one. I got a knife, though." He reaches around behind him and pulls out what looks like a hunting knife with a long serrated blade. He offers it to Matthew, handle first. "Kabar. U.S. Marine issue. You take it." Matthew hesitates and then takes it. When it is in his palm, for a moment Jack's hand is still around the blade and their eyes meet. "It's good that you take it," says Jack. "I want you to take it."

And so, if an attack comes now, things will be more easily decided. The scales have tipped in favour of Matthew's survival. Survival entails responsibilities. Matthew discovers he is disappointed at this turn of events. Then he slips the knife into the pocket on the inside of his jacket. It feels warm.

"Matthew." Jack's voice is strange—thin and hoarse. "I've had some time to think up here."

"And?"

"I can't keep fighting it anymore. I can't let go of it either. Can't get it out of me. This is what's happening now—but it's the end of a fucking chain reaction that started a long time ago. There are other things."

It is only then that Matthew realizes Jack is crying. "What kind of other things?"

"I never told you what I did in Nam. I mean, what I really did." Jack's laugh is filled with the harsh salt-grind of tears. "I never told nobody. Not my brother, not my wife. Fuck." Jack rubs his palms together as though he is cold. "They must have been testing for guys who'd do it. And that's what I can't figure out. How did they know I'd do it? What did they see in me?"

Jack lifts his eyes abruptly. "I'm not making excuses, you understand. I always had a choice. All soldiers have choices.

"You get down in the dark with dark things and you just do it, and then after a while it stops feeling weird. It starts feeling good because disciplining yourself to do these things means you can overcome everything, even your own self—your own sense of what's right. Everything becomes possible then. There's no line that can't be crossed. At first you were afraid, see, that doing these things would mean you were a sick fuck, but it takes almost no time to talk yourself into believing it doesn't mean that at all, because you're on the right team—the good guys. You can overcome anything, even yourself and every Sunday School lesson you've ever been taught, right? Because you have been turned into one tough motherfucker."

He almost looks like a kid then, crazy-eyed and tearful, but still massive and dangerous.

"'Get the information,' they said. 'Get the slant-eyed gook to tell you what we need to know and you'll be saving the lives of your buddies, Jack. Remember what the gooks do to American POWs. Never forget what they do, the slimy yellow bastards. Here, just take this little shiny thing and touch him with it. You can be gentle, in fact it's better if you're gentle. You're doing your duty, soldier. Just don't leave any scars. That's the golden rule. And if you have to do something that might show up on the body later—make sure the body don't show up later.'

"And why do you do it? Because you're in the middle of hell. Because the lines have blurred. Because you've got so you like it. You're in a tent with an interpreter and a VC prisoner. You got to find out if there's a trap waiting for you. You don't want to look like a fucking wuss. And you're scared blue and that makes you crazy-angry. That's how it starts. You want the guy to just fucking talk. If he talks there won't be any need, right, for the other stuff. But he won't fucking talk. He won't fucking TALK! It makes you mad, because if he'd tell you something, you could just stop the whole shit-show before the curtain even goes up, but he's not helping you out. He's this little shit who's making you do terrible things because he won't talk. You *hate* this little slant, then. Which makes things easy. Inevitable.

"You start with just a little flap of skin, maybe. And the gook looks down because he can't believe it didn't hurt that much. Oh, it hurts, and hurts bad, but not *as* bad as he imagined. And he thinks maybe it won't be so terrible and he'll be able to hold out, and be a fucking hard-ass, but he's also got in his head all the shit he'd do to you if the situation was reversed and maybe he starts feeling a little smug because he knows that he's a tougher little fuck than you are. You can't have that, see, you just can't have that because even if he survives this, escapes or something, he has to go back to his people with stories that'll scare the shit out of them. So when he looks down at the flap of skin on his arm that's neat and clean and bearable, that's when you put the sack over his head and you make sure it's a wet sack so he starts to think about not being able to breathe. Then you do something small. Just touch a nerve under the skin and make him jump like a dissected frog in high school biology. It's a shock to the little fuck and he's starting to freak out now and that's just the beginning." Jack's voice is soft and soothing, and Matthew pictures him speaking into the ear of a small man with a wet canvas sack over his head, speaking to him as though Jack were his friend, his lover, his priest.

Jack's eyes are fixed on a point and they do not blink as he talks. His forehead is pinched and his lips pulled back, but he isn't smiling. When he turns his head his eyes remain stationary and the tears fall unimpeded.

"You get a bandage maybe, and fix up the knife wound, because there's blood but it's the sort of thing that might have happened in a righteous fight and if the guy survives and anybody's stupid enough to question you, you can say, look, I didn't hurt him, I gave him medical treatment. And the prisoner is confused now, right, because you've hurt him, but then you've helped him and you talk to him so pretty. But he's not talking, not telling you anything, so you get a field telephone, which runs on batteries and a generator. You start with the hands, see, and then you move on to his nuts.

"You know, I had three friends back in Nam. All black guys. Soul Brothers, we said then. Frankie and Terry got shot, Thaylen got a bamboo stake covered in human shit through the throat. Seems the brothers were always on point, you know? They always got to go first. I stopped making friends after Thaylen." Jack wipes the tears and snot off his face roughly, and hangs his head. His shoulders slope and his hands are mammoth paws. He is a great deadly bear, baited, blinded and beaten, tied to the stake of his nightmares. "Until Anthony. I never got to know another black guy, until Anthony. Fucking Anthony."

At some point Matthew has taken his hands from between his knees and put them over his ears, and it now takes a great effort to pull them away. It has not helped. He has heard everything. Another boundary shifts, another solid piece of ground slips away beneath him. The Killers of Kigali. The Butchers of Bosnia. El Salvadorian death squads. The mass murderers in Chechnya. Iraqi torturers. Palestinian suicide bombers. Israeli hit men. Jack, his friend, who sits before him hiccupping with tears. Jack. Friend. Torturer. Murderer. Matthew is weighted. Filled with stones. Skulls.

"We've all done things, Jack. None of us is innocent."

"I took pleasure in it, Matthew. I took pleasure. Came a time I didn't want to stop. Most of my talk is just bullshit, you know that, but this thing, it's true. And I liked it. How did they know that about me? It had to always have been there. What did they see?" He shudders, deep and violently. "Would it have come out anyway? That's what I just don't know. And then you come along. With your book deal and your little adopted Lebanese family and everybody thinking you're a hero. So like me in some ways. So unlike me. I hated that." Jack raises his face and looks to the sky, but there is nothing there, no moon, no stars, the clouds an opaque nothingness. "There's only one thing for it."

"What's that?" The words are spiny burrs against his tongue.

"Atonement, my friend."

Matthew looks at Jack, his face ravaged with all that he has done and cannot undo, all the acts of violence and cruelty he has committed. Each act and each denial written like an unhealed scar along his skin. And something shifts in Matthew. Shifts to pity. To grief. It makes him sick, and he wishes the killing anger were back. It was so clean, so simple, that anger. But it is as though something dark and swollen has been blasted out of his belly. It is all quite clear. The only difference between him and Jack lies in circumstance and trajectory. And what Matthew chooses to do next.

"And how will you atone, Jack? Kill yourself?"

"Cops will be looking for me. I'm gonna let 'em find me." He speaks slowly, precisely.

"And let *them* kill you?"

Jack shrugs. "Let life take its course."

It is unclear what that course will be, but Matthew nods. It is always unclear.

Jack stands and holds out his hand. "I'm going back up. I do need you to do something, Matthew."

"What?"

"Make sure Anthony's all right, okay? I mean, see that his body gets home to New York. Don't let him be buried in fucking Potter's Field, all right? He's got a sister there. Arcola's her name. Same last name. Find her. Tell her I'm sorry. Bury him with a fucking cookbook or something, okay?"

"Done." It has become very difficult to speak.

"And listen—" His hand is like cement surrounding Matthew's. "You make the call to the cops, all right? You be the one."

"No. I can't do that."

"You have to. For both of us." He steps back. "For Anthony."

"Yes. Fine. I'll make the call."

Jack gives Matthew a hug, fast and strong enough so that his spine pops.

"Fuck, I hate cops," says Jack, and before Matthew can say anything in response, Jack disappears into the back of the cave.

Matthew looks at his watch. It is two-thirty in the morning. His feet are rooted. He does not want to go, because if he does this part of their lives will be over and it will be true that Anthony is dead and that Jack is a ghost. Like the day he stood at his mother's grave. It was his leaving that had been the final good-bye, not hers.

"Good-bye," Matthew says to the cave. He will say good-bye to Anthony later.

Ever after, he will find it difficult to remember the walk out of the wood or much of the walk across the west of Paris. Only that it was filtered through tears that made the city glitter, hard and cold and mockingly radiant.

CHAPTER THIRTY-NINE

He intends to go home, and he almost makes it. He lusts for a bottle of whisky and a bottle of blue pills and several days, or weeks, or months of oblivion. He actually makes it to his building. He stands outside, fully intending to press the code and open the door and go inside. And then he doesn't.

He walks to the phone booth on the corner. He tells the police he knows who is responsible for the dead man on the Champs earlier that night. He tells them where to find him and that they are expected. Then he goes walking, and when he passes a garbage can he takes the sap out of his pocket and drops it in.

Half an hour later he enters Saida's building. As he nears her door he hears voices, hers and Joseph's. Raised voices. The words, however, are in Arabic and he understands nothing. He hesitates for only a moment, and then knocks. Instantly, they stop speaking. Joseph opens the door. His face is swollen on one side, the cut on his cheek has been bandaged, but the eye is also black and swelling. The other one is red as well and swollen from crying.

"Matthew!"

"You tell me!" Saida pushes past her son. "You tell me what is going on now. He will not." She pulls Matthew into the room and stands with her hands on her hips, scowling at them both. Then her expression changes. She goes pale and her hands fly to her mouth. "My God, Matthew. What is it?"

It seems he has started to cry.

"Sit down. Sit down. You are going to tell me," she says, taking him by the arm. "Joseph, make coffee."

It is some time before he gets control of himself. "What's happened? What's happened?" she keeps saying.

There is coffee in front of him. He sips, scalding his lips. He tries to breathe. "You don't know? Joseph?" He glances at Joseph, who shakes his head slightly, then drops his eyes to the floor.

"Would I be asking if I knew? I will slap someone in a moment!"

"It's Anthony," Matthew says.

Saida sits down abruptly. Her hands move to her neck and involuntarily cover her scar.

"Anthony is dead," he says. The words are like something heavy, wet, fallen from a great height. Black-hole words, sucking up all the oxygen.

"How?" Saida says, tears already in her eyes.

"Jack," Matthew says. "He didn't mean to. But it happened anyway."

"What are you saying?"

"On the Champs Élysées. There was a fight."

Saida's head snaps around to Joseph. "You were there."

"Imma." Joseph starts to cry, his lower lip loose and trembling.

"Oh, poor Anthony," wails Saida. And before Matthew knows what is happening Saida is out of her chair, her hands flying, slapping Joseph on the shoulders, the head. "And this is your big hero! This killer! He is the one you want to be like? You still think so?"

"Saida!"

Joseph holds his hands up to shield his face, but doesn't try to stop her.

"Stop," Matthew says, rising. "Please, stop."

She looks at him, stricken. She sits down again, and her spine is very straight. "You must tell me everything. *Everything.*"

Matthew looks at Joseph, who nods. And so he tells her what happened, as best he remembers it, and leaves out only that he thinks Jack was making a drug buy—let her have that at least, that it was only Jack's influence that concerned him and nothing more. When he is finished the three of them stare at the table and don't speak.

"In Lebanon," Saida says at last, "I thought I'd left the violence behind. It is like a curse, following you. When the Palestinians and the Syrians came into Damour, they killed more people than we could count. They burned the houses with people inside. For months afterwards I could not bear anyone to strike a match near me, the smell gagged me. They shot babies in the back of the head. My little nephew, he was your cousin, Joseph, your cousin. They shot him. They shot my brother, Khalil, and his wife. They shot Habib, your father. Your grandfather took Ramzi and me to the church, the Church of Saint Elias, which is his patron saint, you see. There, huddled between the pews, we listened as Father Labaky preached a sermon about the slaughter of the innocents. And then two young men from our village came and stood in front of the church and shot their guns, acting as a diversion so we could escape. It took ten minutes for all of us to get out through the back. There were five hundred of us and we ran to the seashore and got away in boats.

"But my mother was not with us. She would not leave her parents. They were very old and frightened. They lay on a pallet under the dining-room table, too weak to get up. This Libyan mercenary—a mercenary like your hero Jack—he shot them all, my grandparents where they lay, my mother, whom they raped first. All this a neighbour told me, you understand, a neighbour who was also raped by many men, but survived. He even took a picture, this mercenary, with a flashbulb, our neighbour said. This is what those men are like."

Joseph hugs himself. "You never told me this."

"I didn't want you to know. But I was wrong. I see that now. You need to know." Saida turns to Matthew. The expression on her face is difficult to read. There is grief, more than anything else, but also there is something softer. "I'm sorry for you, Matthew. You cared for them both and that is the hardest of all."

"Yes," he says.

It is a long hour as they go over things again and again, trying to make sense of the night's shattering events. Talking about Anthony and what he was like. Matthew thinks of Jack but keeps his name behind his teeth. They talk of funerals. "I will have to come forward. Talk to the police, say that I know them."

"Yes, you will have to do that," says Saida.

"I have to call his sister."

"Yes. That, too."

"And what will you do?"

"Me?" she says.

"Without Ramzi, without Anthony . . ."

"Oh. The restaurant." She rubs her forehead. "It's not right to talk of these things now."

They sit, each in their own sorrows. Matthew thinks, and tries to find words, feeling the sack of skulls on his back shifting, pressing down on his shoulders, his ribs. *And who will we be good for?* Anthony had said that, the day in the Passy Cemetery. Matthew wants to explain to Saida what her family means to him. What she means to him, except he doesn't really know. He only knows he wants to find out. He doesn't want to wander in the dark lands alone anymore. How to explain the hopelessness of self-loathing, the terrible treadmill of it, bringing him always, irrevocably, back to his own loathsome self? How to explain that he wants to spend the rest of his life *not* thinking about himself at all, for doing so seems merely selfish, merely still self-centred, merely useless, exhausting. How to explain that for a moment or two sitting inside Jack's cave, he had balanced, stretched, inched toward another person, one who was as unlovable as Matthew feels himself to be—and that in doing so the appalling ache of self-hatred, indeed, of *self*, had disappeared. Just for a moment, and he hadn't even been aware of the moment until it was gone and left a glimmer of longing for its return, but still. The problem was only compounded by words. What to *do*, that is the question.

"I want . . ." he starts, "I want to, I don't know, get out of my own way. I feel so guilty all the time. It does no good and I want to do something good. To *be* good . . . for someone." He has the urge to cover himself in some way, and crosses his arms over his chest, but this makes it difficult to breathe and so he uncrosses them. But it doesn't help. He feels undefended, embarrassed and exposed, and yet not unsafe, oddly.

Joseph stares at him.

"I thought I might like to learn the restaurant business."

"Don't be silly, Matthew. We are fine. And you are a journalist."

"Not anymore. I almost picked up a gun once . . ." He stops. It is a tale he doesn't want to tell again. "I'm going to finish my book. And after that I'd like to maybe write novels. I'm not a journalist anymore. I'm done with that. It's done with me."

"We'll see."

"I mean it."

"We'll see."

Joseph starts to cry again, and he puts his head down on his folded arms. His shoulders shake. As she caresses her son's shaved head with her left hand, Saida's right hand lies on the table next to her cup. Matthew sits there, looking at her hand with the burn scar on it like something glowing, a piece of cloth rippled over the top of her flesh, red and ivory-bone. He wants to take her by the hand but cannot because he is afraid of hurting the fragile parchment of her skin. So he places his hand next to hers, and waits.

The kitchen is lightening, the shadows becoming less inky in the corners of the room. It is almost dawn, when the sun is still hidden behind the buildings, but through the green leaves of the bamboo that grow in front of Saida's windows comes the argent promise of impending light.

She meets his eyes first. And then, when she takes his hand, the burning in her skin travels up his arm, into his chest. And nothing, thank God, is the same after that.

ACKNOWLEDGMENTS

Immeasurable thanks to my agent, Dean Cooke, who always believed in this book and who did much beyond-the-call-of-duty hand-holding, as did the ever-efficient Samantha North. I am grateful as well to my editor at HarperCollins, Iris Tupholme, for her confidence in me as a writer and her keen editorial vision. Thanks to production editor Katie Hearn, managing editor Noelle Zitzer, copy editor Pamela Erlichman, the wonder-publicist Rob Firing, and Norma Cody for unending good cheer and all those warm welcomes.

There are many other people to whom I owe thanks: Isabel Huggan, for sound advice; Matthew Campbell, for reading an early draft and sharing his experiences as a journalist; Nina Burleigh and Sparkle Hayter, for extremely helpful conversations on what makes war reporters tick; Khahil and Joseph Medawar and their family, who shared not only their wonderful food at La Pinède restaurant in Paris, but also their stories of life in Paris and Lebanon; Monsieur Michel Ruminski, who provided details of the Parisian police's Brigade des Mineurs, as well as unending book deliveries; and Ernest Hunt, Canon of the American Cathedral in Paris, now retired, for allowing me to quote from one of his sermons. The writing of this book was supported by a grant from the Canada Council for the Arts, for which the author is profoundly grateful.

Finally, I would like to thank my husband, Ron, for his support, patience, good humour and kindness. Had it not been for you, this book would never have been written.

Some readers may find a similarity between the Hebron scene and that of accounts of the death of Mohammed al-Dura and the wounding of his father, Jamal. I feel it is important to say that it is in no way my intention to bolster the polemics presently existing in the Middle East, although I admit the account of Mohammed al-Dura and his father inspired the scene in the book, particularly in its symbolic insanity, regardless of which side was ultimately responsible for Mohammed al-Dura's death. However, this is obviously not a factual account and for this reason I have changed the sex of the child involved, as well as the geographic location and narrative details. *The Radiant City* is, above all, a work of fiction, and should not be interpreted any other way.

For those interested in reading more about the various subjects covered in this book, I offer the following list of books that were invaluable to me.

American Psychiatric Association. *Diagnostic and Statistical Manual of Mental Disorders*, 4th ed. Washington, DC: American Psychiatric Association.

Arnett, Peter. *Live from the Battlefield.* New York: Touchstone, 1995.

Ben Jelloun, Tahar. *French Hospitality: Racism and North African Immigrants*. New York: Columbia University Press, 1999.

Darrow, Siobhan. *Flirting with Danger.* London: Virago Press/Little, Brown and Company, U.K., 2000.

Hargreaves, Alec G. *Immigration, "Race" and Ethnicity in Contemporary France*. London: Routledge, 1995.

Hedges, Chris. *War Is a Force That Gives Us Meaning.* New York: PublicAffairs/Perseus Books Group, 2002.

Herr, Michael. *Dispatches*. New York: Vintage Books/Random House, 1991.

Keane, Fergal. *Season of Blood*. London: Penguin Books, 1996.

Loyd, Anthony. *My War Gone By, I Miss It So*. New York: Atlantic Monthly Press, 1999.

Mertus, J., Tesanovic, J., Metikos, H., and Boric, R. (eds.), *The Suitcase: Refugee Voices from Bosnia and Croatia*. Berkeley and Los Angeles, CA: University of California Press, 1997.

O'Nan, Stewart. *The Vietnam Reader*. Toronto: Random House of Canada, 1998.

Politkovskaya, Anna. *A Dirty War: A Russian Reporter in Chechnya*. London: The Harvill Press, 2001.

Prochnau, William. *Once Upon a Distant War*. Toronto: Vintage Books/Random House, 1996.

Rohde, David. *Endgame*. HarperCollins Canada, 1997.

Steele, John. *War Junkie*. London: Corgi and Transworld/Bantam, 2003.

Tzonis, Alexander. *Le Corbusier: The Poetics of Machine and Metaphor*. New York: Universe Publishing, 2001.

THE TYPE

This work is set in Garamond, a typeface created in the sixteenth century by the eminent Parisian engraver and letter founder Claude Garamond. For over four centuries, Garamond has remained a typeface of high repute; almost every manufacturer of type or typesetting equipment has produced its own version. This adaptation was produced in England in the 1920s by the Monotype Corporation, under the supervision of Stanley Morison.